Quin fanned herself with her hat, watching the Maserati as it sped like a silver bullet, sleek and smooth, gleaming in the hot light, gathering momentum.

Then something went haywire. The front of the car whipped right, left. It screeched into a ninety-degree turn, its back end snapping from one side to the other like the hips of a belly dancer. It was headed for the concrete wall.

When it slammed into the wall, the Maserati was doing 110. The explosion hurled a fireball of metal and debris some fifty feet into the air. . . .

Also by T. J. MacGregor
Published by Ballantine Books:

DARK FIELDS

KILL
FLASH

T.J. MacGREGOR

BALLANTINE BOOKS • NEW YORK

For Rob
& mom and dad
because they're the best

And thanks again to Diane Cleaver
and Chris Cox

Library of Congress Catalog Card Number: 86-92084

ISBN 0-345-33754-9

Manufactured in the United States of America

First Edition: June 1987

"The door to the past is a strange door.
It swings open and things pass through it,
but they pass in one direction only.
No man can return across that threshold. . . ."
—Loren Eiseley
from *The Immense Journey*

Fade In

TWO DAYS AFTER the murder, a videotape arrived with his mail.

Gill Kranish, thinking it was one of the dozens of audition tapes his production company received daily, popped it into the VCR in his office. The screen filled with a blurred closeup of a face: a nose that gaped with pores like craters, the liquid blue of an iris, a widening pupil as black as a bean. Then the image cleared. The only sound came from Kranish, who made a noise like hissing steam.

He recognized the place, the person. It was inside the motor home on the set two days ago and the man was J.B. Domer. He was gagged, arms stretched out over his head and tied to the legs of the couch, ankles bound to the other end of the couch so he looked as if he were on a medieval rack, being slowly pulled apart. His head was raised a few inches from the couch. His terrified eyes were following whoever held the camera. The soundlessness, the absolute silence from the screen, seemed to quiver in the air around Kranish's head. An acid taste rolled over his tongue. He wanted to shut off the machine, knew that he should, but he couldn't move. He stared at the screen.

The image tilted, the room widened as the person with the camera stepped back away from Domer. He tried to scream, tendons stood out in his neck, he struggled to yank his hands and arms free.

Kranish blinked. His muscles tightened. His head began to ache. He gritted his teeth as the picture went fuzzy again, then cleared.

Smoke wafted across the front of a TV set in the motor home. It was on. He knew the movie, the scene. It was Spin Weaver and his girlfriend, Molly Drinkwater, arguing because they'd run out of beer and were still five weeks away from Alpha Centauri. The smoke thickened and drifted across Spin's face like a cloud, melting it. Tendrils of flame leaped from within the smoke. Kranish saw them clearly, bright orange, flaring, glowing like the eyes of some primeval beast. Now the camera panned the windows. Tongues of fire zipped along the hem of the curtains that hung in the motor home window, consuming the paisley in a flash.

There was a skip in the film, barely discernible to the untrained eye, but Kranish caught it. The person had either switched the camera off momentarily or film had been spliced in. The hem of Domer's slacks smoldered.

Kranish swallowed hard, slammed his hand against the OFF button, and the screen went black. *Sweet Jesus, he was burned alive.* He opened his mouth to call for someone, but no sound came out. His fingers twitched against the button. The set flickered to life again.

Now Domer was lifting his head, his face gleaming with sweat, eyes wide with horror as the fabric caught fire and tongues of orange raced up his right leg. Domer thrashed against the ropes, bucked, rolled right and left, trying to smother the flames, and his silent screams went on and on, echoing inside Kranish's head, echoing forever.

There was a second skip in the film. Domer's hair was burning. He jerked his head right and left, trying to press his hair against his shoulder. He screamed and screamed into the gag, slammed his head against the couch. Thin flames sucked off Domer's eyebrows, his hair blazed, the flames were blackening the skin on his forehead.

Tears sprang into Kranish's eyes. His knees went soft as putty. His heart rotted in his chest like dead meat. The tape skipped again, a definite break this time. Kranish sat there, paralyzed, the bitterness of bile coating his tongue. He didn't realize he'd been holding his breath until the picture flickered to life again. This time, the camera was outside, panning the flames that licked the belly of the dark September sky. An obscene beauty, Kranish thought dimly, a violent beauty, those flames, spilling orange down the sides of the sky. Then the lens dropped to the source of the flames, to the motor home going up like so much tinder. The windows shattered in a burst of glass that seemed to glisten in the apricot light like radioactive dust. The door blew off its hinges, then suddenly the motor home flew apart at the seams, exploding.

A fireball displaced the sky and the remains of J.B. Domer scattered like motes of dust in a vagrant wind.

The TV went blank and dark as death, and Kranish sank to his knees and wept.

PART ONE

Dailies

"Making movies is a giant crap game."
—Gill Kranish

One

THE THING QUIN later remembered about that morning was how at precisely 10:06 A.M. its perfection cracked like an egg.

It was the sight of the bright red Mercedes that started it, a sleek little number snuggled into her spot under the banyan. Apparently the driver had failed to see the sign that announced parking was only for employees of ST. JAMES & MCCLEARY, PRIVATE EYES. In smaller letters was a warning that all other cars would be towed. Parking spaces in this area were like gold bullion; you hoarded them.

Good-bye, Mercedes, she thought. She would call the towing company as soon as she got inside. Then she noticed the license plate on it that said SPIN and there was only one person in the world with a plate like that. Gill Kranish. The home boy had come home, and she had a good idea what he wanted.

She considered leaving. She could go get a bite to eat or something, and maybe when she returned he'd be gone and she could pretend she'd never seen the car. *Oh, Gill was here? Too bad I missed him.* But Kranish was like the flu. Once he'd arrived, he was tough to get rid of, and sooner or later she would have to deal with him.

Quin parked her Toyota at the other end of the lot, near the hibiscus hedges, and got out. The September heat swam around her, thick as molasses. Strands of her long umber hair dampened against her neck, her cheeks. Her blouse, a fancy little silk number that she should

7

never have worn in this heat, she thought, stuck to her back. Her slacks felt as if they'd been ironed onto her legs.

Four months without rain had checkered the lawn brown, despite a daily dousing from the sprinklers. The withered buds of the geraniums hung their heads like sinners, the usually vibrant purple Mexican heather had faded to lavender, even the hibiscus and ivy seemed to be dying from thirst. The heat, like Kranish, sucked everything dry.

She sneaked in through the back door, so she wouldn't have to go by McCleary's office, where Kranish probably was. She could hear the buzz of voices from Ruth Grimes' TV in the reception area, but otherwise the hall was quiet; that was a good sign. It meant the hoopla that Kranish's arrival had probably generated was over. Or hadn't started yet. In that case, when Kranish exited McCleary's office, the staff would be lined up—ten private eyes, a receptionist, and two secretaries. They'd be whispering about Kranish the executive producer, Kranish the creator of Spin Weaver, Kranish the king like Spielberg. Gill's groupies.

Spare me.

As she rounded the corner toward the staff kitchen, she nearly collided with skinny Joe Bean. He grunted; coffee splashed out of the two cups he was holding, trickled down the sides and onto the rug. He barely noticed. His dark raisin face broke into a grin.

"Quin. You *know* who's in there with Mike?" he whispered.

"Spin Weaver?"

"You knew. You knew Kranish was coming and you didn't tell me. I can't believe it, Quin. I can't believe you'd keep something like that from me."

She laughed. Bean paced around her, the way Richard Pryor did whenever he was in the middle of a hot monologue and the crowds were cracking up, begging for more.

8

"I didn't know. Really. I just saw his car in the parking lot."

"He's a *friend* of Mike's, Quin. How come you never mentioned it?"

"You never asked." She went into the kitchen, briefcase in one hand, her bag of lunch in the other, and Bean followed quickly.

"They're *buddies*, Quin. They grew up together." Bean seemed to have forgotten she was married to McCleary and would therefore know all this. He set his cups on the counter, refilling them.

"Right, I know." She held out an empty cup and Bean filled it, too.

"Now, you know I'm not a sci-fi freak, Quin. But lemme tell you, when I saw the first Spin Weaver flick seven, eight years ago, whatever it was, I thought, He's my man, Spin Weaver's my man. He's—"

"I know, Joe, believe me, I know." *Ole Spin charmed me, too, Bean.* "So what's Kranish doing here, did he say?"

"Business. Something about the fire on the set and Domer's death. You read about it, didn't you?"

"Hmm." And she'd also heard about it from McCleary because Kranish had called him after it had happened. Then it had hit the papers—not because Domer was such a hot item, but because Kranish was executive producer of the movie, a made-for-TV movie being filmed on location in Miami.

"Well, let me get in there with this coffee. I got things to *say* to this man. I want to pick his brain."

She chuckled. "I get the picture, Joe."

Bean took off down the hall, whistling softly under his breath. Quin put her lunch in the fridge, sipped at her coffee, and glanced at herself in the mirror, postponing the inevitable moment when she'd have to walk into McCleary's office and pretend she was glad to see Kranish.

She ran her hand through her hair, but it had frizzed from the humidity and was beyond fixing. Her eyes, a pale ghost blue, were bloodshot at the edges because she hadn't slept well last night. *Gill's fault.* She'd had a hunch she would see him today, that he'd drop by the office, drop by casually, like he just happened to be in the neighborhood.

She touched the corner of her eyes, wishing she'd worn makeup. She rarely did when it was this hot, though, a fact Kranish was sure to notice. Her cheeks seemed too pale, her chin too pointed, her . . . "Oh, stop," she snapped irritably. Kranish made her feel irreparably flawed.

She looked away from the mirror. Maybe she would just walk into her office and shut the door. Kranish's presence here was an invasion. The firm, after all, felt more like home to her than home did because she and McCleary spent so much time here.

It was a comfortable old house in North Miami, large enough for their staff of fifteen, including her and McCleary, with room for expansion. The kitchen was her favorite room, with its high ceiling, Mexican tile floor, and the large window over the sink filled with a patch-work of pines and hedges from which curved a slice of scrubbed blue sky. Sunlight swept through it like a hot wind, striking two of McCleary's most recent paintings that hung on the far wall.

The first, her favorite of the two, depicted a man and woman embracing against a backdrop of flaming vines that curved and twisted, duplicating the shape of the entwined couple. But this morning, the mood of the second painting fit her own. In it a child and dog strolled a country road beneath a dark, sagging sky that threatened rain. They seemed to be walking out of the picture, abandoning the ominous weather, turning their backs on it, just as she should do with Kranish.

They'd met twice. The first time was over a year ago when he'd blown into town to scout locations for the movie, for *Night Flames,* and again about six months ago. They had taken an immediate dislike to each other. It was never verbalized, because people like Kranish

10

didn't operate that way, and in the beginning she'd thought it was just bad chemistry. Now she understood that Gill saw her as competition. He and McCleary were like family, the closest thing to a brother either of them had, and she, as McCleary's wife, was the interloper, the outsider.

During his last visit, five or six months back, he and McCleary had vanished into the Everglades for a five-day canoe trip. She wouldn't have minded going, but wasn't asked. Well, on second thought, she probably wouldn't have gone even if they'd asked. She wasn't fond of bugs and reptiles. But it was the principle of the thing.

Okay, she would get it over with.

She rapped once at McCleary's office door and peeked inside. McCleary's smoky eyes smiled at her and whispered, *Where've you been?*

Doing errands, her shrug replied. "I thought I saw a familiar license plate outside," she said.

Gill glanced around. He wasn't a handsome man. His nose was a shade too long and squashed like a boxer's at the end, and his forehead was too high. There was a lupine quality to his features that disturbed Quin. It was as if an atavistic, predatory hunger skulked beneath his civilized veneer. But his eyes were a wide, Pacific blue, the sort of eyes that could steal a woman's soul, and hypnotized you into forgetting the hint of hunger. His charisma lay in his presence, in the power of his accomplishments, a power that seemed to surround him like an aura of sunlight.

At the moment, though, his expression was petrous, and Quin felt as if she were peering into the mouth of a volcano. Then he grinned and got up and hugged her hello as if she were a long-lost friend.

"Quin, it's great to see you again. You're looking wonderful. And still as thin as ever."

He held her at arm's length, as if she were a child who'd grown two feet since he'd last seen her. Actually they were about the same height, five ten, and Quin wondered if that was part of what he didn't like about her. Maybe her height intimidated him. It wouldn't be the first time it had affected a man that way.

She stepped back. "You're not looking too bad yourself, Gill."

The remark obviously pleased him. He gave a self-conscious smile, twisted the end of his sandy-colored handlebar mustache, ran his hands over his jeans, and gazed down at his Reeboks. "Up until several days ago, things were going along just swell," he murmured. "Now . . ." He shrugged.

"I was sorry to hear about Domer," she said as she sat down.

"That's part of why Gill's here," McCleary interjected.

Kranish turned those blue eyes on her. "I'd like you and Mike to take the case, Quin."

"I didn't know there *was* a case. I thought the fire and the explosion were an accident."

Kranish shifted gears now, so that he oozed *presence.* It was the sort of presence politicians and attorneys had. Or used-car salesmen. Or movie producers. It was a presence that, combined with enormous talent and vision, had made him a multimillionaire in less than ten years, with three of the biggest moneymaking films of all time.

Not bad for a thirty-seven-year-old guy who'd started out with nothing but a dream.

"Yesterday morning, Sergeant Tim Benson from Metro-Dade phoned to tell me the feds determined that the fire in the motor home which led to the explosion was the result of arson. Turpentine. I, uh, also received a videotape last night." He briefly described what was on it, then McCleary held up the tape like an attorney wagging evidence.

"So it was someone in the cast or crew?" she asked.

Kranish nodded. "The security is so tight on the set, it had to be someone inside. We were filming out at Glades Airport, which is in the middle of nowhere. The motor

12

home was one of several we use on location, and J.B. was in there having dinner between takes."

"Do you keep a video camera on the set?" Quin asked.

"Yeah. We have a video historian, too, but he was out sick that night, so some of the camera crew had been using the video camera. Anyway, when we broke for dinner, the camera wasn't turned back in to props. It was left outside with the other equipment. Anyone could've used it." He rubbed his square chin thoughtfully. "I told Mac I'll pay you double whatever your normal fee is, Quin, if you'll take the case."

Double: this, too, was Kranish's style, waving the proverbial carrot to get his way.

"I've got a production schedule to meet," he went on. "Normally, it takes from twenty-one to twenty-eight workdays to shoot a two-hour TV film. I'd already added a week to that in the original budget just to compensate for the vagaries of the weather down here. We'd been shooting five days before the fire and lost three days because of it." He paused, looked down at his hands. "Given the videotape and the note, Sergeant Benson feels that Domer was killed as a message to me."

"What note?" Quin asked.

"This one." McCleary passed her a piece of paper. "It came with the tape."

"I didn't see it until later," Kranish explained, "because it got stuck to the inside of the wrapping paper."

The note was chillingly brief: "THIS IS THE FIRST."

She passed the paper back to McCleary. She was liking this whole thing less and less. "The first murder?"

"We don't know," McCleary replied. "Benson feels someone's trying to sabotage the film."

She shifted her gaze toward him. He'd been sitting back in his chair, listening to the exchange. His cheeks bloomed with color, as if he had a fever. His dark, trim beard was threaded with gray, and his wood-smoke eyes asked: *So what do you think?*

Tell me more, her frown replied.

"Tell her what you have in mind, Gill."

Kranish crossed his legs at the knees and brushed a piece of lint from his jeans. "Mike would be working with Sergeant Benson, on a so-called special task force to investigate J.B.'s death. I would hire you as an extra, Quin, that way you could work from the inside."

"An *extra*?" She laughed. "You mean, as an actress? God, I'd pass out in front of a camera, Gill."

"You'd do fine," he assured her, sitting forward, anxious to convince her, his *presence* rolling out of him in waves. He touched her arm now and then, establishing contact. It sent an electrical chill along the surface of the skin. He kept his incredibly blue eyes latched on to hers. "There wouldn't be that much actual camera stuff, Quin. You could help around the set when you're waiting around. There'd be a lot of Willie Nelsons and—"

"Willie whats?"

"Will notifies. When you're on call for a particular day, but the hour isn't set. It'll give you a chance to get to know everyone. You'll do fine. I know you will."

"Listen, I might be able to pull off a fifteen-second commercial. But this is a Spin Weaver movie. I mean, I'm not the type for—"

Kranish laughed. "You'd play a twenty-first-century secretary to a reporter, Quin. On Alpha Centauri."

"Alpha Centauri," she repeated, and started to laugh. "How can you bring something like Spin, something larger than life, to television?"

"Spin's perfect for television. The characters have made the Spin movies what they are, Quin, not the special effects. I've got a new guy to play Spin who's better than the original. He and the other characters will come across great on the tube. Better than on the screen, probably."

Kranish, the mass audience genius, was no doubt right, she thought. "What's it about?"

His blue eyes blazed. He sat forward. "Spin and Molly get involved in a money laundering investigation."

14

"I would think they'd only use credit by the second half of the twenty-first century."

"It's Old World money that's being paid to a banker who arranges to smuggle periodic shipments of an hallucinogenic drug to Earth. It's a type of cactus that grows in Alpha Centauri's Great Hunger Desert. Two American reporters who live in Settlers' City on the planet are also onto this banker. The story focuses on the reporters' search, Spin's investigation, and the banker's wife and son. One of the reporters is murdered during the course of the investigation and the other one just abandons the whole thing, even though she knows who's behind her friend's murder."

"What's the title mean?" Quin asked.

Kranish shrugged. *"Night Flames?* It's a metaphor for how the surviving reporter views her life after her partner's been killed. Everything's been wiped out—her integrity because she hides what she knows, her career because she abandons it, everything. In the end, Spin tracks her down."

"It sounds ambitious." *I think.*

"It is. We've found some terrific locations here in Miami that with a little help from our design people are ideal for the mood on Alpha."

"Who would have a strong enough vendetta against you, Gill, to sabotage the film?" she asked.

His brows, which were thick and dark, knitted together so they formed an almost continuous line above his eyes. "I don't know. I've worked with most of these people before on my other films. Some of them are old Spin Weaver people. But I'm sure I've made my share of enemies in this business."

I'll bet.

"Since we were shooting on location, that meant dinner had to be catered," Kranish continued. "So we set up a huge tent at one end of the airport. We'd broken for dinner around eight-thirty and were supposed to start shooting again at ten-fifteen or so, when the moon would be about right. The fire was reported at nine-sixteen, I think it was, by the airport security guard."

Ironic, Quin mused, that Domer was torched at night on the set of a movie called *Night Flames*.

Kranish's attention had turned to McCleary. "I'd been trying to catch a short nap in between takes in one of the other motor homes. The noise woke me up."

"What part did Domer play?" Quin asked.

Kranish smiled. "The corrupt banker, the mastermind. He was a terrific villain. Fortunately, we'd shot most of his scenes, which weren't many. I can get one of our stunt people to fill in as needed from here on in."

"We'll need a list of names of cast and crew and who among them you've had run-ins with, Gill," McCleary noted. Then he glanced quickly at Quin and asked: "If we take the case, I mean."

If? Why consult with me if you've already decided, Mac? her look grumbled. But he didn't see it because his eyes were riveted on Kranish again.

"No problem," Kranish replied. "And I'll need some information from you, Quin, so we can get your SAG card."

"What's that?"

"Screen Actors' Guild. Unions, like lawyers, have this business rigged." Then he slapped his palms once against his thighs. "So, when can we get moving on this?"

Quin and McCleary exchanged another glance, which Kranish intercepted. "What's this, marital telepathy or something?"

"Or something." Although she smiled, she was a little miffed at McCleary for having committed them without their discussing it privately. They both had cases they were handling, and only so much could be pushed off onto the other investigators. "We need some time to check with Benson and the coroner and get some facts straight, Gill. How about if I report on Wednesday?"

"Perfect." Then he reached down to his briefcase,

which had been leaning against the leg of his chair, and brought out a flask.

So, Quin thought, nothing much had changed.

"A celebratory drink. Are there any clean cups?"

"Coming up." McCleary opened a drawer in his desk and brought out three Styrofoam cups.

Quin watched Kranish splash generous amounts of vodka into each cup. Her stomach burned just at the sight of it. Then, as though he were sampling a classic vintage of wine, Gill passed his cup under his nose. "Fantastic," he murmured, and raised it.

"To the successful completion of *Night Flames*," McCleary said.

They toasted. Quin touched her cup to her lips and pretended to swallow.

McCleary, she noticed, did not pretend.

Neither did Kranish.

"Now," the big man said. "Let's talk money."

Two

SHE WAS A mythic bird, fleet and lovely, a silver RX7 which, beneath McCleary's hands, glided, darted, whipped from one lane to the other with the speed of light. Her name was Lady, and next to Quin she was the most important woman in his life. She was an anodyne for stress, constipation, and insomnia, and outstripped Advil, Kaopectate, and penicillin. Maybe, with time, she would even ease his disappointment that his closest friend and his wife couldn't stand each other.

He slowed for the exit, stopped at the light, and glanced over at Quin. Her nimble fingers were quickly peeling a kiwi fruit and dropping the bits of skin in a piece of Kleenex in her lap. She'd drawn her thick hair up, off the nape of her neck. Several strands had escaped and curled like commas against the sides of her face. Her sunglasses nested in her hair; sunlight slid along the tips of her lashes and spilled onto her cheeks. She wore a gold chain he'd given her last Christmas from which hung a delicate gold-leaf orchid.

"You want some kiwi? Is that why you're staring?" She looked up quickly. Her eyes, an eerie ghost blue that always startled him, creased at the corners as she smiled.

"I'm appreciating, not staring. There's a difference."

"Flatterer," she murmured, and bit into the kiwi, her expression rapturous. Quin and food, like peas in a pod, were inseparable.

"What network is the movie going to be shown on, Mac, do you know?"

"NBC. Sight unseen, they want it. And the studio doesn't even get to see the dailies. This is Gill's baby, all the way." The light turned green. "You still don't like him, do you, Quin." It was a statement, not accusatory, but puzzled.

"This is only the third time I've met the man. You sure you don't want a bite?" She extended her hand, crowned by the rich and gleaming kiwi.

"No, thanks. That doesn't really answer my question, you know."

She sighed, a small sound of resignation. "No, I don't like him."

Well, he'd asked. And Quin, with her usual candor, had told him. So it was his own fault if he didn't like the answer. "Why not?"

"I don't know."

"C'mon, give me a reason, Quin. I know you have reasons."

"A reason. Okay. Let's see." She wiped her fingers on the Kleenex, then folded it carefully and dropped it in the plastic garbage bag on the floor. "He uses you."

"*Uses* me? How? He's paying us twice our normal fee for investigating a homicide."

She looked out the window. "I don't think we should have this conversation."

McCleary turned left and pulled up in front of the county coroner's office. He switched off the engine; it ticked like a clock in the silence. "Okay. I didn't mean to raise my voice. I'm just curious."

She hooked a leg up under herself, and he watched her mouth. He considered himself something of an expert on mouths, an interest that had started with his painting. Like bodies, mouths had their own unspoken language, a code of twitches, pouts, smiles, and dimples, as well as a variety of shapes and sizes that offered other clues. At the moment, Quin's mouth—bow-shaped and painted coral—was saying, *I don't want to discuss this but you're making me.*

19

"Look, Mac. Maybe it's just me, okay? Maybe I just have a warped sense about people. Yeah, that's probably what it is. Me."

"It's because of that incident on Miami Beach last year, right?"

She shrugged. "Partly. Gill was drunk and assaulted someone and he couldn't buy his way out, so he comes whining to you for help."

It hadn't been like that at all, he thought. Kranish was the one who'd been assaulted, and when he fought back, he and the other man were both arrested. But McCleary didn't want to argue. He hated to argue. He made a visor with one hand, hiding his eyes, and Quin laughed and peeked around the side of it.

"Oh, c'mon," she said. "Let's go see the doc. Just because I don't like Gill doesn't mean I don't like you." Then she kissed him quickly and got out of the car, and he tasted kiwi all the way across the parking lot.

She didn't understand. In many ways, Gill Kranish was the kid brother McCleary didn't have. For the first fifteen years of their lives they'd lived a block from each other in Syracuse, New York. They'd gone through grade school and most of high school together, with Gill as the spacey kid who dreamed of making movies and McCleary as his practical sidekick. Gill's family moved to Miami when he was fifteen, and ever since, he'd considered South Florida his real home, even though he'd left when he was eighteen for Europe and the London Film School. McCleary had spent four out of the next six summers in Europe, traveling around with Gill.

For a while he'd even considered moving to London, until Gill had tried to talk McCleary into accompanying him into the Golden Triangle, the heart of the world's opium trade, where he wanted to investigate material for a script. McCleary had said no way, and Gill had gone alone.

At twenty-four Kranish blew into Hollywood with some minor film credits, his inimitable belief in himself and his dream, and a movie script he'd written based on his experiences in the Golden Triangle. He sold the script, directed the film. The critics loved it, but it bombed at the box office. After that, Kranish left Hollywood and McCleary lost touch with him for nearly three years. Then Kranish burst onto the scene again with his first Spin Weaver film, a sci-fi suspense movie with an off-the-wall, futuristic detective as the central character. It was a hit with both critics and audiences, and eventually became the fourth-biggest moneymaker in the history of films. Like the *Star Wars* saga, it was planned as a series, a kind of space-age soap opera. So far, there had been three Weaver films, with a fourth planned for next year, in addition to *Night Flames*—Spin's first foray onto the tube.

By the time they renewed their friendship, McCleary was working for Metro-Dade, and the years had changed them both. Gill was no longer just a spacey kid with a dream. He was the hottest producer around, and a man who walked the cutting edge of obsession, of frenzy, as if to compensate for the three years he'd lost when he'd left Hollywood after his box office failure. The only time he'd referred to those years, he'd called them the darkest in his life, but he'd never elaborated.

McCleary couldn't blame Quin for not understanding his friendship with Gill. There were times when he didn't either.

The building that housed the county morgue had once been a small apartment building and was part of Miami's Art Deco preservation project. It was pale blue with yellow and green doors, pink trim around the windows, and a lemon stripe that circumvented the top part of the building. There was a neon sign out front that said DADE COUNTY CORONER. It was the sort of place where you could imagine corpses dancing to old thirties tunes once the rooms had cleared out at night. As the last stop before the cemetery, he supposed this building was preferable to most morgues.

They found Doc Smithers in the lab, hunched over a microscope, his bald head reflecting the bright overhead lights like a mirror. On a VCR in a corner of the room, Phil Donahue was interviewing the unmarried parents of an infant who needed a heart transplant.

"Hey, Doc."

"Mac, Quin. By God, it's been a while." He shook McCleary's hand and hugged Quin hello. He reminded McCleary of Tweedle Dum: stray hairs sprouting over his ears like a cat's whiskers, plump cheeks that his wife loved to affectionately pinch, a mischievous glint of humor in his dark eyes. "Tim was in much earlier this morning and mentioned you two might be working on the Domer case."

McCleary jerked a thumb toward the tube. "I didn't know you were a fan of Donahue's."

Smithers made a face. "I'm not. I taped that this morning. I wanted to hear about this baby that needs a heart transplant. He got turned down by a med center in L.A., you know. Because his parents are unmarried and too young, just kids really. Anyway, Donahue nabbed them when they turned custody of the child over to the girl's parents. Now all they need is a heart."

"Did you know that the average American watches TV a little more than seven hours a day?" Quin remarked to no one in particular.

McCleary laughed. "My wife, the trivia expert."

Smithers wrinkled his nose. "Poppycock, as my old man used to say. That means they watch the tube seven hours, work eight hours, sleep eight hours and have approximately one hour left in the day for meals, commuting, sex, and showers."

McCleary pulled two stools up to the counter. "So tell us what you know about the case, Doc."

"Not much, I'm afraid." Smithers ran his hand over

the crown of his bald head, his effervescence hissing out of him like steam. The twitch at the corner of his mouth said, *This may be unpleasant.*

He shuffled over to a refrigerator and brought out an oblong metal container. He set it carefully on the counter and pulled up a stool. As he slumped onto it, his fingers rested lightly on top of the container.

"You understand that an explosion doesn't leave a man much to work with. These are just the smaller pieces of Mr. Domer that were found." He flipped open the lid. McCleary's breakfast skidded like a drunk across the floor of his gut as he stared at a hand, two fingers, and parts of what looked like a foot. His eyes skimmed across bones he couldn't name with bits of flesh still attached. Some items were charred, others were untouched. Everything was tagged and categorized in Smithers' neat, precise script.

"Most of the samples in here are about what you'd expect for an explosion. Based on the blood-sugar level, my guess is Domer hadn't had dinner yet. For whatever that's worth. There was also some alcohol in his blood. Under the index fingernail here"—Smithers gestured toward one of the fingers—"I found some skin and blood, maybe from whoever Domer struggled with, maybe just someone he accidentally scratched at some point during the day. Anyway, if it's the killer, you're looking for someone with type O blood who's hypoglycemic."

"Which means what?" McCleary asked.

"Whereas diabetes is characterized by elevated blood sugar, hypoglycemia means an abnormally low level of sugar in the blood. It can be tolerated by normal people for brief periods of time without any symptoms whatsoever. But if the blood sugar remains low for a prolonged period of time there can be mental confusion, hallucinations, convulsions, and eventually deep coma."

"Could you tell if Domer was dead before the explosion?"

"That would've depended on when the fire was set. He

bled to death, but since I had so little to work with, I don't know from what. Maybe a gunshot wound, maybe a stabbing, I just don't know. But the serotonin levels in his blood indicate he lived at least ten minutes after it happened. I'd say he died between seven and ten in the evening."

"What do the serotonin levels have to do with how long he lived after it happened?" Quin asked.

Smithers' mouth, which was large, with a thin upper lip, formed an O as he yawned and tried to stifle it. "Sorry, it's already been a long day." He jerked a thumb toward the wall drawers where corpses were kept. "Got six in there from last night—a domestic argument with no winner and a drug deal gone bad." He sighed and a small frown burrowed down between his eyes. "Now what'd you ask? Oh, serotonin. Right. It's a powerful neurotransmitter that prevents surges of chemicals in the system that could overwhelm the heart when a person is terrified or angry. From the amount of serotonin in the blood, I could roughly estimate how long he lived."

"It's not much to go on," Quin remarked.

"It's more than we had fifteen minutes ago," McCleary replied. "Doc, would you mind taking a look at this?" He removed the videotape he and Quin had viewed and set it on the table. "You may see something we didn't."

Smithers wrinkled his nose. "*The* videotape?" McCleary nodded. "Benson told me about it. Sure, I'll take a look at it. I've got some stuff here that may help you two." He opened a drawer and brought out a stack of photographs. "These are pictures the crime lab sent over, showing where his remains were found in relation to the motor home. I understand the police still have the area where the explosion occurred sealed off, so it might be worth your while to drive out there."

McCleary nodded. "We were planning to."

On the VCR, the mother of the child was sobbing and Phil Donahue looked on the verge of apoplexy. Smithers turned up the volume, and for several moments Donahue's voice flooded through the autopsy room. A donor had just been found for the child. "I knew it," Smithers said. "See? You see the power of the tube? Drama in the making. Well, this is taped, but you know what I mean. History as it happens zipping into two hundred million homes. Or whatever. Incredible." He turned the volume down again, then closed the lid on his metal box and returned it to the refrigerator. "So what's he like?"

"Who?"

"Gill Kranish."

McCleary shrugged. "A regular guy."

Smithers chortled. He leaned against the refrigerator, hands in his pockets. "Just like Spielberg's a regular guy, huh. I usually don't go to movies, you know. I like to rent and sit at home like the old fart that I am. But Spin Weaver's different. He's like a member of my family. I not only bought those films on cassette, Mike, I've seen each of them at least three times, not to mention Kranish's other stuff. The man's brilliant. Brilliant people are rarely just 'regular guys.' "

"McCleary and Kranish grew up together," Quin commented.

"Yeah?" Smithers brows shot up. "Well, ask him sometime who his technical advisors were on the Weaver films. His forensics stuff was correct down to the last blood cell, and some of the nifty tools he created were pretty damn close to what the field will probably have by the twenty-first century." Smithers tapped his temple. "He filters information differently than the rest of us. Visionaries always do. This movie he's working on, what's it about?"

McCleary briefly explained.

"Same actors?"

"Some. A new Spin Weaver, though."

"Oh, why? What happened to Jackson?"

"He was getting too big for his britches. Gill put him in his place."

"Well, if you two are ever knocking around with some time to kill, Mike, come by. I'd love to meet the man."

"You'd like him." *Most everyone does except my wife.* And whoever was trying to sabotage his film.

Three

THE MERCEDES WHISPERED east on Dania Beach Boulevard, sunlight sliding off its darkly tinted windows like water. Inside, Kranish had the vents turned in his direction so the cool air spilled onto his face, easing the pain in his head somewhat.

At the Dania pier he turned into the parking lot for the public beach and followed a dirt road shrouded in pines. It wound back behind the beach to a half-moon cove where the crew was filming today. He parked between two pines and got out of the car.

Despite his dark sunglasses, the light poked into his eyes like hot darts as he came out of the shade. The pain in his head slid off to one side and pounded against his temples. Jesus, the light down here brutalized like its heat—marvelous for shooting, but deadly to a man with migraines.

He stood at the edge of the cove, watching the activity. Half a dozen technicians were rigging up cables that connected to several huge vans that supplied electricity. Cameras sprouted from mobile platforms like exotic trees. A cluster of boulders, hauled in from the central part of the state, rose from the sand, dark, majestic, symbols of the barrenness that had prompted Alpha Centauri's settlers to live in domes. This slice of beach, of impossibly white, flat sand, and the brilliant backdrop of blue water, were supposed to be just outside the domed city. The water, for all its beauty, was fed by hot mineral springs and poisonous to drink.

"Gill?"

He glanced around. Irene Bedford strolled over, dressed in the shimmering jumpsuit that marked a person as a denizen of Settlers' City. Hers molded itself to her slender hips and legs, and the gold contrasted sharply with her black hair and eyes. Although she was the stunt coordinator for the movie, she was also playing the part of Lynn Weatherspoon, one of the *Centauri Tribune* reporters.

"Hi."

She nodded amicably, but as always, Kranish sensed her remoteness. "You going to be around while they shoot this scene?" she asked him.

"Should I be?"

She slid a hand into the pocket of her jumpsuit, looked down at the ground, then up at him again, cocking her head to one side. "I'd appreciate it if you were. So you can tell me if you think I pulled it off."

"You'll do fine," he assured her.

"Hey, Irene, we're about ready," shouted Patrick 'Patty Cakes' May, the director. Then he waddled quickly across the sand, his bulk equaled only by his capacity as a director. He scratched his unkempt beard and tilted his sunglasses back into his hair. "Gill, one of the cameras is blitzing out. I rigged it for now, but we're gonna need another one from L.A. pronto."

"I'll get Dina on it."

"C'mon, Bedford, back out on the set." Patty Cakes stabbed his thumb in the air. "I gotta talk private with Gill."

"Stay around, Gill," she called, then trotted off across the sand.

"It's going without a hitch, Gill. But I've got some script changes for tomorrow I want you to look at."

"Fine. I'll pick them up before I leave. Also, we're going to have another character, a real small part. The reporter Sammy plays will have a secretary."

Patty Cakes scratched the back of his neck. "A secretary, huh. And who's gonna write her lines?"

"Don't worry about it. We'll go over it."

The director fixed his hands to his ample hips and fell forward at the waist, reaching for his toes. He rose up again. "It worries me when you do things like this, Gill." He flopped forward once more, inhaling, then exhaling with: "We don't need an extra character." Now he straightened again and patted his belly. "Five of these every hour."

Kranish laughed, and it brought a flare of pain to his temple. He rubbed it hard. "Look, Pat, trust me. We need this character."

Patty Cakes finished his exercise. "Trust you. Shit. I've trusted you this far and I'm still alive and working, so what the hell." He frowned; it brought his bushy eyebrows close together, giving him a slightly simian look. "Headache bad?"

Kranish nodded.

"Yeah, I thought so. I can always tell 'cause you get that look in your eye." He patted Kranish paternally on the back. "Get your ass to a doctor, Gill. See you later."

For a long moment, the pain paralyzed him. "Brought on by stress, Mr. Kranish," one physician had told him. "It's psychological," a second doctor had opined. "When did they begin?" a neurologist had asked.

Fourteen or fifteen months ago, Kranish thought, when the pre-production work had begun on *Night Flames*. That was when the migraines started. He thought it odd that none of these learned men had mentioned guilt as the source of the pain.

When he could move again, he turned and walked slowly back to his car, sorry that he couldn't stick around to see Irene's scene, knowing it would be just one more black mark she placed against him. But he couldn't help it. If he stayed, the pain in his head would bring him to his knees, and for an executive producer, betraying such a weakness could prove fatal.

He took one of his pills and then drove recklessly along A-l-A to Hollywood Boulevard. By the time he drew up in front of a building on Young's Circle, he could barely see. He fed two dimes into the meter, then glanced around, his eyes sweeping through the streets. Ever since the fire, he'd been jumpy as hell, looking over his shoulder wherever he went, unable to shake the feeling that he was being followed, that the note, "This is the first," meant that he was next.

He wanted to follow this thought, pursue it, but it made his head throb fiercely and he shook it off and hurried into the building. It was one of the older ones in the Circle, with a huge atrium filled with plants in the center and stairs that twisted through vines and ferns toward a skylight. It was the sort of building which, with a little imagination, could have been used in *Night Flames*. Maybe he could still use it. Larger, more exotic plants, that skylight enlarged perhaps . . .

Hell, he didn't know. His head hurt too much to think about it.

He entered an office off the atrium with a sign on the window that said LEE LING, CHIROPRACTOR & ACUPUNCTURIST. He didn't have an appointment, he never did, but that was why he paid Lee three times her normal fee. Even at home, he never scheduled appointments with dentists or doctors or people like that. He simply appeared, strolled in unannounced. It was convenient, of course, and convenience was one of the many pleasures money bought, but more than that, it meant he was in control. It meant he did not have to hang around anyone's office like he used to do, victimized by another person's schedule.

The air inside was cool, the lighting soft, the music subdued. The walls were pale blue and pearled like clouds. Chinese symbols hung on the walls. Tremendous plants billowed in delicately painted clay pots near the window. He rang the bell, and a moment later Lee Ling appeared. She was slender and short, about thirty, he guessed, although it was hard to tell with Orientals because they aged well. Her sloe eyes matched the shade of her thick black hair that hung nearly to her waist. A Chinese-American from San Francisco, he thought, who carried the imprint of her heritage in her soft voice and in eyes that seemed to see everything.

"Gill, what a nice surprise." She leaned over the counter and brushed her cheek against his. The touch of that skin, as soft as a baby's, seemed to absorb the pain in his head like a sponge. "I am most sorry about the tragedy, Gill. I read about it in the paper, saw it on the news." She waved a hand. "Well, it is everywhere. You are having headaches again?"

"Worse than before."

She nodded. "Please, go down the hall to the second room. I must tell my other patient she can leave now."

Her businesslike manner amused him. She gave no indication they'd ever been lovers. "Put up your OUT TO LUNCH sign while we're back here," Kranish told her. "And lock the door."

She nodded. Ordinarily, he couldn't have cared less about the front door. But since Domer's death, paranoia had rooted inside him and unfolded like ferns. It made him nervous to think how easily anyone could just waltz in the front door, sneak down the hall, and blow him away.

He undressed, then slipped on a colorful brocade robe. The air in the room smelled faintly of lilacs. The soft music drifted around him. His head continued to pound, but not as badly as before. He closed his eyes, trying to practice the visualization techniques Lee had taught him for controlling the pain. *Imagine your head packed in snow, imagine. . . .*

She came in and closed the door. "So it is an acupressure treatment you would like?" she asked, washing her hands at the sink against the wall.

"And then a massage."

"Where is the pain, Gill?"

"At my right temple and some across the top of my head."

She came up behind him and placed her fingertips against his temples. She rubbed slowly, gently, talking to him quietly, and Kranish floated away in the music of her voice. After a while, he didn't know how long, she lowered the head of the chair, so it flattened out like a table, and instructed him to turn over on his stomach. She pressed her thumbs to the center of his left foot and began to massage an acupressure point, then switched to the same spot on his right foot. The pain in his head began to recede.

"I've been having more intense headaches," he murmured. "Sometimes it's almost like I black out."

"Where you actually faint or you simply can't remember?"

"Can't remember."

"You will excuse me for saying so, Gill, but I believe that is due to drinking and stress, not to the headaches. The headaches are only a symptom."

A symptom. Yeah. He nearly laughed, but when he opened his mouth, the laughter wasn't there, he couldn't cough it up. He whispered, "Someone's trying to kill me. I feel like someone's trying to kill me and what happened to J.B. was meant for me."

Her voice touched him as lightly as feathers. "You punish yourself with such thoughts, Gill. You believe that someone is trying to kill you because you feel guilty about something."

"Maybe you missed your calling, Lee. You should've been a shrink."

"That, my friend, is exactly part of what I am. I am like the hairdresser to whom people spill their secrets. The body never lies."

The pressure of her thumbs against his foot warmed his insides until the warmth became a heat that focused in his groin. Kranish felt himself getting hard. He mentioned it and Lee laughed softly. "The bottom of the feet are erogenous zones. But we've had this discussion before."

He opened his eyes and gazed down the length of the

chair at her. She was watching him, her inscrutable smile hinting at her dark chest of wonders. It had been three months since he'd flown her out to California and they'd spent four days at his cottage north of San Francisco. Four days that had ended with Dina's unexpected arrival. He'd seen Lee since, here in the office, but things had been strictly professional.

She knew what he was thinking, because she said, "Dina is with you on location?"

"Yes. She's manning the office at the hotel."

"Ah." Lee began kneading his calves, his ankles. "She has recovered?"

Kranish chuckled. He had a sharp, sudden image of prim and proper Dina moaning softly on silk sheets the color of eggshells as he and Lee initiated her, drew her into an erotic web of sentience. "She doesn't mention it."

Lee laughed. "We will have to see sometime what the evening taught her."

"I don't think she's too enthused about a repeat performance."

Lee flicked her hair off her shoulders and gazed down at him with that implacable Oriental tranquility. "That is what she would have you believe, Gill. Just as you would like to believe that someone wants to kill you."

Was she mocking him? Making fun of him? Jesus, you could never tell with her because her face hid so much. He felt an irrational urge to strike her, to rip off her starched white uniform and pull her down onto the chair and rape her.

But the urge passed. Her dark eyes sucked at him just as they had always done, luring him into a wind tunnel of strange desires. "I'll have a car pick you up tonight," he said.

Her hands kneaded his toes. "And Dina will be there?"

He closed his eyes, allowing himself to imagine, for just a moment, a repeat of what had happened in San Francisco. Softly, he said, "Sure, Dina will be there."

Four

GLADES AIRPORT LAY at the edge of the Everglades, in the heart of Dade County's farming community. There was no tower, only two small hangars, and a general aviation school which ran a flight training program. McCleary didn't see many planes parked in the field, maybe three or four dozen in all, and of these, at least ten were crop dusters.

They circumvented the field by car first, checking the number of entrances. There were only two. Both had been guarded the night of the fire. Although it was possible an outsider could have flown in, killed Domer, and left, McCleary admitted the insider theory was certainly the most promising. A man in Kranish's position probably made enemies the way missionaries made converts.

He parked in front of the general aviation building. The hot afternoon sun brutalized the stillness; a wall of sweat sprang across his back.

"Maybe we should move to Colorado, Mac," Quin grumbled, cleaning her sunglasses with a piece of Kleenex, then slipping them back on.

"We don't ski."

"So what. We'd be snow bunnies."

"How about a cabin in the Smokies for the summer? Something simpler?"

"Can we afford that?" she asked hopefully.

"No. But we can't afford five new computers for the firm, either, and we're going to get those."

But she didn't want to hear about computers. She was now fixated on a cabin in the Smokies. "We could get a place with a balcony that has a fantastic view, see."

"And we'd leave Miami in June and come back in October, right?"

"Now you're talking."

"What're we going to live on?"

She made a face. "I wish you weren't so practical."

The inside of the building was cool as a cave, and nearly as quiet, except for the drone of a TV set against the wall. When, McCleary wondered, had televisions impinged on the workplace? The morgue, a general aviation office, and come to think of it, even Ruth Grimes, the firm receptionist, had a set behind her desk. *For hurricane reports,* she said, but McCleary suspected she was an avid fan of the soaps. No wonder surveys had determined that Americans derived more pleasure from TV than they did from sex, food, hobbies, religion, or marriage. He could almost believe it.

"Afternoon," said the brunette at the desk who was polishing her nails. She waved one of her hands now to dry the polish. "If you're here about renting a plane or taking lessons, everyone's out to lunch."

"No planes, no lessons," Quin replied. "We'd like to ask you a few questions, though."

The woman's hands stopped waving. "You're cops, right?"

"Private detectives." McCleary dropped his ID on her desk. She barely looked at it.

"Oh. Private eyes. Well, I was close. Ever since this thing happened, there've been cops and feds and reporters and all kinds of people poking around outside, probably looking for souvenirs or something. Sick. So what do you want to know? Was I here the night of the fire? Yes. I had a bit part in the film, see, playing just what I do right here. Only I got to wear one of those fancy jumpsuits and sailed in here on some weird contraption that looks like a hot air balloon. That's how the Centaurians get around the dome. Anyway, did I see anything? You bet, flames shootin' about eighty feet high. Do I know who did it? Nope. Anything else?"

Who wound *her* up? "Yeah, what's your name?" McCleary asked.

"Loretta. Loretta Sweeney." She blew on her nails, scrutinizing them like a plastic surgeon admiring her artistry, and waved her hands once more. Then she touched her tongue to her thumbnail. "Damn, still wet. I need some of that spray stuff that dries 'em real quick." She looked at McCleary again. "I was just in here minding my own business that night because I was going to go on after dinner and I had some work to finish up. Around eight or a little after, these two guys from the film came waltzing in. Lenny Moorhouse and Sammy Devereaux. You'd probably recognize Sammy. He's played the bad guy in a couple of the Weaver films. Now he's playing an obsessed reporter." She frowned. "I think.

"Anyway, they wanted to look through some of the aviation charts, so I sent them into one of the offices. Then sometime after nine, Gus Wright, the airport security guard, comes tearing in here shoutin' about a fire. About two minutes later there was an explosion. It broke one of the windows in the back office there. And that, friends, is all I know. You should probably be talkin' to Gus. He can tell you more than I can."

"Where is he?"

She gestured vaguely toward the wall. "Out there makin' his rounds. You'll see him. He's in a jeep."

"Thanks," McCleary said.

"Uh, I wouldn't go poking around the sealed area if I were you. Gus has already chased off about half a dozen people today," she warned, then leaned forward and switched the channel on the television.

The main tarp that covered the remains of the motor home was about a quarter of a mile away. Beyond it, rising like anthills from the flatness, lay other smaller tarps covering more debris. The black field of asphalt lay

36

between them and it seemed impossibly far in the heat, so they drove over. McCleary divided the photos Smithers had given them and passed half to Quin. They stepped out of the car.

"This one shows the layout of where the motor home was in relation to everything else," he said, holding up a black-and-white eight-by-ten glossy.

Quin studied the photo and looked around. "So we're almost due north right here. At roughly six o'clock is the hangar where they were filming, nine o'clock is where the dinner tent was, three o'clock is the second hangar and general aviation building. Got it. Now what do I do with these things, anyway?"

"Just try to get a mental picture of where Domer's remains were found in relation to everything else."

"Gross." She walked off with her photos.

McCleary lifted the edge of the main tarp and propped it up with a stick. Waves of heat, trapped under the tarp in ninety-plus degrees for a week, rolled over him, riddled with pothers of ashes and the effluvium of smoke, burned flesh, decay. He peered into a chancrous landscape, blistered, scarred: there, part of a toilet, the door of a refrigerator, twisted pipes, the splintered remains of a TV; here, a charred mattress, half the frame of a couch, a cushion with stuffing spilling out, a sparge of weeds that had broken through the asphalt since the fire. He began matching the photos with what he was looking at: femur bone, found there by the refrigerator door; right leg, found at a sixty degree angle to the toilet; right hand to the far left by those twisted pipes.

California had the Hillside Strangler, the Skid Row Slasher, the Walk-in Killer, and Charles Manson. Yet Miami boasted cocaine cowboys and the highest homicide rate in the nation.

And now here's another one for you, Miami, the scattered vestiges of a man's anatomy.

(knock it off, chum. it's not my fault. i hate complain-

ers, so if you can't do something about it, then just shut
up.)

Testy as always.

(you would be, too, if you hadn't had any rain for four
months.)

He worked his way slowly around the tarp. When he
met up with Quin, she was sitting back on her heels,
the photos in a half moon circle around her. Her eyes
were closed.

"You praying?" he asked.

"Sure, Mac." Her eyes fluttered open. "I'm doing kill
flashes."

He crouched beside her, the bone white sunlight pool-
ing around them. "Kill flashes? Is that like hot flashes?"

She lifted her hair off the nape of her neck with one
hand and fanned herself with the empty folder with the
other. "It's like right brain bridge."

He'd been married to the woman for nearly a year and
this was the first he'd ever heard of "kill flashes" and
"right brain bridge."

"You never told me you play bridge."

"I don't. But my mother does. She says the secret to
winning at bridge tournaments is to *not* think about what
you're doing. You just play whatever drops into place
behind your eyes. Right brain bridge. A kill flash is like
that. It's a way of perceiving. In some cases, you need to
have everything lit up before you can see the pattern.
That would be like using a flash to take a picture in a
room where the light is dim. The flash exposes everything. But in other cases, you want to kill the flash and
try to discern the pattern in the play of shadows."

Like painting, he thought. "So what'd you see?"

She shrugged and gathered up her photographs. "Nothing. We don't have enough facts yet."

"If it's facts y'all be wantin', folks, I suggest y'all goes
to the po-leece," said a gruff voice behind them.

McCleary looked around at a short, white-haired man
in a brown uniform. His face was bright pink, with thin

38

white creases at his eyes as if he'd spent half his life squinting into the brutal subtropical sun. He wore thick glasses that distorted his dark eyes, so they looked small and mean.

"You Gus?" McCleary asked.

"Gus Wright. Who're you?"

McCleary introduced himself and Quin, then showed Wright their IDs because he looked like the kind of man who wouldn't cooperate otherwise.

"Dicks, huh. Who hired ya?"

"Gill Kranish, the executive producer."

Wright squeezed an eye shut against the bright glare. "I guess it's okay y'all be lookin' round then. Had so many people out here the last few days I'm gettin' sick of it. Snoopy reporters been makin' real pests of theirselves." He brought a cigar out of his pocket, skinned the paper from it, lit it.

"I understand you called in the fire that night," Quin said.

"Shore did, ma'am." The words tumbled out in a puff of smoke. "I was doin' my rounds, mindin' my own business, and I sees these flames in the winder' of the motor home. I ran up to it, touched the knob, and it was so hot I knew if I opened the door I's a goner. Then one of them winders blew, so I hotfooted it on over to the general aviation buildin' to call the fire department."

"You see anyone around the motor home before it happened?"

Wright tapped his cigar; an ash the size of a dog turd dropped to the ground. "Looky here, Mr. Mack-Leary. I do my job. I don't want no trouble with the po-leece."

A man with a need to confess, McCleary thought, and nodded. "Right. I understand. Whatever you say would be kept confidential."

Wright didn't look convinced, but he said, "Well, 'round 'bout seven-thirty that night, when they was still shootin' the scene near the hangar down yonder, I was ridin' along the fence." He pointed to the east at the fence that separated the airport property from an empty field. "I saw the stunt woman knockin' at Mr. Domer's door."

"You know her name?" Quin asked.

"Sure. Irene. Irene Bedford. She's the stunt coordinator. It was almost dark then, and the only reason I noticed her at all is 'cause the motor home had this little stoop, with a porch light. Well, a while later, I's comin' 'round again, must've been about twenty minutes later, and I could hear them arguin'. One of them winders must've been open. So, bein' the nosy ole man I am, I stops the jeep 'n lights me a ci-gar, and, sittin' out there by the fence, I hear her shoutin' that he's nothin' but a whoremaster and he uses people and other stuff like that."

"What kind of stuff?" Quin asked.

"Don't 'member exactly, ma'am, but not very nice stuff, I can tell you that. Not too much later, she comes a'marchin' outa that motor home, slammin' the door behind her."

"About what time was that?" McCleary asked.

"Oh, I'd say it was pretty close to eight o'clock. I's hungry by then, so I moseys on over to the smaller hangar, right near the general aviation building. I usually eat my suppers there."

He settled down at the desk in the little office, he said, finished his sandwich, and decided to take a snooze. He turned off the lamp, removed his glasses, and put his head on the desk. "Next thing I know, I hear this creakin' sound outside and realize it's the door to the shack openin'. There's this little storage shack connected to the smaller hangar. Anyhows, I could hear someone inside, breathing real hard, like they'd been runnin'."

He paused and held out his arms, where a crop of goosebumps had erupted. "That's what it done to me, that breathing, the sound of water in the sink in there . . . it was like a goose had just strolled 'cross my grave. So I just sits there, real still like, waitin' for the person to leave. When I finally heard the door closin', I got up nice and slow and went over to the door and put my ear to the wood. I didn' hear nothin', so I opened it. Well, I didn't see nothin', neither, 'cause I'd forgotten to put on my glasses."

"You didn't look outside to see who'd been in the shack?" Quin asked.

"No, ma'am, I didn't want to know. But after I put on my glasses, I went in the shack and had a look 'round with my flashlight." He stopped, ran a finger alongside his nose. "C'mere, I'll show you what I done found."

They walked over to his jeep with him. From the back, he brought out a paper bag. "This was shoved down in one of them garbage bins." He reached into the bag with a pair of pliers and retrieved a plastic container that had probably contained Clorox or a similar cleanser. He set it down and with a handkerchief unscrewed the top. "Take a good whiff of that."

McCleary did. The odor was turpentine. He looked over at Quin.

You run with it, her eyes said.

"Why didn't you just give it to the police?" McCleary asked.

"I told y'all, I don't want no trouble. I'm mighty sorry a man lost his life in that fire, don't be misunderstand'n me, but with these movie people, ya just don't know. They think the law don't apply to them. Hell, they've got so much money, maybe they'd try to pin this thing on *me.*"

"You didn't touch this, did you? I mean with your hands?"

Wright smiled. "No siree."

"Did you find anything else?"

"Yup." He reached into the bag again, reminding McCleary of a shopping center Santa Claus. But what he withdrew had nothing to do with Christmas. It was a plastic baggie with a steak knife inside covered with dried blood.

"You've been carrying this stuff around with you since the night of the explosion?"

"Yup." He rubbed his chin. "Guess I been feelin' guilty 'bout not goin' to the po-leece, figured sooner or later someone'd come along who I could trust." He replaced the items in the bag, picked it up, and handed it to McCleary. "It's yours. But so help me, if y'all break your word and the cops come around askin' me questions, Mr. Mack-Leary, I'll deny this-here conversation to the grave."

McCleary felt like kissing the old man.

"Mr. Wright, when you left the hangar, is that when you saw the fire?" Quin asked.

"Yes, ma'am. And I ran over there, like I says, and realized the place was too far gone for me to do somethin', so I took off for the buildin' and called. Then I scooted back to the hangar and gathered up what I'd found."

"You mind showing us the shack?" McCleary asked.

"Mind?" He chuckled. "It'd be a relief."

"Great. Let me put this stuff in the car."

Five

KRANISH STOOD OUTSIDE his suite in the penthouse of the Prince Hotel on Miami Beach. He had the corner penthouse, the largest, and the hall here was darker than he would've liked because there wasn't a window. The stairway door was just behind him, and he glanced back at it several times, expecting the killer to suddenly burst through with turpentine and a match.

His key was in the lock, but he couldn't turn it, was afraid to open the door and step into the darkness. His fear shamed him. It was coiled like a beast at the bottom of his gut, and the beast gnawed at his intestines, working its way upward toward his heart. *Did Domer feel fear like this? I'm sorry, J.B., I'm sorry.*

He knuckled an eye, wishing he'd stayed someplace where the elevator wouldn't ascend to the penthouse without a key. Then he would be absolutely certain no one was waiting behind the door for him, or in the stairwell, waiting with turpentine and a match, or a bullet with his name on it.

He turned the key, sucked in his breath, nudged the door open with his foot. A rush of cool air licked at his face. He swallowed hard and pushed the door open wider, the blackness yawning at him now. The tip of his shoe connected with something, then he lunged for the light switch. His eyes swept through the front room—furniture in soft blues and celery greens, chrome and glass tables, a plum-colored rug, the moon rising in the sliding glass porch doors, illuminating a slice of the vast, black sea.

And there, off to the right, the twinkling lights of Miami, perdurable. *No one's been here, you idiot.*

He looked down. His shoe had kicked a stack of mail Dina or someone from the office had delivered. He scooped it up, dropped it on the coffee table, strolled over to the VCR across the room, and popped in a Spin Weaver tape. *Spin in Space.* He stepped back, watching as the credits rolled, and the scene opened on Spin and Molly Drinkwater.

His phone rang.

He ignored it and fixed himself a drink and wondered if Spielberg ever watched *E.T.*, puzzling over how he'd produced such a masterpiece. It was how Kranish felt every time he watched one of the Spin Weaver films. He'd never been able to figure out from what dark corner of his mind Spin had sprung. As a kid, he'd been fascinated with electronics, with the future, with space, but science fiction per se hadn't interested him at all. If anything, he supposed that Spin Weaver was the sort of man he would like to be: ordinary, but quirky, honest, and direct, a man who felt things deeply enough to be moved by the play of shadows on a woman's cheek.

The curious and disturbing thing about Spin was that after each film, Kranish was always certain his sci-fi detective had slipped back into the soup of his unconscious, that there would be no continuing saga. It was as though Spin had assumed a life of his own and at any moment might choose to vanish as rapidly as he'd appeared. The irony, of course, was that Kranish felt absolutely powerless over the character *he* had created. The character, he thought, who'd brought accolades from the critics and millions from the public and who'd shoved Kranish's name into the upper echelons of the Hollywood power structure. He did not control Spin Weaver; Spin controlled him. It was as simple and complex as that.

A knock at the door prompted him to pop out the tape. He slipped off his shoes and strolled across the room with the drink in his hand. He reached out to open the door, then yanked his hand back as though the knob had burned him. In his mind, he saw himself opening the door and looking down the barrel of a gun. "Who is it?"

"Dina, Gill."

He unlocked the door. Dina was nibbling on a cracker, and dabbed at her mouth with the back of her hand. Her pale green eyes smiled at him. "Your paranoia's showing, Gill."

"Only to you."

She stood about five foot five, and he had to lean down to kiss her hello. Her mouth tasted salty, from the cracker. Her shoulder felt thin beneath his hand, insubstantial. Her light chocolate hair smelled faintly of shampoo. She wasn't pretty; she was cute. She was the kind of woman who would never end up on the screen, but behind it, running the entire operation.

"How about a drink?"

"Thanks, I'd love one."

They walked into the living room. "I hired the McClearys."

He watched her cross the room toward the bar. She moved quickly, but with an air of singularity, purpose, not impatience. Thin, he thought, but with curves in all the right places. She opened a can of peanuts and dipped her fingers inside. A nibbler; she contended it kept her thin. "I figured you had. I still think you should let the police deal with it, but it's your money."

"Quin's going on the payroll Wednesday."

"Okay, I'll take care of it. I'll need her—"

"I know, I've got all the information." He motioned at the coffee table where his yellow legal pad was. She came back across the room with her Scotch-and-soda and a handful of peanuts. "How about if I fix us dinner tonight and we eat in?"

"'Yeah, I'd like that. I'm famished. You cook, I clean up." She sipped at her drink and started talking about what had happened on the set today, updating him.

Kranish had had numerous assistants through the years,

but none did the job as well as Dina. She kept her finger on the pulse of the production. If he wanted to know how a particular crew or cast member felt about something, he had only to ask her, and if she didn't know, she would find out. He consulted her on everything from scripts to personnel problems and she was his liaison with the unions, the network, writers, and his L.A. office. She wasn't brilliant, but she possessed a perspicacity about the movie industry that often astonished him.

He'd met her six years ago, when she'd applied for a secretarial job in his L.A. office—one of seventy-five applicants. When he'd told her someone would get back to her once he'd made his decision, she'd laughed. "Why look any further, Mr. Kranish? I'm the best person for the job." Her hubris had impressed and amused him.

"What makes you think you're the best?" he'd asked.

"Try me for a month and I'll show you."

So he did. She was recently divorced and had no children, no commitments. Consequently, she threw herself into the work as if she'd been doing it for years. At the end of a month he'd given her a raise and promoted her to office manager. Within a year she'd become his personal assistant. Three years ago they'd become lovers, and from the beginning she'd known about his other women. It was fine with her, she said, because she would continue to see other men. He supposed she did; he had never asked. It didn't matter. Jealousy was as alien to Kranish as the Pill was to devout Catholics.

In the many years they'd worked together, their most serious disagreement had been about his hiring the McClearys. She believed it was a waste of money because cops were paid to do the same thing private eyes did. But as far as Kranish was concerned, cops—like politicians, like any public servant—were perfect examples of the Peter Principle, raised to the highest level of their incompetence. If you wanted a service, you had to pay for it, and pay better than anyone else. So now he would sleep more soundly at night, knowing the McClearys were being paid twice what they usually were to finger the person who intended to sabotage this film.

The doorbell rang, and Kranish glanced at his watch. Lee Ling was right on time. "I'll go start dinner, why don't you get the door," he suggested.

"Are you in?"

He laughed. "Yup, I'm in."

"Even to Patty Cakes?"

"Especially to Patty Cakes."

Kranish went into the kitchen. He loved to cook, and whenever he was going to be on location Dina forwarded a list of items that should be stocked in his kitchen. The list included spices, herbs, certain types of cooking utensils, and things like flour and brown sugar and so on. Tonight's meal, he thought, would fit the occasion— something with a touch of eroticism.

He got out his box of recipes and flipped through them, thinking of the hidden camera in the bedroom. It was a neat and sophisticated piece of equipment that had been developed as a result of the Spin films. Like a pet, it accompanied him to every location, and its clone was installed in his bedroom at home. In the last nine years it had recorded more of Kranish's life than the gossip columns. The resulting videotapes comprised a private collection that he enjoyed viewing as he might the dailies on a movie, looking for ways he could've improved his performance or the lighting or what the women might've done differently.

He thought of it as celluloid voyeurism. There was nothing quite like capturing the image of a woman at the moment of her deepest pleasure and doing it without her knowledge. It was like trapping a bit of her soul and possessing it forever: the ultimate form of control.

He heard the women in the front room, ice clinking in a glass, then Lee poked her head into the kitchen. "Hi, Gill, I understand you're the chef tonight," she said, and winked at him. "Make it yummy, hmmm?"

"Count on it."

Dina didn't come into the kitchen, but Kranish knew she hadn't left. She would stick out the evening because now that she knew Lee was here, she wouldn't turn him loose alone with the competition. She would hang on like an irrepressible itch even when things started heating up. That was how it had happened last time, at the cottage north of San Francisco. And that was how it would happen tonight.

He prepared his special meal, relieved that tonight, for a while, he would forget about death and murder and his film. But a part of his mind kept chipping away at the puzzle. Had the killer viewed his tape of Domer's death before he'd mailed it to Kranish? Had he watched and relived every moment of Domer's torture, his slow death?

Yeah, Kranish thought. And then he'd laughed and packaged the tape and his note and mailed them. The tape was a statement, a promise that read: I will destroy your film. But it didn't tell him why. It didn't tell him if the killer knew about his dark secret of a decade ago or if he was just a looney-tune. It told him only that the killer worshipped control as deeply as Kranish himself did.

Perhaps that was what frightened him most of all.

He awakened suddenly, from a nightmare which was gone as soon as he'd opened his eyes. His mouth tasted dry. His head ached, but not too badly. He glanced to his side, where light from the lamp spilled across Dina's back. Her cheek was pressed to the bed, her mouth was slightly open, her hair curled damply on her cheeks. Lee Ling was gone.

He got up and padded out into the living room. Lee stood at the porch doors, in the half-light from the bar, gazing out into the dark. Her obsidian hair fell to the middle of her back. She turned when she saw his reflection in the glass, her nakedness seeming to suck at the light, to mold it to her bones, her skin.

"You're leaving?"

"No. I'm having wine." She held the glass out to him and he sipped from it. The image of her in the glass captivated him—the curve of her spine, buttocks, the river of hair. It was as if she were rising out of the dark like an apparition. He handed the glass back to her, slipping his arms around her tiny waist. Her breasts grazed his chest as he kissed her. She pulled away, shaking her head. "This isn't what you want to do. Straight sex doesn't interest you much anymore, Gill." Her mouth curved with one of her secretive smiles.

"Is that what you think?"

"That's what I know. I believe that at some point it will cause you much trouble, Gill."

He thought of the hidden camera, of nine years of hidden cameras, and laughed. "I doubt it."

She crooked a finger at him and moved toward the bedroom. "I'll show you what you really want."

"What I want," Kranish said, annoyed by her certainty, "is to finish this wine."

He picked up the glass she'd left on the coffee table, opened the sliding doors, and stepped out on the wide balcony, into the windy warmth of the September night. This was the choice penthouse, offering dual views—Miami as a city of lights, and the black Atlantic. Contrasts and dichotomies, Kranish thought, like the two women. *Like life and death*.

He drained the wine and went back into the bedroom. He stretched out alongside Lee. "You want Dina to awaken while you're making love to me," she whispered. "That's what you want, Gill."

He ran his hand along her smooth and silky thigh, turning her toward him so the camera could capture her face. Her tongue teased his. Coolly, deliberately, he stroked her thigh until goosebumps rose on her arms, then kissed her, ran his tongue over her nipple, letting it linger there until it grew as hard as a pebble, then he slid two fingers between her legs. His tongue traveled down across her stomach, and now she rolled onto her back, arms thrown over her head, hands gripping the brass headboard, and beside her, Dina stirred.

Kranish held Lee at the hips.

Dina lifted her head.

Lee cried out as he thrust himself into her.

Dina, smiling sleepily at first, as though she thought she were dreaming, now rose to the occasion.

Kranish thought of the camera's ubiquitous eye, capturing their souls, chasing away death. Yes, that was the heart of his obsession. The cameras somehow cheated death.

Six

1.

TIM BENSON REACHED into the OUT basket on his desk and set one file after another in front of McCleary. "Here's my investigative report, Mac, the report from the feds on how the fire started, the statements we took from forty-seven members of the cast and crew and probably ten people from the catering company, Smithers' autopsy report—"

McCleary held up his hands and laughed. "Okay, okay, that's fine. That's enough. It'll take me all day to wade through this stuff."

"You don't know how glad I am that Kranish hired you, Mac." Benson pushed his glasses back on his nose with his index finger. He was a thin, wiry man in his forties. He had an almost prissy mouth which, when he was disturbed about something, shrank by degrees because he would roll his lips together. As he was doing now. He usually moved with the quickness of Pan, but this morning his energy seemed attentuated. He sighed as he sat back. "This case is—what? Six days old? A week? Whatever. It's already burned me out, Mac. With you around, though, it's like old times."

'Old times' meant the ten years McCleary had spent in this building as a homicide detective. Although Benson had been assigned to the robbery division back then, they'd worked as partners from time to time. Now Benson was full-time homicide and mired in the vagarious pitfalls that came with the job.

"How many of these alibis have checked out?" McCleary asked.

Benson rubbed his jaw. "That's part of the problem. There were forty-seven people eating dinner in the tent between eight-thirty and ten-fifteen that night. It's not like summer camp where you have to sign in and out, so the only way we could verify where people were was by who they sat with, talked with, that kind of thing."

"And?"

"There're about two dozen folks who ate dinner early and left. According to the payroll sheets, eight of those checked out for the day. Then there were ten, mostly technicians, who vouched for each other's whereabouts." He grinned. "Basic math one-oh-one, huh. So okay, that left us with no alibis for Irene Bedford, Sammy Devereaux, Lenny Moorhouse, and Maia Fox."

"What about the video historian? He's the obvious guy to talk to."

"Bruce Harmon. Yeah, I spoke to him. His alibi checks out right down the line. He wasn't on the set that night. He was at home in bed with the flu. I spoke to his doctor, who came by his apartment with some penicillin, and then with a woman in his graduate program, who stayed part of the night just in case he needed anything. He said there's a video camera always on the set, but when I talked with the prop guy, he said it wasn't checked in on the break, that it was just lying around outside with the cameras, so anyone could've used it."

"Yeah, Gill told me. The receptionist at Glades Airport mentioned that Devereaux and Moorhouse came into the general aviation building shortly after eight. Did they tell you?"

"No." Benson gave an indignant snort. "These damn Hollywood people. They're *weird,* Mac. Why would they lie about something like that when it's their alibis?"

"Probably because they've got something to hide."

"I get the feeling *all* of these people have skeletons rattling around in their lives."

"So that leaves us with Bedford, Devereaux, and Moorhouse, and Maia Fox."

"Right. And after what the airport security guy told you, I'd say our best shot right now is Irene Bedford. The thing that bothers me is that the Bedford woman has known Kranish for years, since the first Spin Weaver film. So why would she want to sabotage this film?"

"Maybe she doesn't. Maybe she just wanted to kill Domer and make it seem like the murder was directed at Gill. What about Moorhouse and Maia Fox?"

"Well, there was some professional jealousy between Moorhouse and Domer. Moorhouse auditioned for Domer's part and didn't get it. That also created some antagonism between him and Gill. Or so I've heard. Oh, about that treasure trove you and Quin brought in. The blood on the steak knife was definitely Domer's. The crime lab's sending that plastic container to Tallahassee. The state's got a new seventy-thousand-dollar argon-ion laser that can pick prints off a wet duck. So if there're prints on the container, it'll find them." He paused. "I talked to that old geezer Wright, you know. He never said diddly squat to me about the container or the steak knife or any of it. I should arrest him for withholding information."

"He's just a scared old man, Tim."

"Yeah. Well." He rolled his lips again. "Even though the doc says the skin found under Domer's nail might not belong to the killer, I'm having everyone come in for blood tests. It can't hurt. Oh, also"—he reached into his drawer and dropped an envelope in front of McCleary— "one more thing. I thought that might come in handy."

He opened it. Inside was a plastic embossed ID card with his picture on it. The photo had been taken shortly before he'd resigned from Metro-Dade sixteen months ago. He looked—what? Haunted? Feverish? His dark hair was gray at the temples, his smoky eyes were drawn in a parody of a smile, his mustache drooped at the ends, as if with fatigue. He didn't have a beard then, and his jaw seemed too square, somehow, making his face seem asymmetrical.

Under the picture, in bold black letters, was HOMICIDE SPECIAL TASK FORCE, and next to that, in print almost too small to read, his vital statistics. "Thanks. This will probably make life a little easier."

"You going to be seeing any of those people today?"

"I have an appointment with Bedford tomorrow. I thought I'd spend today going through all this stuff." He tapped the files. "You mind if I use one of the offices to wade through this?"

"Got one all ready."

He followed Benson into the familiar hall, where the air smelled of two-day-old coffee and resonated with the tap of computer keys from the secretarial area. He almost expected to pass the ghost of his old self: the chief of homicide who'd resigned after he'd shot his partner, a woman he'd loved so blindly that in retrospect it was embarrassing. Robin Peters: lovely, deadly, and mad as a hatter. She'd killed Grant Bell, whom Quin had been living with at the time, and more than a half dozen other men before a bullet from his .357 had ended her life— and perhaps part of himself as well.

He hadn't touched the Magnum since.

Benson opened the door to McCleary's old office. "We made it into a conference room after you left, Mac."

He felt an odd twist in his gut as he stepped inside. The plants and paintings were gone, but the room still reminded him of the bow of a ship. The far wall was glass and overlooked downtown Miami, awash in a sea of harsh September light that seemed to flatten the city, strip it of depth, rendering it two-dimensional.

"If you need anything, just holler."

"Thanks."

When the door closed, McCleary walked over to the window and continued his ongoing dialogue with the city.

Ahoy, Miami.
(welcome back, mccleary)
It's not like I really left.
(you did in spirit)
I did not. I still live here.
Then the city seemed to quiver in the light, as if seized by a massive chuckle, and McCleary realized his ambivalent feelings about Miami would never change.
Don't be smug.
(see you around, chum. you got work to do)
"Yeah, yeah," he mumbled, and sat down at the conference table, spread out the files, and went to work.

2.

To Quin, Lazy Lake was a South Florida anomaly, a little Walden in the heart of an asphalt desert. The thirty-acre town lay within the city limits of Fort Lauderdale, and was built around a freshwater lake that had originally been a rock quarry. There were fewer than three dozen residents and several dirt roads that wound past the sixteen homes.

Pines and tremendous banyan trees with braided trunks proliferated like vestiges of some ancient civilization across its acres. Their branches bridged the main road, hid the homes in their folds, and cast shadows that undulated across the surface of the lake, keeping time to some internal rhythm. The town's mayor, Marielle Lindstrom, was a freelance writer, a former columnist for the *Fort Lauderdale News*, and a good friend of Quin's.

Her home, which she'd inherited from her husband, a surgeon twenty years older than she who'd died four years ago, was on the eastern side of the lake, in a cul-de-sac. Tucked into a holt of pines and banyans, it was built from cypress and tiered like a wedding cake in back, with the final layer a redwood deck that led to a dock. It was here where they sat that Tuesday afternoon, the air so sweet and clean and quiet it made Quin's heart ache.

"Ever since you called last night, I've been *dying* to hear all about this," Marielle said, plucking a plump blue grape from a tray filled with goodies and popping it in her mouth. "I could've been writing scripts all these years."

"I try to forget that he knows Kranish."

Her mouth twitched into a smile. "So it's like that, is it. Okay, start at the beginning."

So Quin talked as the windy warmth of the September afternoon danced through the tall, thick branches of the banyans. Birds trilled. The ducks who made their homes in the lake's nooks and crannies floated by, as serene as enchanted swans. Squirrels chattered and scampered across the deck, snatching up nuts that Marielle tossed them.

"My kinda stuff, for sure," she said when Quin had finished. "Murder and intrigue among the rich and famous. So what do you want me to do? Pose as a writer from *TV Guide*? No problem." She fell forward at the waist, flipped her thick coppery hair to the front, then whipped it back as she sat up again. "Do I look weird enough to be a writer covering TV?"

Quin laughed. "What I need is information, articles, interviews, whatever, on these people." She opened her purse and brought out a list of names taken from those Kranish had given McCleary.

Marielle combed her fingers through her hair and read out loud: " 'Sammy Devereaux, Maia Fox, Irene Bedford, Will Clarke, J.B. Domer, Lenny Moorhouse, Rose Leen.' These are the major actors?"

"Bedford's also the stunt coordinator. The rest are people who were on the set that night. Cast, crew, extras."

"Devereaux and Maia Fox. Spin Weaver people."

"Yeah, Devereaux plays a reporter this time around. Maia's still playing Spin's gal Friday, Molly Drinkwater. And Will Clarke is going to be the new Spin Weaver. I think Gill's got his sights on Spin eventually being picked up as a TV series and that he's looking at *Night Flames* as the pilot."

"It'd be about time." She glanced at the list again. "These other people aren't too well known, though."

"Unknowns are cheaper. Also, I think Gill likes making stars as much as he likes making movies. Look at what *Raiders of the Lost Ark* did for Harrison Ford. Anyway, so Gill gets these people for less money, and in return this is their big break."

"Mutually convenient. You looking for anything in particular?" Another grape vanished into her mouth.

"I'm not sure. Basically, I need to know if any of these people have a grudge against Gill. Maybe some sort of disagreement or altercation that appeared in the press, stuff like that. Also, see if you can find out if anyone on the list has hypoglycemia."

"What about background checks, criminal records, that sort of thing?"

"The firm's handling that part."

"Have Irene Bedford and Maia Fox ever been involved with Kranish? Jealousy's always a good motive for murder."

"I don't know. I'll have Mac ask him."

"I'll check the gossips, too, and see what I can dig up."

"Fine." Quin took her checkbook from her purse. "How much, Ellie?"

She waved her hand. "Poo. We'll worry about that later."

"C'mon."

"Look, I'll bill you by the hour, okay? I don't know how long it's going to take to dig this stuff up. Now c'mon, let's go for a swim. I hope you brought your suit."

Before Quin could reply, Marielle had whipped off her T-shirt and stepped out of her shorts. She already had her suit on. She dived off the end of the dock and surfaced in the middle of the lake, the ducks making lazy circles around her, squawking about the intrusion.

"It's great. Go change," she called.

Quin changed in the three-walled stall that enclosed the outdoor shower and ran for the lake. She executed a nearly flawless shallow dive and moved in a graceful crawl through the sun-kissed waters. They swam to the wooden raft that floated in the center of the lake. From here, Quin could see the FOR SALE sign on the iron fence that surrounded the old home with the overgrown yard that was Marielle's closest neighbor.

"How much do they want for the old Randolph place?" Quin asked.

"Three hundred and fifty grand," Marielle replied, stretching out on her stomach, her arms dangling over the side of the raft. "It's been on the market two years. I bet you and Mac could get it for two hundred and fifty."

Quin laughed. "Right. On what? American Express? If we can get the credit, we're going to go into hock for new computers for the firm."

She rested her chin on her hands and gazed at the dark waters. The ducks, four of them, moved steadily toward the dock, drifting in and out of shadows. Beyond them, on the far shore, the shaggy heads of the banyans dipped low over the water. Lichenous rocks gleamed wetly in slices of opaline light.

"How're things with you and Mac?"

"Good. Except for Kranish. He idolizes the man. I can't stand him. It's like in-laws."

"Ah. Right. In-laws." She sat up, stretched out her legs, rested back on her hands, and tilted her face to the sun. She was a thin woman in her late thirties whom Quin had met five or six years ago, when Marielle's husband had been named in a medical malpractice suit. He'd hired Quin and her then partner, Trevor Forsythe, to help prove his innocence. "Do you know my ex-sister-in-law is still bugging me about a stupid love seat in the hall? I finally told her she could come over and get the damn thing. Yeah. Tell me about in-laws. Technically, she's not even my in-law anymore, since Mark is dead."

"You still miss him, don't you."

Her expression softened. "Sure. Mark was a good man, generous, and we had a wonderful eight years together. But things go on, and you adjust."

"You seeing anyone?" Quin asked.

Marielle shrugged. "I guess you could say I'm free-lancing." She said it with a laugh, but it lacked mirth. "You know any male writers?"

"Not a one."

"Too bad. I think I'd like to meet a writer, Quin." She ran her fingers through her wet hair. "I'd like to meet a guy I could work with. Like you and Mac. Every time I see you two together, I wonder if you realize how lucky you are. You don't just have a good marriage, you *work* together. You know how hard that is to pull off?"

Luck: sometimes it came wrapped in deceptive packages, Quin thought on her way home. A homicide had brought McCleary into her life, and much of that time seemed remote now, as if it had happened to someone else. Yet, in retrospect, certain memories had assumed an almost preternatural clarity: discovering Grant Bell's body on the kitchen floor of his townhouse; her initial dislike for McCleary, the investigating homicide officer; uncovering evidence of Bell's numerous duplicities as well as the dozen Colombian emeralds he'd smuggled out of South America; and Robin, blown out of their lives by the explosion from McCleary's .357.

She thought briefly of the emeralds, worth millions, which the state had claimed once the gems had gone through probate with the rest of Grant's estate. She and McCleary could have appealed, of course, but it would have taken years and money, lots of it. Their lawyer doubted they would win, since the emeralds were stolen to begin with. So they'd dropped the whole thing. How could you miss what you'd never had?

There were occasional moments, like now, when the dry cackle of the past wandered through her thoughts like a restless ghost, but mostly it was a yardstick for measuring the present. *I have come this far since. . . .*

By the time Quin neared the house, she was anticipating a leisurely evening with McCleary—dinner, a swim in the pool they'd installed in the back yard five months ago, romance. This would be her last night at home for a while. Kranish had suggested she move into a condo on Miami Beach where some of the cast and crew were staying.

She'd protested at first, but of course Kranish knew the value of logic. It would make her look more legit, he'd said. It would be more convenient, he'd said, since it was located next door to the Prince Hotel, where his production offices were. It would give her access to the cast and crew, he'd said. Again. And again.

So tomorrow she would pack up her Toyota with its ersatz plate that, if checked, would show the car belonged to a Quin St. James, formerly of New York State. Occupation? Actress. Age? Thirty-five. Address? The Atlantic Towers, 542 Collins Avenue, Miami Beach.

Oh yeah, McCleary, she thought with a delight bordering on lechery. Watch out.

Then she saw Kranish's red Mercedes and Benson's Honda in the driveway. Her thoughts of romance shut down as fast as a half-hour sitcom. She parked at the curb because there wasn't room in the driveway.

Benson, McCleary, and Kranish were huddled around the dining-room table like spies, with Merlin sprawled at McCleary's feet. There was a chorus of hellos, but only Merlin rose to greet her. Quin mustered a gaiety she didn't feel, then scooped Merlin up and carried him into the kitchen.

The air smelled of dinner. There were stacks of dirty dishes in the sink, spaghetti sauce splattered on the burners, sauce crusted on the counter. The clean stuff in the dishwasher was still in there because, of course, no one had thought to put it away. None of this would have been so bad if they'd thought to leave her some leftovers. But there wasn't even a ribbon of pasta she could gnaw on.

The final indignity, she thought, and yanked open the fridge. She plucked an apple out of the fruit bin to tide her over until she could prepare something for herself.

But how the hell was she going to fix anything without cleaning up the mess? And why should *she* clean up *their* mess?

Quin got on the phone and called the nearest pizza place. She ordered a salad and a small pizza with everything on it but anchovies. Then she stood at the sink, fuming. In the next room, McCleary called out. She ignored him. She helped herself to a beer and stood at the window, peering out into the yard, where the crepuscular shadows were lengthening. McCleary came to the doorway.

"Could you take a look at this? Gill got something in the mail yesterday."

"Sure."

She didn't turn around, and after a moment he came up behind her. "Something wrong?"

Quin turned. McCleary's smoke eyes were frowning, puzzled. "You could've at least left me something to eat, Mac."

"I did. But Benson didn't realize it was for you and he ate it."

At least Kranish hadn't eaten it, she thought.

"And I'm going to clean up the mess, don't worry."

"Who cooked?"

"Gill."

"Then let him clean up the goddamn mess."

"Would you come and take a look at this?" he asked quietly, in the *reasonable* voice that said he didn't want to argue and why was she so bent out of shape, anyway?

The object of their concern was a note that had been typed on a sheet of paper:

Ta Chuang/The Power of the Great

The union of movement and strength gives the meaning of THE POWER OF THE GREAT. That which is truly great does not degenerate into mere force, but remains inwardly united with the fundamental principles of right and of justice.

The changing line in the third place: Whereas an inferior man revels in power when he comes into possession of it, the superior man never makes this mistake.

Which of us is the superior man?

"What do the six lines mean?" she asked. "And what's the x on the third line?"

"We don't know," Benson replied.

Quin pulled up a chair between McCleary and Kranish and sat down. "The Ta Chong or Chang or however you pronounce it sounds Chinese, like a quote from something Chinese."

"Yeah." Kranish nodded. "That's what we thought."

"So do you know anyone who's into Oriental stuff?"

"His acupuncturist," McCleary replied, "who Gill swears would never send something like this."

Right, Quin thought. That was always the story.

"It's out of the question," Kranish said. "Besides, she wasn't anywhere near the set the night of the explosion."

"Maybe the note doesn't have anything to do with Domer's death," she commented.

Benson nodded. "Yeah, it might not. It might be from some sicko who read about Domer's death in the paper. Whenever a murder gets a lot of publicity, we get crank calls and letters. But just the same, I think we should talk to the acupuncturist. What's her name, Gill?"

He sighed and ran a hand over his face. "Lee Ling. She's got an office on Hollywood Boulevard."

Benson scribbled down the address, then McCleary took the note into his den and made copies of it. "I'll drop the original off at the station on my way home," Benson said. "It's probably filled with prints, all smudged. But you never know. In the meantime, I think we should all concentrate on finding out where this passage came from."

The doorbell rang. It was the delivery boy with Quin's dinner. McCleary brought in paper plates and they all nibbled on pizza, then Quin made coffee and Kranish came out and started cleaning up the dishes. Neither of them spoke for a few minutes. She felt he was waiting for her to say something like, *Oh, don't bother with the dishes, Gill. I'll get them.* But all she said was, "Do you take sugar in your coffee, Gill?"

"Just black, thanks, hon."

He glanced over at her just at the moment when she was looking at him, and something funny happened to the air. It was rather like being in a smoky singles' bar where you'd just been propositioned, where the smell of stale smoke and spilled beer and the faint tinge of sweat was somehow erotic. Quin quickly averted her eyes, and because she just wanted him to go away she told him never mind about the dishes, she would get them, and would he just take out the coffee?

It wasn't until later, lying upstairs in the dark, that she suspected she had done precisely what he had wanted her to do, that he had manipulated the situation, that he had manipulated her. She got up and walked to the doorway, then down the stairs to McCleary's den. They were still out there by the pool, McCleary and Kranish, talking and drinking.

They were talking about the old days when they were kids in Syracuse, New York. Their bond, she thought, was a common childhood of dreams, forged during long, endless winters and summers as evanescent as butterflies. McCleary, the only boy among four sisters, must've gravitated toward Gill like the Earth toward the sun. She tried to imagine him then, his full height of six feet at fifteen, a basketball player whose bookish, spacey friend sat on the sidelines.

Now they were trying to remember the names of women they'd met when McCleary had visited Kranish in Europe years ago. Ice clinked in a glass; distantly she heard the wail of a train. *Remember that woman in Holland who wanted both of us?* Kranish laughed. Sure, McCleary said, he remembered. *You ever tried that, Mac?*

McCleary chuckled. "No."

"I don't mean since you've been married to Quin. I mean ever."

"Nope, Gill, can't say that I have."

"That's your problem, Mac. You're too damned straight." Kranish slurred his words, and Quin heard McCleary chuckle again and tell Kranish he was drunk and it was late. But Kranish wasn't about to be put off and told McCleary he ought to come to work for him for two and a half grand a week.

"Why? I like what I'm doing."

"Right, Mac. You were better off in homicide. You're doing this other shit, insurance and malpractice cases, because of Quin."

"C'mon, let's call it quits for tonight. Why don't you stay in the guest bedroom."

Quin, shaking with fury at Kranish for impugning her when she wasn't there to defend herself, and at McCleary for proffering the extra bedroom, scurried up the back stairs. She felt like a twelve-year-old kid who'd eavesdropped on her parents and found out she was adopted. She crawled under the sheets, raw and injured in a way she didn't fully understand, and pulled Merlin against her.

A few minutes later she heard Kranish's sharp, drunken

laugh, then McCleary came into the bedroom and shut the door. She wanted to leap up and screech that he was blind, that Kranish wasn't his friend. *He's manipulating you just like he did me tonight.*

In the bathroom, water ran, the toilet flushed, she heard McCleary brushing his teeth. These were small, familiar sounds which any other night would have comforted her, reassured her that her life was in order. Now the sounds merely irritated her. And when the bed sighed as he got into it, she nearly snapped at him.

Merlin wiggled free of her arm, padded blithely over her waist and settled between her and McCleary like a referee.

"You asleep?" he whispered.

She remained on her side, her back to him. When she didn't respond, he settled down and she stared into the empty dark.

Seven

THE ONLY ACTING experience Quin had was in college, when she'd played a dragon in *The Skin of Our Teeth*. She'd worn a dragon costume that hadn't fit right, her dragon's head had no ventilation, and within twenty minutes of her appearance in the first scene she'd fainted dead away from the heat and stage fright. Now, as she prepared for her first scene in *Night Flames*, as a *Centauri Tribune* secretary, she wondered how she'd let Gill talk her into this. His celluloid world was as alien to her as Indonesia.

They were shooting at one of the Miami Beach hotels, in an Art Deco soda fountain that had been converted into a bar that reminded her of a cave. The walls had been painted black and were now curved, so there were no right angles. The domed skylight, which fit the pattern of Settlers' City on Alpha Centauri, had been rebuilt especially for *Night Flames*. It had been widened so the prismatic glass now extended about a quarter of the way down the black walls.

The bar itself was shaped like an S and still bore its Art Deco colors—pale pinks, celery greens, powder blues. But above it hung vertical slats for glasses and mugs that looked like the bars of a xylophone. They were different colors and were strung from the dome so they seemed to float above the room. On the far wall was a tremendous clock that showed the time for New York, Alpha Centauri, and the star base where Spin Weaver lived when he wasn't on assignment. It resembled a crab—not just any crab, of course, but one of the giant and deadly sand crabs that inhabited the planet's Great Hunger Desert. A crab which had developed a taste for humans.

Quin stood outside the bar in a courtyard, drowning in the smells of ocean and sand. She wore a shimmering green jumpsuit made of a fabric as soft and flimsy as Kleenex. It crossed her chest like an X, leaving most of her back exposed, and hugged her legs like stockings. The belt at her waist was supposed to be glass that was as flexible as plastic, made from the sand of the Great Hunger Desert. In truth, it was some sort of metal. She wore the sleek thick-soled boots that characterized all denizens of Settlers' City. But the boots were unsuited to the climate of *this* planet, she thought. Her feet felt as if they'd been steamed. She wasn't exactly crazy about the outfit, either. It showed too much.

And yet no one seemed to notice, even though everywhere she looked there were people: cameramen and electricians; a director, first assistant director, second assistant director, and a second second assistant director; the wardrobe mistress and her two assistants; the makeup and hairstyle guy and *his* assistant; the script supervisor and her assistant; the prop master and his assistants; four production assistants and their assistants and on and on ad infinitum. The courtyard swarmed with assistants to the assistants to the assistants. It was like watching a colony of ants or a hive of bees where there was a clearly delineated hierarchy.

Technicians were the drones, a clique apart, with its own union, its own rules. They didn't associate much with the others. PAs, or production assistants, were the low guys, the lackeys of the group directly involved with the production. They spent an inordinate amount of time scurrying around with clipboards, passing out script revisions, Tic-Tacs, cigarettes, and whatever else happened to be in demand. They also shouted a lot—for attention, for quiet, and at each other. The higher-ups, like the assistant directors, pretty much ignored them unless they wanted something.

The primary actors were an echelon apart to whom everyone else catered—except Kranish, the undisputed royalty of the hive, and Patty Cakes May, the director. Extras and people with bit parts like Quin were rather like drifters, she decided, the nomads who crossed boundaries because it didn't much matter *what* they did as long as they were on time.

She stepped aside as a pair of technicians moved past, and nearly tripped on the thick electrical cables snaking through the courtyard. The technicians were pushing dollies on which were mounted huge lights like satellite dishes. They disappeared through the doorway of the soda fountain. Two cameras were positioned outside, near the doorway, and there was another pair inside. Canvas chairs with the stars' individual names on them formed a half-moon circle about five yards from where she stood. They were all empty, because the stars were still in their motor homes or in makeup or not on call until later.

In the heart of the chaos was Bruce Harmon, the video historian. He wore a T-shirt the pale blue of Crest toothpaste, loose-fitting white pants, and sandals. A gold earring glittered in his right ear. He wandered around with his video camera, recording it all for his doctoral thesis from the University of Miami. Quin had heard that Kranish eventually would release the footage as a documentary.

"Pretty weird, huh," said Harmon, strolling over to her, his camera aimed up at her face because she was almost half a foot taller than he.

Quin covered her face with her hands and peeked out at him through splayed fingers.

"Party pooper," he murmured, grinning at her as he lowered the camera.

"How long's your documentary going to be?" Her hands dropped away from her face.

"Oh, I won't know that until I edit it. I'll probably

shoot eight or ten thousand feet of film. I've even been following the cast and crew home, so I can get them in their natural settings."

"They don't object?"

He snickered. "Most of the time they don't know." He frowned a little. "Hey, I don't think we've been introduced. I'm Bruce Harmon."

"I know. I'm Quin St. James."

They moved out of the way as an electrician swept by, trailing more cables. "How'd you know my name?" Harmon asked. His small blue eyes wrinkled as he smiled, and his nostrils flared like a rabbit's. He was sort of cute, she decided, if you could ignore the intrusive presence of his camera.

"I got the impression everyone knows who you are."

This obviously pleased him. He twisted the earring in his ear, a small, self-conscious habit, and flicked his pony-tail off his collar. "My function is to record facts, see. I don't judge those facts. I'm a video historian. Video's where everything's at. MTV's proven that."

"Your thesis is on video?"

"And how it relates to television. I think of myself as the invisible man on the set, the ghost of *Night Flames.*" He laughed at this, an Elmer Fudd laugh, a *yuk, yuk,* like he had something stuck in his throat. "The camera's eye never closes, see, and I drift around, I get the stars at their best and their worst, I get the crew, the behind-the-scenes stuff. Do you know Gill never did this for any of the Spin Weaver films? You got any idea what those would've been worth if he had? Jee-zus, I hate to think."

"Excuse me, excuse me," murmured one of the camera-men, hurrying past them with a crate in his arms that was almost as big as he was. Quin and Harmon moved closer to the low wall behind her, with Harmon standing practically on top of her.

"I suppose the police questioned you, huh?"

He shrugged. "Yeah, sure. I was the obvious choice." He smiled a little at this. "But fortunately for me, I was zonked out at home, flat on my back with a fever and a bad flu. Shit, it coulda been anyone." He paused. "Except you, since you hadn't even started yet."

Quin didn't want to seem too interested in the murder, so she changed the subject. "Do you get a percentage if your film's released as a documentary or something?"

"You bet. It's my pie in the sky. That'll be my retirement."

"How'd you get this job, anyway?"

Harmon opened his mouth, but now Patty Cakes waddled past, griping to himself. Harmon stepped to Quin's side and sat on the wall. "I feel like a mannequin," he complained, then lifted the camera and shot Patty Cakes' receding rear end. "I shoot asses, that's how I got the job."

Quin laughed.

"Gill ran an ad in the *Herald*," Harmon went on. "There must've been eighty or a hundred people who applied for the job. You had to have a two-minute video with your initial application. Mail in. Out of those, they chose twenty people to come in for personal interviews and to submit a three-to-five-minute video. I made it to the finals, and when I went in there, I'd already decided I was gonna get the job."

"What was your video on?"

"A montage of filmmaking in South Florida—*Miami Vice, Harry & Son, Porky's Revenge* . . . movies and pilots and TV shows. It was stuff I'd been collecting for a while." He shifted the camera to his other shoulder. "You always ask so many questions?"

Quin smiled. "You trying to tell me I'm being nosy, Bruce?"

He turned the earring in his lobe. "Listen, arrogance is the disease of choice in this business. Most people here don't give a damn about anyone else. Rose Leen's the exception. I guess you are, too." His eyes darted left, watching Kranish as he strolled onto the set. She could feel the stir in the air that his arrival created. "Mark my words, Quin. Fifty, a hundred years from now, Gill Kranish is going to be more of a legend than he is already."

Kranish and Patty Cakes were conferring now with one of the assistant directors and a couple of technicians. Even if she'd never seen Kranish before, she would've known he was the head honcho. He was oozing *presence*, control, mystique. He wore sunglasses so dark they were nearly black, tailored khaki slacks, and an expensive but casual blue shirt that no doubt matched the color of his eyes. From time to time he twisted the ends of his handlebar mustache.

Harmon excused himself and darted off through the percolating heat with his camera, ponytail bouncing, his shadow a bulbous shape that puddled and shifted at his feet. He paused at Kranish's group, shooting them, and Kranish glanced up and he and Harmon spoke for a few minutes. Then Kranish strolled over to where she was. The air turned funny again, as it had last night, charged with that sexual electricity that seemed to be as much a part of Kranish as the color of his eyes.

He tilted his sunglasses back into his hair, and his gaze swept blatantly from her face to her feet, as though he were undressing her. She stifled an urge to cover herself.

"You look great, Quin, like a true resident of Centauri."

"I'm not sure if that's a compliment or not."

"It is." He laughed and reached out, adjusting her belt. She stiffened, irritated by his presumptuous attitude. Kranish, sensitized to the nuances of people who worked under him, understood and smiled. "You don't have to wait out here, you know. You can use the honey wagon."

"I wanted to watch."

She wished he would put his sunglasses back on. His eyes disturbed her. As if reading her mind, he dropped the glasses back on his nose. "Well, you'll do fine." Then he touched her arm, his fingers cool and dry against her skin, and she winced inside, as if jolted. "I know you will. Talk to you later."

Quin watched him stroll off through the crowd, then turned her attention to the script, mentally repeating her lines until the words were an enjambment of verbs strung together like beads, of adjectives, nouns, and conjunctions effacing periods, commas, hyphens. She finally gave up.

Her scene would be brief, thank God. As Barb the *Centauri Tribune* secretary, she and reporter Juke Farber, played by Sammy Devereaux, would be sitting at a back table, keeping an eye on Spin Weaver, whose presence in the city disturbed Farber. She had only a few lines, none of them memorable. This time there would be no dragon costume and no audience—except for the four dozen or more members of the cast and crew. But her stage fright rode her like a demon: wet palms, a dry mouth, a tight ball in her gut, a burning in her eyes. Yeah, she was in fine shape.

"Y'all about ready?" Devereaux asked, stopping beside her, already in character with his Florida cracker drawl.

"Sure thing."

"Ah may ad-lib a couple of lines, so just play along. Gill encourages us to do that."

"Okay."

Devereaux passed his hand over his black hair as if to make sure it hadn't fallen out since he'd last looked in the mirror. His sparse, pointed features gave him a predatory look. Combined with the drawl he'd developed for this part, he could've passed for a redneck, the kind *Easy Rider* made so infamous, knocking off beers from morning to midnight and driving around in a pickup truck with a rifle slung across the back. "Ah consider this a most important scene because it's when Juke Farber commits himself to investigatin' the launderin' scam. He suspects Spin's here for the same reason, and that bothers him, because he's afraid Spin will crack the case before he gets his story."

In other words, *Don't mess it up, girlie.*

"Right. I agree about the importance of the scene."

"You do?" he asked, genuinely surprised.

"Oh, absolutely. To Farber, getting the story is everything. To Spin, the important thing is the rightness or wrongness of what's going on."

"Well, ah couldn't have said it better mahself." Devereaux smiled widely, and Quin squashed an urge to pinch his cheek. *Don't you worry your little puddin' face now, Sammy boy. Ah got mah shit together.*

She sat down finally on the wall. It was barely noon, but she felt like she'd already put in a full day's work. At seven this morning she'd checked into the production office in the Prince Hotel. The production manager, a slightly overweight and glib man named Greg Hess, handed her a stack of papers and instructed her to sign on the dotted lines. When she said she wanted to read the material first, he laughed and leaned back in his chair and told her *no* one ever read the stuff.

"But if you want to, go ahead. You'll be paid every Monday. Gill already gave me your Social Security number and stuff. You'll be getting your SAG card *maybe* before we're finished shooting. Check in with Dina Talbott at the end of the hall to see if she's got any other stuff for you."

"Class dismissed?" Quin quipped as she picked up the stack of papers.

Hess laughed. "Yup. You're due on the set at eight-thirty. It's about two blocks south of here."

From his office, she proceeded to Kranish's, where Dina Talbott was. The office was actually a suite of rooms with a temporary feel to them, as though at any moment things could be folded, packed, and moved. Quin was surprised to find out the woman knew about her and McCleary, but she was, after all, Kranish's personal assistant. Dina closed the door, and while she stroked a ceramic koala bear on her desk, stroked it as though it were living, she gave Quin a little speech about how if she needed anything, anything at all, to just give her a call. Quin had the distinct impression that she was simply regurgitating what Gill had asked her to say.

Then Dina handed Quin another packet of information and sent her off to the set, and now here she was. *The big time.*

Besides Devereaux, she'd met Moorhouse (handsome, arrogant); Will Clarke, (a likable twenty-five-year-old guy who might've hailed from Kansas or Idaho, the heartland of America); Rose Leen (warm, funny, plump as a plum); Maia Fox (flighty, spacey); and Irene Bedford, (aggressive, straightforward). She'd also met most of the crew. She'd expected snobs; most of them were not, at least not with her. She'd expected eccentrics; they were definitely that.

"The fans," drolled Dina Talbott, stopping in front of her. She gestured toward the beach, where people had lined up, watching the activity. "Cute, huh." She uttered 'cute' as though the fans were adorable pets, and nudged her sunglasses back on her pert little nose. Then she reached into her purse and brought out a bag of peanuts. She dipped her fingers inside, offered the pack to Quin, who quickly accepted.

"Without the fans, where would the stars be?" Quin asked rhetorically.

Dina found the remark amusing. "The star-stoking machinery isn't the fans, Quin. It's the media." She nodded toward Bruce the historian. "He and the still photographer are probably the most important people on the set, you know. Next to Gill. They're getting it *all* in visuals."

"Ah disagree," Devereaux piped up. "The fans are everything, and our boy Gill, the mass audience genius, plays 'em like the piano." Dina's expression said, *He's a know-it-all*, but if Devereaux saw it, he gave no indication. He shaded his eyes with a hand and gazed out toward the beach. "Ah usually go over and talk to them when ah'm finished with a scene. Sign a few autographs, that kind of thing. After all, if it weren't for them, where would any of us be?"

But Dina had already turned away. Quin decided she didn't like the woman very much.

"Okay, we're ready to go!" shouted Patty Cakes, rubbing his dark beard. "Will, Quin, Sammy, let's go. Inside. Someone get those extras."

They took their places inside the smoky bar. Devereaux, wearing a black jumpsuit of heavier material than Quin's, brushed at the front, flicking away invisible bits of lint, and he and Quin took a table at the back. The bar filled up.

A production assistant snapped a clapper board in front of the table; the cameras rolled. For one horrible instant Quin thought of herself as the dragon and nearly lost her nerve and ran. But then she saw Kranish, standing off to the side, and knew she couldn't humiliate herself in front of him. Besides, Devereaux, as Farber, had already begun to speak. He was peering at her over the top of his menu.

FARBER (whispering): That's him, Barb, right over there near the cashier, standing next to the redheaded girl.

BARB (glancing around, then back): *That's* Spin Weaver? He looks awfully young. But he's cute.

FARBER (rolling his eyes): Cute? Cute isn't the point. Look at him, will you? He's not here on vacation. Oh, he's made it seem like he's visiting his mother here in the city, but I'm telling you that's just a front. He and Molly are onto this story. I know they are.

Quin hesitated. Devereaux had just ad-libbed a line, and she wasn't sure where to take it. So she said the first thing that came to mind: "So he probably felt a need for some of his mother's chicken noodle soup, Juke. You're jumping to conclusions."

Devereaux seized the line and ran with it: "I'm not writing a story on chicken noodle soup, Barb."

"Cut!" Patty Cakes shouted. "I love it. Perfect."

That's it? Good God, what had she been doing all these years, knocking herself out as a teacher and then as a private eye when these people probably made five times what she and McCleary did in a year?

"Okay," Patty Cakes said. "We're going to do the same thing from another angle. Keep in that ad-lib. Stay where you are."

"Good line, Quin," Devereaux commented as Patty Cakes hurried over to the cameras. Then he sighed. "It's a fine life, wouldn't you say?"

And weird, Sammy mah boy, very weird.

Eight

MIAMI BEACH: LITTLE old ladies trudging through the heat along Collins Avenue, young women zipped inside tans as sleek as the hides of palominos, sparges of color that were Art Deco buildings, old wealth, fields of concrete, glimmers of the Atlantic. To McCleary, the beach typified South Florida at its best—and its worst.

He parked in the underground garage at the Prince Hotel on Collins Avenue, in one of the spots marked in yellow for the staff of *Night Flames*. Then he walked next door to the Atlantic Towers, where Quin and other members of the cast and crew were staying.

The building, like so many on Miami Beach, was an aging but gracious matron that dated from the early sixties. Her recent facelift had left her with a cloying glitter that insulted rather than improved her appearance. Her lobby, which had once been ceramic tile, was now marble. Gone were the luxuriant tropical plants near the window. Now, fake ivy and fake rubber trees sprouted from huge and expensive ceramic pots. The formerly violet walls were hidden by shiny wallpaper which, if he looked at it too long, would give him a headache. The chandelier was lopsided. Progress. Ha.

He continued through the lobby to the pool area. The brilliant sunlight rendered the world in elemental hues, like a Japanese painting—startling blue sky, a ribbon of lavender along the horizon, white beach, lapis waters. There were maybe a half dozen sun worshippers stretched out on lounge chairs around the Towers' swimming pool, and another handful were in the water. It was like walking into a Club Med commercial.

An ocean breeze lessened the impact of the heat, and music from a radio slipped through the air like smoke. He went over to the poolside bar, where he was supposed to meet Irene Bedford, and sat on one of the stools. He ordered iced tea from the bartender, a young guy with a pierced ear who wore a bathing suit and T-shirt, and glanced back at the Towers, wondering which floor Quin's room was on.

He swiveled around and saw a tall, sinewy brunette in a bikini approaching the bar. Her face, framed by thick raven hair that fell to her shoulders, was unremarkable, but her body compensated for the lack: long, tanned legs, a thin waist, breasts that were exquisitely shaped, not an ounce of fat. She moved with a phlegmatic grace, the sort born of quick reflexes and athletic control.

"Mr. McCleary?" He nodded. "I'm Irene Bedford." They shook hands. Her palm was rough and dry and her grip, strong. "Let's move over to one of the tables, where we'll have some privacy."

There was a tall glass of something sweating on her table, a pair of sunglasses, and an issue of *Redbook*. "I've already given my statement to Sergeant Benson," she said as they sat down.

"I know, but there're a couple of points that were unclear to me."

"Really? Like what?" She flicked her hair off her shoulders and slipped on her sunglasses, which annoyed him. Stripped of the input from her eyes, he concentrated on her mouth. Soft lines, fullness, expressive, but tight at the corners, a mouth that could plunge from a smile to a pout in the blink of an eye. *Moody*.

McCleary flipped open his notebook. Although he knew what he wanted to ask and had nothing written on the page he'd turned to, he'd learned to flow with people's expectations. And Irene Bedford was the sort of woman who expected a detective to consult his notes. He reiterated

78

her statement to Benson that she'd walked with Domer back to the motor home around five, and left about fifteen minutes later. That was correct, was it not? Oh yes, absolutely, she said.

Then he skipped around. How long had she been seeing Domer (about a year); where was she from originally (New York); how old was she (thirty-two); how did she get to be a stunt woman (a long story). When he was certain she was beginning to think he was wasting her time and his, he said, "I understand you visited Mr. Domer's motor home about seven-thirty the night of the fire."

"I just told you when I last saw him."

Slick, he thought, not so much as a tic under the eye or the kick of a pulse in her throat. "Someone saw you enter at seven-thirty, Ms. Bedford, heard you and Domer arguing, and saw you leave in a huff about eight. Now, why don't you tell me what you were arguing about."

She sat forward, pushed her sunglasses back into her hair. Her dark eyes regarded him with contempt—and a flicker of fear. "Who told you that?"

"The airport security guard."

She lowered her gaze, stirred the liquid in her glass, looked up again. "Even if it were true, Mr. McCleary, my relationship with J.B. is no one's business."

"Let's say it *is* true. It doesn't mean you killed him. All it means is that you lied to Sergeant Benson. Why?"

"Unless you've got a warrant, Mr. McCleary, I'm not obligated to answer your questions. Now if you'll excuse me." She scooted back her chair, got up, and walked away.

McCleary sat there, staring after her, the hot sun hurting his eyes. Not bad. It had taken him all of ten minutes to blow that one. And now, for the rest of the day, her possible motives would stalk him like his shadow.

He finished his iced tea and was about to get up when he noticed a slender guy in a lemon-colored guayabera shirt walking off in the direction Irene had gone. There was something distinctly familiar about him—the layered cut of his blond hair, the rapacious set of his handsome face, even the high-topped tennis shoes and the reflective shades. Sure. Charles Roberts, ex-surfer boy turned big-time dick. The last McCleary had heard, Roberts was raking in a small fortune doing private-eye work for some heavy-duty racketeering types. So why was he following Irene Bedford?

McCleary waited until Roberts had stepped inside the building, then quickly followed. He spotted him in the alcove where the mailboxes were and strolled over.

"Surfer Charlie. What a surprise."

Roberts' head whipped around so fast his reflective shades nearly slid off his face. "Mike. Mike McCleary." He jammed his hands in the pocket of his slacks. "That beard threw me. I like it. Nice disguise."

So, McCleary thought. Roberts hadn't recognized him outside. "It saves me about five minutes in the morning. You living here now?"

Roberts whipped off his shades. "Me?" He laughed. Nervously. "Here? No way."

"Just casing mailboxes, huh," McCleary remarked.

"Actually, I'm uh . . ."

"Looking for Irene Bedford's apartment number?"

"Who?"

"Who hired you, Charlie?"

His mouth, which was full and large, dimpled at a corner when he smiled—a beautiful, specious smile that whispered, *Me? Little ole me?* "You know I can't tell you that, Mike. It's confidential. But while we're on the subject, how'd *you* get involved? And what'd the Bedford dame have to say for herself?"

"Still the same old Charlie, chasing the big tsunami in the sky."

He twirled his shades, glanced down at his sandals, raised his eyes again. "It beats the hell out of insurance and malpractice cases, Mike." His mouth was really saying, *Insurance and malpractice are the dregs of the private-eye biz, ole buddy.* "I'll tell you what. Let's cut a deal. You tell me what you know and I'll tell you what I know."

"Including who hired you?"

"No. That's not part of the deal."

"Then I guess there isn't any deal." McCleary tapped his fingers against the wall of mailboxes. "By the way, the names aren't on the mailboxes. It'd probably be simpler just to call the front desk and ask for her. Then they'd give you the apartment number, and you could figure out when she isn't going to be home and break in and go through the place."

"That's a fine idea, Mike, but they don't give out apartment numbers."

"Oh. Well. Too bad. See you around, Charlie."

He felt surfer boy's eyes boring through his back as he walked across the lobby.

He returned to the Prince Hotel and rode the elevator to the fifth floor, where Kranish's production offices were. This was the hub, the nerve center, where every detail involved in shooting the film was coordinated.

From here came the daily call sheets, specifying who should be on the set and when and which scenes would be shot. From here came script changes, entered on a computer system identical to the ones the McClearys hoped to purchase for the firm, and copied on a Xerox machine that collated, stapled, and did everything but slap the paper against the glass. The production office also handled anything to do with publicity—from requests for interviews with the actors to issuing statements about Domer's death. Here was the wardrobe department, makeup, set design, budget, all the behind-the-scenes details that to the average person, McCleary included, were celluloid alchemy, a twentieth-century mystery.

When Gill had given him a tour of the place, McCleary had experienced a surge of pride and respect for the empire he'd constructed. It was a long way from the streets of Syracuse, New York.

He stopped in Gill's office at the end of the hall. It had a sense of impermanence about it, yet it was comfortable, with soft pink and lavender walls, a glass and chrome coffee table, dove gray couch, and matching chairs. Except for a Spin Weaver poster that looked as if it had been put up hastily, the walls were bare. A VCR and a large Quasar television dominated the far end of the room. Here was where Gill viewed the dailies once they'd been transferred to videotape. At the moment, the set was tuned to what looked like a documentary on China. But the sound had been turned off, and Beethoven's Ninth Symphony whispered from a radio.

Dina Talbott glanced up from her typewriter when he walked in, and smiled warmly. "He's not here, Mr. McCleary. He had to go over to the set. But he left strict instructions that I'm supposed to supply you with whatever you need. So what'll it be?" She cupped her chin in one hand while the fingers of her other hand stroked a small ceramic koala bear. "Phone numbers? Bios? Addresses? What?"

So she knew, he thought.

"It's okay, I know about Gill hiring you and your wife," she added quickly, sensing what lay behind his hesitation.

A friendly mouth, he noted, one that invited trust and yet had a difficult time giving it in return. She was petite, with pale green eyes and light brown hair parted on the side. He guessed she was thirty, maybe thirty-one, and while she wasn't a knockout, she was attractive. And like Gill, she radiated a certain presence, but not one that smacked of ambition or drive or obsession. Her presence was softer, peaceful, as though she possessed some inner reservoir of strength that could deal with almost anything. Although he'd spoken to her many times when Gill was in L.A., they'd never met.

"Two things. Will Gill be free around eight for dinner, and I need Maia Fox's current address. The only thing I had on the sheet Gill gave me was a P.O. box."

She flipped open an appointment book. "He should be free at seven-thirty. You want him to meet you somewhere?"

McCleary gave her the name of a restaurant in Coconut Grove, and she jotted it down in the appointment book. "He always takes a look at this at the end of the day. Now. Maia's address." She swiveled in her chair, pulled open a drawer in a nearby filing cabinet, retrieved several sheets of paper, and passed them to him. "It should be on there. We had a change for her on the call sheet, though. Let me see." Another sheet of paper, another brief consultation: "She's on call at five. She'll probably be home until four."

"How do you keep track of all this?" he asked, amazed at her efficiency.

She laughed. "Gill likes things done a certain way. So that's how I do them."

"You've worked for him a long time, haven't you?"

"Six, seven years, sometimes I forget." She opened her desk drawer and brought out a packet of Saltine crackers. She nibbled on one, sipped from the mug of coffee to her right. "But long enough to know he's a brilliant man." She smiled self-consciously. "He hates that word, you now. Brilliant. He says people in Hollywood throw it around too much. But in his case, it happens to be true." Her voice was soft with obeisance. "And this movie . . . well, I think it's going to be his best. Despite J.B.'s death. Spin's introduction to TV."

"Another obsession."

She smiled. "All his movies have been obsessions. I think it's been like that ever since his first movie flopped."

"How long has he had migraines?" McCleary asked, thinking of how the other night at the house, Kranish had asked for an ice pack for his head.

"Oh." *Zip*: her smile flattened out. "For a while. A year, maybe more. He refuses to see a doctor, so what can you do?" She smiled ruefully, the way a mother might who was fretting over a child's stubbornness. "He'll have to go eventually, though, because his last attack lasted twenty-four hours."

There was a knock at the door and a short guy with a toothy grin and black hair pulled into a ponytail stepped in. A gold earring glimmered in his right ear. "Hi, Mrs. Talbott." He had a video camera in one hand, resting on his shoulder. "You mind if I get a few shots of you and of Gill's office?"

"I guess it's okay, Bruce."

"Mrs.?" McCleary asked. "I didn't know you were married."

"Divorced," she replied.

Harmon butted in by extending a stubby hand. "Hi, I don't think we've met. I'm Bruce Harmon. You're Detective McCleary, right?"

"Right," McCleary replied. Harmon's palm was calloused and dry and his grip was as limp as a corpse's.

"Bruce is our historian," Dina explained. "Gill hired him to document the making of *Night Flames*."

So this was the weird little dude who'd been out with the flu the night Domer was killed. "I understand you were sick the night of the murder."

Harmon grinned. "And my alibi checks out, Detective McCleary." He panned Dina's desk, started to turn the camera on McCleary, then reconsidered. "I don't suppose you should be in this."

"Not unless you're planning on including the murder and the investigation in your documentary."

Harmon yukked. "Actually, with you in the documentary, Detective McCleary, it'd be a video version of *Blow-up* or something."

"*Blow-up?*"

"Yeah, you know. That 1966 film with Vanessa Redgrave where the photographer thinks he's photographed a murder. That may be one of my favorite movies of all time. What's your favorite movie, Detective?"

"*The Last Unicorn.*"

Harmon's mouth—a rather ordinary mouth, McCleary

noted—plunged at the corners. "That was *animated*, Detective. I mean a *real* movie."

McCleary laughed and resisted the urge to tug on his ponytail. "I'd have to think about it." He glanced back at Dina. "Thanks, Dina."

"You're welcome, Mr. McCleary."

"Mike," he corrected.

"And I'm Bruce," Harmon echoed, and laughed.

Nine

His HEAD BEGAN to throb the moment he stepped into his suite. The heat, he thought, it was the goddamn heat. The white concrete in the hotel courtyard had reflected light like a mirror, there had been no awning for shade, the air-conditioning in the bar hadn't worked well. The heat and the usual anxieties about how the scene had come across.

Did Spielberg go through this shit?

Kranish made himself a vodka on the rocks with a twist of lime and paced around the living room like a caged animal for a while. Then he stood on the porch watching the surf and drinking in the skyline of Miami. When he went back inside, he ordered lunch through room service.

He walked into the bedroom, where the air still smelled of Lee Ling's perfume, of silk and lust, and he stared at the unmade bed, at the quilt that had slid to the floor and puddled there like unfinished patchwork. He smiled and returned to the living room and flipped through his collection of tapes. It included everything from forty-year-old classics to *E.T.* to tapes like the one he'd made last night. He found it, and slipped it into the VCR.

He sat Indian style on the floor, sipping at his drink, rubbing his temple, and kept his eyes fixed on the screen. There, Dina undressing, shy as a nun, the discs of her spine like steps. Now Lee Ling emerged from the bathroom, her impudicity as casual as a porn queen's, and Kranish entered through the door, and Dina turned, and no one's expression was the same. Dina's face remained shy, embarrassed; Lee Ling was smiling; Kranish simply walked toward the bed and slid into it, face down, and sighed.

Lee approached the bed, sat down, and began kneading Kranish's feet as Dina just stood at the side of the room, watching, her arms covering her breasts. As Lee's hands worked up Kranish's legs, her hair fell forward, brushing his back. Dina's expression changed; Kranish could see her sucking in her breath. She moved over to the bed, looked down at him, at Lee, and said, "I get the feeling you're the one who's going to have all the fun, Gill, since you're the only man."

On the screen, Kranish opened his eyes and smiled. "So who do you suggest I call, Dina?"

"How about McCleary?" She laughed, and Kranish felt as irritated with the comment now as he had been last night.

On the screen, he suddenly turned over and reached for Lee, pulling her up toward him, and now, seeing Dina's face, he knew she understood he'd done it to get back at her for the remark about McCleary. She stopped laughing, her mouth flattened out into a thin, white line. She brushed strands of hair behind her ear and sat stiffly at the edge of the bed, watching as Kranish embraced Lee.

Kranish sipped at his drink and grinned.

On the screen, Lee Ling lifted her head and smiled at Dina and tugged at her hand, urging her over into the middle of the bed. Dina giggled like a young girl and rolled in beside Kranish.

"Now it will be more fair," cooed Lee, and straddled Dina's legs and began running her fingers through Dina's hair, down the sides of her face, to her shoulders and over her breasts.

Kranish froze the frame. He leaned closer, noticing the wide, utterly startled look in Dina's eyes, and behind that look, something darker, the lure of the forbidden. He stared at Lee's long fingers, dark against Dina's white skin, and then unfroze the frame and watched as those fingers pinched and teased Dina's nipples.

The muscles in Dina's stomach began to quiver. Lee moved lower on the bed, and now Kranish saw himself kissing Dina, then lifting his head to kiss Lee as he drew his hand over Dina's hip, then between her thighs.

Lee, with her Oriental sensibilities for balance, Kranish supposed, dropped forward, her mouth moving across Dina's shoulders and breasts as Kranish stroked her until her pelvis arched, until she ground her hips against his hand. Then there was only a kaleidoscope of arms and legs, curves and smooth slow shapes that were a shoulder, a heel, buttocks. . . .

The doorbell rang. Kranish shut off the tape, annoyed by the interruption. "Who is it?" he asked before unlocking the door.

"Room service, sir."

Kranish unlocked the door. The bellboy, a young kid with stylishly cut hair and a bad complexion, said, "You ordered lunch, Mr. Kranish?"

"Yes, that's right." Kranish lifted the top of the dish, picked up a knife and fork and cut a slice in his steak. "It's too rare. I asked for a *medium* steak. Take it back."

The bellboy consulted his order. "Sir, right here it says rare steak for—"

"Take . . . it . . . back." Kranish enunciated each word clearly, crisply, just in case the kid was hard of hearing. Then he shut the door and, after a moment, heard the wheels of the cart clicking down the hall. He rubbed his temple, where the pain clung like adhesive, and went back into the living room to finish watching his tape. As he was refreshing his drink, someone else knocked at the door. "I'm not here," he said quietly, pouring two shots of vodka over ice.

Another knock, more insistent this time, then: "Gill? It's Dina."

Usually, when she stopped by instead of calling, it meant trouble—ego problems on the set, a change in the

88

script, plans that had fallen through at the last minute. He quickly removed the tape from the VCR, slid it under a cushion, and padded down the hall to open the door.

"Let me guess. Lenny has decided he hates his line in the next scene, right?"

She laughed. "Wrong." She stretched up on her toes, kissed him hello, and strolled into the suite.

"Will Clarke has decided to forego show biz?"

"Pessimist. I've never met such a pessimist." She plopped down into one of the pale blue chairs and kicked off her shoes with a sigh. Her white dress hiked up to her thighs, the fabric rustling against her silk stockings. "I just got a call from the shipping company. The Maserati came in last night. You want me to let the others know so the car can be broken in tomorrow night after they've finished shooting?"

Kranish sat at the edge of the couch, sipped at his vodka. It burned his stomach, and he set it aside. "Yeah, that'd be fine. Have the company bring the car over to the hotel tomorrow sometime. Greg Hess can sign for it."

She lit one of her occasional cigarettes. "Let's see. What else. Oh, Mike McCleary wants to know if you'd like to have dinner in the Grove tonight."

"Sure. Anything else?"

Dina tapped her cigarette against the ashtray. Her hair fell along one side of her face, and when she lifted her head again, her expression was soft, almost coy. She smiled. "Yeah, last night was interesting." Color swept into her face; he realized it embarrassed her to talk about it and that 'interesting' was probably going to be the extent of her observation.

"How was it interesting?"

C'mon, Dina, describe it for me. Tell me. For once in your life get past your Catholic childhood.

"It just was." She looked away, stabbed out her cigarette, pressed her hands to the armrests, and pushed herself to her feet. She walked over to the bar, opened the pint-sized fridge, and helped herself to a can of juice and some dried fruit. Even in bed, she was a nibbler, he thought. She leaned on the bar, gazing at him across the room. "I think Orientals are fascinating people, don't you?" *Nibble nibble.*

Kranish reached for his unfinished vodka and walked over to the bar. He opened a bottle of soda and poured half of it in the glass. "Orientals. Yeah, I suppose they're fascinating people, Dina." He sat on a bar stool. She was leaning toward him, sipping at her juice, biting into dried fruit, smiling this cockeyed smile. "So describe what was interesting about last night."

She touched her fingertip to his chin, then tweaked the end of his mustache. "You're impossible. I was here, isn't that enough?" Then she laughed and tipped her head back, finishing the juice. "But I think we should do it again. With someone else. Someone neither of us knows, Gill."

He laughed, and swung around on the stool, watching her as she crossed the room again. "That's a switch."

She sank into the chair again. "C'mon, I'm serious. You're the one who's always talking about breaking down sexual boundaries and all, so let's do it, then. I want to see you with someone neither of us knows."

Kranish laughed again, delighted. "I've created a monster."

Her smile possessed the unmistakable imprint of a challenge. "Well?"

"Sure, okay. What the hell." He glanced at his watch. "I've got to get back to the set." He walked over to the chair and pulled her to her feet. He cupped her face in his hands, enjoying the scent of her perfume, the softness of her hair against his skin. Her arms encircled his waist, and as he kissed her, Lee Ling's voice whispered through his head: *Straight sex doesn't interest you much anymore, Gill.* It was true, he thought, and for a moment he envied McCleary's monogamous relationship with Quin and his irritating *straightness.* But it bothered him to

90

think about it too deeply, and he stepped away from Dina. "I've got to run. C'mon."

As they were leaving, the bellboy was arriving with Kranish's new steak. "You can take it back," Kranish snapped. "I'm due back on the set. Next time get the order right."

He and Dina walked past him toward the elevator. The bellboy shot them a bird.

Ten

MAIA FOX LIVED in a houseboat docked behind an expensive home on Star Island, about four blocks from Domer's place. The island was one of perhaps half a dozen that dotted Biscayne Bay and were connected to each other by bridges. It seemed an odd place for a houseboat, but it fit McCleary's idea of Maia Fox.

In one of her films that he'd seen, she'd played a wacko inventor who created a drug that enabled people to travel through time. In the other three, she was Spin Weaver's zany girlfriend, Molly Drinkwater, part klutz, part bombshell, sharp as a tack. He expected a woman who was a cross between Goldie Hawn and Diane Keaton.

As he approached the houseboat, he saw two low canvas chairs positioned across from each other on the roof. In front of them was a video camera aimed at Maia Fox, who sat in the left-hand chair, reading from a script. He stood there, watching her, not wanting to interrupt, and listened.

"Spin, I'm telling you I don't like it. I think this whole thing's dangerous. You're talking like you've been doing exo-drugs or something."

She scrambled to the other chair and, in a deeper voice, which McCleary presumed was supposed to be male, replied: "Now, Molly, no one says you've got to stick with this. Catch the next shuttle back to the star base."

She moved back to the other chair. "Don't patronize

me, Spin, I mean it." Then she slammed the script against the chair and McCleary applauded.

Maia shielded her eyes with her hand and gazed out across the lawn at him. "This is private property, you know."

"I'd like to ask you some questions about J.B."

"You a reporter?"

"No," he replied, and introduced himself.

"Oh." She switched off the camera, hopped down from the roof, and stood at the railing, a hand on her slender hip. "C'mon aboard. We can talk over here in the shade. It's cooler."

The shade she referred to was an awning that extended about five feet over the back of the houseboat. It shielded two wicker chairs with bright orange pillows and a wicker table with a vase of fresh flowers on it. She dabbed at her damp face with the back of her hand and slumped into a chair with a sigh. "Did you think that little scene sounded all right?" she asked.

"Terrific. Is that this afternoon's scene?"

She combed her fingers through her short, curly dark hair. "Yes. It's where Spin and Molly have their first disagreement about the case. They've actually been hired by the corrupt banker's wife, which Rose Leen plays. Anyway, she's got a hunch the whole thing's dangerous."

"What's an exo-drug?"

"The hallucinogen that the banker's been smuggling to Earth. Well, *he's* not the smuggler, he just arranges for the stuff to be smuggled on cargo ships. It's the source of his dirty Old World money." She glanced at him. "You think I got the inflection right?"

"It sounded fine to me."

"I've been taping my practice sessions, just to see how they look," she explained, then went on, talking with her hands, explaining what she hoped to communicate in the scene.

McCleary decided she was as pretty offscreen as she was on. Her eyes were the color of India ink, her complexion creamy, soft, and her mouth, infinitely intriguing. Her body wasn't bad either, zipped as it was into shorts that were very short and tight and buttoned into a sleeveless etamine blouse the same color as the bay. But when she went on for at least fifteen minutes about the scene, he wondered if she was avoiding the issue of J.B.—or simply didn't care.

". . . anyway. Now all I need to do is make sure that when Spin and I meet with Juke Farber, the reporter, Sammy Devereaux doesn't ad-lib too much. He loves to do that. And it can screw things up. He's sometimes a real pain to work with. He always stays in character, too, with that Southern accent, which gets on my nerves."

"How was J.B. to work with?"

She snapped her fingers. "A breeze. He'd been in the business a long time, knocking around Hollywood in these grade B movies and stuff. But he was a pro. This film could've been his ticket. What a drag, though, to become famous posthumously, don't you think? Death frightens me, I'll be honest with you. I mean . . . my God, who knows for sure what it is?" She giggled. "Remember that scene in *Sleeper* where Keaton and Woody Allen are on that hill, watching the VW go over the side, and she turns to him and says, 'You know what? "Dog" is "God" backwards.' Well, that's how I feel when I think about death. All these books are being written on death and dying and near death experiences, but suppose . . . suppose it's *nothing*?" The last word came out in a sibilant whisper.

She was Spin Weaver's girlfriend all over again, but as Joe Bean would've said, her elevator didn't reach the top floor. "What was your relationship with J.B.?"

She shrugged, stretched out her legs, crossed them at the ankles, and folded her hands on her flat stomach. "Offscreen? We screwed when it was mutually convenient. But that got messy because one night we were down here on the houseboat and Irene caught us together. Gawd, I thought she was gonna split a vessel in her brain or something. Unbelievable. I mean, we were just screwing, right? We weren't professing undying love to each other. But oh no, Irene didn't understand that. Actually, she never understood J.B. at all, but I guess that's another story." She paused, leaned over the railing, and pointed at a school of fish that leaped out of the water. Light quilled their wiggling ghost shapes a pale silver, and for breathless moments they seemed suspended a foot above the bay. Then they fell in a swoop, shadowing the water, and swam away.

"You fish, Mike?"

"Not in years."

"When Gill was scouting locations down here last year, he brought me and J.B. with him and we went fishing in the Everglades one weekend. Strange place to go fishing, considering how close the Atlantic is. But I'll try just about anything once. Things got sort of weird that night, though, because we were camping on this chickee, a wooden platform above the water, and Gill sort of rolls over next to me during the night and we started going at it. I'd never been with Gill before, but hey, like I said, I'll try anything once. Then J.B. woke up and I thought they were going to get into a fight, but Gill says, 'Hey, there's enough of Maia to go around. Right, Maia?' So I says, 'Sure thing, Gill.' So we spent the rest of our fishing weekend screwing there on the chickee."

The question Kranish had asked about whether McCleary had ever been with two women floated through his mind.

"Bye, fish," she said softly, waggling her fingers as the fish leaped once more, farther from the houseboat this time, then disappeared.

"Is there anything between you and Gill now?"

She sat back, shrugged, winked an eye shut, and looked over at him. Her long lashes cast shadows on her dimpled cheeks. "Sometimes, when we're both in the mood, yeah, but Gill bugs me." She paused and looked over at McCleary. "And this is strictly *off* the record, Detective."

"Right."

"Well, Gill's heavy into this control trip, see. I mean, the man has to be controlling *everything* in his personal environment or it drives him bonkers. Unless he's drinking. Then it's six sheets to the wind and who gives a shit. So between this control stuff and his drinking, he's gotten a little too strange for me. He goes into these weirded-out spaces sometimes where he starts talking about how *Night Flames* is going to bring Spin Weaver to a larger audience and all through the miracle of television." She touched his arm. Her hand was cool, soft, the fingers delicate and long. "You want to hear something strange?"

Something else? "What."

"Right before we began shooting on this film, J.B. had this party out at his place. Big deal thing, see. So you know what Gill does? He gets J.B. and me in the same room and he wants us to make love while he gets the thing on video. I'd had a bit to drink that night, so at first I went along with it. We locked the library door and stuff and J.B. and I get snug on the rug, but then Gill starts directing us, you know, telling us what to do to each other. So I told him no way and got up and left. He's tried to pull that shit on other people, too."

"Like who?"

"Oh, Irene, for one. See, he's got this mistaken impression that just because he's one of the most powerful producers in Hollywood, he can make people do what he wants. He's like a spoiled kid. Okay, so it works with some people, but I wasn't having any of it that night. Sex on video, for Christ's sake."

"And what'd Irene do?" McCleary asked.

Maia gave him a small, secretive smile. "Guess you should ask Irene about that, Detective. You got any leads on who killed Domer?"

"No."

Her hand was still on his arm, and her nails moved gently over his wrist, creating spicules of quick, pleasant sensations he didn't want to think about too closely. "Well, it could've been almost anyone, that's what I

96

think. Sammy was jealous of J.B., and Lenny Moorhouse auditioned for J.B.'s part and didn't get it, and then there's Irene."

"Do any of those people hold grudges against Gill?"

Her expression was nonplussed, then she burst out laughing. "Detective McCleary, people *always* hold grudges against producers as powerful as Gill. Sometimes it's just the ole 'How come you're successful and I'm not?' routine, but other times it's warranted."

"You think it's possible any of those grudges are strong enough for someone to get back at Gill by sabotaging the film?"

She shrugged. "I wouldn't presume to guess what dark motives people have, Detective McCleary. But sure, it's possible. Anything's possible."

"When did you last see J.B. the night of the fire?"

"Around five, when his scene was over." She removed her hand from his arm; his skin burned from her touch.

"According to the statement you gave Sergeant Benson, you—"

"Benson," she sighed. "Benson. I can't tell you how *bad* he pissed me off. Okay, here's the truth, McCleary. You want to hear it?"

He nodded. The air had gone deadly still. Maia fanned herself with a magazine and gazed out over the water.

"During dinner, I went for a ride in a wonderful little plane called a Pitt Special. It belongs to this mechanic out at the airport. He'd come up to me earlier in the day and asked me for an autograph and we got to talking and he told me about his plane and I asked him to take me up. We flew around and did loops and stuff, then we landed and went back to my dressing room. We were there until I heard the sirens." She crossed her heart. "Honest to God truth."

"What's his name?"

"Francis." She laughed. "Good Catholic man. Francis. I don't know his last name. You can find him out at Glades Airport."

"Why didn't you just tell Benson that?"

She made a face, rolled her lower lip between her teeth, a gesture that reminded him of Robin Peters. "Oh, Benson. He's so . . . so *straight*." She touched his arm again. "What about you, Mike? You as straight as Benson?"

"Worse."

Her black eyes, riant and almost mocking, studied him. Then her fingers marched down his arm to his hand and stopped at his wedding ring. "I've been known to revitalize floundering marriages."

"Mine's not floundering." But he wondered, suddenly, how true that was. He stood. "Thanks again for your time, Maia."

Her eyes followed him up, then she pushed herself to her feet with a sigh and walked with him to the other side of the houseboat. "So, McCleary. If you ever decide your marriage is floundering, or if your marriage isn't floundering and you want to have a few laughs, you know where I am."

If he'd been single, he might've taken her up on the offer. But because he wasn't, she became cute the way a Kewpie doll was cute, and he felt like ruffling her hair and patting her on the head. Instead, he chuckled. "Righto, Maia."

Dinner in the Grove that night with Kranish was like old times, like the summers in Europe drinking wine in sidewalk cafés. They talked films, books, plays; Syracuse and Hollywood and Europe. Once, he asked Kranish if he'd ever had an affair with Maia and Kranish laughed and leaned across the table and said, "Mike, I enjoy women. Women are part of what makes moviemaking the best business in the world. I wouldn't say Maia and I had an affair, exactly, but yeah, it hasn't been strictly platonic."

"What about Irene Bedford?"

Kranish rolled his eyes. "History, ages ago."

And what about you with a camera, Gill? Is that true too? But he somehow couldn't bring himself to ask it.

"Have you talked to Lee yet?" Kranish asked.

"No, I'll do it tomorrow."

"Show her the note, will you? I tried calling her today, but her assistant said she'd taken the day off. She might know where the passage came from."

"She might also have sent it."

"Naw, no way."

They lingered over coffee, and as the restaurant filled up, people who'd recognized Kranish began approaching the table. Some just wanted to tell him how much they enjoyed his Spin Weaver films, others asked for autographs, and still others offered condolences about J.B., as though Kranish had been a member of the man's family. Instead of brushing people off, Kranish chatted with them all, inviting several to join them for a drink. Before long, there were more than a dozen people crowded around their table.

They moved to a larger table. More people joined them, and one young man had a guitar and they all began to sing. At first, McCleary figured Kranish was just basking in the adulation that rode tandem with success. But after a while he realized it was more than that. Kranish's gift was his ability to communicate with people, to transmute their sorrows, their dreams and triumphs, into film. Few in the industry did it better, and part of it was because of nights like this when Kranish shed his *producer* persona. Now he was just Gill Kranish, human being, in whom the spacey kid with the dream still lived and breathed.

McCleary wished Quin could've been here to see it.

Eleven

THE MOTOR HOME had cost over a hundred grand and was a clone of the one in which J.B. Domer had met his demise. Quin wasn't immune to its numerous luxuries: a rug so thick your curling toes could sink from sight; a comfortable couch that converted into a double bed; a TV and a VCR where the second Spin movie was now showing for whoever wanted to watch; an assortment of books and a small kitchen with a fully stocked refrigerator. She was supposed to go through the rack of Centauri clothes and choose something appropriate for her scene, where she would observe a meeting between the banker's wife, played by Rose Leen, and Spin Weaver. The meeting would be shot first, and then Quin's scene.

She went through the rack and chose a chatoyant blue silk tunic with floppy white slacks. It was more conservative than what she'd worn the other day, and would be subject to Kranish's approval, but she lacked the patience to look further. It was 5:15 Friday morning, the beginning of her third day on the job, and she was hungry and tired. There was something obscene about being up this early, before the sun, traffic, before most of the birds. But Kranish wanted a sunrise scene and like Caesar, what Kranish decreed became law. Even if it meant convincing the city of Coconut Grove to block off Peacock Park for three hours.

There was a knock at the door, then Rose Leen poked her head inside the motor home. "Hey, hon, they just brought out the coffee and Danishes. I got you some, if you're interested."

"Oh God, you read my mind."

A table with goodies had been set up on the other side of the motor home, and people now crowded around it, murmuring. Rose patted the chair beside her own, where Quin's coffee and Danish were. The temperature already hovered in the low eighties. The humidity was thick as pea soup and pressed against her chest with a weight twice that of gravity. But despite the heat, she sipped gratefully at the steaming cup of coffee and bit into the Danish as if she hadn't eaten in weeks.

"Slow down on that roll or you'll get sick," Rose admonished, flicking her black braid over her shoulder. Her plump cheeks dimpled when she grinned. She reminded Quin of a carnival gypsy, the sort of woman you would find reading Tarot cards in a tent, decked out in a turban and a silk robe.

She played Joanne Corliss in *Night Flames,* a woman whose life was falling apart like crumb cake. She was married to Frank Corliss, the head honcho's assistant and the man who actually arranged the shipments of exo-drugs to Earth. Caught between her love for her husband and the urgings of her conscience, she would finally meet with Spin Weaver in today's scene, to give him information.

She was already dressed for the scene in a black, short-sleeved jumpsuit that slimmed her hips. She wore a gold chain around her neck from which hung a slender gold chip that bore the emblem of a dome with a dollar sign in the center. On a planet like Alpha Centauri, where settlers were known primarily by their professions, the emblem marked her as a member of a banking family.

"So who's on the rampage today, Rose?"

"I hear Patty Cakes got up on the wrong side of the bed. And Maia's in one of the motor homes, sacked out. She partied too much last night."

"Who with this time?"

"Greg Hess. Or so I hear."

During the last two days, Rose had filled her in on the cast and crew—who to stay clear of, who was reliable, who had ego problems. She was affable without affectations and seemed to lack the compulsive edge to her personality that characterized almost everyone else Quin had met—specifically, that people seemed to be using their experience on *Night Flames* as a stepping stone to something better. One of the motor-home drivers, for instance, had written a script he hoped to sell to Kranish before they finished shooting the film. The assistant to one of the production assistants hoped to become a director. And so on. Everyone had an angle, a grand and intricate plan called ambition. Except for Rose.

"How about Kranish?" she asked.

Rose shrugged. "He's tricky to read. He's the sort who'll be smiling one minute and on a rampage the next. It's the Gemini in him. He's a typical Gemini, the twins, two faces, two sides."

"Sounds like schizophrenia to me," Quin remarked, and Rose laughed.

"Yeah, Geminis do things like insisting scenes be shot at sunrise. It wouldn't surprise me in the least if his moon was in Capricorn. That's a real stubborn combination. Capricorn moons love to control things." She glanced over at Quin, her eyes as black as wet streets. "I don't suppose you've had to talk to the police, since you weren't here when the fire happened, huh." She stroked the tip of her braid with her thumb and sipped at her coffee.

Quin shook her head.

"Well, they've got this new detective on the case, McCleary, so I had to review my statement with him. I asked him what would've happened if I'd been, say, in my dressing room when the fire happened, instead of having dinner with the cameraman. He told me I wouldn't have a verifiable alibi then, unless I was with someone in the dressing room, which would've made me a suspect. So it's all timing, Quin, everything in life is timing—even your guilt or innocence. That's been one of the things I've learned from all this." She chuckled. "It's like being married and your husband demands to know where you were between X hours and Z hours and you tell him you were window shopping and he says, 'Prove it.' Now, how do you prove you were window shopping? So what happens is that he decides you've been unfaithful and you get divorced."

"That really happened? About the window shopping?"

"Yeah. We got divorced, and by then I'd had it with the West Coast. EST and health food and exercise freaks and then the Beverly Hills crowd with their la-de-dah airs. So I packed up the car with my clothes and my two cats and drove to the Catskills and did summer stock for a while. Then I did a spoofy horror film, and then it was winter and I was freezing my ass off, so I drove south. I got a part in a play at the Burt Reynolds Theater in Jupiter. When that ended, Gill contacted me about this. Here I am, me, Hepburn, and Tracy. My cats," she added. "That's my story. What's yours?"

Quin laughed. "Nothing that interesting." She explained she'd taught for a while (but didn't say where), then decided teaching was boring and got hired for a walk-on part in a low-budget film (but didn't say which one). There were strings of similar low-budget films after that and acting lessons and a few plays, and then this film, her break, even though the part was small. The story sounded so good, she almost believed it.

"Where's your hubby?" Rose asked.

"What?"

Rose took Quin's hand, admiring her wedding ring. "Pretty. Is your husband in New York?"

Wonderful, Quin thought. They'd mapped out everything but this. Was she supposed to be married, divorced, widowed, single, what? Before she had a chance to reply, Bruce Harmon materialized as if out of thin air and brought his faithful video camera within inches of Quin and Rose.

"All right, ladies, a little smile, a dance, something good."

Rose's middle finger shot up.

Harmon's camera dipped toward the ground, and he peered at her over the edge of it. "Why is it everyone shoots me a bird?" he asked ruefully.

Rose chuckled. "Do a nice close-up, Brucie baby."

His hand went to his ear, where he twisted his earring. "Pooh," he said after a pensive moment, and walked away.

Rose and Quin laughed. "He's sort of like a Dudley Moore," Rose commented. "Now tell me about your hubby."

Dudley Moore or John Wayne: it didn't make any difference to Quin *who* Bruce the Historian was. He'd given her some time to think of an answer. She loved him for it. Her husband, she told Rose, was a New York real estate broker.

"First marriage?"

"Yes."

"Make it your only one, hon. Take it from someone who knows. I've been married twice. It's too confusing."

"How long have you known Gill?"

"Oh, dear. Let me think. I guess about six years, seven, something like that. Since the second Spin movie. I had a bit part in it."

"What do you think of him?"

Rose's plump cheeks danced with shadows as she leaned toward Quin. "Hon, that's not a real wise question to just go asking people. I mean, it's fine that you ask me. But just be careful. He's a powerful man who doesn't like people nosing around in his business. I've seen him make and break careers with just a memo."

"Thanks for the advice." She finished her coffee, knew she should keep her mouth shut, but couldn't. "So you don't like him?"

Rose laughed. "Gill? I adore him. He's the best in the business. He works hard, he plays hard, he knows what he wants when it comes to anything having to do with movies. He can be extremely generous, and he can also be a sonuvabitch. You just have to know how to read him, when to stay out of his way."

"Rosie, here's your transportation," shouted Patty Cakes.

He was squashed into a little two-seater roofless car called a Buggy, a primary mode of transportation on Alpha Centauri. It had been designed specifically for *Night Flames* and resembled a dune buggy, except that it was paneled in translucent squares that had supposedly been made from the sand of the Great Hunger Desert. It was also solar-powered, shaped roughly like a bullet, and rode close to the ground. Patty Cakes putted to a stop in front of the motor home and unfolded himself from behind the steering wheel.

"We're about ready, so I thought I'd pick you up. Madam," he said, then bowed deeply at the waist and gestured toward the Buggy.

Rose laughed with delight and took Patty Cakes' out-stretched hand. "Such service. You coming, Quin?"

"Uh, I don't think there's room, Rose."

Patty Cakes grinned and held up a finger. "Wrong." He walked around to the back of the Buggy and flipped open a third seat. "You'll fit fine."

Quin climbed in with a laugh and off they chugged through the dark of Peacock Park. On Alpha Centauri this verdant bastion was known as the Edge—the edge of Settlers' City, the edge of the poison sea.

Just beyond the park, the bay was a slate blue mirror. Isolated lights from the buildings circumventing the bay twinkled against the waters, as lucid as stars. Although there were only a few bystanders and a handful of reporters, barricades lined Main Highway and McFarlane Road. Production assistants darted about like hummingbirds. They pulled to a stop at the periphery of the chaos.

The scene would actually be shot in the Buggy, at the juncture where the jogging path divided. Quin supposed the fork was symbolic of the sudden division in Joanne

Corliss' life. Rose walked over to where Kranish was. He hugged her affectionately, Quin noticed, and then touched her hair with that same proprietary air she'd sensed when he'd adjusted her belt her first day on the set.

"Hi, Quin." Will Clarke stopped beside her, a cup of coffee in his hand, steam rising up around his face.

"Aren't you on?" Quin asked him.

He laughed. "I lay you odds they stand there another five minutes. Time enough to finish my coffee."

Just looking at him, she could understand why Kranish had cast him in the Weaver role. He seemed innocent, as though there weren't a wicked bone in his body. Yet there was something infinitely rueful about his huge blue eyes. The combination of youth and wisdom was appealing.

He ran his fingers through his thick khaki hair and muttered, "Do I look nervous?"

Quin laughed. "Hardly. Why, are you?"

"Terrified. Once I get in front of the camera, I'm fine, but before . . . forget it. Gill keeps telling me I'll outgrow it."

"Well, you don't look nervous. Believe me."

He grinned, then Patty Cakes was shouting, "Okay, let's move it!" and Will Clarke darted off in his denim jeans and plain shirt, an ordinary hero who got to wear ordinary clothes on this extraordinary planet.

"Quiet on the set!" someone shouted. "Take one, scene twenty-two. Quiet on the set, quiet. Someone tell those bystanders to shut up!"

A hush fell over the park. The cameras moved in. One of the giant lights flicked on. It looked like a UFO or an insect that had been mutated through germ warfare or something. Its illumination was softened by a translucent screen. "We're rolling!" Patty Cakes shouted as the clapper board barked.

And here came Rose, putting along in the Buggy, looking very much a dignified lady of Settlers' City. And here rolled the cameras, following her through the overhang of trees, and there, at the edge of the poisonous sea, stood Spin Weaver. Then something happened to the Buggy. It coughed, it sputtered and suddenly died. "Aw shit," Rose mumbled.

Patty Cakes yelled, "Cut! Cut!"

Quin's stomach rumbled for more food. She hurried back through the dark toward the honey wagons, figuring she could grab another Danish and a cup of coffee before they had resolved the problem with the Buggy.

Birds warbled in the predawn stillness. Distantly, she heard a screech of brakes. She thought about her conversation with Benson yesterday afternoon. He'd stopped by the studio, where they were shooting, to talk with one of the crew, and had told her the results of the blood tests were in. Bedford, like half the cast and crew, was a type O, but there'd been no evidence of hypoglycemia in *her* blood or anyone else's. Then he went on to say he and McCleary were going to have dinner with Kranish that evening, and if there was time, they might even go fishing this weekend, the three of them, and wasn't Kranish a swell guy?

"Fishing? You're going fishing? Where?"

"Maybe in the Everglades, we're not sure."

And she'd thought, Here we go again. McCleary hadn't mentioned anything about a fishing trip when he'd called last night. He didn't even *like* to fish. But then, he somehow ended up doing all sorts of things he didn't normally do when he was with Kranish.

The honey wagon area was deserted now, illuminated only by the lights above the dressing room doors. With the motor homes to the left of it, the scene reminded her of a wagon circle. There should've been a camp fire burning, and scouts keeping a lookout for Indians. But there wasn't even a security guard around. She helped herself to another cup of coffee and stood under a banyan in the lightening dark, gazing off across the park to where a family of ducks waddled toward the pond. Her gaze swung around to the motor home where the racks of

107

clothes were. In her mind's eye, she saw flames zipping along J.B. Domer's slacks, his hair catching fire, his skin turning black.

She thought she saw a light inside, but when she blinked it was gone. She decided it had been a reflection from one of the windows on the other side of the vehicle.

She kept watching, though, and when she saw the light again, considered alerting one of the security guards. But suppose it was just someone from the cast or crew? She walked closer for a better look. By the time she reached the door, the light was gone. She tried the knob. It was unlocked and shouldn't have been, but she didn't hear anything inside. Where were the security people, anyway? She knocked, waited a moment, then opened the door and peeked inside. She could make out the shadow which was the clothes rack; the air smelled of aftershave. She stepped inside, closed the door. "Hello," she called out, but the emptiness tossed her voice back at her.

She was beginning to feel foolish when she heard something, a small noise like a grunt, from the back, where the bathroom and closet were located. *Someone's in there taking a crap, Quin. March on out.*

But if so, why hadn't the person responded when she'd called out? Frowning, waiting until her eyes adjusted to the dark, she tiptoed to the back, rapped on the bathroom door. When there was no answer, she tried the knob. It was locked.

She backed toward the clothes rack, pulled it toward the bathroom door until it was almost touching, then hurried to the front door. She opened it, but without leaving, and slammed it shut. She scooped up a ceramic flower vase from the coffee table and positioned herself to the right of the clothes rack. If the rack didn't stop the intruder, then the vase would.

Reason and curiosity waffled inside her; she shook aside reason and remained where she was.

Something squeaked behind her. Her head whipped

around; she glimpsed a figure flying out of the closet. Then the person slammed into her and she stumbled back into the clothes, into the perfumed scent of silk and designer labels, arms pinwheeling, seeking an anchor. The rack rolled, and down she went. Her last thought before a warm and inky black swam over her was that the man's blond hair was refulgent, lighting up the dark like a sun.

Twelve

1.

AN OVOID TANGERINE light nibbled at the heart of the blackness, and the guardian of movie and TV stars said, *Hello Quin. Do you have your union card?*

Gill said—

I don't care what Gill said. If you don't have your SAG card, you'll have to leave. Only union actors are allowed in here.

I've applied for it, but it just hasn't arrived yet. It's coming in the mail.

I'm sorry, that's not good enough, Quin. Saint Weaver will show you to the gate.

At the gate, Spin Weaver, who looked nothing like Will Clarke, patted her on the head like a child. *When Gill and McCleary went fishing, Gill used your SAG card as bait, Quin. I wish I could help you, but what the guardian says goes.*

Who's the guardian? I never saw his face.

And Spin laughed and laughed. *Only union card members know that. Sorry.*

When she came to, she saw McCleary's face, his smoky eyes, his beard. "Mac," she said. "Mac."

She reached out to touch his beard but felt skin that was soft, butter smooth. She blinked and it wasn't McCleary's face now, but a woman's. Gray light filled the motor home. The TV was on. Spin and Molly were arguing. *Listen, Molly, it's different, that's all,* he said. *A friendship between men is just . . . well, different.*

Yeah, like McCleary and Gill, she thought, and tried to sit up. She almost expected to see Bruce Harmon swing through the motor home, camera in hand.

"Hey, take it easy." Irene spoke gently and helped Quin over to the couch. The clothes rack was in the middle of the room. Skirts and blouses, dresses and jumpsuits had slipped off their hangers and puddled in colorful heaps on the floor. An ache drummed behind her eyes, and tendrils of pain burned at the back of her skull.

"What happened?" Irene asked.

In a halting voice, Quin explained and pointed at the bathroom door. "I thought he was in here, because the door was locked. But he was hiding in the closet."

Irene tried the door. "It's still locked." She stood there, hands on her slender hips, glancing around. "It doesn't look like anything's missing."

The outside door flew open, banged against the wall, and warm air riffled through the motor home, following Kranish inside. "Did anyone call an ambulance?" he barked at Irene.

"I think someone in security did."

"I don't need an ambulance," Quin protested.

"What happened?" Kranish asked.

"I was coming back over here for coffee," Irene began, "and saw this guy sprinting across the park toward Main Highway. I came in here to get a copy of the script and found Quin." She snapped her fingers. "The scripts. That's what's missing. We kept extra copies of the script in here. On the counter."

Kranish turned his eyes on Quin. They knotted with umbras like bruises. "Did you get a look at him?"

"Just that he had blond hair. I think."

"You *think*? You don't know for sure?"

"Lay off, Gill," Irene snapped. "The woman's been banged on the head, for God's sakes."

Quin asked Irene to tell the security man she did *not* need an ambulance. But Kranish, speaking with authority, told her to have her head X-rayed. She didn't appreciate him telling her anything, thank you. "I'm fine. But I think I'd like to go back to the Towers."

Kranish nodded. "No problem. We'll shoot around you. I'll drive you and take a cab back."

"I can drive myself, thanks."

"I'll drive you," Irene offered. Quin opened her mouth to protest, but Irene shook her head. "Nope, I insist."

She was suddenly too tired to argue. "Okay, thanks."

Irene said, "I'll go see what we can do about canceling that ambulance." Then she left.

Quin glanced at the screen. Now Spin skulked through a room in a space station, and he whispered to Molly: *Even the way dust falls might provide a clue.* The desire to curl up on a couch and abandon herself to Spin's adventure tugged at her. But Kranish was making noises about examining the back of her head. His fingers stepped through her hair, brushed the tender spot, and she winced.

"Ouch. Right there."

"It didn't break the skin, that's good." He sat beside her on the couch. "I had dinner with Mike last night."

And the night before that. "I know. I spoke to him."

"He thinks Irene is our best suspect at the moment."

She didn't agree, but wasn't up to debating the point.

"What do you think?"

"I don't know. My head hurts too much to think." She cosseted the back of her neck.

"Here, I'll do that. I'm famous for my neck rubs."

Quin sat forward and closed her eyes as his hands kneaded the tight muscles in her neck, her back and shoulders. She eyed the screen, where Molly Drinkwater stood over Spin, who sat on the edge of a bed. Her smile burned. *You ready to rock 'n' roll, Spin?*

And Spin looked around with a mischievous glint in his eyes. *Here? You want to do it here, Molly?*

"Mike hasn't been able to find that mechanic Maia

supposedly spent the evening with," Kranish said. With his free hand, he reached for the remote control device and aimed it at the VCR, shutting it off.

Bye, Spin, she thought dreamily. *Catch you later.* "I thought he was at Glades Airport."

"He was fired. They don't have any forwarding address."

Her neck was feeling better, she said, but his hands kept moving, down along her spine, massaging the muscles on either side of her backbone. She felt like purring. She wanted to sleep. She was hungry. Swollen with her elemental needs, she closed her eyes and surrendered to sentience. Gill's hands were at her shoulders again, her upper arms, and he was leaning into her, his breath as warm as a baby's against her hair as he went on about Maia's phantom mechanic.

She knew the hands were his, that they were no longer impersonal, that they were kneading her muscles as a lover's might. She disliked the man, but she didn't move away, didn't stop him, and knew if she turned, he would embrace her, she would feel his mouth against hers. The visceral tug of Kranish's magnetism spread warmly through her insides, her nipples tightened, and for a moment, just a moment, she nearly capitulated to the sexual heat that emanated from him. Then her spine went rigid and she moved quickly away.

"I feel better now, Gill. Thanks."

Their eyes locked, and she knew that he understood what had nearly happened. She hated the gleam of triumph in the tilt of his chin; she hated him, she did.

The door opened and Irene came in. "Okay with the ambulance, Quin. You all set?" Her eyes darted to Kranish, then back to Quin as if she could feel the vestiges of what had just taken place.

Quin stood and slung her purse over her shoulder. Kranish rose and walked outside with them. She could feel him behind her, his eyes on her back, peeling away her clothes. "I'll check on you later, Quin," he said, and moved off across the park.

Don't do me any favors, Gill.

"I can drive myself to the Towers, Irene. Thanks."

"No way. I'll take a cab back."

Patches of pearled sky bled through the trees. The thickly heated air slid like silk through Quin's fingers as she handed Irene the keys to her Toyota. *Would a murderess do this? Go out of her way like this?*

They sped east. In the lightness of mind the blow to her head had caused, Quin's thoughts were flung back to Kranish's hands at her shoulders. She forced herself to concentrate, instead, on the sorcery of Miami. Yes, it was safer to think of the familiar, the erratic skyline like jagged peaks, the perfect cerulean blue of the sky where pagodas of distant clouds fractured the tropical light, the sinews of highways and interstates looping across and beneath each other, creating geometric shapes. Closer, more immediately, swirling in the stark beauty, was violence. And this, she knew, had its own shape.

"Can you remember anything else about this guy besides the blond hair, Quin?" Irene asked.

"No, everything happened too fast."

"Tall? Short? Fat? Thin?"

She thought about it. "Tall and slender. Yeah, I'm pretty sure he was tall and slender. A surfer type."

"Damn. It's got to be the same guy."

"You've seen him?"

"If he's the guy I'm thinking of, yes. I saw him hanging around the pool at the Towers Wednesday afternoon. In fact, I noticed him when that Detective McCleary was talking to me. And then yesterday, I thought I saw him again when we were shooting at the studios."

"Did you mention it to McCleary?"

Irene made a face. "No way. I'm sick of cops. First Benson, now McCleary, poking around with their questions about my relationship with J.B. It's none of their business."

"They're just trying to find out who killed him."

"They can damn well do it without my help. The man's

gone. Nothing's going to bring him back." Her voice had spiraled to a whisper, then she gave a quick, nervous laugh. "Like Steve McQueen used to tell me, strum your guitar and mind your own business."

"*The* Steve McQueen?"

Irene smiled. "*The* Steve McQueen. He's the reason I'm in this business. I used to hang around a cycle shop in L.A. when I was fourteen, begging Roger, the owner, to give me a job. He finally did, on Saturdays. The shop was a hangout for McQueen, Clint Eastwood, Peter Fonda, Paul Newman, guys like that. They used to come in and talk bikes with Roger and race dirt bikes out on the desert."

She seemed relieved to talk about something else, and Quin was content to listen. She was swept along in Irene's quick, staccato voice; it abraded the drumming in her head.

"So I'm in there one day, taking an engine apart, and McQueen comes over to me and asks what the problem is with the bike. I told him. He wants to know how I know. I told him that, too. Then he wants to know if I can ride as well as I talk and I showed him, and after that I used to race with these guys on weekends. Pretty soon, I was learning how to lay down a bike and jump a bike, and after that I graduated to cars and then into gags." She shrugged like it was no big deal.

"How many stunt women are there in the States?"

"Oh, maybe ten. There're four hundred and fifty people registered as stunt men and women with the Screen Actors' Guild, but just because you can spin out a car doesn't mean you can do gags. I'd say twenty percent of the four-fifty make eighty percent of the money."

She pulled into the Towers' parking lot, turned off the engine, handed Quin her keys. "Here you go. Take it easy, okay? If you start getting dizzy or anything, you should go to the ER for X rays. I got banged up real bad once when I did this gag where I rolled a car. I started having dizzy spells, and it turned out I had a hairline skull fracture. So be careful, huh?"

Relief blazed through her as she entered the apartment with its cool air and huge rooms and a thick charcoal gray rug that soothed her feet. The white and black furniture seemed to strip the world of dimension; she felt like she was walking through the back door of a dream. Any minute now, the guy with the blond hair would burst into the room, only this time he would carry a Samurai sword and a Polaroid camera.

Oh yeah, she was in great shape.

Her head throbbed, but not so much that she could forget she was hungry. She was usually hungry, but it was worse when she felt anxious. Then she consumed food at an alarming rate, as though her anxiety were something that could be broken down, digested, and diffused through her system like nutrients. She fixed herself an omelet, toast, and bacon, cleaned half a cantaloupe, and sliced up cheese. As she ate, part of her worked away at what had happened. "Leave it alone," she muttered, polishing off the meal.

She pushed away from the table and shuffled down the hall to the bathroom. She ran hot water for a bath, the steam rising upward toward her face. While she soaked in a hot tub, it happened again, so this time she just let it come, accompanied by quick, sharp flashes from the tape the killer had sent Kranish. She reviewed the facts: *Between seven and nine-sixteen, when the fire was reported, you entered J.B.'s motor home, stabbed him with a steak knife, splashed turpentine around the motor home, and set it on fire. No one saw you enter or leave.*

Unless it was Irene Bedford, whom the airport security guard had seen enter the motor home at 7:30 and leave about 8:00. After a heated argument. Maybe she'd gone over to the tent for dinner, making sure she'd been seen, then sneaked back to Domer's motor home with the steak knife and turpentine.

And then you went over to the shack, where old man Wright heard you.

Quin cleared her mind and tried a kill flash with Irene as the killer, then Maia. But neither one seemed to fit. She couldn't even establish a possible scenario for the murder at this point because she lacked a vital clue to the killer's motive. Revenge? Jealousy? What? Right-brain problem solving was where intuition leaped the gaps between the facts. But they still didn't have enough facts.

At the heart of detection is the art of listening: a Spin Weaver line.

The hot water and steam seeped through her pores until she grew drowsy and closed her eyes. She finally got out of the tub and wiggled beneath the covers of the big double bed. She was asleep in moments. She dreamed of a square attic door that wouldn't open. She pounded it with her fists, hit it with a metal bar, drilled at it, held a blowtorch under it, and still it wouldn't give. She prayed over it, and Saint Weaver appeared to her and said, *You can't get in without the union card, Quin. Sorry.* Then he rang a bell and kept ringing it and ringing it until the sharp, hurtful sound penetrated the mush of her brain.

She awakened in a sweat, the phone pealing.

It was Marielle, a familiar voice from her own life, calling from Lazy Lake.

2.

McCleary had never liked spying on a person through one-way windows. There was something about it that smacked of a police state, of Big Brother. Besides, there was no surprise left in the routine anymore. Every ordinary Joe knew about one-way windows and police interrogations. Lenny Moorhouse, in fact, waiting by himself in the room, strolled right up to the window and pressed his handsome face to the glass. "Hey, in there, who do you think you're foolin'?"

Wayne O'Donald, the department shrink who was sitting at the console of a computer, whispered, "That boy's pretty proud of himself for having his shit together."

Then Benson came into the room and Moorhouse moved away from the window. His nose had left a smudge on the glass. He sat across from Benson's desk, one leg thrown over the other. "So? You want me to give my statement again, Sergeant?"

McCleary guessed he was in his mid-thirties. His features were so finely chiseled they might have been embossed on the face of a coin. There was a kind of arrogant solopsism about him which McCleary had come to expect in most of Kranish's people, as if Moorhouse considered himself a sun around which the planets revolved.

"His pulse just leaped to eighty," O'Donald remarked, eyeing the computer screen.

Kranish nodded his approval; McCleary asked O'Donald to turn up the volume.

Benson was doing his *aw shucks* routine, softening up Moorhouse by asking him how he'd gotten the part of Frank Corliss in the film. "Through the usual channels," Moorhouse replied. "I read for the part in L.A. Patty Cakes asked me if I wanted to practice for a few minutes before I read, and I decided to just go in there cold. I'd read the script, so I knew what it was about. Anyway, the minute I was finished, I knew I had the part. But they brought me back twice again to read."

"He's starting to relax now, Mac," O'Donald said. "Why don't you go on in."

As McCleary entered the room, Benson made the introductions and explained that McCleary was part of the special task force working on the case. McCleary noted how Moorhouse's features tightened just enough to create an impression of exaggerated patience.

"I'd like to ask you a couple of things," McCleary said.

"I already gave my statement to Sergeant Benson." Defensive now.

"Just pretend you've been called in for a second reading," McCleary snapped. "Didn't you audition for the part Domer got?"

He seemed to take great interest in his hands now, examining the nails, picking at them. "Yeah. I didn't get it. So what?"

"Why didn't you get it?"

"Because Gill apparently thought Domer was better for the part." He smiled. "That's how it is in this business. You either get used to it or you get out."

"Or maybe sometimes you get even?"

Moorhouse's head jerked up, his eyes blazed. "If I'm being accused of something, then spit it out, don't fuck around by playing games, Detective."

"No one's accusing you of anything." McCleary's voice became the paragon of patience. "But I do have some questions concerning your whereabouts the night of the fire. Correct me if I'm wrong, but you stated that you left the dinner tent that evening about eight-fifteen and went back to your dressing room to rehearse your lines. However, you were seen leaving the tent with Mr. Devereaux, and the two of you strolled over to the general aviation building. You care to tell me why you lied?"

"What's that got to do with J.B.?" Moorhouse snapped.

McCleary leaned toward him. "It establishes your alibi, Mr. Moorhouse, that's what."

He rubbed his hands across his jeans, lowered his eyes. He was quiet so long McCleary thought he'd fallen asleep. "Okay, it's true," he said quietly.

"Then why lie about it?" Benson asked.

Another long silence, as if Moorhouse were weighing the consequences of what he was about to say, then: "Because of Sammy's religious stuff."

"I don't understand."

"His *religion*," Moorhouse repeated. "He's a Born Again."

McCleary rubbed his beard. "I guess I'm an obtuse man, Mr. Moorhouse. What's his religion got to do with why you would lie about a walk to the general aviation building?"

Moorhouse sighed and stared at the floor. When he finally spoke, his voice was soft. "Sammy and I were together. Or we would've been, except for that idiot receptionist in the other room."

"I can't hear you." Benson's cosseting *aw shucks* stuff vanished. McCleary shot him a *Lighten up* look. But Benson ignored it. "I said, I can't hear you, Lenny."

He fixed his eyes on Benson. "Sammy and I were going to be together, I mean . . ."

"Together, right, we realize you walked *together* to the building, Lenny. You've already said that."

"Back off, Tim," McCleary demanded.

But it was too late. Moorhouse was already on his feet. *"Together, Sergeant,"* he shouted. "We were going to *fuck,* is that clear enough for you?"

Benson flashed a pugnacious grin. "Yeah, that's clear enough, Lenny. So why didn't you? Why should a receptionist stop you?"

Moorhouse's face gleamed like a damp strawberry. He glared at Benson, then at McCleary, then down at his hands. "Because he's . . . still afraid. His religion, his family, the fear of AIDS, Jesus, I don't know."

"So you were going to become lovers, right?" Benson's voice poked at Moorhouse like hot needles. McCleary could see it, could see that Benson had pushed him too far, because he suddenly stormed out of the room, slamming the door behind him.

"Christ, Tim," McCleary muttered.

"He disgusts me." Benson spat the words and ran a hand over his hair. Then, remembering they were being observed, his head whipped toward the one-way mirror. "Got all that, O'Donald?" he shouted. "Want me to repeat it so you can make sure you've got it verbatim?" He left the room in a huff.

McCleary stared after him, and O'Donald's voice crackled over the intercom. "How about a cup of coffee, Mike? I've got a fresh pot on in my office."

"Sure."

"I'll meet you upstairs."

O'Donald's office, like the man himself, was eccentric. A high-tech clock shaped like a palm tree adorned the far wall. There was a lamp on the desk that looked suspiciously phallic, dozens of psychiatric journals jammed in with books on the shelves, and a four-foot vase near the window with a death mask painted on it. The room possessed a cursory neatness, as if at any moment papers and magazines might pop out of nooks where they'd been shoved and everything would suddenly slide back into disorder.

"I've drawn up some preliminary conclusions on this guy, Mike," O'Donald said, setting his pipe in an ashtray. He plucked a sheaf of papers from the OUT basket. "The copy of that note helped."

"You have any idea where it's from?"

"No, but I'm working on it." His walnut eyes studied McCleary for a moment. "I don't know if the person's male or female. But I think the killer feels he—or she—adheres to a different set of rules than the rest of us. Superior rules, God's rules, if you will." He read from the note Kranish had received: " 'That which is truly great does not degenerate into mere force, but remains inwardly united with the fundamental principles of right and of justice.' "

O'Donald looked up. "*He* is the one on the side of what is correct and just. And then this little passage: 'Whereas an inferior man revels in power when he comes into possession of it, the superior man never makes this mistake.' Then the final riddle: 'which of us is the superior man?' It's almost like he's telling Kranish, the executive producer, the guy with the *clout*, that he doesn't have any power at all because hey, guess what? J.B. Domer is dead, the killer even got it on film, the production schedule was delayed, and Kranish lost a motor home worth more than a hundred grand."

McCleary's temple had begun to ache, and it took a moment for what O'Donald was saying to sink in. "So you're confirming what we've thought all along—that Gill's the real target."

"Yup."

"But *who*? If it's an inside job, which I'm pretty convinced it is, then whoever's doing it stands to lose if the film is sabotaged."

"That wouldn't matter, because the desire to strike back at Gill would be stronger than anything else. 'Which of us is the superior man?' The killer's going to *show* Gill who the superior man is."

McCleary sipped at his coffee; it soured in his stomach. "That would mean that J.B. was chosen at random."

"Not necessarily. It might have been a convenient way to accomplish two things at once, Mac." He rubbed his hands over his face and sighed. "Nefarious intents abound," he said quietly. "My motto is to never overlook anything. Which reminds me." He sat forward again, tapping his fingers against the edge of his desk. "You look like hell."

"Must be the beard."

O'Donald's laughter was a small, strange sound, like a hiccup that didn't quite make it. "How's Quin, anyway?"

"She's fine."

The dark eyes bore through him. "Uh-huh." He fingered a pencil now. "Did you know cops have one of the highest divorce rates in the country, Mike?"

"I'm not a cop anymore."

"I'm not necessarily talking about you. Take Benson, for example. Approaching burnout after more than a decade in the department. Beginning to have serious communication problems with his wife. Cops have made an art out of shunting their emotions aside. That's Benson's problem. He's been doing it so long that all this

122

stuff wells up inside him and he . . . explodes. Like today."

McCleary didn't know whether he was relieved that the conversation had veered toward Benson or annoyed that the story about Benson might be a parable that related to him. It bothered him on a visceral level, though, as if O'Donald's observations had bypassed certain synapses and dived straight for his gut. "I'm sure Tim'll work it out."

O'Donald's fingers moved down the length of the pencil, playing it like a flute. "But you—I never see you explode, Mike. I get the feeling there's lots of stuff locked up inside you. Stuff from that business with Robin. I was watching you in there today, and you know what I saw? A man wound up like the proverbial top. I figure that's why you told Benson to lighten up on Lenny Moorhouse. It hit a little too close to home, didn't it?"

He thought about Quin's chilliness on the phone last night, when he'd mentioned he and Kranish were going out to dinner. He thought of how he'd known she was awake the night before she started on the set and how she'd lain there with her back to him.

You like seeing my brain being picked apart, don't you, Miami. Admit it.

(oh please, chum, don't blame your travails on me)

It's your fault.

(looky here. you try my shoes for a day, okay? besides the heat and the drought, i've got smugglers to deal with. and the mob. and these shitty little punks beating up on old ladies. then i've got another gang stealing cars outa mall parking lots. you think you've got problems, mccleary? you got *no* idea, chum)

"I suppose now you'll send me a bill for seventy-five bucks."

O'Donald smiled, but it lacked mirth. "You bet."

McCleary tapped the desk top once, and stood. "I've got to run. Let me know if you come up with anything else."

"Right. Hey, Mike."

"Yeah?" McCleary stopped in the doorway.

"Just because Robin turned out to be a nut case doesn't mean you have to spend the rest of your life locked up in an emotional cocoon."

"What is this, anyway? *I'm Okay But You're Fucked Up*?"

O'Donald laughed again, but this time it rang sincere. "Hey, I like that. See you around."

McCleary hurried down the hall, relieved to be away from O'Donald's prying eyes. What'd he know, anyway? Shrinks were always loonier than the people they treated. "Smart ass," he grumbled, and wondered why his stomach felt as if a nest of worms had been turned loose inside.

Thirteen

Kranish was in his Mercedes, talking to his L.A. office on the mobile phone, when Irene came up and knocked on the window. In the reflection of the overhead branches in the glass she seemed unreal, as if she'd been spun from the shadows. He motioned for her to go around to the passenger side. She did and slid inside. He jotted down several messages, most from the network, then hung up, and Irene said, "You still up to your old tricks, Gill?"

She smiled as she said it, but her arms were folded at her waist, as if for protection, and her shapely legs were crossed tightly at the knees. The air from the vents ruffled her hair. She smelled faintly of lilac soap. Tiny beads of sweat crossed her upper lip. She sat rigidly in the seat. It was funny what the body language of a woman you'd slept with told you, he thought. Irene, the police's primary suspect, was pissed, and what the hell, maybe she would suddenly splash turpentine in his face and light a match.

"Tricks? What tricks?" He watched her hands, making sure they didn't suddenly dart forward.

"You know, the trick where you put the moves on the newest addition to the set. That trick, Gill."

A sense of déjà vu flooded through him. They'd had this conversation before, he and Irene, and almost verbatim, on the set of the first Spin film. *History*, he'd told McCleary when he'd asked about his relationship with Irene. Yeah, it was history, all right, but back then it wasn't.

She'd seen him talking with an extra he'd hired just the day before and marched up to him in the middle of it and said she wanted to speak to him privately. Then she'd accused him of 'putting the moves' on the woman. In that instance, it happened not to be true, but he hadn't denied it because she wouldn't have believed him, since it *had* been true so many other times.

"Who's the newest addition to the set?" he asked.

"Quin."

Kranish almost laughed. He was tempted to tell her a few things about Quin—like who she was and how she'd known exactly what she was doing when she'd allowed him to massage her neck and back. She'd wanted him to touch her. The problem, though, was that he couldn't figure out if it was because she was attracted to him or so resentful of his friendship with McCleary that she'd wanted something to happen so she could later yell, 'Assault!' and finish off the friendship in one fell swoop. "Quin, right."

"She's relatively new to this business, Gill. Leave her alone."

Her hands moved, and for an instant he flinched, expecting the warm splash of turpentine, the hot flare of a match. But her hands dropped to her lap, and Kranish stared at them. Were those hands capable of setting a man on fire? And then shooting a videotape of the whole thing? Years ago, he would've said no. He would've thought of how soft those hands were, how accomplished. He wondered if Irene hated him. He would have to view the tape of her he had and see if he could detect the capacity for such hatred. But maybe that tape didn't count. It was eight or nine years old and things had changed. They had changed. Their relationship had changed.

"Do you hate me?" he blurted.

Astonishment manacled her face. But he didn't know if it was caused by the question or the fact that he'd asked. She looked quickly away, at her hands. "No. I've known you too long to hate you."

Did you torch Domer, Irene?

She glanced up then, almost as if she'd heard his silent question. "You know, Gill, there's no telling what you'd produce if you weren't so continually sidetracked by women."

"It's not women."

"Oh, really? You could've fooled me."

It was sex, he thought.

No, that wasn't quite right either. It was the exploration of a woman's psyche that intrigued him, the search for her weakest point which, when triggered, would bind her to him enough so he could mold her will, sculpt it. He'd reached that point finally with Dina, and it was the sort of thing you found out about a woman only by making love to her, by discovering what she liked, how to please her, how to create an addiction in her for sex with you. His pursuit was a hobby, a small passion, and he excelled at it. In some ways it wasn't all that different from making movies. In both cases you had to define the opiate—and supply it.

"You know what I'm talking about, Gill," she said.

He nodded. "Sex. You're talking about sex."

Her black eyes scrutinized him without seeming to. "Forget I even said anything." She sighed; it made her nipples stand out against her yellow tank top. Then she reached for the handle, started to swing the door open, but Kranish's fingers closed around her arm. She glanced back, startled. "What?"

"You never really answered my question."

"About hating you?"

He nodded and her face softened and Kranish leaned toward her and touched his mouth to the smooth tanned curve of her shoulder. He remembered the taste of her skin. Funny, that he could forget things like names, but never the way a woman tasted or smelled.

When he looked at her again, her eyes were closed,

her head rested back against the seat. "Like that," she whispered. "That's what I hate. The way you still try to control me when you do things like that."

"Like what? Kissing your shoulder?"

"No, damn it, the *way* you do it." She opened her eyes now. "The way you do it at precisely the minute you're telling me I didn't really say whether I hate you or not." She reached for his hand, brought it to her breast, held it there. "Go ahead, Gill. Go ahead and do what you used to do. You know, the little number with your thumb. I've never met a man since who can do it like you can. Or maybe the tongue trick, that used to make me feel like I was unraveling at the seams, Gill. Remember how I used to beg for more? Huh? Remember? And I was too young and too stupid to realize it was just part of your repertoire of body moves, that it didn't mean anything more to you than a dog scratching to get rid of an itch."

She laughed and knocked his hand away. "No, I don't hate you, Gill. I think you're brilliant. I'd work with you on any movie, for TV, theaters, a commercial, in any locale in the world, and I'd be proud to see my name rolling in the credits on any film you make. But I think you're a mess inside. There's something missing in you." She tapped her chest. "In here. You try to hide it by doing things for people, you know, small considerate things, or big important things like giving an unknown a break because you remember how it was before you hit the big time. But basically, you're fucked up, Gill, and I feel sorry for you."

She opened the door, and he watched her walk off through the umbrageous park toward her car. The echo of her words warbled in the air around him, then fell like birds struck down by the heat.

If she weren't the best stunt woman in the business, he would've called her back and fired her. Instead, he slammed the Mercedes into gear and peeled out of the park.

Fourteen

As Rose turned her 1975 Fleetwood Cadillac through the late afternoon shadows that slipped across the Florida International University campus, Quin glanced back at the troupes. A carnival train, she thought. Rose's car took the lead, followed by Maia Fox, Bruce Harmon, and Lenny Moorhouse in her plum-colored BMW, and Irene with Greg Hess, the production manager, in a pickup truck, towing the Maserati. The car would be used in one of the scenes taking place on Earth.

Marielle had stopped by the hotel unexpectedly, on her way home from the Dadeland Mall, and she was in the back seat with Will Clarke. Quin had introduced her as a 'friend from Lazy Lake' with whom she'd gone to college. No one questioned it. McCleary, of course, wouldn't have approved that she'd immixed elements of her dual lives, but so what. She needed the help.

She'd called and told him about what had happened to her on the set. She knew by his reaction that Kranish had neglected to notify him. It didn't surprise her. She could've had a cracked skull, for Christ's sakes, but Kranish had more important things to attend to.

"Everyone still with us, Will?" Rose asked, glancing at him in the rearview mirror.

"Yup." His all-American face appeared between them, chin resting on the edge of the seat. "Who gets to drive 'er first?"

"Lenny. That's only fair," Rose replied. "If it weren't for Lenny, we wouldn't even *have* a Maserati in this film.

He bugged Gill until he finally consented just to shut him up. Too bad Sammy couldn't make it. He would've enjoyed this."

"Where is he?" Will asked.

"He had an appointment with that Detective McCleary."

Quin felt Marielle's eyes burning holes in her back.

"I bought a bottle of champagne, but it's not the good stuff," Will said.

Rose waved a hand in the air. "It'll do, as long as it's champagne. That's the tradition."

She pulled alongside an old, low-slung shack that looked like a deserted Quonset hut. Years ago, this had been a military base. Then the military had moved out and the state had built a university, but the runway and a few oddities like the Quonset hut and the control tower had remained. The ribbon of black asphalt—cracked, with tussocks of grass poking through—tore straight for the horizon for at least a mile and a half, then ended abruptly at a lake. Surrounding the lake was deep green grass the likes of which Quin hadn't seen since last spring. Beyond the lake and to its right was a concrete wall that divided the campus from a pasture where horses grazed.

As they got out of the car, the heat made Quin suck in her breath. It sheathed the asphalt like a second skin and quivered in waves inches above it. She pulled a straw hat down snugly on her head and slipped on her sunglasses, watching as Irene and Lenny Moorhouse unhitched the Maserati from the pickup. Harmon was setting up his video camera, and Marielle wandered off to talk to him.

Rose made a face at the camera as he aimed it at her. "Close-ups, Brucie baby, don't forget the close-ups," she called. "And if any of them are good, I want stills for my portfolio."

"I want nudes, Rose," Harmon shouted back, then laughed his weird laugh, his *yuk yuk* laugh.

"Okay," Moorhouse called, clapping his hands like a schoolteacher. "Let's get the show going. Where's the champagne?"

"I'll get it," Will volunteered and sprinted back to the Caddy.

Moorhouse ran a cloth over the Maserati's hood, wiping it down. Irene opened the door, inserted the key in the ignition, and tightened her hands on the steering wheel. "Beautiful," she murmured. "It's just beautiful." She poked her head out. "Lenny, I think you should get first shot at her. If it hadn't been for you, Frank Corliss would've been driving a Chrysler or something."

Moorhouse chuckled and rapped his knuckles on the windshield. "You want to come along as navigator?"

"I'll wait my turn."

Rose pulled a bag of Fritos out of her purse and munched noisily as they waited. Then she wiggled the bag in the air and shouted, "Bruce, get the Fritos bag. Maybe we can make a commercial out of it." Quin's stomach growled loudly, and Rose offered her the bag. "Here, can't have anyone starving to death."

Maia Fox dabbed at her pretty face with a monogrammed handkerchief. "C'mon, guys, it's hot out here."

Will raced back with the champagne and everyone crowded around the car. Will passed Moorhouse the bottle of champagne. He held it above his head. "I can't see breaking this baby, so let's pop her and pass the bottle around. Bruce, make sure you get this on film."

Harmon peeked out from behind his camera. "Just save me a sip, man."

Moments later there was a soft but audible pop and stuff spumed from the bottle. "To a successful *Night Flames*," Moorhouse said, "with no more tragedies." Then he took a swig and passed the bottle to Maia, and on it went around the circle.

"Go! Go! Go!" they began to chant as Moorhouse sidled over to the car and climbed in.

Marielle glanced at Quin and flashed a thumbs-up that said: *Maybe I can get a celebrity piece outa this*. The camera moved closer as the door shut. The engine revved. Through the windshield, Quin saw Moorhouse strap himself in. Rose held a red kerchief in front of the car. "On your mark," they all shouted. "Get set. *Go!*"

Rose's arm sliced down through the air like a guillotine. The Maserati's tires shrieked against the black pavement and it blasted away in a cloud of smoke and flying pebbles. The slipstream seemed to suck at them, pulling them forward en masse for several hundred feet.

"Look at her fly!" Irene shouted.

Quin fanned herself with her hat and shaded her eyes with her other hand, watching the Maserati as it sped like a silver bullet, sleek and smooth, gleaming in the hot light, gathering momentum. The horizon seemed to reach down and kiss the shiny roof. Any minute now, Quin expected the car to suddenly sprout wings and leap toward the skies like a phoenix or a dragon. Instead, it reached the end of the runway, bounced onto the patch of grass, and swung around the lake, graceful as a gazelle.

Spicules of light flew off the hood like water, then struck the Maserati's windshield, bleeding all over it, silver against the emerald green, the cerulean sky curving overhead, embracing it. The car headed back toward them to the sound of applause and shouts urging Moorhouse on. Their voices beat the still September air like the wings of a dozen birds. *Go, go, go*: the chant encompassed more than a car and a man moving like the speed of light. It was a collective paean for the success of the film.

Then something went haywire. The front of the car whipped right, left. It screeched into a ninety-degree turn, its back end snapping from one side to the other like the hips of a belly dancer. It was headed for the concrete wall that divided the campus from a neighboring pasture.

Spin's breath echoed in Quin's head: *Death whispers and even the deaf hear her coming. . . .*

"The brakes, slam on the brakes!" someone shouted.

The horn blared once, twice, and still the brake lights didn't flash and still the car kept flying toward the concrete wall. Then the horn grew in a crescive shriek that was the sound of a wounded animal, a terrified man, a peal for help, salvation, forgiveness, something.

When it slammed into the concrete wall, the Maserati was doing 110. The explosion hurled a fireball of metal and debris some fifty feet into the air, then it showered onto the dry pasture, and the dozen horses grazing there sprang into a mindless stampede.

For a long moment, no one did anything. The silence trembled with the pounding of hooves against the ground, the air filled with the smell of gasoline, of burning vegetation, cloth, skin. Quin felt as if her legs had sunk into the ground knee deep, as if the sun had slid from the sky and melted over her head and shoulders like hot wax.

Then everyone moved at once, like a film speeded up. Irene sprinted toward the pickup, it screeched off into the heat, the towbar banging the ground behind it. A moment later, Rose's Caddy and Maia's BMW followed, and Quin and Marielle were alone in the heat.

Quin blinked sweat from her eyes. A huge pressure balled in her chest, a nameless something, a swirling malaise that shouted, *There were no brakes no brakes*. So why didn't he turn? It pushed its way into the air on the heels of her sob and pursued her as she tore across the desert of asphalt toward the nearest building—and a phone.

Harmon's camera whirred on.

PART TWO

Jump Cuts

"The dead speak.
We just don't know how to listen."
—Spin Weaver

Fifteen

1.

SAMMY DEVEREAUX, THE obsessed *Centauri Tribune* reporter Juke Farber in the film, lived in a comfortable home in Coral Gables with his wife and two kids. Although he was polite and cooperative, McCleary sensed an underlying suspicion of law enforcement people.

"I've told Sergeant Benson and I'm telling you, Detective McCleary, that I ate and went back to my dressing room. I have no way of proving that, of course. Now if that makes me a suspect in this whole thing, well, so be it. The good Lord must be testing me."

McCleary doubted 'the good Lawd' had anything to do with it. But if He did, He might question Devereaux's omission of the facts—that he and Lenny Moorhouse had walked over to the general aviation building to 'be together,' as Moorhouse had put it. "And about what time was it you left the dinner tent?"

"A bit after eight, I think it was."

"Dinner didn't start until eight-thirty."

"You can usually get in early for a tray. I was quite tired that night, because we'd been on call since, oh, around seven that morning. I was hoping to use one of the motor homes to nap for a bit, but they were all occupied."

"By J.B. and who else?"

Devereaux ran a hand over his thick black hair and sipped from his glass of juice. They were sitting on the

137

patio. Thick hibiscus hedges grew halfway up the screen, and tremendous pink and red blossoms drank up the water from the revolving sprinklers nearby. From inside the house McCleary heard rock music, the television, a phone ringing, a dog barking. The usual family noises for a Friday evening.

"I don't remember, except that Gill was using one of them."

"Was there any professional jealousy between you and J.B.?"

Devereaux laughed. "Between me and J.B.? I've been in this business for about fifteen years and have made more money at it than J.B. could ever have hoped to make. Besides, the Lord places such temptations in front of us to be *overcome*, as challenges. And I must say I have more talent in my little pinky here"—he held it up, wiggled it—"than J.B. had in his whole body."

McCleary wondered what the *Lawd* thought of Devereaux's vanity. He missed being handsome by a certain sparseness in his features—a thin, hawkish nose, a lack of flesh around his chin so that it seemed pointed, eyes that were a shade too small, a mouth with underdeveloped lips. But even if he'd looked like Redford, his hubris would've somehow destroyed it.

"What's your blood type, Mr. Devereaux?" he asked, even though he knew.

Devereaux sighed. "O. Type O. Just like fifty percent of the population. We're the universal donors, you know. I must tell you we *all* resented the implication of those blood tests. The other night the Lord came to me in a dream, Detective McCleary." He leaned forward, his face a rete of tiny wrinkles and lines in the waning sunlight. "And it was His message that J.B. was a victim of a random killing."

"I see. Did He happen to mention the killer's name?"

"No. No, He did not. I have asked for guidance in that area, but . . ." He paused. A slow smile worked at his mouth. "I do believe you are poking fun at me, Detective McCleary."

Ah do believe Ah may puke, Mr. Devereaux.

"You don't think anyone in the cast and crew had a reason to see Mr. Domer dead?"

He looked thoughtful. "Perhaps. J.B.'s biggest problem in life, you see, was his pagan lifestyle."

"Pagan."

"Unchristian." His fingers stroked his sweating glass, and he didn't meet McCleary's eyes. "In some circles, I believe it's called satyriasis." When McCleary didn't respond, Devereaux lowered his voice. "His, uh, inability to keep his pants on."

"Delicately put," McCleary laughed.

"J.B. was worse than Gill."

"Gill?"

It was obviously something that had slipped out, because Devereaux suddenly seemed nervous. Very nervous. He twisted his wedding ring, cleared his throat, said, "What I meant was that J.B. wasn't exactly a puritan."

"Tell me about Gill, Mr. Devereaux."

"Look, that has nothing to do with Domer, okay, Detective? Just forget I said anything."

Fear, McCleary thought. Devereaux wasn't just nervous, he was scared of Gill. "I'm afraid that's not good enough."

Devereaux's mouth gave a little twitch that said, *I don't wanna do this, Detective. But you're making me.* "Look." He leaned toward McCleary and lowered his voice as though he were afraid his house was bugged. "If it weren't for Gill Kranish, I would probably still be starving in Hollywood, Detective. You understand? The rogue I played in the Spin Weaver movies made me a very rich man. I admire and respect Gill. I—"

"It won't go any farther than the two of us."

Devereaux sighed and sat back. "You're not seeing the picture, are you? Gill is a powerful man. There're probably two producers in Hollywood who've got more clout than he does, and even that's open to debate. What he does with his private life, Detective, is his own business."

"Mr. Devereaux, you're talking like it was forty years ago. C'mon, Rock Hudson died of AIDS, Stacey Keach did time in England for possession of cocaine, everyone's dirty laundry is front-page news. So what?"

"It's not the same thing. Gill remains a very private man. It's not my business if there are rumors about orgies and a private video collection that would place some very important people in compromising positions."

McCleary was struck again by that odd feeling that they weren't talking about the same Gill Kranish. This was the second time there'd been allusions to something to do with Kranish and an invasion of privacy. He didn't know what to say, so he turned the subject back to Devereaux. "I suppose that you lied to the police, then, to protect your reputation?"

"Lied to the police? I told you that—"

"And Lenny Moorhouse says differently, Mr. Devereaux. He says you two are involved with each other. Or about to be involved. That's why you met in the aviation center that night. And I suspect that maybe, just maybe, you didn't meet that night, that he killed Domer and you're covering up for him."

Devereaux's hawkish face turned meek. He blinked several times, as if to clear his vision. He stopped twisting the wedding band on his finger and glanced quickly over his shoulder to make sure the door was closed.

"Okay, it's true," he whispered in a cracked voice. "We . . . I mean, yes, what he says is essentially true. But I didn't lie for him. He *was* there in the aviation center that night, we *did* meet, he didn't kill J.B."

The hunch spot between McCleary's eyes burned. He knew Devereaux was telling the truth, and he felt suddenly soiled. "Look, I—"

"I am a married man. A father," Devereaux went on in a hushed voice. Sweat had erupted on his forehead.

140

He dabbed at it with a monogrammed handkerchief and stared at his hands as he talked. "I . . . I care for Lenny, but I've never acted on it because I . . . I also care for my family. Is that so wrong?" He lifted his eyes. McCleary recognized supplication, a need for someone to pat him on the shoulder and assure him he was doing just fine because, hey, the world is a pretty fucked-up place and all you can do is try to get along.

"I understand. I don't intend to go to your family or anything, Mr. Devereaux. Really. I'm just trying to figure out who killed Domer."

Devereaux looked visibly relieved.

Inside the house, the phone rang.

"I would appreciate it if—"

The doors slid open and Devereaux's wife poked her head out. "It's for you, Sammy."

He pushed away from the table and went inside. Mrs. Devereaux asked McCleary if she could get him anything. He shook his head and thanked her and she went back indoors. McCleary sat there, musing over the puzzle of Kranish. Video collections, orgies, more women than any man could possibly keep track of—fact or fiction? Truth or just malicious rumors? But all that aside, what had disturbed him most of all was that Kranish hadn't bothered to call him about Quin until hours after she'd been knocked out. And by then he'd already spoken to her.

When Devereaux returned a few minutes later he looked utterly defeated. His shoulders sagged. His face had drained of color.

"That was Rose. Rose Leen. There . . . there's been an accident. With the Maserati. Lenny was driving the Maserati. It . . . it went out of control. He . . . he's dead." His voice ended as a sibilant whisper.

By midnight, the verdict on the accident was in: the Maserati had been sabotaged.

This edict was handed down by a short, wiry fellow

141

named Ray whose coriaceous face was the color of hot tar. He was an ex–race car driver and, according to Benson, now the best auto mechanic in South Florida. He walked with a limp, the result of an accident which had prompted his departure from professional racing ten years ago. Since nothing of the car had remained to examine, they'd given Ray a copy of Bruce Harmon's videotape to view to see if he could determine what had happened. Now Ray slipped the videotape in the station's VCR and fast-forwarded it to the moment when a smiling Moorhouse entered the car.

Who would have ever thought, McCleary wondered, that the weird little dude with the camera would actually prove useful?

They watched as the Maserati shot toward the end of the runway. Just as it whipped around the bend of the lake so it was headed back toward the runway, the front end zigged right, zagged left, and Ray froze the frame. He turned to them, a slight man who, against the white of the wall, looked almost undernourished.

"Here's where the boy first knows he's in a heap of trouble. He's trying to bleed off some speed by playing with the steering. He probably done took his foot off the accelerator a couple of seconds before that."

"What kind of trouble?" McCleary asked.

Ray held up his hand. "Patience. You be seeing shortly."

He started the video again. The Maserati had made a ninety-degree turn and was bearing down toward the concrete wall. The back of it fishtailed, dust flew. Ray stopped the tape once more.

"What he shoulda done here, in my opinion, was head back toward the lake. Or hell, gone into the lake if he'd had to. But instead, he's headin' in a straight line for oh-blivion. My way of thinkin', there's two reasons a man would do somethin' that stupid." A cloud of smoke from his cigarette rose around his head. "Because he's scared shitless or because there's something wrong with the steering mechanism. I reckon he wasn't scared shitless, because he knew enough to try to correct the problem when he realized he was in trouble. So I gotta go with the second reason. The steering."

Small sounds in the room pulsed through the brief silence: the hum of the VCR, a wheeze from Ray, a phone ringing somewhere down the hall. *Sabotaged:* an ugly word, McCleary mused, but not surprising.

"So we've got brakes and a steering mechanism," Benson said. "How difficult is it to tamper with those two things?"

Ray sat back, hooking his hands behind his head. "Not difficult if you know what you're doing. Without taking a look at the car, I can't be sure what was done. But I can tell you for sure that *something* was done."

"How long would it take to sabotage the car?" McCleary asked.

Ray stabbed out his cigarette in a nearby ashtray. "Again, that depends. My guess is that the brake line was cut, so the brakes were gone from the beginning, but he didn't know it because he didn't need 'em until he rounded the lake. The steering mechanism, though, that was screwed up just enough so it'd fail once the car was movin'. Where was the car kept, anyhow?"

"It'd just arrived from the West Coast," McCleary explained, "and was being kept in a warehouse. It was towed to the production offices by the firm that shipped it and then towed out to the airport by some people on the cast and crew."

"I'd sure be checking out the warehouse if I was you."

Benson's jaw seemed to sag with defeat. "We probably won't find squat, Mac."

"It's worth a look."

"Listen to your friend," Ray said to Benson, then laid a thin, bony hand on Benson's shoulder. "You know what your problem is, boy? You oughta retire from police work. Don't wait around like I did for an accident to do you in. I was sittin' real pretty, see, and feelin' damn smug, too, thinkin' that in ten years of doing the race car circuit, all I'd gotten were a couple of busted bones and a wrenched back. And I was sittin' so pretty I forgot that trouble's got a way of sneakin' up on you. Next thing I know, *bang.* . . ." He slapped his hands together once, crackling the still air. "I got a busted hip socket that they had to remove and replace with metal. So now I got my second love, see, working on cars. That's what you need, boy. A second love."

Benson knuckled an eye. "You're assuming my first love is homicide, Ray. I'm not so sure that's true."

"Well, shee-it. Then get out of it." He stood. "Now I gotta be gettin' some sleep, guys. If you need anything else, just holler."

Benson went downstairs with Ray, and McCleary rewound the videotape to watch it again. Who knew cars well enough to cut a brake line and tamper with the steering mechanism? Irene Bedford, for sure. She'd started as a stunt woman driving cars.

And Quin had pointed out that she'd told Moorhouse to take first crack at the Maserati.

The air-conditioning clicked on, swirling the remaining smoke from Ray's cigarette. His eyes burned, his body ached, his brain screamed for sleep. When Benson returned to the office, McCleary said, "I think you should put a tail on the Bedford woman, Tim."

"Yeah, I agree. I'll get on it. What about Devereaux? Maybe he wanted Moorhouse dead so he'd keep his mouth shut about their hot little romance, or beginning romance. Or whatever the hell it was."

"Maybe. But if the point is to sabotage the film to get back at Gill, how does Devereaux figure in?"

Benson ran a hand over his face, stifling a yawn. "Hell, you said it yourself. He's scared shitless of Gill. Besides, we're overlooking that Charlie Roberts, Mike. Why would he take scripts from the trailer?"

McCleary's head swam. "I don't know. Let's get outa here. I need some sleep." Too many unknowns, he thought as they descended in the elevator. Even if the picture, as it stood now, were completely exposed, what would it tell him?

Zip, buddy boy.

So maybe Quin was right. Maybe it was a matter of poking around in the shadows, poking around in . . . *Gill's private life.* Christ.

Outside, a lopsided moon squatted low in the sky. Jasmine sweetened the air. McCleary followed Benson out of the parking lot, then turned south, driving with his windows down. In the distance, lightning burst against the horizon, perforating the edge of the sky. A distant storm that would probably not reach land. Too bad. They were entering their seventeenth week without rain. Patches of the Everglades were burning, and sometimes at night he could smell the smoke, woven in with the fecund scents of ferns just beneath the window.

His thoughts wandered back to Moorhouse, blown to smithereens like Domer. A clean, quick death, someone had remarked when the firemen had been squelching the flames. *Clean & Quick,* like a new kind of bathtub cleanser. But what about Moorhouse's terror, which must've made those last few moments seem like months? Were they *clean? quick?*

McCleary felt the flutters of his own mortality and pressed his foot against the accelerator. He wanted to get home. Roll into bed. Hold Quin. Talk to the cat. Moorhouse's death had left a chasmal darkness inside him that begged to be filled, lighted. Death always did that to him. Sometimes his life sprouted around him like some grotesque caricature of a life, its shape distorted, excessive where it should've been lean, sparse where it should've been full, and then death blew in, whipping it into shape. Maybe the source of his addiction to homicide was a need to be constantly reminded of death so he could fully appreciate life.

(sicko, chum. you see me getting all bent out of shape just because i lead the nation in homicides?)

Who asked you, anyway, Miami.

Quin couldn't stand the idea of another night alone. She'd come home, but now she couldn't sleep, so she went skinny-dipping. Moonlight poured through the screen, into the patio, illuminating dried leaves that floated on the surface of the water like thin paper ships. Somewhere distant, a dove cooed. The night air smelled sweet. Of life, Quin thought. She needed that smell. She needed it to drive out the image of the Maserati, blown to dust.

A light came on in the house and spilled through the kitchen window. A moment later, McCleary came out onto the patio and crouched at the edge of the pool. Quin backstroked toward him. "How's the water?" he asked.

He looked . . . his age, she thought. "Perfect. I left some dinner for you in the oven. How'd it go?"

"It was sabotage."

She nodded. "Brakes?"

"And the steering mechanism."

"C'mon in."

He grinned. "Be right back."

He started to rise, but Quin reached out, took hold of his hand, and yanked. He tumbled into the pool with a laugh, grabbed her around the waist, and dunked her good. She shot to the surface, sputtering.

"You never did play fair," he said, pouring water out of one of his shoes. He removed the other and set it next to its twin. He unbuttoned his shirt as he moved toward the steps at the shallow end.

Quin laughed and swam alongside him.

He told her about his meeting with Devereaux and about running into Charlie Roberts Wednesday afternoon at the Towers. "I think he's the guy who knocked you over the head."

"Charlie Roberts. Why's that name so familiar?"

"Remember that Toyota case Bean handled a while back?"

Quin made a face. "Oh, yeah. The one we lost, right? There was that PI who dug up some damaging interdepartmental memos about the steering mechanism on the Toyota. That Charlie Roberts?"

McCleary nodded and stripped off his shirt. He wrung it out and draped it carefully over the metal railing. So neat, Quin thought, even now, in the pool. "The same."

"I don't suppose he told you who he's working for."

"He may when I threaten him with an assault charge."

"If I remember correctly, Charlie doesn't scare too easily. What I'd like to know is why he took copies of the script."

Off came the rest of his clothes, wrung out and draped, just like his shirt.

"I think you must've run a Chinese laundry in a past life, Mac."

"And you were my mistress," he said.

She swam away from him on her back, moonlight filling the distance between them. "And I worked for you and you fired me."

He laughed and did a breaststroke toward her. "And now I'm paying for it."

Then he dived suddenly and grabbed her around the legs and she went under. They shot to the surface, laughing. The water changed the texture of his skin, his hands were silk at her waist, his mouth tasted of chlorine and fear. Yes, she could taste his fear as surely as she did his hunger.

His tongue licked water from the tip of her nose as his hands moved over the curve of her shoulders, the slope of her back and buttocks, around to the steps of her ribs and the swells of her breasts. He sculpted her from the hot night, his mouth creating the hollow in her throat where a pulse leaped against his tongue, his fingers forming peaks of her nipples, his hands loosening and tightening the muscles across her stomach.

She took him in her hands and he murmured something she didn't catch. His hand rested between her thighs as lightly as clouds, then his finger slid inside her. He pressed her back against the steps, stroking her so slowly, so gently, she thought she would die of wanting him. She thought, briefly, of Kranish, of what happened that morning. For a moment, just a moment, it was Kranish's mouth, Kranish's hands, she could see his face in her mind, his smile of triumph, and then McCleary's strokes drove Kranish out of her, almost as if he sensed her thoughts. He held her against the steps, his mouth against her neck, her throat, her eyes and breasts, devouring her.

His finger slid, stopped, slid, almost driving her into a frenzy. *Don't stop, please stop, don't stop, why did I think of Gill, Jesus, why.* . . . His tongue slid the length of her, defining her, moving lower until she was impaled against the steps like a butterfly. Her body had never felt so sensitive, he was pressing her thighs farther apart, she whispered something but he didn't listen, didn't hear her.

His tongue touched her, teased, then his finger again, in and out, a rhythm like music, oh God, yes, like music, and then his tongue, everything sharper than before, every texture different, every sensation new, and she could barely breathe, her womb was on fire, she gripped the railing as she lifted her hips, wanting more, more, consumed with a heat like greed. His hands slid beneath her, splashing water that was cold where she was hot. She made soft sounds, murmuring something to which he paid no heed, and his tongue kept on and on and she cried out and then suddenly he was inside her, filling her, and she clutched at him as everything inside her convulsed.

She couldn't move anymore, but he kept thrusting, long and slow, quick and hot, and her arms came loose from his neck and she fell back and one hand grappled for the edge of the pool as pleasure melded into pain and pain became pleasure. He was trying to climb inside her, he was, he was trying to climb inside her, and she came again, sucking at the air, her lungs filling with it like kites, and she soared, soared. Then he gripped her hard at the waist and his insides erupted.

Quin held on to him, opened her eyes and saw a single star in the bruised night sky, blurring, sliding toward them. And then she saw movement at the patio door. "Jesus," she hissed, "Jesus. Mac. Someone's out there. I just saw someone at the side of the house."

They scrambled out of the pool, and a few moments later the doorbell rang.

It was Kranish.

Sixteen

1.

QUIN MADE A pot of coffee, then fussed around, cutting up cheese and celery and radishes, and adding chocolate chip cookies for a plate of munchie food. Sex made her ravenous. Anxiety made her ravenous. Combine the two and her hunger deepened to immedicable proportions.

She didn't want to turn around and look at Kranish. The mere thought of doing so made her insides shrivel like a cupful of prunes. How long had he been standing out there? *Did you enjoy it, Gill? Is voyeurism the subject of your next film?*

McCleary had answered the door in a towel, then scampered upstairs after Quin to dress, the two of *them* acting as guilty as children. It was Kranish who should've been feeling like shit, she thought. But now he and McCleary sat at the kitchen table, snug as bugs. "I'm sorry about coming by here so late," Kranish apologized. "But I wanted to know what was determined about the car, Mac. I kept ringing the bell and no one answered. I was about to leave and decided to try the side door."

Sure, Gill. And then you stood there, watching.

McCleary told him what they'd determined about the car accident, and she heard Kranish saying, yes, he'd expected as much, and then he went on and she shut off her hearing so she wouldn't have to listen to him.

As she set the plate of food on the table with three mugs, Kranish asked, "How's your head, Quin?"

He said it as if to remind her of what had happened or almost happened in the trailer today. He said it with a smirk in his voice that hinted at what he'd seen as a Peeping Tom at the side of the house. "Just a knot."

"You gave us quite a scare this morning."

And how're your migraines, Gill? How're your ulcers, your damaged liver? How could McCleary just sit there as though nothing had happened? "Well, I'm fine now."

She nibbled at some radishes, devoured a chocolate chip cookie, then got up and poured coffee, her thighs aching, her body begging for sleep. She drank half of her coffee, ate some more, listening only dimly to the sound of their voices. Then she pushed away from the table with a yawn. "I've got to get some sleep," she said. "See you two in the morning."

She fled the kitchen, and as soon as she was inside the bedroom she hugged her arms against her, squeezed her eyes shut, and in her mind saw the silhouette at the side of the house again. Then she felt Kranish's hands massaging her neck and back this morning in the trailer and hurried into the shower. She turned the water on hot and let it pour over her. *Was it fun, Gill? Did you get off on it?*

Quin finally got out of the shower and slipped under the covers with a shudder and closed her eyes, but sleep wouldn't come. She could hear the drone of their voices through the walls, drifting through the air-conditioning vents. She knew McCleary was telling Kranish that perhaps he should consider canceling the movie, and she knew Kranish would shake his head and say no, he couldn't. *Night Flames*, he would say, would bring Spin to a mass audience; it was destined for Emmy nominations.

The movie, movie, movie, she was sick to death of the movie, she was . . . *The Movie.* Was it being sabotaged because of its content? Was that possible? She got up and turned on the light and opened a drawer in the nightstand. She brought out a copy of the script. NIGHT FLAMES BY HANNAH DAVIDSON. Who was Hannah Davidson?

Kranish *must* have hired her because Spin was *his* creation, and no one else would use Spin as a character. Did that mean the idea for the script was her idea or his?

She stared at the title page, light spilling across it from the lamp, then went through it, plucking out words, phrases, dialogue. *KILL FLASH.* She shut off the light, set the script on the floor, and lay back. Shadows waltzed across the walls, the ceiling. As her eyes grew accustomed to the dark, she began to detect patterns that swirled like fingerprints. In the center of one pattern, Kranish's face took shape. *Money laundering . . . drugs . . . two reporters, one who's killed . . . corrupt bank officers . . .* Twentieth-century stuff transposed to the twenty-first century.

After a while, she heard footsteps on the stairs, then McCleary came into the room. She sat up and turned on the light. He looked at her. "Did Gill leave?" she asked.

McCleary nodded and yawned and went into the bathroom. She followed him, standing in the door as he washed his face and told him her idea about the script. Then she blurted, "He was just standing there watching us, Mac."

He sighed; it was a cloying sound. "Quin, he explained what he was doing. He was going to knock on the glass door."

"But he *stood* there. He stood there and watched, and I don't give a damn what he *says* he was doing; I *know* what he was doing."

McCleary rubbed his face with the towel, brushed his teeth, and she stared at his back, waiting for a reply. He was angry; she saw it in the tension of his shoulders. He rinsed out his mouth and lifted his head, watching her in the mirror. "No matter what Gill does or says, you take it personally, don't you. You're *looking* for reasons to hate the man."

It was true. She resented Kranish. His mere presence spalled her patience, her tolerance. Every time she saw him her invidious list of black marks against him grew.

Kranish's list of sins. Kranish who'd watched her and McCleary in the pool, who'd probably heard her cry out, Kranish whose face had appeared like an apparition in her head in the middle of it all. Great, this was just great.

"I don't have to *look* for reasons to dislike him, Mac."

He turned, leaning against the sink, arms folded across his chest. "So what do you want to do, Quin? Drop the case?" His voice had lost any semblance of patience.

"I don't know."

He lit into her then, telling her she was unfair, that two men had been killed and all she could think about was how much she disliked Kranish, and on and on, and she just stood there until she no longer heard him.

"You're not listening."

"I am. I *am* listening. I just can't believe what you're saying."

"Oh, fuck it." He marched past her into the bedroom. He slid down under the covers as if into a cocoon, and rolled on his side, his back to her.

"I hate it when you get like this," she snapped. "When you do this silence routine." When he didn't move, didn't say anything, she grabbed the pillow, yanked a blanket off the bed, and stomped downstairs. She threw everything on the couch, switched on the television, marched into the kitchen for something to eat, and returned. Merlin was curled up on the blanket. She sat down, bit into her apple with a vengeance. On Cinemax, Bill Murray and Dan Akroyd were busting ghosts. On HBO, *Romancing the Stone* was showing for the fortieth time. On Showtime, *The Last Starfighter* battled aliens in a distant universe. Presto, chango, and into your home rushed the past, present, and future, the familiar and the unimagined. With a quick flick of her fingers she could tune into any of twenty-eight stations. Their stereo TV was cable ready, but she wasn't.

What the hell were they doing with cable TV anyhow? When did they watch it? How much a month did they pay for the blasted thing?

She switched the set off, tossed out her apple core, brushed her teeth again, and slid under the covers in the dark. She would leave in the morning before McCleary woke up. Otherwise, they would circle each other warily, each waiting for the other to continue the argument, end it, or simply ignore it. And because she could never tolerate long bouts of silence, not that kind of silence, she would say something like, "Let's be friends." And if he were feeling friendly, he would laugh and they'd make up. But if he were still feeling out of sorts, he would walk away. Just like that, he would walk away.

Well, she was tired of being the one who always made the first gesture toward reconciliation.

2.

Surfer Charlie lived in an expensive yuppie complex in South Miami. To McCleary, it looked like a small, self-contained walled city dedicated to the pursuit of long life through exercise. There were tennis courts and swimming pools, Jacuzzis, a gym, and a running track. Since it was Saturday, there were people outside in the fulgent sunlight doing all these things, but without much conviction, as if they were bored with it all. At least, that's the way it appeared to McCleary.

He wound through the complex, looking for Roberts' building. It was one of four facing the canal, and he noted that most of the cars parked in front were trendy and expensive. Water, of course, made these buildings more desirable. Forget that the canal looked polluted or that the trees along it sagged from the long drought. It was exactly the sort of place McCleary had imagined Surfer Charlie would live.

He walked into the courtyard, checked the mailboxes for the number of Roberts' apartment, then rang the doorbell. He heard music inside, loud music. A woman in a leotard and leg warmers opened the door a moment later, her pretty and vacuous face sheathed in perspiration.

"Hi," she said over the volume of the music, and suddenly glued a hand to either hip and bent at the waist. "One, two, three . . . You looking for Charlie?"

"Uh, yes."

Now she bent to the other side. "One, two, three . . . I'm doing my workout tape," she huffed. "Charlie can't stand Jane Fonda, so he's out on the courts."

"Which court, do you know?" There were at least three dozen of them.

"Fourteen. Self-service."

He strolled through the clubhouse and out by the pool and courts. He passed a poolside bar advertising fruit juices, Tofutti cocktails, and the usual assortment of drinks with exotic names like Miami Whammy. He found court fourteen and stood at the fence, watching Surfer Charlie engaged in what looked like battle. As a machine hurtled tennis balls across the net, Roberts bounced from one side of the court to the other, forward and backward, and missed most of the shots.

McCleary pushed open the grated door and sat down on a bench. *Whoosh* went the machine, out shot a ball, and Roberts loped toward it, brought his racket back, and slammed the ball. Heat poured into the court.

"Hi, Mike," called Roberts, without looking away from the machine. "What brings you over here?"

"An information exchange."

"Oh, yeah?" Roberts glanced over at him with interest, and the machine spit out a ball that whistled past his head. He positioned himself for the next ball, missed it. "About what?"

"About why you wanted copies of the script for Kranish's film." *And while we're at it, did you sabotage the Maserati?*

"I'm afraid I don't know what you're talking about."

McCleary walked over to the machine and turned it off. He stood facing Roberts across the net. His erubescent face glistened with sweat. "I guess I can always file assault charges against you for knocking out my wife, Charlie. If that's what you'd prefer."

He tapped the edge of his racket against the net. He was wearing his reflective shades again; miniature images of McCleary danced back at him. "Like I said, I don't know what you're talking about. Turn on the machine, will you? I've still got ten minutes of balls in there."

McCleary fudged the truth a little. "She ended up in ER, Charlie. And correct me if I'm mistaken, but I think we could also get you for a B&E charge, for breaking into the motor home. On top of it, you stole some scripts. Petty theft."

Roberts whipped his towel from the net, wiped his face. "Let me see if I've got this straight. You're saying that I broke into one of the motor homes on the set of Kranish's movie. That I stole some scripts. That in the process I also knocked out your wife." He rubbed his chin, looked down at the court, then up again. "Seems to me the question should be what your wife is doing in a new career as an actress, Mike."

Suit yourself, Bozo. "See you in court."

As McCleary passed the machine, he switched it on full speed. It coughed, rattled, and suddenly vomited balls that whizzed through the hot air, slamming into the net, skimming it, and banged against the fence. Roberts yelped and shouted, "Mike, hold on. Hold on just a goddamn minute."

McCleary waited in the doorway as Roberts turned off the machine and hurried over.

"Yeah?"

"Look, my job is to keep tabs on things, okay? That's all I know."

The next logical question, of course, was who Roberts' client was. But surfer boy, anticipating it, shook his head. "I can't tell you that."

McCleary laughed. "Don't give me that confidentiality crap, Charlie."

"It's got nothin' to do with confidentiality. I'm covering my own ass. My client is *not* someone to piss off,

Mike. And if you keep meddling in this, he may just get pissed off at you."

"Horseshit, Charlie. He'll be too busy trying to bail you outa jail. For assault and murder." McCleary started to turn away, but Roberts caught his arm.

"Murder? Who?"

"Lenny Moorhouse, whose car was sabotaged. Don't you read the papers, Charlie? And of course, if they get you for *his* murder, then they'll probably also get you for Domer's."

"Look, man, we've had our differences, but I'm trying to be fair without compromising myself." He lowered his voice, as though he were afraid of being heard. "These people get back at you, Mike. And they do it through the people closest to you."

This did *not* sound like horseshit. It might've been the only thing surfer boy had ever uttered that McCleary believed. His clients, after all, were the type who did you in first and asked questions later. He thought suddenly of how empty the bed was when he'd gotten up this morning, of how he'd stormed around the house, angry because Quin had left before he'd gotten up and they'd never resolved their dispute. Now his anger had just been sucked out by the foul wind of Roberts' proclamation.

"What's your client's interest in the film?"

"I don't know. My job is just to keep tabs on things."

"And steal scripts," McCleary added.

Surfer boy shrugged.

"Listen good, Charlie. If *anything* happens to my wife, I'm holding you responsible. I don't just get back. I get even."

Roberts smiled slowly. "Seems to me I recall something a while back, Mike, when you shot and killed your partner. Robin Peters, I think that was her name. So what'd *she* do, kick you outa bed?"

If they hadn't been on a tennis court in full view of probably a dozen tennis players, McCleary might've shoved Roberts' teeth down his throat. As it was, his hand clenched and his muscles sang for retribution. He turned, slamming the gate behind him, and Roberts shrieked with pain.

McCleary looked back and saw Roberts gripping the fingers on his right hand, his *tennis* hand, his face skewed in pain. "My fingers, you bastard, you just slammed the gate on my fingers!"

"Oops, too bad. See you around, surfer boy."

McCleary whistled all the way back to his car. It had turned out to be a pretty fine morning after all.

3.

The Carlyle Hotel on Miami Beach was an Art Deco monument. Painted pale lemon, its ledges were trimmed in blue, and the space between the floors in front bore bold stripes of flamingo pink. Quin found a parking space in front, and as soon as she stepped inside spotted Marielle at one of the paisley booths.

"You look miserable," she said as Quin sat down.

"Gee, thanks. I needed that."

"Is it the knock on the head or a bad night?"

"Bad night."

"I didn't sleep so great, either. I closed my eyes and kept seeing exploding cars. It was like a sequence from *Miami Vice* or something, but real."

Quin explained what had happened after McCleary had gotten home. Marielle listened, and then she smiled and said, "So Gill Kranish is a bit kinky, huh. It doesn't surprise me."

"Kinky isn't strong enough. How about perverted."

Marielle sat forward, her hair a copper explosion around her head. "Now don't take this the wrong way, Quin. But despite how much you've been telling me you dislike this guy, how come I get the feeling you're attracted to him?"

Quin stared at her, appalled and indignant, a vitriolic denial rolling down her tongue that dissolved in a bitterness like acid. She sat back, feeling utterly deflated. "I guess because I am." She spoke softy, the admission creating a huge ache in her chest. "He *exudes* this . . . Christ, I don't know. I was going to say sexuality, Ellie, but it's more than that. It's like he's challenging me or—"

"Quin, the man has enormous appeal. So stop flagellating yourself for reacting to it, okay? And consider this. Maybe he's envious of your and McCleary's relationship, your marriage, and is trying to come between you two by seducing you so he can then hold it up in McCleary's face and say, *See? What's so special about Quin?*"

"Well, I sure don't have to go to bed with the man for him to come between Mac and me. He's already done that pretty well."

"So you and Mac had an argument. Big deal. Don't worry about it. I've got some stuff to show you." Marielle picked up a folder from the booth and opened it. "I went back through eight or nine years of Hollywood gossip stuff and counted forty-two women Kranish has been linked with romantically." She was removing clips as she spoke, and Quin glanced at photos of Kranish with a parade of lovely women. "Here are a couple of interesting ones—Kranish with an Oriental woman, Lee Ling, and another one with his assistant, Dina Talbott."

Well, Quin thought. So many surprises. Lee Ling the acupuncturist and Dina the minion.

"Both of those items are recent," Marielle pointed out. "But this one isn't." She brought out another clipping dated ten years ago of Kranish with an attractive blonde. The brief article identified her as Pam Spenser of Miami. The picture had been snapped as the couple left a Miami disco, when Kranish was still relatively unknown.

"Who is she?" Quin asked.

"I don't know. I only found this one item. Anyway, you take this stuff with you. I made copies."

Quin thought of her kill flash last night. "Ellie, could you check back through the last ten or twelve years and see if you can find anything about a reporter killed while investigating a story?"

Marielle chuckled. "Hon, I don't have to check back ten or twelve years for something like this. Shit, it happens all the time. Journalists abducted in Beirut, journalists killed in Nicaragua . . ."

"No, I mean something that corresponds with the plot of *Night Flames*."

"Okay, I'll look. But why?"

"I'm not sure. A new angle, I guess. I've got a copy of the script in my car that I can give you. Oh, and take a look at this." She brought out a copy of the note Kranish had received. "What do you make of this? It's the best lead we've got to date. If we can figure out what it means."

Marielle glanced at it, and read out loud: " 'The union of movement and strength gives the meaning of THE POWER OF THE GREAT.' " She paused and lapsed into silence. When she glanced up again, she was frowning. "I might be wrong, but I think this is from the I Ching, Quin."

"What's that?"

"I guess you could call it a philosophy of sorts. The only reason I know about it is because the Swiss psychologist Carl Jung wrote the introduction to the Richard Wilhelm version of the book. Jung was one of my pet projects for a while when I did a series of articles on the pros and cons of psychoanalysis. Anyway, the text is believed to date back to the twelfth century B.C."

"You said it's a philosophy?"

Her coppery curls bobbed. "The yin and yang, that's what it's really about. The dark and the light, good and bad, male and female. The roots of both Confucianism and Taoism have their roots in the I Ching. But it's also an expression of the Chinese mind-set. While the Western mind very patiently dissects, analyzes, classifies, weighs, and isolates, the Oriental mind seeks wholes. We nibble; they gulp."

"What're the six lines?"

"A hexagram."

"Which means?"

A waitress interrupted them and they ordered lunch. When she'd walked away, Marielle continued.

"Jung was always looking for the common thread that united men, so his research focused on the unconscious—dreams, fantasies, mythology. His interest in the I Ching came about because of his friendship with Wilhelm, a German guy who lived most of his life in China and devoted his life to studying the I Ching—and translating it. The book operates on a mathematical premise, really. Fifty yarrow sticks—which in ancient China were made of bamboo—are divided six times through a rather complicated process and assigned numerical equivalents. There are only sixty-four possible hexagrams that can result. These represent sixty-four *typical* situations an individual might experience. The lines in a hexagram represent stages in the situation."

"Situations like this one, in other words—THE POWER OF THE GREAT," Quin said.

"Right." She reached into her purse, opened her wallet, and brought out three pennies. "Since yarrow sticks are a rather cumbersome way of doing the I Ching, there's a shortcut that can be done with coins. Supposedly you should use Chinese coins, but pennies will do. The face on the coin would be a yang line or unbroken, with a numerical value of three. The tail would be the yin line, with a numerical value of two. By throwing the coins six times, you can come up with only one or two of sixty-four possible hexagrams."

"What's this stuff about the changing line mean?" Quin asked.

Marielle dug a pencil out of her purse and copied the hexagram on the napkin. On the third solid line, she placed an X in the middle. "It means this situation is going to change. The yang or solid line in the third place is changing to a yin or broken line. Sometimes you can have a hexagram where *every* line is a changing line. It's advice, a warning. If you do this, then this will happen. Jung, after studying the I Ching, felt it was a way of exploring one's own unconscious."

"How?"

"He believed the I Ching was an example of synchronicity—it took the coincidence of events in time and space as meaning something more than mere chance. When you divide the yarrow sticks, what you come up with is supposedly an accurate depiction of your particular situation or state of mind at a given time. The Chinese saw it as a way of uncovering patterns in their lives." She tapped the hexagram with the tip of her pencil. "The solid line changes to a broken, which will result in a completely new hexagram. Instead of four solid and two broken, you'll have three of each."

Quin sat forward, suddenly excited. If this had come from the killer and not some sicko in the great wasteland of Miami, then it was part of the shadowy pattern she'd been looking for. "Listen, when we finish here, how about going by the mall with me? I want a copy of the I Ching."

"To the mall," echoed Marielle.

It was the battle cry of an intrepid shopper.

Seventeen

McCLEARY WASN'T SURPRISED to see Joe Bean's car parked in front of the firm, even though it was Saturday. Bean not only enjoyed what he did, he liked the percentage he received on each case he handled and the hefty bonus for every case he brought in. Saturday was his day for drumming up business.

McCleary trotted up the steps, carefully stepping around the welcome mat that bore the firm's name. The sight of the logo that he'd designed reminded him he'd done pitifully little painting these past few months. It seemed to go through stages. Like marriage, he thought.

He paused at Ruth Grimes' desk when a poster behind her typewriter caught his eye. It was a theater billboard from the third Spin movie, signed in Kranish's florid script: "To Ruth, the best always, Gill Kranish."

The poster had always been there, but Kranish had signed it his first day in the office, and Ruth had since gotten it reframed. He knew she'd also received a videotape of the second Spin movie, when she'd mentioned to Kranish that it was her favorite, but she hadn't been able to buy a copy anywhere because it was always sold out. Kranish's small miracles, he thought, and wondered what it meant.

"Hey, Bean," he called when he was inside.

"Yo, back here, my man." Bean was sitting at the table in the staff kitchen, writing up an ad. "My latest recruiting scheme. But I don't seem to be having much luck with a cutesy jingle, Mac."

"Here's a jingle for you. He's blond and skinny, has a laugh like a whinny, and surfed like a ninny till he became a private eye."

Bean laughed. "The last line doesn't rhyme, Mac, but it's got to be Charlie Roberts."

"Yup."

"Lemme guess. What could the young stud have done now? Messed up one of our cases like he did with that Toyota fiasco?"

"Close."

McCleary explained and Bean sat back, turning his pen around in his hand. "I'll tail him, if that's what you want. Believe me, it'd be a pleasure to find out what that shithead's up to."

"You must read minds, Bean."

His white teeth lined up in his mouth as he grinned. "It's one of my better talents."

"Can you and Rusty handle round-the-clock surveillance alone?"

"I'll get my bro to help us out. We can rotate. When do you want us to start?"

"How about tomorrow morning? Or late tonight? I want to know everything he does, Bean. Who he sees, where he goes, who he talks to, and if he appears anywhere near that set. I'll pay you extra for the time."

Bean tapped a quick beat on the edge of the table with his pen. "Mac, you could pay me zip and it wouldn't make *no* difference to me. You forget, that Toyota case was *my* deal, and that asshole screwed it up. *This* will be a pleasure." He stood. "Gotta go make some calls. Oh, Benson called. He said the note Kranish got was filled with smudged prints and the Argon laser wasn't able to pick anything off the steak knife the geezer out at the airport gave you. Also, I brought in the mail. Yours is in your office."

"Thanks, Bean. And keep me posted on Charlie Roberts' games."

McCleary poured a cup of coffee and padded down the

hall to his office, consulting his list of things to do today and tomorrow: *See Surfer Boy, ride out to Maserati warehouse, talk to Irene Bedford, ask Gill about scriptwriter Hannah Davidson, check with Greg Hess on time Maserati was signed in* . . . He stopped, crossed through *See Surfer Boy* and checked off *ride out to warehouse.* That'd be next, taking a look at where the Maserati had been stored. The most important item, apologizing to Quin, was conspicuously absent. But why should *he* apologize? What exactly had he done except point out that she was looking for reasons to dislike Kranish?

All right, he admitted that Kranish shouldn't have dropped by at almost two in the morning, and it was irritating that he would be presumptuous enough to go around to the side of the house when no one had answered the doorbell. But Quin's assumption that Kranish had been spying on them was ridiculous. Kranish had some unusual pursuits, yeah, no one would argue that point, but voyeurism with friends? No way.

He sat at his desk and began going through the mail—a few bills, a couple of checks, bank statements, and a small square package addressed to him. He opened it. Inside a rectangular, plain wooden box was a videotape. *Tape number two?* Was he going to find a play-by-play recount of the last moments of Lenny Moorhouse's life? It seemed unlikely, since only Lenny had been in the car, and even if there'd been a camera hidden in it somewhere, it would've gone up in smoke when the car had.

He went down the hall to Quin's office and slid the tape in the VCR's slot. He sat back and switched on the machine. The image flickered, then cleared. McCleary frowned, sat slowly forward, then got up, walked over to the machine, crouched, backed away from the set, froze the frame. It was a long shot of a room—nightstands, an open closet door, a deep blue rug, a mirrored ceiling. Against the panorama of a bed as huge and blue as a summer sky were Kranish, Maia Fox, and J.B. Domer. *We went fishing in the Everglades one weekend . . . things got sort of weird.* . . . So what was this, a postscript to the fishing weekend?

He unfroze the frame. It was like watching *Emanuelle in Bangkok* or something on the Playboy channel, except there wasn't much dialogue and he knew the actors. He noted that neither man touched the other; their attentions were focused on Maia, who looked to be having the time of her life, thrashing about on the bed, making soft, purring sounds. But her every movement seemed orchestrated for the camera, he thought, as though this were just another performance for her—more fun, more enticing, yet still a performance.

McCleary watched with a curious detachment, wondering where and when the little scenario had taken place and why it had been mailed to him. The angle of the camera remained the same, and McCleary guessed it was fixed to a tripod. But because so much of the room was visible, including the mirrored ceiling, he suspected a wide-angle lens had been used.

Now and then someone would say something like *Turn that way, how's this feel, sit up, roll over.* If he'd been listening just to the sound, he might've thought the tape had been recorded at a dog training school. *Heel, Rover. Bark. Play dead.*

There was a momentary pause in the film, as though the camera had been shut off, then Maia's grin filled the screen. It grew smaller and more distant as she backed away. She was dressed in a black bra with matching underwear and black net stockings with high heels, and she was twirling a top hat and miming a song.

"That's it, baby, belt it out," said an offscreen voice McCleary knew was Domer's. "Make us believe you're out in front of Carnegie Hall, performing for three thousand people."

Kranish, wearing a matching top hat but nothing else, came up behind her just as she thrust her arms out in a great, silent finale in which she twirled the hat and dropped it on her head. His arms tightened around her, a hand

166

covering each breast, and she laughed and leaned back into him. Her hat tilted forward, low on her forehead, obscuring her eyes.

Then Domer strolled into the picture with a bottle of something and three glasses and they all laughed and toasted and drank. There was another break in the film, and when the image returned, the three of them were sitting Indian style in the middle of the great big bed, drinking some more. The light in the room had changed—the shadows were longer and thinner. McCleary guessed it was now mid- or late afternoon. There were smudges of mascara under Maia's eyes; both men's chins were shadowed with stubble.

They were speaking in low, hushed voices, as if they were afraid of being overheard. Something about films. Domer lit what McCleary guessed was a joint, puffed on it, passed it around. Maia started coughing. Kranish, wearing a robe now like the other two, patted her paternally on the back, then began kneading her shoulders, and her head dropped like a flower's and she hummed, softly, puffed again on the joint, then shrugged off her robe. McCleary saw the look Kranish and Domer exchanged over her head, a sly, knowing look that spoke volumes about what was coming next.

They ravaged her—not violently, not cruelly, but with each movement, each tease, orchestrated as if to test her endurance, the parameters of her sentience, her sexuality. At some point she ceased being aware of the camera—McCleary could see it in the way her expression changed. She bit down on her lower lip, her face sparkled with perspiration, her hands gripped the sheets, the edge of the bed, she whipped her head from side to side on the pillow. They were doing her, McCleary thought dimly, and now there was something cruel and mean about it because they brought her to the edge again and again and left her hanging until she was sobbing and bolted out of the bed shouting, "I hate you, you're mean and spiteful, both of you. I hate you." Then she ran off the screen, and a moment later McCleary heard a door slam.

"Who's going to coax her out this time?" Domer asked, smiling.

"Your turn," Kranish said, running a hand over his head and studying his nails as though the whole thing bored him. Then he looked directly at the camera, as if remembering it was there, and added: "Turn off that damn thing."

The screen went blank. McCleary remained where he was, Quin's voice whispering through the quiet: *He was standing there watching us.*

He rose swiftly, popped out the tape, and turned off the VCR.

Buildings, like people, possessed distinctive scents, and the Prince Hotel was no exception. The cool air in the lobby was redolent with the fragrance of fresh flowers that graced antique crystal vases, the lingering smell of perfume, a trace of stale smoke, of history.

There was a certain Old World grandness about the place in its sweeping staircase and antique mirrors, pale pink marble floors and chandeliers. But as if to temper the elegance, homey touches had been added: the old granddaddy clock near the elevators on the fifth floor, the framed watercolors by Dade County schoolchildren on the walls, plants in tremendous clay pots. And at the end of the hall, a sweeping view of the Miami skyline. It was, McCleary thought, the ideal spot for Kranish's temporary production offices.

Although it was Saturday and the offices should have been empty, Moorhouse's death had changed all that. Greg Hess, the production office manager, and his staff of six, were answering phones, playing the computers, fielding calls from the press, and scheduling auditions for actors to take over Moorhouse's part. McCleary stood in the doorway for several moments, watching the frenzy, listening. Then he walked over to Hess and said, "Can you pull yourself away from this for a couple of minutes?"

Hess, fixed in front of the computer as if he'd been glued there, looked up at McCleary like he'd never seen him before, and laughed. "You must be kidding. I haven't even got the time to take a piss, Mr. McCleary."

"Good. Then it's time for a break."

Hess sighed, reached for a cigarette, lit it, sat back. "So?"

"In the hall."

"Christ," he mumbled and got up.

Like the Pillsbury Dough Boy, he was plump through the middle, had black bean eyes, a button for a nose, and an uneven mouth with a prominent upper lip that could curl into a sneer just as easily as it could a smile. He leaned against the wall next to the granddaddy clock near the elevators.

"Tell me how the Maserati was shipped here, by whom, what time you signed it in, all of it," McCleary said without preface.

"Look, I already told Sergeant Benson—"

"Tell me."

Hess sighed and smoke slid from between his teeth. He reached out and flipped an ash into the nearest plant. "Okay, the car arrived Thursday sometime. It was shipped by the Fernwell Moving Company about sixteen days ago from L.A. When it arrived, they called Gill's office. Dina then sent around a memo notifying everyone."

"Why would *everyone* have to know?"

Hess ground his cigarette butt into the soil in the clay pot and thrust his hands into the pockets of his khaki shorts. "Me because I had to check it over and then accept the delivery; the car guy because he had to get the vehicle washed down, waxed, checked over; the set decorator so he could check the color against whatever color scheme he'd chosen for the scenes in which the car appeared; the actors because of this little initiation ceremony they do on all of Gill's movies with things like cars; the director so he could decide if he wanted to move up shooting for the car scenes . . ." He paused. "And so on."

"So the memo came out and then what?"

"Then it was delivered around four Friday afternoon. Here, to the hotel. The company towed it over, and I went outside and did a spot check for things like chipped paint or whatever. I checked the invoice and then signed the baby in."

"Who decided when the car would be broken in?"

"Gill. Well, actually Dina asks Gill and Gill gives everyone a date and time, and if that's not good, someone will object and then they change it. Very democratic process, actually."

"And when did everyone leave here to go out to the airstrip?"

"Oh, maybe five-thirty."

"Where was the car for that hour and a half?"

"The hotel garage, Mr. McCleary. Under lock and key."

"That area's accessible to employees, though."

Hess understood what McCleary was driving at. "Forget it," he said. "No one would sabotage a car down there. It's too busy. The valets are in and out of there, getting cars."

If that were true, and McCleary had no reason to believe it wasn't, then it meant the Maserati was sabotaged at the warehouse, probably Thursday sometime after the workers had left. "How many people knew where the car was kept, Mr. Hess?"

He rolled his eyes, lit another cigarette. "Anyone who wanted to know. The paperwork was on my desk."

"So where were you Thursday evening?"

"Oh, brother." A pother of smoke billowed from his mouth. He shifted his weight from one foot to the other. Glanced at his watch. "You know what a jump cut is, Detective?"

"Should I?"

Hess laughed. "Hey, that's good, that's very good. 'Should I?' Yeah, maybe I oughta ask myself the same question sometime. Well, Detective, a jump cut is this great little technique where the scene changes suddenly and unexpectedly. It's used to jar the viewer, to show emotional confusion. Well, that's how I feel. Like I'm in this continual jump cut. You know what kinda chaos Lenny's murder has caused around here?"

"It was a simple question. How about giving me a simple answer."

"Simple. Right. Okay. My whereabouts Thursday evening. I left here around eleven and drove my fat ass to the nearest Seven/Eleven and bought me a six-pack of Budweiser Beer and proceeded to pop a can in the parking lot and guzzle it down. I then flew out to Maia Fox's little houseboat and spent the next few hours getting blasted. We in show biz tend to be excessive in our lifestyles. I'm sure you've noticed, huh, Detective."

"Did you stay overnight at Maia's?" An image from the videotape insinuated itself.

"Overnight. That implies that Maia and I are lovers, which we are not. We're friends. But yes, I stayed there for a while because I had passed out."

"What time did you leave?"

Another flick of his wrist sent another ash flying into the clay pot. "Leave. Shit. Three. Four. I don't really know. But I went back to the Towers, and I don't exactly remember the ride home. That's a jump cut, Detective." His smile ended in a straight line. "Oh, and yes, I did go out to the airport with everyone. I believe you saw me there." He looked down at his feet, then up again. "Just between you and me, Detective. I put in about fifteen hours a day. I haven't got the fucking time to murder anyone, even if I were so inclined, which I often am."

"Where were you the night of the fire?"

"Here, right here, and you can ask anyone in the production office."

McCleary tried to remember if he'd seen a list of blood types for the production office people. He didn't think he had. Interesting. Someone in Benson's office had really screwed *that* up. He wondered if Hess had low blood sugar and type O blood.

"One more question. Do you have an address for Hannah Davidson? Or a phone number?"

"The *Night Flames* scriptwriter?" Hess rubbed his chin. "No, I think you'd have to go through the Writers' Guild of America or whatever it's called."

"Do you know anything about her?"

"Personally? Nope. But I can tell you one thing about scriptwriters. If they'd do their job right the first time, *my* job would be a lot easier. Script changes we got, Detective, coming outa the kazoo."

"Who does them?"

"Patty Cakes or Gill, or sometimes the actors initiate them."

"Has the original script changed drastically since you started shooting?"

"Actually, it's been easier than working on a pilot or a series. No major plot changes, mostly just dialogue and stuff. . . . And losing two of the actors," he finished quietly.

"That's not major?"

Hess' arms dropped to his sides. "Look, Mr. McCleary. I value human life as much as the next person, okay?" Two deep lines had thrust down each side of his nose. "But we're talking in terms of script right now."

"Mind if I use your phone?"

"In the office. Help yourself."

"Great. And thanks for your time."

"Hey, yeah, sure. Don't mention it. I needed to take a piss anyway."

McCleary returned to the office and dialed Kranish's suite. There wasn't any answer, so he left a message at the desk for Kranish to call him. On his way out, McCleary saw Bruce Harmon, the video historian, shuffling out the door toward Collins Avenue. McCleary hurried after him.

"Hey, Mr. Harmon."

He glanced around, his ponytail swinging as his body did, his camera perched on his shoulder. "Oh, Mr. McCleary."

"I just wanted to thank you for the videotape of the accident. It, uh, helped establish what happened."

Harmon winked an eye shut against the glare. "Like *Blow-up,* huh."

It took McCleary a couple of seconds to remember Harmon's favorite movie was *Blow-up.* "Right, yeah. Except which frame do we blow up to find the murderer?"

"Yeah." Harmon nodded. "I guess that's something of a problem. Listen, could you give me a lift to a gas station? My car's being temperamental, and I hitched a ride over here with a neighbor this morning."

"Sure. I'm parked just down the street."

"Thanks, I appreciate it."

During the drive to a gas station on the other side of the causeway, Harmon talked and McCleary listened. Or tried to listen, at any rate. Harmon was one of those people who seized on whatever thought he had at the moment and verbalized it. It was like being sucked into a tunnel where the wind blew fierce and hard, where the walls were too smooth to grab onto, to dig your fingers into it, so after a while McCleary stopped trying.

As nearly as he could determine, Harmon mentioned or discussed: *Blow-up,* bilingualism, his dissertation, his mother's brownies, that his girlfriend had moved out, a cockroach named Fat Friday that lived under his kitchen sink, his darkroom, Kranish, and the Moonies. He talked as if he hadn't spoken to another human being in decades, as if he'd been in solitary confinement, subsisting on hope and grits and videotapes.

McCleary pulled up to the garage. Harmon slid out with his faithful camera and grinned. "I never know when to shut up. Sorry. And thanks for the ride."

McCleary watched him walk off through the September light—a young man who spent more time recording life than he did living it. He wondered if Gill Kranish had reached the same point, but for different reasons, and in a different way.

Eighteen

KRANISH LAY IN the dark of his bedroom, a cold cloth over his eyes. The pain in his head was like hot knives being driven into his skull just above his right eye. It hurt when he breathed too hard, when he moved, when he tried to think. The phone had been ringing relentlessly, and each separate peal had clashed inside his skull like cymbals, the agony so deep all he could do was grit his teeth until it stopped.

He'd taken two of his pills, but nothing had happened yet. He needed Dina to float into the bedroom with her cool voice and pack his head in ice. He had tried to visualize his head lying in snow, the way Lee Ling had taught him, but it didn't work; his thoughts refused to cooperate. He wondered if in Spin Weaver's time medical science had cured migraines, if Spielberg suffered migraines, if his head was going to explode and some hideous alien lifeform would wiggle out.

The migraine had started when he'd left the McClearys. He remembered the horrible white light slicing into his eyeball like a laser, he remembered fumbling in his glove compartment for his pills, he remembered pulling into a parking lot somewhere, and then there was nothing. A void. A blank. He'd lost two hours.

You're punishing yourself for something: who had said that to him? Lee Ling? Yeah, it was the sort of thing she would say. Why wasn't she here doing her magic on his feet? How could a man with as much money as he had be lying here alone, pressure mounting in his head like steam in a volcano? *Who sabotaged the Maserati? Who torched Domer? Who's trying to ruin me?*

He rolled over, grimacing as the pain followed, as it slid to the right of his eye, into his temple. He hit the switch on his phone that would make the damn thing ring in his office. There. Peace. Silence. He would sleep. The pills would begin to work. He would awaken refreshed, reborn. And then he would return some calls and attack the mountain of paperwork in the living room. Production reports, financial reports, payroll reports. . . .

He shut his eyes, but was afraid to sleep. Had he locked the front door? Could someone get into the apartment through the porch? Had it mattered to the killer who died in the car accident? *Did the killer think I would drive the car first?*

After a while the questions simply became a rhythm like rain against a window, like the noise of a train, and Kranish dozed off. He was fourteen years old and living in Syracuse again. It was winter. He and McCleary were walking home from school, the air so cold their breath seemed to freeze as they exhaled, the gray sky sagging like an old woman's belly with the promise of snow flurries.

They had cut through a vacant lot and were talking about movies, not paying much attention to anything around them, when suddenly a snowball slammed into the back of Kranish's head. He lost his balance and pitched forward, his books flying, snow melting down the back of his neck, his head singing with pain. He fell face down into a snowbank. His glasses were knocked off. The white world went fuzzy, he pushed himself up, patting around for his glasses, squinting. Then he heard McCleary shout, "Watch out, Gill!"

He twisted around but it was too late because two guys in leather jackets had grabbed him by the arms and lifted him up. They held his arms tightly, Big Jim and his brother Jack, and one of them said, "Hey, Krano, you dropped these. And since I'm in a generous mood today,

175

I'm gonna return them to you." He dropped Kranish's glasses back on his nose. One lens was gone and the other was cracked so that everything Kranish looked at was double.

"You busted them," Kranish muttered.

"You're lucky we didn't bust your ass instead. You and your pal over here are on our street."

McCleary was pinned up against a wall, where one of Big Jim's friends held a knife on him. "Hey, it was a mistake, okay?" McCleary was saying, patting the air with his hands. "We weren't paying any attention to where we were going."

"Who asked you, Macko," snapped Big Jim, and pulled out a switchblade.

Jack howled with laughter. Kranish was dimly aware of McCleary shouting something, then there was a scuffle against the wall and Big Jim yelled, "Jesus, Les, don't kill Macko. Not yet." Then he stepped toward Kranish, who backed away, slowly, staring at Big Jim's knife, blinking to clear his vision because he kept seeing two of everything. "Now I want you to say you're sorry, Krano. Say, 'We're sorry for coming down your street, Jim. We will *never* do it again.' "

"Get fucked," Kranish hissed.

"Oh, my, that wasn't nice at all, Krano. Don't your mama teach you better manners than that? Hey, Les, bring Macko over here. Let's see if he's got better manners than Krano."

McCleary stumbled into Kranish's vision. His mouth was bleeding. He wasn't trying to reason with Big Jim or Les anymore. He wasn't saying anything. "Now, Macko, let's see if you've got better manners." Then Big Jim squeezed an arm around Kranish's neck and touched the tip of the knife to the corner of Kranish's eye. "Now let's hear it, Macko. 'We are sorry for coming down your street, Jim. We will never do it again.' "

McCleary glared at him, Kranish felt the knife pricking the tender skin at the corner of his eye, he was afraid to breathe too deeply, afraid to move. Blood trickled warmly down his cheek and froze. When McCleary didn't speak, Big Jim said, "Macko, I'm gonna tell you this just once. If you don't apologize for yourself and your pansy friend here, I am gonna slide this here knife into his eye. Got that?"

Tears leaked out of Kranish's eyes, the cold light glistened brightly on the top of the knife, his heart had shriveled like an old dead fish. He heard McCleary saying the words, reciting them, then he snapped, "That good enough?"

"Maybe, maybe not," Big Jim replied, not moving the knife away from Kranish's eye, not loosening his arm around Kranish's neck, not giving an inch. The hairs in his nose had frozen, the blood on his cheek possessed weight, mass. "Now what I want is for Krano here to kneel at my feet and suck my cock, that's what I want."

"Hey, Jim," said Jack. "I think we'd better—"

"Shut up, who asked ya." He spun Kranish around and pushed hard on his shoulders, forcing him to the ground. McCleary shouted something, there was another scuffle, and Big Jim grabbed hold of Kranish's face and jerked his head around so he could see McCleary out cold in the snow. "No help from your buddy Macko, Krano. So now be a good boy and do like I said."

Kranish was weeping now, dropping to his knees, the knife cold against his throat, then someone kicked him from behind and he fell forward and a hand came down over his head, shoving his face into the snow. He tried to scream, but couldn't, there was snow in his mouth, his nose, and now someone was ripping down his jeans and he knew what was going to happen, he felt the cold air slapping his buttocks and he struggled to leap up, but they held him down. Down.

Kranish bolted out of the dream, screaming, his heart drumming in his ears, the cold taste of the snow frozen on his tongue, the stink of his fear thick in the room.

Then he fell back, breathing hard, squeezing his eyes shut, fighting back the miasma of the dream.

But the images kept pummeling him as if they'd followed him out of the dream. He stumbled into the bathroom, the shower, and turned the water on cold. It poured over him, and he dropped his head back, letting the water pound into his mouth and the back of his throat, and little by little the dream's hold on him began to ebb.

Kranish pressed his forehead against the cold, wet tile. He remembered how they'd left him there in the field when they were finished with him and that he'd lain there sobbing, wishing he were dead. Kranish finally struggled to his feet and found McCleary on the other side of the field, tied to a tree, just coming around. He hadn't seen any of it and Kranish never told him; his shame was too great, too deep.

But seventeen years later, Kranish had run into Big Jim on the set of a TV movie and had gotten him fired. Then he spread the word and no one would hire big tough Jim who wanted so badly to be an actor, to make it. The last Kranish heard, he'd blown out his brains in a motel in East L.A. A fitting end, he thought, for the man who had taught him the value of control and who had, in the space of perhaps fifteen minutes, shut down Kranish's heart forever.

He turned off the shower, stripped his soaking underwear, wrapped a towel around himself, and walked back into the bedroom. Someone was knocking at the front door. As he went to answer it, he realized his headache was gone. He was hungry. He was ready to tackle the mountains of paperwork.

"Who is it?" he asked.

"It's Patrick. You okay?"

Kranish unlocked the door. Patty Cakes frowned at him. "Jesus, Gill, I've been calling half the morning. I was getting worried."

"C'mon in."

Kranish got dressed, then they went into the kitchen where he made himself and Patty Cakes brunch. They had a couple of drinks, and for a while it was like old times, the two of them conspiring over script changes, camera angles, and the nuances of a particular scene. At one point, Patty Cakes cupped his fat chin in his palm and said, "You know, sometimes I wish there actually was a Settlers' City on Alpha Centauri. I'd be there."

But then the conversation turned serious. About Domer. About Moorhouse. About looking for Moorhouse's replacement. Patty Cakes' bushy black eyebrows bled together with concern, with worry. "Listen, Gill. I've been thinking. You've been involved with a lot of women over the years and . . . well, hell, I've seen some of your tapes, and maybe one of the women knows about it and—"

"Who, Pat? Irene? Dina? Maia? My fucking acupuncturist? You think I haven't considered that?" He rose suddenly from the chair and cleared the table. He ran water in the sink. Squirted in soap. Patty Cakes didn't say anything, but after a while he got up. His hand weighed heavily on Kranish's shoulder.

"One way or another, Gill, *Night Flames* is gonna be finished and it's gonna win Emmys. I've got to run. Thanks for the brunch."

And then he was gone, gone faster than Kranish would've thought possible, and he was alone again.

He felt, suddenly, like weeping, and he didn't know why. He felt . . . oh Christ, he didn't know anymore.

He washed the dishes, rinsed them, stacked them in the rack on the counter. His fingers became Quin's last night, in the kitchen after he'd seen her and McCleary in the pool. He hadn't meant to watch, he'd simply wanted answers about Moorhouse, the car. But then when he'd seen them, there in the pool, the two of them painted in moonlight, he'd been unable to move. To speak. A crescive loneliness had risen in him like a tide, consuming him until she'd cried out. Her cry had struck him bone deep, a body cry, visceral, and he'd felt her shudder and then McCleary's. No tape had ever done that.

The doorbell rang.

He ignored it.

Then it rang again, once, twice, three times. He slammed a plate into the rack, flung the dish towel over his shoulder, and marched into the living room. He opened the door with the chain still on it and peeked out and saw Dina, her arms piled high with packages. He laughed and unfastened the chain.

"You found the mall," he said.

She swept into the hallway, trailing the scent of a new perfume, and continued to the living room, where she let the packages tumble to the couch. "Wait until you see this stuff I bought, Gill." She looked up, frowned. "You just get up? You look awful."

"No, I had a migraine."

Concern limned her features. "Are you okay now?"

"Yeah, I'm fine." *Except for the two hours I can't remember, and the dream about Big Jim, and Quin and McCleary, and . . .*

"I wish you'd go to a doctor, Gill."

"I don't want to talk about doctors. Show me your buys."

He cupped her face in his hands, kissing her lightly, wanting desperately to feel tenderness toward her. He wondered what it would be like to kiss a woman and feel a hot tightness in his chest that was both sweet and bitter, a tightness that was love. McCleary knew that tightness; Kranish had seen it. He'd heard it in the way Quin cried out.

"You worry too much. So what's in the packages?"

"Stuff for tonight."

"Tonight?" Had he forgotten a party? A date for dinner? "What's happening tonight?"

She'd opened one of the boxes and was holding a dress up to herself. It was a deep emerald green that complemented her eyes. "Do you like it?"

"Yes, it's beautiful." She folded it carefully and set it aside and opened another box. "Here's some stuff for you."

Kranish laughed. "Okay, what's the occasion?"

She brushed a strand of hair away from her cheek with the back of her hand. "We need to get out. Away from . . . from everything that's been happening." She spoke softly, with a weariness that made him notice the deep shadows beneath her eyes. "Let's just be crazy for an evening, Gill."

"Okay," he chuckled, "we'll be crazy for an evening. What do you have in mind?"

"Remember what we talked about? About, uh, someone neither of us knows?"

He smiled. "And that's what's on the agenda for tonight?"

"Yup. I mean"—she grew flustered—"if you're game."

He wanted to say no, he was sorry, but he'd changed his mind. What would be the point? But he didn't say it, he didn't, even though a part of him wanted to because otherwise it would just be him and Dina or himself alone or himself and Patty Cakes or . . . He heard himself say, "It'll have to be someplace where I'm not going to be recognized."

"I already thought of that. We'll disguise you." She opened another box and brought out a bottle of hair rinse, glasses, a hat, and clothes.

Kranish laughed. Maybe it wasn't such a bad idea. "I suppose you've got a place picked out?"

"A club in Miami." She was laying items out on the coffee table now and turned to him, hands on her hips. She eyed him with a professional detachment. "Okay, let's see what kinda disguise we can come up with here. We'll do a trial run."

"You're a nut," he said, running his hand over her hip. She smiled coyly and playfully slapped his hand away.

Nineteen

THE WAREHOUSE WHERE the Maserati had been stored
sprouted like a weed among other weeds in an industri-
ally zoned section west of Miami. Here were clothing
outlets, furniture wholesalers, shoe factories, a garage
where Triple A trucks were kept, a walled-in graveyard
for retired Greyhound buses.

Since it was Saturday, the place was deserted, stripped
of people and cars. There were no trees, either, and the
relentless September heat poured down, bleaching the
sides of buildings, being sucked into block after block of
black asphalt. It was like a small town where germ warfare had decimated the population. The desolation made
McCleary feel as if he were the last man on Earth.

He parked Lady alongside the fence and got out. The
air smelled of decay, of grease and oil, dust and exhaust.
Part of it was due to the warehouse's propinquity to the
interstate on one side and the airport on the other. But
the huge garbage bin that brimmed with refuse just inside
the fence probably didn't help either.

The FERNWELL MOVING sign that crowned the warehouse was as corroded as the chain-link fence that embraced it. The first big blow that came through Dade, he
thought, and this thing was going to flop over like a dying
fish. The padlock wasn't much better. He knocked the
edge of his fist against it, smiled as it came loose, and
nudged the fence open with the tip of his shoe.

The company fellow who'd towed the car over to the
Prince Hotel had told Benson the Maserati had arrived

early Thursday afternoon. It had been brought here and checked for dents, scrapes, scratches, then Kranish's office was called. The car had been delivered to the Prince Hotel Friday afternoon, and between five-thirty and six the gang had towed it out to the airport on a truck Irene Bedford was driving.

Yeah, it kept coming back to Irene.

But the Oriental woman bothered him too. She'd been out of town since yesterday and wasn't due back until this evening. Like Bedford, she'd been or was involved with Kranish.

And Maia? He still hadn't tracked down her phantom mechanic, but she'd confirmed that Thursday evening she'd been with Greg Hess. *Gill and Irene, Irene and Domer, Domer and Maia, Maia and Gill, Gill and Dina.* A sort of incest. Then there was Devereaux and dead, dead Moorhouse.

Moorhouse hadn't been the intended victim; any number of people could've driven the car before he did. The driver had been expendable. The purpose of the sabotage was to eliminate another actor in the film and the destruction of a custom-made vehicle which, like the motor home, had been worth more than a hundred thousand. *Studio funds.* Kranish had to answer to the studio. Kranish, again, was the target.

The bay door on the warehouse seemed to be electronically controlled, which led McCleary to think the fence had never been intended as anything more than a temporary deterrent. There were two windows along either side, about seven feet up. They didn't look like the kind that opened, neither was broken, and both were heavily tinted. He watched the ground as he made his way around to the back. He didn't expect anything as miraculous as a perfectly preserved footprint, particularly since it hadn't rained in so long. But a little memento would've been nice. Like a Social Security card lying in the dirt. Or a business card. *I was here. Call me at . . .*

He stopped at the back door and brought his face close

to the crack along the jamb and the door. Dead bolt. The wood wasn't splintered; he doubted anyone had gotten in this way. Then how? Near the roof were two windows, but the only way anyone could get through them was with a ladder. And then there would be the problem of climbing down inside the warehouse.

No, there had to be an easier way. Like a key.

McCleary returned to the side of the building and gazed up at the windows. Then he ran out to the gate, opened it up wide, and drove Lady inside. He stopped at the windows, got out, removed his sneakers, and scrambled onto the hood and then the roof. Perfect. He sat down, eye level with the glass.

He pressed his fingers against the panes, ran them around the edges, and at the bottom felt a cool draft. And a groove in the metal. He hopped down, slipped his feet into his sneakers again, unlocked the hatchback, flipped open the lid of his toolbox. He chose a long, flat-edged screwdriver. After climbing back onto the car, he slipped the screwdriver against the bottom edge of the glass, fixed it into the groove, and bore down. The window gave a little. He repeated the process with a thicker screwdriver, and when it was open enough so he could get his fingers under, he heaved. He shoved it up and burst out laughing.

Ladders? Keys? Ha. He'd forgotten the first rule in pulling a B&E: look for the *easy* way in.

But would the saboteur have driven his—*her?*—car inside the gate? McCleary glanced around, wondering what might have been used instead of a car. His gaze fastened on the dumpster, which sat on four wheels. A heave-ho and the thing would probably roll like a skateboard. The riddle solved for the moment, he tied his sneakers, climbed through the window, and dropped about five feet to a low-lying counter against the wall.

Inside was a tractor as yellow as a canary, a Pontiac Fiero the green of seedless grapes, a Piper Cub, and stacks of wooden crates. He poked around for a while, turning on lights, flipping switches at random, peering through the window into a tiny office so cluttered it reminded him of Quin's desk at home.

The hunch spot between his eyes had been burning fiercely ever since he'd pushed himself through the window, and it got worse as he began to inspect the counters, drawers, and lifts. He ran his hands over the metal tracks, clearing away dirt, grime, metal filings. This lift? Was this where the killer had snipped away like a surgeon? *How long did it take you?*

He found a broom against the wall and swished it under the counter he'd stepped on when he entered. Out came motes of dust, an army of plump, pugnacious ants, roaches that probably wore brass knuckles, cigarette butts. The inside of the garage was an oven, and before long his shirt was drenched and his hair was plastered against the sides of his head.

He stopped for a breather. He removed his T-shirt and sat on the counter, back against the cool wall, wiping his face with his shirt. What now? More dust? More bugs?

He pulled his legs up, rested his chin on a knee, and stared at the floor. That was when he saw it, snuggled into a pother of dust like an infant in a cradle. He plucked it out quickly, as though it might suddenly grow legs and scamper away, and felt a momentary disappointment when he realized it was only a coin. He sat back on the counter again, examining it.

The coin was bronze, with a tiny square cut in the middle. On one side, positioned at each of the four sides of the square, were designs, all different. On the reverse side were two designs. The thing was pitted, green in spots, and looked older than time.

McCleary was about to get down from the counter and move over to where the light was better, but he heard a noise outside: the definite crunch of footsteps against the dried grass. His car was out there, the door open, the hatchback open, his toolbox on the ground, the keys in the ignition. Incriminating?

Oh, hello, Officer. . . .

But suppose . . .

He grappled for a nearby wrench, moved into a crouch. He watched the window, prepared to leap up like a jack-in-the-box and pummel the head that poked through.

Now he heard the person climbing onto Lady's roof. He stood slowly, back against the wall, the wrench raised above his head, his breath shallow, heart hammering. He saw a dark crown and tightened his grip on the wrench. He was bringing his arm down when the person's head suddenly jerked toward him. For a distended moment, their eyes locked. Then his arm fell and he laughed.

"Quin."

"Mac." She scrambled through the hole like Alice into Wonderland and dropped down beside him, a smudge on her cheek. He saw the .38 in her hand.

"Disarm yourself, woman," he said, gesturing toward the gun with the wrench.

She laughed. "Look who's talking. God, I thought I was going to climb in here and see you injured or something."

He slid down the wall to a sitting position and she followed like a mimic. "How'd you find me?"

"I called the office and Bean said he'd seen you early this morning."

"Oh. Right." He wiped his face with his shirt again.

"Did you pay Charlie Roberts a visit?"

"Yeah." He told her about Charlie and his conversation with Greg Hess and then, hesitantly, about the videotape he'd received in the mail that morning.

Quin didn't say anything. But McCleary felt their argument last night swelling between them, pressing in against the heat as if the warehouse was a hot air balloon and their argument was a pair of giant arms, squeezing the balloon like a pimple. Quin drew her legs up against her and wrapped her arms around them. "So instead of a videotape of Moorhouse's death, the killer sends you a

186

sex tape. For what? Is it supposed to be a clue? Is it to malign Gill? What?"

"I don't know. I don't know what it means." He glanced at her. "Except that it means maybe you were right about Gill, Quin, about last night."

She just nodded.

"It means that I really don't know anything about a man I've known all my life. That's what it means. Christ, maybe Gill's sabotaging his own movie, Quin. He talks about these migraines he has, where he blacks out and can't remember things."

She reached for his hand and kissed the back of it and held it. "Why would Gill sabotage his own movie? It doesn't make sense. This is his magnum opus for television, Mac."

Yeah, she was right.

"Besides, I want you to see something. I had lunch with Marielle today. You know that note Gill got in the mail? Well, Ellie recognized it as a passage out of the I Ching."

She brought a book from her purse, a large, thick book that made him imagine her purse as a bottomless lake from which would rise other books, secrets, monsters. She explained about the I Ching, and when he paged through it, the symbols reminded him of the designs on the coin he'd found. He showed it to her. They walked over to where the light was better and he saw that the designs were similar. Definitely Oriental.

"Now, the hexagram Kranish received was taken out of context to make a point about inferior and superior men and their uses of power. But the changing line is a warning to him." She read from the book: " 'Whereas an inferior man revels in power when he comes into possession of it, the superior man never makes this mistake.' By following the guidelines in the book, the hexagram has to change because the solid line is changing to broken. That brings us to *this* hexagram. . . ." She flipped forward in the book to hexagram 54, The Marrying

Maiden. "If whoever sent the note is following the guidelines in the book, then this should be the next hexagram. But I've read and reread this thing, looking for something that might give us a clue, and I haven't found zip. When are you going to see this Lee Ling woman?"

"I looked her up in the phone book and got her address. I'm going to stop by there this evening. Besides her, do you know of anyone in the cast or crew who's into Oriental philosophies?"

"No. But Rose Leen probably does. She asked me to lunch at her place tomorrow, Mac. It'll give me a chance to get some information out of her away from the set."

"Get information how? By telling her who you are?"

"If I have to."

Before McCleary could protest, Quin rushed on. Rose, she pointed out, had an alibi for the night of Domer's death, she knew everyone in the cast and crew, they had no reason not to confide in her. "Sooner or later, I've got to open up to someone, Mac, if we want to push ahead. The answer to all this lies with Kranish. Rose has known him a long time. Maybe she even knows something about where the scriptwriter got her story."

McCleary didn't care for the idea of Quin blowing her cover, but conceded she had a point. "Play it by ear, okay? If you can get the information without making her suspicious, great. But otherwise do whatever you think is best."

She smiled, but it was thin, restrained. "I wasn't asking your permission, you know." Her mouth cockled with distaste, as if she'd bitten into a lime.

McCleary touched a finger to it, easing the pucker, and she laughed and he kissed her. When she pulled back, her smile was a real smile. She touched his beard, and for a moment he fantasized about swooping her up in his arms and carrying her over to the tractor or the inside of the Piper Cub and making love to her in the smell of grease and oil.

188

"Nice, you. But at heart, McCleary, you're still a bossy cop." She walked back over to the counter, slipped the I Ching book in her purse, slung her purse over her shoulder. "I'm starved. Let's go find something to eat."

"You'd eat lunch with a bossy cop?" he asked as they hoisted themselves up onto the counter so they could climb back outside.

"Only if he listens to an idea I've got."

"You just told me your idea about Rose."

"That was my first idea." She slid through the window and was sitting on Lady's roof, polishing an apple on her shirt sleeve as he emerged. "You want a hint?" she asked.

McCleary lowered himself to the roof and sat beside her. She passed him the apple. The heat pounded their backs. McCleary bit into the apple and passed it back to her. "Okay, a hint."

"I think tonight we should take a look around Charlie Roberts' place and try to figure out why he stole those scripts."

"Uh-huh." He passed the apple back to her. "That's called B and E, Quin."

She glanced at him, her eerie blue eyes laughing. "Yeah, I know. And what do you call climbing through that window?"

Lee Ling lived in an old section of Dania about five blocks from the beach. The house was small, old enough to have hurricane awnings that drooped over the windows like eyelids, and a carport rather than a garage. Two tremendous banyans stood at either side of the house, providing perpetual shade. Except for them and the grass, there was no other shrubbery. The effect, from a distance, was one of geometric precision, as though the house had been sketched into the landscape, McCleary thought.

The doorbell chimed rather than rang. A young woman who matched the gossip column clipping Quin had shown him answered the door. She was lovely in the way most

Orientals are—slender and slight, with eyes so dark they were nearly black, and thick black hair that shone. Her flawless skin was as smooth as a pearl. Her mouth was small, nicely shaped, a precise, methodical mouth, he decided. McCleary was disappointed that she wore jeans and a work shirt instead of a kimono. "Yes? I may help you?"

He introduced himself. She invited him in.

The living room glistened with neatness. A pale lemon-colored couch with plump cushions and matching chairs graced one wall. The only other furniture in the room was a large, square table that sat low to the floor and was surrounded with pillows that grew from it like flowers; a Japanese screen that separated the living room from the hall; a pine case that looked as if it housed a television or a stereo or both. The light, softened by the rice-paper screen that covered the front windows, seemed to create a soft blur to the room, as if he were seeing it through thin wisps of angel hair. He smelled incense.

She sat on one of the pillows. He did the same. "You would like to know my relationship with Gill, yes, Detective?"

"For starters."

She folded her long fingers on the surface of the table. "I am his acupuncturist. More accurately, his acupressurist. He is not crazy about acupuncture needles, and acupressure works just as well for his problem. You know about his migraines?"

He nodded. "Where did you meet him?"

"In Los Angeles, about five years ago. He started coming to me then because he suffered acute insomnia."

"And you've been lovers since then?" he asked.

Her smile whispered of enigmas, of secrets too vast and complex to explain. "No. Actually, we are not lovers, Detective. We are"—she thought about it a moment—"explorers. Yes, Gill and I are explorers."

"Explorers." Terrific, he thought. He came for answers and she was talking like Marco Polo.

"In each man, Detective McCleary, there is a female

principle Carl Jung called the animus. In women, the corresponding male principle is called the anima. The Chinese think of these principles as the yin and the yang. Gill and I attempt to bring out these opposites in each other by exploring our sexuality."

Wonderful: it sounded like a lecture from Masters and Johnson. "Who do you think is trying to sabotage his film, Ms. Ling?"

Another enigmatic smile, then she said: "Gill is self-destructive, Detective. That trait is manifested in many different ways—through his creative genius, his inability to love, to be monogamous, his need for control, his sudden and sometimes compulsive good deeds. I will give you an example. Two years ago, my sister needed a kidney transplant. She had no medical insurance. I could not afford to pay for the operation. Gill went to my sister's doctor, unknown to me, and arranged to pay for everything. I didn't find out until six months later, when the doctor finally told me. Gill still doesn't know that I know. He paid, Detective McCleary, approximately two hundred thousand dollars to save the life of a woman he'd never met."

Goosebumps dotted McCleary's arm.

"On another occasion, which I heard about through a mutual friend, he flew a badly burned child from Nicaragua to the Shriners' Hospital here in the States and paid *her* medical bills. There are a number of stories like that, not all dealing with hospitals. So when you ask who I think might be sabotaging this film, I can only tell you that the answer lies within Gill himself."

"He received this in the mail, Ms. Ling." McCleary took out a copy of the note. "It's a passage from the I Ching."

She glanced at it. "The Wilhelm edition. Yes, I'm familiar with it. As with any translation, there are some inconsistencies and errors, but the book is perhaps the best English translation of the I Ching." Her small, pre-

191

cise mouth curved into a small, knowing smile. "You believe that I sent this, yes?"

"It certainly looks like a good possibility."

She laughed then. It was a delightful sound, filled with lightness, air, sun. "I am not the only person Gill knows who is interested in Oriental philosophies and religions, Detective. Gill himself is no stranger to Oriental thought.

"His first film was based on his sojourn in Burma, specifically in the Golden Triangle, the heart of opium trade in the world. There he consorted with the exiled Chinese Kuomintang army men. He smoked pipes with opium warlords. There is also the stunt woman, Irene Bedford, Detective. Once a year she travels to the Orient to 'cleanse' herself. Dina Talbott consults a Chinese herbalist when she is in California and is an advocate of Chinese astrology. Maia Fox meditates daily and is a student of the Kama Sutra." She leaned forward, arms parallel to the table. "Californians try everything once," she finished, and laughed.

"Do you have a VCR?" McCleary asked.

She grinned. It dimpled her mouth. "Of course. All we second-generation Chinese are thoroughly modern." She pointed at the pine cabinet. McCleary brought a copy of the videotape out of his back pocket. "Someone sent this to me."

A moment later, the screen flickered to life. He ran about five minutes of it, Lee Ling saying nothing, just watching. When he turned it off, she said, "Why would this be sent to you?"

"I don't know. You don't seem surprised by the fact that Gill taped it."

She sat back on the pillow, her legs stretched out in front of her and crossed at the ankles. "No, it doesn't surprise me. Films are his passion. Why shouldn't he make films for himself? But it raises some personal questions," she added with a thin smile. "Yes, I have to admit it does that."

"What sorts of personal questions?" McCleary prodded, sinking onto the pillow again.

She brought her legs up, crossed them, and sat with her spine as rigid as a cigar-store Indian. She breathed slowly and deeply. "I would not appreciate being photographed in such a manner. Questions like that, Detective."

It was the first time he detected an acerbic note in her tone. "And who would the other woman have been in such a situation, Miss Ling?"

"With me?" She dropped her head back and studied the ceiling. "Maia, Dina, several other women in Los Angeles."

Dina? McCleary tried to imagine it and couldn't. "So this is like his hobby."

"Perhaps 'avocation' would be a better choice of words."

Something of what he was feeling must have shown on his face, because she suddenly asked him how long he had *really* known Kranish. Then she smiled and hastily added, "In all fairness, I should tell you that I know he hired you and your wife to look into the murder of Mr. Domer. But that is all that I know."

He experienced an acute annoyance with Kranish. Dina knew about him and Quin, this woman knew, by tomorrow Rose Leen would know. So much for Quin's cover.

"You are pleading the fifth?" she asked, drawing him back.

"We lived around the corner from each other when we were kids," he said. "I've known him since I was two."

Her head moved slowly, up, down. The rigidness in her spine slackened a little. Her eyes seemed to darken, and he had the sudden and uncomfortable feeling that she knew exactly what he was thinking. "So you're feeling surprised, perhaps hurt, and certainly somewhat confused about a man you thought you knew."

That's about it, lady. But he neither confirmed nor denied what she said.

She sat forward, hands laced together on the tabletop

once more. "You know how we Chinese are big on old sayings and parables, yes, Detective?"

McCleary chuckled. "So I've heard."

"Well, here is one for you. 'The future is hidden from the men who make it.' "

He supposed it was Confucius, even though it didn't sound like him. But he wasn't going to ask.

"Anatole France," she said. "It is the key to the riddle of Gill Kranish. Twenty years from now, he and Spielberg will be men whom others speak of with awe, visionaries in the film industry who brought us, as a race, one step closer to our future by showing us the alternatives. Even *Night Flames*, Detective, shows us something important—the price of truth and the effects of withheld truths. And yet, for all of Gill's visionary prowess, his own future exists only as an abstract for him. Oh, he has goals and dreams and plans, but he doesn't really see himself inside these things, as a part of them. Even love exists as an abstract for him. That's part of why he's so carnal. It's his way of making this abstract idea of love concrete. But it is also what will eventually kill him."

"I'm not sure I understand."

"Someone is murdering his actors. And murder is not an abstract."

Twenty

THE POSEIDON CLUB on Miami Beach had once been a bowling alley. Then, five years ago, an entrepreneurial Cuban had bought the place, gutted it, and rebuilt it. Now it was five levels with several bars, a restaurant, a disco, and a nightclub on the uppermost level with a domed glass ceiling and a hundred-dollar-a-head cover charge.

It had been Dina's choice, and a good one. The room smelled sweetly of power, wealth, of deals discussed and discreetly sealed. It was a place whose rules Kranish understood. The bottom line was that money was king. As long as you minded your own business and didn't make trouble, and of course paid your bill, anything could be purchased—political clout, information, freedom, drugs, sex, death. The very air intoxicated him, acted on him like an aphrodisiac. His pores opened like flowers, absorbing the taste and feel of the air as though it were sunlight.

He could hear the rustle of silk within the murmur of voices, laughter rippling through the music, the clink of glasses, a blender whirring. When a woman in white accidentally brushed up against him, an electric chill swept along his arms. He and Dina paused in the doorway, at the fringe of the crowd.

The maître d', a rather pompous-looking fellow with thick white hair, informed them they would have a ten-minute wait for a seat. Kranish reached into his pocket, drew out a fifty-dollar bill, and pressed it into the man's hand. "We'd like seats near the window."

The man smiled magnanimously and tucked the bill in his pocket. "Yes, sir. Right this way, please," he said, scrapping the ten-minute wait.

He led them to a table at a wall of glass that overlooked Biscayne Bay and the lights of Miami. "Is this what you had in mind, sir?"

"It's fine."

"If I can be of further service, sir, let me know. My name is Harold." He smiled again, a knowing smile this time that said, *what is your pleasure, sir?*

Kranish twisted the end of his mustache and looked at Dina. She was sitting forward, watching him, her fingertips pressed together at her chin. He glanced back at Harold. "I think we'd like to order something first."

"Certainly, sir. I'll send a waiter right over."

Harold hurried away. Dina lit a cigarette and dropped her head back, exhaling with a sigh. "You don't look like Gill Kranish," she remarked.

"That must mean my disguise is good, huh," he laughed.

His hair and mustache were now black, he wore wire-rim glasses, and he was dressed in a T-shirt and jacket like Sonny Crockett. He didn't look or feel like himself, except that his head was beginning to ache. But he told himself it was caused by a flutter of concern in the back of his mind that he shouldn't be doing this. He'd always indulged in his little hobby only with women he knew, because it was easier to maintain control over the situation. A stranger brought certain risks—a psychological quirk that might erupt without warning, the threat of discovery, potential lawsuits, whatever. And yet, the risk somehow sweetened everything. It tightened his nerves like guitar strings, stirred feelings he hadn't experienced since the first Spin Weaver film.

A waiter approached the table and they ordered a bottle of Dom Pérignon and an escargot appetizer. Dina's eyes moved slowly around the bar, slid into the room beyond it, then returned to Kranish. She smiled and held up her glass to his when the waiter had left.

"A toast to an interesting evening," she said.

They clicked glasses. Moonlight limned the curve of her chin and seemed to heighten the green in her eyes. Kranish reached out and rested his fingers against the back of her hand. He stroked her knuckles, the soft skin between her thumb and forefinger, and felt a momentary prick of loneliness. *I should be feeling something special.* Something special, he thought, like he used to feel with Pam Spenser when . . .

Not now, don't think about that now. What the hell was wrong with him, going soppy like that tonight? Here?

"I think she should be someone young," Dina said. "Don't you?"

"How young?"

She laughed. "Above the age for statutory rape, Gill." She lowered her voice and leaned toward him. "Relax, will you?"

Relax. Right. He was perfectly relaxed. In control. He was Gill Kranish, who'd made an art of control. He finished his glass of champagne and poured himself another and began to scan the area, just as Dina was doing. His gaze stopped on two women—a blonde sitting by herself at the bar and a redhead talking with the bartender about four seats away. Both looked to be in their early twenties. Dina followed his gaze.

"I hate redheads," she murmured.

"How about blondes?"

In the moonlight, her smile seemed distorted, Kranish thought, almost predatory. "Hmm, yes, I think the blonde would be fine."

For an instant, Kranish felt like a member of Hitler's upper echelons, perusing the human cattle for a suitable woman. An acescent taste coated his tongue. The ache in his head throbbed a little harder. Once again he started to tell Dina this wasn't such a great idea, that he didn't feel like playing. But instead, he imposed parameters.

"We don't want to go back to the hotel," he said.

"Oh? We're going to go neck at the beach?" The jibe in her voice aggravated him.

"No. We'll stay at Maia's houseboat. She's gone for the weekend."

Dina sat back, her lower lip thrust out in a pout. "Maia. Oh, yeah, that's great, Gill. And suppose she comes home early? What then?"

"She won't. She said she was going up the coast and would be back Monday in time for her scenes. It's either there or not at all, Dina."

She considered this, then she was all smiles again, leaning forward, refilling their glasses, asking him to order another bottle, and how were they going to let the blonde know they were interested, hmm?

Kranish, buoyed by a sense of control once more, smiled confidently and signaled for Harold. The maître d' nodded and came right over, the moonlight parting like water with his passage. He told the man what he wanted, tipped him another thirty dollars. A few minutes later, a glass of Dom Pérignon was set down in front of the blonde. The bartender said something to her and she glanced back at Dina and Kranish. She looked like a young Meryl Streep, and her smile was lovely enough to light up the dark side of the moon.

Only later, when she was dead, would he remember that when she'd joined him at the table his arms had broken out in gooseflesh, as if someone had just strolled over his grave.

Twenty-one

1.

BY TEN THAT evening, Quin and McCleary were parked alongside Bean's Datsun beneath a canopy of banyan trees. From there they had a view of the front and side of Charlie Roberts' townhouse.

It was one of four pink stucco buildings with black trim that faced a canal. They were all clones of each other that looked part Spanish, part eclectic South Florida. The entrance to the courtyard was arched; caliginous light spilled from black iron lamps that jutted from a pair of posts. Off to Quin's left was a dirty canal where a family of ducks drifted through the dim orange glow of the parking lot lamps. On the other side of the canal lay old concrete block houses that looked like loaves of bread.

She turned her attention back to the building. Another couple, dressed in Saturday-night finery, was getting into a BMW. A few minutes ago a couple of teenagers had pulled away in a van. In fact, for the last hour the townhouse had been losing residents at an alarming rate, as if an evacuation were in progress. But so far there'd been no sight of Charlie Roberts. His navy blue El Dorado was still parked in front of the porch at the side of the building. The lights in his windows still blazed. Damn him, anyway, she thought. She was hungry and she had to go to the bathroom and she was tired of sitting here. Why couldn't he be like every other yuppie in his building, stepping out for a night in sin city?

Quin opened Lady's glove compartment and reached for the baggie of dry-roasted peanuts she always kept stocked inside. There were maybe a dozen peanuts in the bag. The corners of her mouth plunged. "Mac, you ate all the peanuts and didn't refill the bag."

He glanced over at her, as if just remembering her presence. Ever since he'd gotten back from his meeting with the acupuncturist he'd been rather withdrawn, pensive. "Oh, sorry. I got stuck in traffic coming back from the beach the other day and I got hungry."

"Thanks a lot."

"Wait. Hold on a sec. I just remembered." He dug down inside a pocket on his door and brought out a bag of dried fruit. "It's kinda old, but it should hold you."

"Great. Perfect." He passed it to her like a gift and she wrinkled her nose and looked up. "They're prunes."

"Best I can do, kiddo."

She opened the bag, plucked out a prune, nibbled on it, and McCleary whispered, "Hey, here comes our boy."

She knew the minute she saw him that he was the man in the trailer that day. He stood about six feet, was slender but not thin, and there was no mistaking that blond hair, that tan. An ex-surfer for sure. And tonight he wore tailored khaki slacks, a pale pink shirt, a tie, and he seemed to be in a rush. He walked briskly through the courtyard arch, consulting his watch, then paused at the El Dorado, drumming his fingers on the roof, staring into the courtyard, glancing at his watch again.

A woman hurried from the courtyard and Roberts snapped, "What took you so long, anyway?"

"Relax, Charlie. *No* one ever arrives at parties on time."

They both got into the car, the doors slammed, the engine revved. They were sealed into the vehicle like astronauts in a space shuttle, and the El Dorado blasted away, burning rubber.

A pair of joggers dashed by. Another couple left the building. The walkie-talkie on the seat between the

McClearys crackled. McCleary picked it up and Bean said, "If you two are all set, I'll keep watch out here. Over."

"We're going in through the porch, Bean. Use the light signals on the walkie-talkie to warn us. One flash means the El Dorado's parking out front, two flashes and it's parking at the side. Over."

"You got it, my man, over and out."

McCleary passed the walkie-talkie to Quin. She clipped it on her belt, McCleary checked his tool pouch, and they got out of the car.

The three porches on this side of the building were screened in, with sliding glass doors that opened onto a living room. Light from the first apartment bled through curtains that covered the door. The second apartment was black. A dim yellow bulb glowed on Roberts' porch.

"I bet you a quarter the porch door's locked," McCleary said.

"I bet you a buck it isn't."

"You're on."

Quin lost. McCleary had to slit the screen around the porch door handle while she stood watch. He peeled back a corner of the screen, reached inside, and flipped back the lock. They stepped onto the porch and tried the sliding glass door. It was unlocked. McCleary slid the door open, pushed aside the vertical blinds, and they slipped into the cool twilight of Charlie Roberts' townhouse.

For a moment, as she stood there inhaling the air in someone else's house, someone else's life, she felt like a voyeur. Perhaps this was something of what Kranish experienced when he'd spied on them. Or when he, Domer, and Maia had made their sick little videotape. Her heart pounded, her palms dampened, adrenaline coursed through her veins, her insides turned spongy. But the sensation was paradoxical—the quick rush from doing something forbidden was tempered with discomfort that she actually felt high.

A floor lamp burned in a corner of the L-shaped room, splashing light across the Mexican tile floors. Fake beams split the high ceiling into quarters. A black iron spiral staircase twisted to the second floor. Roberts made a damned comfortable living, Quin decided, and she bet only a fraction of his income came from being a private eye.

"What we're looking for will probably be in Charlie's den," McCleary whispered. "Let's take a look upstairs."

On the second floor, they passed the master bedroom, where skirts and shirts and slacks littered the unmade bed and puddled over the sides onto a gray rug. Makeup and perfume bottles stood at attention on the dresser in front of the mirror. Quin noted there was a door that led outside to a balcony that circumvented the entire second story and looked out onto the courtyard.

In a guest bedroom, there was nothing of interest except a white cat stretched out on top of a TV that blinked at them with insouciance. The room at the end of the hall was dark. McCleary switched on the flashlight.

There were three four-drawer filing cabinets against the walls, papers stacked on the desk, a phone with two lines, a Canon copier. From the looks of it, this was where Roberts operated his private-eye business.

"What're we looking for exactly?" Quin asked, kneeling in front of the first filing cabinet.

"I don't know. Just pull anything that looks interesting or incriminating."

"We're going to *take* the stuff?"

"Some of it, yeah. Let's give Charlie something to get nervous about."

"You have a criminal mind, Mac."

He balanced the flashlight on the edge of the middle filing cabinet as he chuckled. "No doubt a vestige from a former life. You take the middle cabinet, okay?"

"Right." She opened the top drawer. "Was your life as a criminal the one where I was your mistress?"

"Yeah, and I ended up in prison for adultery, not for my other crimes."

"Men never ended up in prison for adultery. Women did."

He glanced over at her, smiling. "Wrong life, I guess."

For the better part of an hour they sifted through Roberts' files and found that he was a man involved in more than B&Es into motor homes. They recognized the names of racketeers, drug dealers, and crooked politicians for whom he'd done investigative work. The files they plucked out to take with them proliferated like viruses until they finally had to stop and condense the material.

And that was when the light on the walkie-talkie flashed twice, the red glowing in the den like a tiny setting sun.

"Our boy's back and he's parking at the side of the building," McCleary hissed, swooping up a handful of files and shutting the drawer. "C'mon."

"We'll never make it downstairs before he's inside the house, Mac. There's a door in the master bedroom. Let's use that."

"Where's it go?"

"Out onto the second-floor landing."

They rushed down the hall and into the master bedroom. Downstairs, Quin heard Roberts' voice. He sounded angry. Or drunk. Or both. Had he noticed the screen was torn? Now the woman was saying, "I'll get the money. Just calm down, will you?" Quin heard footsteps on the stairs. Paroxysms of fear tightened her gut as McCleary fumbled with the chain. Sweat leaped across the back of her neck. The footsteps on the stairs paused, and the woman said, "Hey, Charlie, where's the grass? I want to take a couple of joints."

Hurry, Mac. Just hurry. She winced as the door squeaked when he carefully drew it open, winced again when she heard Roberts shout a reply. Then they were outside on the landing, their arms filled with files, and

McCleary was trying to shut the door quietly, trying to be neat and precise as usual. "Leave it, Mac," she hissed.

He did.

They scurried left, toward the red EXIT sign. As Quin threw open the door to the stairwell, some of the files slid out of her arms. Papers sailed to the floor. The door sighed shut. She grabbed at the files, the papers, jamming everything into her arms, and McCleary opened the door again and she fled through it, into the stairwell.

There were no lights. The dark bit down over them like a whale's mouth, and for a long moment all she heard was her breathing and his. She leaned against the wall. The cool of the concrete through her damp blouse felt good against her skin. The air smelled fusty and tickled her nose, but she couldn't scratch it without setting down the files. She leaned against the wall, rubbed her face against her shoulder, but couldn't reach her nose. She was afraid she would sneeze.

"Mac, c'mere, quick," she whispered.

He inched closer to her and she rubbed her nose against his shoulder and sighed.

"Better?" he asked with amusement.

"Much."

"You're weird, Quin."

"Gee, thanks."

The flashlight came on; the beam found the stairs. "C'mon," McCleary said. "Let's get away from this door and then call Bean to find out if they've left yet."

They moved to the landing on the first floor. Quin set her files down and unclipped the walkie-talkie from her belt. "Joe?" she whispered.

"Yo. Surfer boy's standing outside at his porch door, looking mighty interested in something. The woman's still inside. Where are you?"

Shit, she thought. The screen. They were almost home free and Roberts had to notice the screen McCleary had cut. "We're in a stairwell. Flash when they've gone."

"Right. Keep the line open."

Swell. Keep the line open while her bladder felt like it was going to pop any minute and her stomach began to fuss for food again. She sat down on a step, and McCleary lowered himself to the one beneath her. He turned off the flashlight. The blackness swam around them.

"Mac?"

"Hmm."

"I was wondering about something."

"What's that?"

"Since we've been married, have you ever felt the urge to sleep with anyone else?"

"No." The silence fell between them again, then he added: "Have you?"

"No. Have you been attracted to any other women?"

He laughed quietly. "You pick odd places for conversations like this, Quin."

"Well, there's nothing else to do. C'mon, answer my question. Have you been attracted to any other women since we've been married?"

"Sure." His voice seemed disembodied in the dark, and she shifted on the step until her shoulder brushed his. There, that was better.

"Like who?"

"Oh, I don't know. You see a woman on the street, and you wonder what it would be like."

"No, I mean specifically. If you were single, say, who would you have slept with that you've met since we got married."

Another laugh, just as soft, as good-natured. "Oh, c'mon, Quin, I don't know. I . . . okay, let's see. All right, when I first met Maia Fox, I was attracted to her. But after I saw the tape, I wasn't. How's that?"

She wondered if Maia had come on to him, and poked him in the shoulder. "You're humoring me."

"No, I'm not. That's the truth, really. What about you?"

She started to tell him about Kranish, about the raw sexuality he exuded, about what had happened—or almost happened—in the motor home. She wanted to explain how when she'd viewed the videotape earlier this evening, she'd felt an almost overwhelming pathos for Kranish. But she didn't know where to begin, and then Bean's voice cut through her musings. "Hey, they've split."

"Thanks, Joe, we're on our way."

They pushed through the door into the courtyard. A warm breeze pursued them to the cupola of shadows beneath the banyans where Bean and Lady were parked. Quin thought of their unfinished conversation, of the unspoken words curling like smoke in the dark of the stairwell. It was just as well. Some things, she decided, were better off left unsaid.

2.

Bruce Harmon sat outside the Poseidon Club in his beat-up Chevy, his video camera on the seat beside him. It was hot and uncomfortable in the car, and a cold beer would've been nice. But no way was he going to go inside and risk being seen by either Kranish or Dina. He'd ventured this far, and no sense in blowing it now.

Following the cast and crew around had started as a fluke, a postscript to his documentary on the making of *Night Flames*. He'd thought it would be interesting to observe these people in their private lives away from the set. But in the last few days it had become more than just a casual pursuit, something he did in his free time. He'd found himself planning for these sojourns as if for a cross-country journey, choosing his targets with the same care he might've picked out a motel or a restaurant or a tourist attraction. He was nervous about following Kranish, the legend, to learn about Kranish, the man, but wasn't this part of the recording of history?

He reached under his seat for his thermos of iced coffee. It wasn't cold anymore because the ice had melted, and it wasn't a frosted beer, but it was better than nothing. He sipped at it, his eyes never leaving the front door of the club.

The club had valet parking, but he'd noticed that Kranish hadn't used it. He'd left the Mercedes in a metered parking spot around the corner, and he and Dina had walked to the club, her arm linked in his. Something about Kranish had struck him as odd, a subtle change in the way he walked or the color of his hair or maybe the way he was dressed. Harmon couldn't pinpoint it, exactly, and finally dismissed it.

He capped the thermos and grinned as he saw them exiting the club. At the corner, Kranish stopped and Dina hurried on to the Mercedes. He stood there, watching the door of the club as though he were waiting for someone. Harmon slid a little lower in his seat.

After a moment, a blonde stepped out of a crowd just leaving the club and walked toward Kranish. As they spoke, he could see how she tilted her head toward him, a stray breeze rustling her pretty hair. Then they walked on toward the Mercedes.

Harmon started up the Chevy.

Twenty-two

THE MERCEDES ROSE over the bridge to Star Island, the noise of the tires against metal making Kranish clench his teeth. His head ached, he'd had too much to drink, he didn't know if he wanted to go through with this. What the hell was the point? Why was he here? He'd lost two of his major actors, the network was screaming about the escalating production cost, someone was trying to sabotage his film. And here he was, cruising through the navy blue dark of Miami Beach like he'd never had a problem in his life.

Everything inside the car seemed suddenly excessive, cloying: the murmur of Dina's voice, drawing the woman out, the thick scent of the woman's perfume, the music from the radio. Jesus, he couldn't even remember her full name. Lynette Someone who looked like Meryl Streep and worked as a stew for United. The cheap air passage enabled her to live in Miami but fly out of Houston, she said, and since she'd been undergoing analysis, she had come to truly appreciate the beauty of flying. Of being free like that. She had, in fact, realized she was too free to be tied down to her boyfriend, who wanted to get married, but she wasn't ready, might never be ready. After all, she was only twenty-three, and why be in a hurry? The point of her analysis was to learn how to be open to the flow, to let it nudge you in the right direction, so some nights, like tonight, she would just come to the Poseidon Club by herself and wait for a sign.

"A sign?" Dina asked.

"Yes, you know, a sign. When Mr. Kranish here bought me a drink, I knew that was the signal from my unconscious. The nudge." She sat back, and Kranish glanced at Dina and she looked at him and smiled. *A sign. Great, terrific. I buy a loony stew a drink and suddenly it's a sign from the soup of the collective unconscious. It's God nibbling at her ear.* He wished she hadn't recognized him. He wished she'd never heard of Spin Weaver. He wished . . . oh Christ, he didn't know. That his head would stop pounding.

He stopped in front of the house where Maia's houseboat was docked. Dina slid out and opened the gates, and Kranish drove on through. The Meryl Streep Doppelgänger was leaning forward from the back seat, her arm brushing his shoulder. She was saying something about Tahiti, which was on United's route, and how she would like to retire to the South Pacific because she'd never been anyplace as sensual. Well, on second thought, she added, maybe Brazil was more sensual. She supposed anyplace could be sensual if you were with the right person. Didn't he agree?

He stopped the Mercedes, and Dina got back in. "We're staying at this wonderful little houseboat," Dina explained, as the headlights lit up the backyard. "There, you can see it there." She pointed at the moonstruck houseboat hugging the seawall.

"Oh, how precious, really. It's like . . . oh, what's that author's name. I can never remember her name," Lynette gushed. "Wait. Anaïs Nin, the French diarist. She lived on a houseboat in Paris for a while. Great. How great. She was into the flow too, you know."

Kranish pulled the Mercedes up onto the grass, parallel to a row of tall thin pines. As they got out of the car and started toward the houseboat, their footsteps echoed in Kranish's head. It was as if the ground were the skin for a drum against which everything pounded and reverberated: their footsteps, the whistle of a tug out in the bay, the pulse of blood through their legs, the bark of a

209

dog several houses away. He grimaced with pain and patted his pockets for his migraine pills. It hadn't reached immedicable proportions yet, and if he took a pill now, it wouldn't. When he couldn't find the pills, he remembered he'd left them in the pockets of another pair of slacks.

They'd reached the houseboat. Kranish stepped on first, reached into the potted plant where Maia kept her key, and unlocked the door. Moonlight flooded the galley, and the air smelled of salt. He turned on the generator, the air-conditioning, and shut the windows. Then he walked into the middle room. It looked like a sitting room in a New England farmhouse—round braided rugs, pine floors, wooden shelves filled with books and videos, a coffee table, a TV in the corner, a leather hassock in front of a rocking chair. Very Maia, he thought, and went into the last room.

He flipped on the light. A bed dominated the room. The covers were turned down for the night, the corners were neatly tucked in, there was even a pair of slippers at the edge of a braided rug. An afghan draped the back of a rocker near the window. Pure and pristine, he mused, as if Maia were still a small child living in her parents' farmhouse in Connecticut.

"It's just the neatest place," he heard Lynette saying, and as he turned, a ribbon of pain stabbed into the bone above his eye. *A drink, I need a drink and some aspirin. Yeah, maybe aspirin will do it.*

Lynette and Dina had already made themselves comfortable in the sitting room and Dina was fixing drinks and now the stew was fixing up three lines of coke on a compact mirror. Kranish went into the bathroom and took two aspirins, and when he returned, Dina and the stew were snorting up the coke, and the stew, still calling him 'Mr. Kranish,' said, "We left a line for you."

A drink, aspirin, a little coke: hell, he'd blast his migraine out of his head, he thought, and did the line.

Someone put on music. They did more coke. Had

more drinks. The air tightened around them. Color flared in Dina's cheeks. Lynette, smiling tristfully like Streep in *The French Lieutenant's Woman,* asked Kranish to dance and pressed herself against him as the pain in his head kept coming, wave after wave. Dina suggested they all go for a swim. After that, Kranish's mind seemed to blink on and off, so that later his memories were chopped up—bright flares of images connected by nothing but huge pits of blackness.

He remembered how in the water, this Meryl Streep look-alike had rubbed up against him and he'd kissed her and she'd whispered, "Does *she* have to stick around?"

But he didn't know what he'd said or if he'd said anything at all. He didn't recall climbing back onto the boat or going into the bedroom. His next memory was of himself and Dina tantalizing Lynette just as he and Lee Ling had done to Dina and how Dina smiled at him as though she had passed some sort of test, as though she'd been initiated into the great secrets of the Kama Sutra. He remembered the expression on Lynette's face, a look even Streep wouldn't have been able to pull off, of astonishment and hunger and perhaps fear.

Then there was nothing except pain, a terrible squeezing in his head, as if the cells in his brain were mutating, enlarging. He knew he was dying. He knew his head was going to burst because the pain was too huge, too massive to contain. He didn't know how long the pain lasted. But his next memory was of a shadow passing against the window. He wanted to see what it was, check it out, but he became aware of Dina's voice, then Lynette sobbing. He saw her face, squashed like an apple that had been too long in the sun, her eyes red and swollen, her hand clutching the sheet against her as she shouted for Dina to get out, to leave her alone, that she hadn't wanted to be with Dina in the first place.

He remembered Lynette lunging from the bed, trailing the sheet behind her as she sobbed, and he and Dina ran after her, to calm her. She tripped over the sheet and fell and smacked her head on the coffee table and slumped to the floor like a rag doll.

From that point on, he remembered everything. He stood absolutely still, staring at her, at the way the light puddled on her breast and how the sheet draped her like a Grecian garment. Then he saw the blood oozing from her temple and he began to weep, Jesus, he wept like a child, fists knuckling his eyes, his chest heaving. He wept because he knew she was dead, and they had killed her.

It was a few moments before he realized Dina was shaking him. "Gill, snap out of it. Come on. We've got to get the body out of here."

She was right.

The body.

They had to get rid of the body.

No, it was an accident. They would call the police and explain. . . . Sure. He would call McCleary first and McCleary would call Benson and everything would be straightened out. An accident, anyone could see that. She had run, they had tried to calm her, she had tripped, bumped her head. . . .

"Gill," hissed Dina.

"I'm calling the cops," he said, and turned to move, but she caught his arm.

"The cops?" Her voice shrieked with alarm, and he grabbed hold of her and pressed his hand over her mouth.

"Not so *loud,* Dina. Christ."

She shoved his hand away. Her voice hissed like hot oil in a pan. "She's dead, Gill. This isn't a movie. I felt for a pulse and she's dead."

"It was an accident, for Christ's sakes. She—"

Dina started to laugh, an erratic, hysterical sound. "Oh yeah, that's great. You're going to call the police and explain how it was an accident and tomorrow every newspaper in the country will be reading about Gill and Dina and Lynette the Stew. Hey, that's great, Gill. That's really great." She dragged her fingers through her hair. "At the *minimum,* we would get charged with manslaughter, Gill. That means a trial. You know the kinds of things that might come out in a trial?"

Everything. Private tapes, his drinking, his women, everything.

"And we'd go to prison," Dina finished. "*Prison,* Gill. No thanks, I'm not going to prison. Look," she gripped his arm, "all we do is roll her over into the water. No one at the bar saw us leave with her. The tide will carry her out into the bay. She'll just be another Miami statistic. Gill, listen to me, please."

He looked at Dina, pleading, then drew his eyes from her and gazed at Lynette, draped like a Grecian goddess. In the blackness of his mind, he saw his life as a labyrinth layered with secrets. Here, the day in the field with Big Jim, his cowardice swelling like a tumor in his silence; his flight from Hollywood after his first film had bombed because he couldn't face defeat; and a decade ago, the death of Pam Spenser, when he was so afraid that whoever murdered her would come after him that he'd never come forward and had fled again. Now this.

But what other choice was there? If he was arrested for manslaughter, *Night Flames* would never be made. And if that happened, then what the hell did any of it mean?

He went numb.

He nodded.

He stepped toward Lynette the Stew like a mummy. He heard his knees crack as he crouched beside her. When he spoke, his voice sounded dead. "Is it high tide?"

"Yes."

"Check outside and see if there's anyone around."

She went into the bedroom to dress. Kranish felt for a pulse at Lynette's neck. The skin was still warm. Jesus, the skin was still warm, but she was dead. No pulse. No brain waves. *Gone, buddy boy, gone.*

He yanked his fingers away from her neck and picked up his slacks from the chair, wondering how they'd gotten there. He pulled them on, wiggled into his shirt, slipped on his shoes. He was perfectly sober; his migraine was gone. His thoughts, in fact, were more lucid than they had been for months, so clear that it occurred to him that HE might've set the fire in Domer's trailer and tampered with the Maserati. He might have done these things during one of his blackouts, as a punishment to himself for what had happened ten years ago. Yes, it was possible.

He felt odd, considering the possibility that he might be a murderer. But why not? He was capable of rolling a dead woman over the side of a houseboat, wasn't he? So why shouldn't he be capable of plotting out a murder? Several murders? He could very well have sent himself the videotape of Domer's death and the note. Sure, the ultimate cowardly act would be for his psyche to split down the middle like an atom, and go to war with its other half.

Dark against light.

Moon against sun.

Yin against yang.

He was a coward, that was the long and short of it. And from this cowardice had sprung Spin Weaver, twenty-first-century space hero, an ordinary, likable man with a host of odd quirks and more courage that Kranish had in his little finger. Spin Weaver was his antithesis.

"Gill?" She was whispering, her voice a harsh grating sound. "It's clear outside."

"Grab that end of the sheet."

They carried the body out onto the deck of the houseboat in the white cocoon of the sheet. He felt nothing. They unrolled her from the sheet and Kranish stared at her, at the curve of her hip, her long legs, the wound at her temple. Then he pushed the body off the deck and it tumbled into the bay. With an oar, he pushed her away from the side, her blond hair floating like bleached seaweed around her head, and slowly the current claimed her.

Neither of them saw the man with the video camera pressed into the hedge at the far end of the property.

214

Twenty-three

1.

"HI, TIM, IT'S Mike. Hope I didn't wake you, but if I did, I'll buy you breakfast or something."

It was seven Sunday morning, and Benson, instead of yawning, laughed. "That sounds like a guilty conscience speaking. You didn't wake me. The chief did. What's up?"

"Could you run a background check on a guy named Everett Winthrop? He's connected somehow with Charlie Roberts."

"Roberts, huh, you bet. Give me what you've got."

McCleary glanced at the label on the file taken from Roberts' den: WINTHROP, EVERETT. Inside was a sheet of paper with Winthrop's address on it (the Sanctuary in Boca Raton); a fee ($3,000 a week plus expenses); and a payment schedule (every Monday). Another sheet listed dates, and next to each date Roberts had jotted a word or phrase like *Observation of daily routine* or *Tailing*. What had caught McCleary's attention were entries for Wednesday, 9/15, and yesterday, 9/18: *I. Bedford, Atlantic Towers* and, in red ink, *McCleary, horse's ass*.

"I don't have much except that he lives in the Sanctuary in Boca Raton, Tim."

"Then he's got bucks, Mac. Big ones. I'll run this through and get back to you. Oh, I've got Greg Hess and his production people scheduled for blood tests tomorrow morning. Anything else?"

"Yeah, a couple of things." McCleary gave Benson a brief update, and when he'd finished, a silence rang hollowly along the line. "You still there?"

"Yeah. Yeah, I'm here. A fucking videotape? Gill just doesn't seem the type, Mac."

Yeah, no kidding.

"Have you talked to him yet?"

"No, I'm driving over to the Prince this morning."

"I'll be at the station all day if you need me. I've got a new case. A woman's body was hauled in from the bay around five this morning. We're going to try to establish an ID, then the Doc's going to come in special this afternoon and do an autopsy."

Good going, Miami.

(who asked you, pal?)

"Has your tail turned up anything on the Bedford woman?"

"Nope. Zip. But I finally tracked down Maia Fox's phantom mechanic, Mac. He went by the airport to pick up his last paycheck and that Loretta woman got his phone number. He confirmed he'd been with Maia. Showed me his log book where the flight was written down. A log is a legal document."

Well, so much for Maia Fox as a suspect in Domer's death. "I'll call you later. Good luck with the new case."

Benson snorted. "Mac, if luck had anything to do with anything, we'd all be rich and retired."

As he hung up, Quin strolled into his den and handed him a cup of coffee. She was wearing running shorts, a nylon T-shirt, and running shoes. "You look like you're dressed for a marathon."

"No, just the preliminaries." She sat on the edge of the couch. "Last night I dreamed I was being chased, Mac, by whoever killed Domer and Moorhouse. The person was carrying this *huge* Butane lighter, and every time he lit it, the flames licked at my back and, well, I think the person caught me in the end. Or would've

216

caught me if I hadn't woken up. So I decided it's time for me to start running."

McCleary laughed. "Because of a dream?"

"This dream was very specific."

"You already swim four times a week. There's nothing wrong with swimming."

"Yeah, it's a good all-around exercise, but it's not as aerobic as running. At least I don't think it is." She paused. "You trying to discourage me or something?"

He laughed again, delighted he would finally have company on his runs. "Discourage you? No way. Let me get dressed." He stood. "We'll go two miles, running and walking, so you can get used to it."

The morning was overcast and warm, but not uncomfortable. A slight breeze stirred the eucalyptus and pines that bordered the McClearys' street, bringing with it the smell of smoke from the burning Everglades. In fact, everything they passed bore the evidence of a seventeen-week drought. Lawns were a patchwork of brown, hedges drooped, flowers had wilted, even the birdsongs sounded weighted with fatigue.

They chatted as they ran, their shoes pounding the pavement, the brown grass, their voices quick and clipped. McCleary told her about the body hauled out of the bay and elaborated on his conversation with Lee Ling. "No wonder you were so reticent last night. Gill almost sounds like that Fertipton fellow on the old TV show *The Millionaire*."

"Yeah, something like that."

She glanced over at him. "I guess there're a lot of sides to Gill no one knows about." She pointed at the dancing sprinklers in the park. "I'll race you, Mac."

"You're on."

They ran down a shallow slope into the deserted park, neck to neck. Quin was surprisingly fast, arms hugging her sides, her hands closed but not too tightly. McCleary purposely dropped back a few paces, liking the sight of her from behind, her damp hair loose in the warm air, her long legs narrowing the distance to the sprinklers. His heart swelled with emotion, swelled like a balloon in a sudden gust of wind, and he raced after her and they burst through the spray, laughing, gulping at the water.

Quin dropped her head back, and her sunglasses tumbled into the grass. She closed her eyes and let the water pour over her like rain. Her blouse turned transparent as ice, water beaded on her legs, her arms, her throat, and glistened in her hair like jewels. McCleary suddenly wished he had his sketchpad. He wanted to preserve this image of Quin with her head thrown back, her arms held out as if in supplication to the sky, her skin sheathed in a silvery light. She seemed almost mythical, like something shaped from the elements, from wind and air and water.

Then she moved, she brought her head forward, and for an instant, McCleary thought she was dissolving like powder in water, that he would blink and she would vanish. It frightened him. He stepped toward her, touching her, reassuring himself that she wasn't dissolving. The sprinklers went off, almost as if the act of his touching her had caused it to happen, and Quin laughed a little at the expression on his face. "Hey, what's wrong?"

"Nothing. Nothing's wrong." But he hugged her tightly, utterly afraid that he would lose her, that the miasma surrounding Kranish would creep toward her like black, greasy smoke. He whispered that he loved her, and she hugged him back, nibbling like a fish at his earlobe. Then she stepped away, her ghost blue eyes searching his face as if she hoped to find what had prompted the declaration.

He tugged on her hand. *Home?* his eyes asked.

Home, her smile replied.

So they ran for another mile through the park, water dripping from their clothes, sloshing in their shoes. The miasma ebbed, but in the back of McCleary's mind he could feel its weight, its mass, its chill.

218

2.

Quin left the house at 11:30 for her noon lunch date with Rose. Fifteen minutes later she was sitting in a traffic jam on the Arthur Godfrey Causeway. The bridge to Miami Beach had gotten jammed when it opened to admit a boat. The thing was just frozen there, yawning like the mouth of a shark, the metal glinting brightly in the heat, and there were probably forty cars behind her and another forty in front, and even if she made a U-turn there in the middle of the road, the next bridge was ten minutes away. She sat there fuming.

This was the sort of thing Miami residents expected during the week, when they planned for traffic jams the way people in other parts of the country planned for the future. But on *Sunday,* for God's sake?

Five minutes into her wait, the radiator needle on the Toyota swung into the red zone and she had to turn off the engine. Roll down the windows. The heat, reflected off the black concrete, blistered the air, rolled into the car, and seemed to bubble against the windshield. Her stomach growled. She was thirsty. She had to go to the bathroom. These three needs seemed to pursue her relentlessly, and why oh why the hell did they always manifest themselves when she was stuck somewhere?

Fifteen minutes after she slowed to a halt, the bridge crept down. It creaked and moaned so loudly she had visions of the thing collapsing as eighty cars scrambled over it.

At 12:10, Quin hurried off the elevator on the fourth floor of the Atlantic Towers. She was late for lunch with Rose, she was hot, sticky, she needed a shower. She dug in her purse for the key to her apartment, and then she rounded the corner and saw the envelope tacked on the door. There was nothing special about it. The bold black letters of her name, QUIN MCCLEARY, rose starkly against the white field of the paper. The silver tack gleamed like a singular eye. She knew what it was. She stood in front of her door, staring at it, at her name, just staring, and she knew what it was.

Her fingers left perspiration stains on the envelope as she removed it. She unlocked her door but didn't step into the room. Her eyes darted about, clawing apart the shadows there in the corner, where sunlight didn't reach, seeking some small sign that someone was inside. She reached into her purse and drew out her .38. Her thumb knocked off the safety hammer. She came in, listening closely for something other than the pulse of the room, but heard nothing.

Just the same, she kept the door open and swept through the apartment, checking closets and showers and the porch and even under the bed. When she was satisfied no one was hiding inside, she shut the front door, locked it, and sat down in the kitchen to open the envelope.

The note, like the one Kranish had received, was typed:

Keui Mei/The Marrying Maiden

Every relationship between individuals bears within it the danger that wrong turns may be taken, leading to endless misunderstandings and disagreements. Therefore, it is necessary constantly to remain mindful of the end.

A changing line in the second place: here the girl is left behind in loneliness; the man of her choice has either become unfaithful or has died.

Suppose the girl herself dies? Where oh where would that leave the unfaithful spouse?

A slow chill fanned out across Quin's spine. She read the note through twice, and then again. Her phone rang. She reached for the receiver automatically.

"Yes? Hello?"

"Quin? It's Rose. You coming?"

"Oh. Rose. Right. I just got in. I'll be up in a jiffy. I got stuck in traffic. Right. See you in a minute."

"You okay, Quin? You sound funny."

"Sure. I'm fine, Rose." *Just dandy, Rose, no problem.* She hung up, fingering the envelope, glancing at the note, then at the envelope again. There was something off about all this, but her thoughts fluttered too fast to catch it, pin it down. She reached for her purse and took out the I Ching book. With a changing line in the second place, the hexagram of The Marrying Maiden would change to . . . She flipped the pages. Number 51, The Arousing. Quin read it through. Certain words leaped off at the page at her—violence, shock, thunder, terror.

Vie-oh-lence, terr-or: she sounded the words out phonetically, like the English teacher she'd been, and decided *Sshh-ock* was the cleanest and sharpest of the four. *Shock.* Yes, there was no mistaking what that meant. The word itself seem to spring from the tip of her tongue like a high diver or a bolt of electricity. But hey, *terr-or* was pretty clear too, now wasn't it. Sure. There was *The Terror, Terror by Night, Terror in the Aisles, Terror in the Wax Museum, Terror on the 40th Floor* . . . And now there was Quin's terror, borne of the suspicion that she was next, that the note was fingering her for death.

Rose's apartment was a clone of Quin's, except the decor was chocolate brown, pinks, and golds instead of black, white, and gray. The porch doors were thrown open to the sea breeze. Two cats, a calico and a white Persian, were comfortably ensconced in separate chairs. The Sunday *Herald* littered the coffee table and the floor. Half-filled glasses were abandoned on the dining-room table, the end tables, on the bookcase. Quin guessed Rose was one of those people who used a new glass every time she had something to drink.

She wore slacks and a blouse with huge hibiscus flowers on it that looked real enough to attract bees. Her hair, free of the braid, hung loose and wavy past her shoulders. She looked, Quin thought, like a gracefully aging hippie.

"This lasagna will cure everything from menstrual cramps to stage fright, hon," Rose was saying as she popped open the oven and brought out a tray. "I make the best lasagna outside Italy." The cats were sitting patiently at Rose's feet, watching her, as she set down the steaming tray.

"So who're your friends, Rose?"

"The calico is Tracy and the white Persian is Hepburn. They're the two who accompanied me from California. In the beginning, they weren't crazy about being cooped up in here all the time. But after I explained the realities of Miami Beach to them, they decided they liked the retiree life."

A small black-and-white TV sat on top of the refrigerator. On the screen, Julia Child was up to her elbows in dough as she chatted away. "I got this lasagna recipe from *that* woman," Rose explained, nodding her head toward the television. She scooped portions of the lasagna into the cats' bowls and set them on the floor, then brought the tray over to the table. There was also a salad with everything but anchovies, hot Italian bread, a bottle of wine.

Rose chattered about the man they'd hired to replace Lenny Moorhouse, talked about stocks, the film, books, movies. Her thoughts roamed, her mouth followed. Now that she was here, Quin wasn't sure where or how to begin. So over coffee, she just jumped in.

The story rolled out into the lingering aromas of melted cheese and pasta. Rose simply folded her hands on the tabletop, rings gleaming on six of her ten fingers, and listened. When Quin was finished explaining everything, Rose shook her head. "You know, I've always said that the problem with this business is that you never know for sure when your friends are acting." She reached into her pocket and withdrew a piece of folded paper. "Speaking of the I Ching, I found this under my front door this morning."

Chien/The Arousing

> When a man has learned within his heart what fear and trembling mean, he is safeguarded against any terror produced by outside influences. . . . He remains so composed and reverent in spirit that the sacrificial rite is not interrupted.

Instead of one changing line, however, there were three—in the first, second, and sixth places, marked by an X and two circles. Quin brought out the I Ching book and Rose got a pad and pencil. She figured that the new hexagram would be based on the changing lines.

"Before Completion," Rose said. "The last hexagram in the book, number sixty-four. I certainly don't like the sound of *that*. But what changing lines will there be in Before Completion?"

"I don't know. C'mon, let's do the dishes and drive over to the station."

"I knew there was something off about you, Quin," Rose commented as they cleared the table. "But I just couldn't quite put it together."

That was it, Quin thought. That was what had been bothering her, that someone had *put something together*. "Rose, what's my name? I mean, what name do you know me by?"

"Huh?"

"My name, what's my name?"

"Quin. Quin St. James. I mean—"

"Exactly. Quin St. James." She set the dishes in the sink, plucked her note from her purse, and held it up so Rose could see the name on the envelope. QUIN MCCLEARY. The killer had figured out who she was.

Twenty-four

KRANISH WISHED MCCLEARY would just say it, whatever it was. They'd been sitting in the hotel dining room since 10:30, hot light streaming through the picture window, splashing across the table, glinting off the silverware, and this *thing* he had to say was stalled between them.

But maybe it wasn't McCleary at all. Maybe it was his own guilt that stood between them, his need to confess what had happened last night. *It was an accident, Mac. Really. I blacked out, and when I came to I . . .*

Yeah, sure. Right. *I was scared shitless, man, so I wrapped her body in a sheet and rolled her into Biscayne Bay.* He and Dina had swept through the houseboat like those old Mr. Clean commercials, and then they'd driven back here, to the Prince Hotel. She'd gone to her room and he'd gone to his, and the only time he'd slept, he'd dreamed of Pam Spenser and Big Jim. *The past is never past:* Spin Weaver, yes, thank you very much, Spin.

Jesus.

Kranish blinked and slipped on his sunglasses. The light was too bright. McCleary was saying something to him. He stared at McCleary's mouth, clutched at the words, willed them to have sound. ". . . I got something in the mail yesterday, Gill, and I'm not sure how or if it fits into the murders. I think you should take a look at it."

"Another note?"

"Uh, no, not exactly." McCleary reached into his brief-case. He set a videotape on the table. "This."

224

"Of *Moorhouse?* Is that what this is?"

"No. Not Moorhouse."

"There's a VCR in my office." He stood, scribbled his name across the bottom of the bill, added a twenty percent tip, and they left.

Dina was typing at her desk when they entered the office. Kranish hadn't seen her since they'd returned to the hotel last night, and the sight of her was like a hot poker in his chest. The sound of her voice as she greeted them triggered a quick flash of memories: Dina helping him roll the body into the bay, Dina sobbing, "We can't go to the police," the sour taste of his own panic. But she smiled at him, at McCleary, smiled as if her life were sailing as serene as a swan in waters that had never known darkness. *It's going to be okay,* he told himself. *Everything will be fine. Lynette the Stew will just be another statistic.*

"How about some coffee, Mac?"

"Thanks, I'd love some."

"Go in and make yourself comfortable. I'll get the coffee."

McCleary went into the office, and when Kranish turned around, everything about Dina had changed. Her shoulders tensed, her fingers absently and quickly stroked the stupid ceramic koala bear on her desk, her mouth twitched, her eyes shouted: *What's McCleary doing here? Did you tell him? Did you did you did you. . . .*

"I'll get the coffee," she murmured, rising so quickly she knocked some papers to the floor. They crouched at the same time to retrieve them, and Kranish touched her hand. She yanked her arm back as though his skin had burned her. "Did you tell him?" she hissed. "Did you, Gill? Jesus, I can't believe you would do—"

He took her roughly by the shoulders and urged her out into the hall, pinning her against the wall. He gripped her shoulders. "Calm down, Dina. I haven't said anything, I don't intend to say anything. He's got some stuff about the case he wants to discuss with me, that's all, okay?"

Her eyes filled with tears, and she nodded mutely. "The . . . the body was discovered. I heard it on the news, Gill. I'm afraid, I—"

"Stop it."

"I . . . I . . . I . . ." She sniffled. Ran her hand across her nose. "I'm okay."

Kranish let go of her. Neither of them moved. For a distended, uncomfortable moment, they stared at each other. Her lower lip quivered. The green of her eyes was as pale as old celery, light from the fire exit to his left limned the curve of her chin. *Distrust, suspicion, and murder, that's what we're made of, you and me.* It was a dim, almost lazy thought, tapping the edge of his mind like a cloud. And with it came his utter certainty that she believed he had killed Domer and Moorhouse, that he was sabotaging his own film.

You'll betray me in the end, won't you, Dina?

He stepped away from her. "McCleary takes his coffee with cream." His voice was quiet, hoarse. Her head bobbed, just once, and he walked away from her, fear spreading through his bones, rumbling in his blood like the hooves of a dozen horses pounding across the Great Hunger Desert.

He smiled as he stepped into the office and closed the door. McCleary was sitting on the couch, looking nervous and ill at ease. The tape, Kranish noticed, was already in the machine. He switched it on. The skin across his forehead tightened. He stood there, feet rooted to the floor, watching himself and Domer with Maia Fox. A bright white ball of panic swelled behind his eyes. *How? How did someone get ahold of this? Isn't it upstairs, in the collection? Isn't it . . . Oh Jesus.*

He reached out and turned the machine off. He was aware of the brittle silence in the room, the wall of sweat that sprang across the forest of his skin, the stiffness in his legs as he walked across the room. He sank into the chair behind his desk and only then did he glance at McCleary.

The expression on his face reminded Kranish of how McCleary had looked that day he'd untied him from the tree, after Big Jim and his boys had left: distress, confusion, anger. The difference, though, was that more than twenty years lay between then and now, and the emotions were stronger, bolder, almost colorful.

Sorry, Mac, but I'm not who you think I am. "What do you want me to say?" Kranish asked finally.

McCleary looked down at his hands, rubbed them together, stood, ran a hand over his hair. He paced restlessly around the room, hands in his pockets. "For starters, you can answer a couple of questions, Gill. Is it your film? Did Maia and Domer have copies? Who else might've had copies?"

Kranish dry-washed his face with his hands. "Yes, it's my film, and no, to my knowledge neither Domer nor Maia ever had copies of it. As far as I know, that's the only copy."

"Did you keep it at your place in L.A.?"

There was a knock at the door and Dina came in with their coffee. She set the mugs down on the coffee table. "Mike, Quin just called. You're supposed to get in touch with her at the station."

"Okay, thanks, Dina."

Her eyes darted to Kranish. "Gill, I'm going to get a bite to eat."

"Downstairs?"

She nodded. He said he would join her when he and McCleary had finished. Her smile was thin, rueful, and she left as quietly as a geisha, closing the door behind her.

Kranish sipped at his coffee.

McCleary asked, "When was the tape filmed?"

"Not long after we'd scouted locations for *Night Flames*. It was made in L.A."

"And you kept it in L.A.?"

"It was here. In my suite. I brought it with me." Jesus,

why was it so hot in the room? Had Dina turned off the air-conditioning? Why was he having so much trouble getting the words out?

"Any particular reason?"

"Reason?" His look was as blank as glass.

"Yeah, any particular reason you brought the tape here?"

Kranish got up, walked over to the bookcase, opened a cabinet beneath the shelves. He brought out a bottle of Kahlua and splashed a generous amount in his coffee. "You want some?"

"No."

McCleary's clipped response struck Kranish as sanctimonious, judgmental. It pissed him off. He slammed the cabinet doors shut and leaned against the bookcase. "You want answers? Fine, I'll give you answers. But don't give me this provincial moralizing shit, Mike."

McCleary had been staring into his mug, and now he lifted his eyes slowly. Kranish felt the hairs rising at the back of his neck. "Let's get something straight, Gill. *You* hired *me* to investigate a murder. I assumed you had enough sense to realize that I can't operate in a vacuum. I need information. *Accurate* information. Now, if you don't think you can provide it, if there are things you need to withhold, then fine. Get yourself another investigator because, frankly, I don't need fucking surprises like this."

He stood and walked over to the VCR, popped the tape out of the machine, dropped it on Kranish's desk. "When you make up your mind, let me know."

He started for the door. Kranish almost shouted, *No one walks out on me, no one, you asshole.* But the crushing past of a thirty-five-year friendship shoved him forward, killing the shout. His hand fell on McCleary's shoulder. "Wait, Mike. Hold on. Okay. I apologize."

McCleary turned around. "Then I need the truth, Gill. If the killer thought this tape was important enough to

228

send to me, then I need to know why. You're the only one who can provide information that might tell us why."

"Right. I understand." He gulped at the rest of his coffee. The Kahlua in it burned his stomach. "I brought the tape with me here because . . ." *Why? Why do you travel with your skin tapes, Gill? Huh? Gimme one good reason.*

"I mean, the tape is part of a collection. My collection."

He saw a flicker of something in McCleary's eyes, but couldn't decipher it.

Kranish paced back across the room. "There are probably fifty tapes, maybe more. I usually bring a selection along with me when I'm on location."

McCleary was leaning against the door, hands in his pockets, when Kranish turned around. "I don't give a shit how many tapes there are, Gill. I want to know who's in them. Who besides Maia and Domer? Did the people involved always know about the camera? I mean, was the camera always there in full view?"

"No."

"No," McCleary repeated. "Okay, no, what? Elaborate."

Kranish pressed his back against the bookcase again. His head was beginning to ache. He felt nauseous. He kept seeing the body rolling, rolling, rolling into the bay. McCleary came over to him. "Gill, the motive for what happened to Domer and Moorhouse may lie with these tapes. If you want to see *Night Flames* completed, if you want to see your masterpiece on the tube, Gill, then tell me what I need to know."

Kranish turned away, brought out the Kahlua, filled his mug to the brim. "Except with Maia and a few other women whom I haven't seen in years, the camera is always hidden." In the mug, he imagined the dark lens of the camera staring up at him, recording, whirring away.

"Do you have a tape with Irene on it?"

"Yes. Maia, Irene, Dina, Lee Ling."

"What men besides Domer?"

"None here in town."

"What other women?"

"Women in L.A. The women I mentioned are the only ones who're here in Miami."

"Is it your camera?"

"Yes."

"Did you install it yourself?"

"Yes."

"Who else knows about these tapes?"

"Jesus, Mike, I don't know. I mean, there are some tapes that just have women on them, and once in a while, some of us guys get together and—"

"Who, Gill. Give me names of people who know you have the tapes and travel with them."

Kranish gulped again at the Kahlua. "Well, Patty Cakes and Greg Hess have both seen some of the tapes, but I doubt if they know I travel with them."

"But neither of them have been involved?"

"No."

"Isn't it possible people might know about the tapes through rumors?"

"Of course it's possible. This business thrives on rumors, on gossip."

"Did you know a tape was missing?"

"No."

"Do you have the only key to your suite?"

"Yes."

"How many suites are there on the top floor?"

"Three. One at either end of the hall and another in the middle. Mine's a corner penthouse."

McCleary was moving around the room now, restless as a ghost. "So it's possible someone could've gotten in without being seen." He stopped. "I'd like to take a look at the suite, Gill."

"Okay." He drained the remaining Kahlua. Pain now spanned his head from temple to temple like a bridge. His eyes felt raw. He locked the office and they went upstairs.

230

McCleary moved around the front room in the penthouse like a thief, noting the placement of objects, the type of lock on the porch doors, testing the lock on the front door, examining it. He paused in front of the VCR, his gaze sweeping across the shelves of videotapes. "These are all your collection?"

"No. Some are just films—stuff that was shown in theaters, other stuff that ran only on television."

"But the tape of Maia and Domer was in here?"

"Yes." Kranish plucked out a tape. "They're dated." He pointed at the white tag.

"This is dated several days ago."

Kranish almost laughed. Of all the tapes he could've chosen, he'd picked the one of Dina and Lee Ling from the other night. "Yes." He slipped it back in its slot.

"I'd like to see the camera."

"In here."

They walked into the bedroom. The blinds and curtains were drawn, the bed was unmade, the sheets twisted. Kranish turned on the lights. He was so nauseous now, he felt like he was going to throw up.

"You don't get room service?" McCleary asked.

"Not unless I'm here. Then I call housekeeping and they come up and clean." He stopped in front of a potted plant. The rubber tree had thick, glistening leaves that brushed the ceiling. He parted the leaves with his hands, and the lens of the camera poked through like a dog's nose.

McCleary nodded and walked out. Kranish glanced at the satin sheets. As tangled and twisted as they were, he was tempted to lie down, close his eyes, pull the cool sheet up over his head, and pretend that last night hadn't happened. But he knew that the moment he shut his eyes, he would see the woman's body again. He would see it rolling, rolling. . . .

He fixed the leaves and returned to the front room. McCleary was standing at the porch doors, hands deep in his pockets as he gazed out at the ocean. Kranish had a sudden image of a younger McCleary dribbling across a basketball court as feet pounded in the stands and people cheered him on. Then the ball flew out of his hands and dropped through the basket for the final, winning point in the game and the gymnasium exploded. He thought of how his own heart had burst with pride.

"It changes things, doesn't it, Mac? I mean, with us. With our friendship."

"Nothing will do that." He said this quietly, but Kranish thought it lacked conviction. Then McCleary turned around, and when he spoke, his voice was as dark and hard as his eyes. "Gill, if you wanted to fuck monkeys, that would be your business. The problem is that now every time you tell me something, I'm going to wonder what you *aren't* telling me."

"What else do you want to know?"

"A couple of things. The scriptwriter for *Night Flames*, Hannah Davidson. Tell me about her. Spin is *your* creation, so how come her name's on the script?"

"Because I hired her to write it. Why? What's she got to do with—"

"I don't know. Maybe nothing. Just bear with me, okay? Where did she get the story?"

Kranish knew what McCleary was driving at, and in his head he heard Spin whisper: *the past is never past.* "Where does any writer get stories? Out of her head, I guess. I read the script and I loved it."

"Did you give her guidelines?"

"Sure. I had some ideas and we discussed them and she gave me her input and we talked some more and then she wrote the script. She knew the characters. And since this will be the first time Spin's been on television and the first time Will Clarke appears as Spin, I wanted fresh writing. She provided it."

"I'd like to talk to her."

"Fine, I'll give you her number in L.A. I don't know if she's there, but you can try it. Why do you want to talk to her?"

"Well, it occurred to me that maybe part of the reason someone is sabotaging this film is because there's something in it the person doesn't want to come out. It might be why the script was stolen. The guy who broke into the motor home that day and knocked out Quin is a PI named Charlie Roberts. A man named Everett Winthrop hired him. I don't know who Winthrop is yet, but we're running a check on him. At this point, I want to have all the bases covered, Gill."

Then ask me about my blackouts, Mac. Ask me if I can remember what I was doing when Domer was torched. Ask me if I sabotaged the Maserati. Ask me, Jesus, just ask and I'll tell you how my mind shuts down, how . . .

He turned away and scribbled Hannah's phone number on a scrap of paper. His fingers were so rigid the tendons ached. His head was pounding now; the vision in his right eye was going fuzzy. He handed the number to McCleary. "Anything else?"

"One more thing. Are all the tapes as, uh, graphic as the one that was mailed to me? Are people's faces always visible?"

"Yes, most of the time. If you think there's anything you can glean from them, Mike, then take them."

McCleary looked acutely embarrassed. "I don't need to see them. But if I were you, I'd put them in a safe-deposit box or something, Gill. Next time someone might decide to blackmail you."

Kranish walked McCleary to the door. The air seemed weighted, oppressive. He dug into his child self, looking for some event in the past that he could mention, that they could laugh about, an event that, in remembering, would bind them again. But the only thing that came to mind was the day of Big Jim, the goddamn day his heart had frozen.

"I'll be in touch, Gill."

"Right. Thanks."

Then McCleary walked into the hall and Kranish closed the door, leaning into it, his eyes squeezed shut as he fought back the flares of pain in his head. He didn't hear McCleary's footsteps receding down the hall. Kranish knew McCleary was standing there, staring at the floor, his shoulders stooping beneath the weight of thirty-five years.

Twenty-five

1.

As MCCLEARY BEGAN his four-mile run Monday morning, he felt like a rat in a dead-end alley. None of his leads was panning out. No one answered at Hannah Davidson's number. Benson had been unable to turn up a shred of information on Everett Winthrop. The computer analysis of the various possibilities of I Ching hexagrams wasn't much help because they didn't really know what they were looking for. The tail on Irene Bedford had nothing to report. *Zip, zero, nada.*

The notes Quin and Rose had received had prompted Benson to assign one of his men to act as a bodyguard when they were on the set and another guy who would do nothing but keep watch on the Atlantic Towers. McCleary, feeling out of sorts after his meeting with Kranish, had overreacted to the notes. He'd demanded—not suggested—that Quin drop out of the case. Their subsequent argument had probably been the most intense—and briefest—of their marriage. She'd simply looked at him as if he'd lost his mind and told him she was sick to death of his being a bossy cop and she was staying with the case, seeing it through, and that was that.

As McCleary jogged through the park, the trees opened up in a V that filled with the cerulean blue of a flawless sky. Some of his miasma bled away, and he felt less trapped. Always, in the past, when he'd reached what he believed was a dead end in a case, something had broken. One of those blind alleys had developed fissures, then gaping holes, and surrendered its secrets. It would happen with this case, too, he was sure of it. The question was when. The question was whether it would happen before or after an attempt had been made on Quin's life.

Why'd she have to be so pigheaded about everything, anyway?

He emerged from the park and started the last mile toward home, mentally composing his list of things to do today. He would call the Screenwriters' Guild to get the name of Hannah Davidson's agent. Maybe he or she would have a forwarding number for her. He would give Joe Bean a call and see if there was any news on Charlie Roberts. And at some point today, he would do something for himself. He would drive out to the computer store and find out where the firm stood on the credit approval for the new equipment.

(feel better now, mccleary?)

Yes, but not because of anything you did for me, Miami.

(bitch, bitch, bitch)

As McCleary pounded down the street toward the house, the heat riding his shoulders like an albatross, he saw Bean's black Datsun 240Z in the driveway. He was sitting on the front steps, a red baseball cap pulled low over his eyes. He flipped up the tongue and grinned at McCleary.

"Look at you, white boy. Youse must be de only honkie out runnin' in dat dere heat, and nows you jus' drippin' wid sweat and all . . . Jee-zuz."

McCleary laughed and whipped his towel off the railing, where it was draped, and wiped his face with it. He was too winded to say anything except, "Water."

"Bet yo ass you needs water, honkie. Dat and some sense'll save yo soul."

McCleary unlocked the door and Bean followed him into the kitchen, clucking his tongue as McCleary tipped the pitcher to his mouth and drank. "Don't tell Quin I just did that, Bean. Hey, put on some coffee while I take a quick shower, then I'll fix you some breakfast."

"Hurry, my man. You're gonna love the stories I got for you on Charlie Roberts."

Over a breakfast of omelets and cinnamon toast, Bean told McCleary about his twenty-four-hour watch on Roberts. When he'd arrived at Roberts' place early Sunday morning, the El Dorado was parked where it had been Saturday night.

"So I parked under the banyan again and waited. Charlie and his woman came out after a bit—she was late again—and I followed. They go for breakfast at the Hilton. They go to church." He laughed. "Charlie Roberts in church. Christ. I nearly puked. Then they drive out to Kendall, to this little concrete house, and I gather it's the woman's parents' place, because this older couple comes out and the woman says, 'Mama,' and there's a lot of hugging and kissing.

"Okay, so they stay there, have lunch. Then they go home and play a couple sets of tennis. Then Charlie's inside for maybe forty minutes and I suddenly see him barrel outa the house like his ass is on fire. He leaps in the Caddy and I followed him to the Sanctuary, in Boca Raton."

McCleary sat forward. "That's where Everett Winthrop lives."

"You got that right, Mac. Ever seen that place? Now let me tell you, that is WASP country. There's an eight-foot wall around the development and a very unpleasant guard at the gate. But I waited until surfer boy had driven on through, then I drove up to the guardhouse, and this man struts out and sees that I am *not* a WASP.

"I told him I was with the man in the El Dorado. 'Sure, pal, and what might that man's name be, anyhoo?' he says. So I told him. He gets all polite and says he'll have to call ahead to see if Mr. Winthrop's expecting me.

" 'Winthrop?' I say. 'Charlie said we were going to see a man about an investment. Who's Winthrop?' The guard chuckles and rolls forward onto the balls of his feet, you know, and tells me that Mr. Everett Winthrop is *only* vice-prez in charge of investments at Coast Bank. Then he dials Winthrop's number and I give him a fake name. He struts back all nasty again and says Winthrop's never heard of me.''

McCleary laughed. "You're brilliant, Bean."

"There wasn't anyplace to wait around, so I drove back to Charlie's place. He got home around seven. He and the missy left later and had dinner at the Café de Paris in Lauderdale. Then they went dancing and got home around one-thirty."

"Who's on now?"

"Rusty. Then my bro goes on this evening. You want us to stay on this a couple more days?"

"Yeah. But what I'd like you to do is keep an eye on Quin, Joe."

"On Quin?"

"Yeah, but don't be obvious about it," McCleary replied, and explained.

Bean left around nine and McCleary placed a call to the Screenwriters' Guild in New York. A young woman who bubbled with enthusiasm answered.

"I'm trying to locate a screenwriter named Hannah Davidson. I was wondering if you might know how I could contact her."

He swiveled his chair around and gazed out the kitchen window into the backyard.

"Has she actually sold a screenplay? We only take writers who've made at least one sale."

"Yes."

"Okay, then we'd have her *if* she's east of the Mississippi. Otherwise, she'd be registered with our West Coast office. And all that's assuming she's written for producers who're registered with the Guild."

"I don't understand."

"We have about twenty-five hundred producers who've signed with the Guild, agreeing to pay certain rates, give

238

writers credits for scripts, that kind of thing. Writers who sign with us agree not to work with independent film producers unless that producer becomes a signatory to the Guild."

"Do you have a full listing of producers who're signatories or just those on the East Coast?"

"Full listing."

"Is Gill Kranish a signatory?"

She laughed as if she thought he was joking. "You bet."

"Then I need to know if Hannah Davidson is a member of the Guild."

"Hold on."

McCleary watched Merlin out by the pool, stalking a bird. The light burned his black fur almost red.

"Sir? I don't have anything on her for the East Coast. Let me give you the number for our West Coast office."

McCleary jotted down the number and thanked her. The woman added that the Guild could give out the phone number for a client's agent, but not for the client.

"I understand. Thanks again."

A beginning, he thought. A little dent in the blind alley.

2.

Quin stood at the edge of the limestone quarry, shading her eyes against the bone white light, the heat beating at her back. As far as the eye could see, there was nothing but the white dust and sharp, jagged rocks that rose against the thin blue sky like buildings, like a city. An alien landscape, that was what it was supposed to be, and that was what it looked like.

This was the Great Hunger Desert on Alpha Centauri, the plain of death that bordered the dome of Settlers' City on the planet. This, she thought, was where Rose Leen as Joanne Corliss would meet again with Spin Weaver and hand over evidence that would incriminate her husband and his boss in the money laundering scam. Rose and Will Clarke would sit on that blinding white rock over there and she would tell him how her husband had been working with a pair of exo-drug smugglers. She would explain how the hallucinogenic was smuggled to Earth on cargo ships. Two weeks after an arrival, her husband would meet with a Centaurian who would have upwards of a million dollars in Old World cash to launder.

And Spin, of course, would be recording the information with an implanted transmitter.

"Hey, Quin, could you c'mere a second?"

She glanced back, and the Great Hunger Desert vanished. There were trees, hedges, an oasis of green. Rose was leaning out of the wardrobe motor home, her hair loose, exploding around her face and shoulders. "What's wrong?" Quin walked over to the door, where it was shaded, and pushed her sunglasses back into her hair.

"What about this outfit?" Rose asked.

She wore a silvery, short-sleeved jumpsuit with silver boots. The necklace at her throat was supposed to be the shell of a mini sand turtle from the red dunes on the other side of the planet. It was actually a chip of mother of pearl that had been shaped like a turtle's shell and dyed.

"I think you look great. What's the problem?"

Rose turned, offering a profile, and slapped her ass. "I look grotesque, that's the problem. This is all that Julia Child's pasta."

"You look terrific, really."

Quin stepped in out of the heat and was surprised to see the bodyguard, Corporal Vic James, sitting in the driver's seat. "Hi, Vic."

He glanced up from the gun magazine he was paging through. "Hi, Quin. You have a scene today?"

"Much later. I'm just hanging out. Hey, Vic. Don't you think Rose looks great?"

"Especially when you see the other choice," he replied.

Rose made a face and whipped up a red jumpsuit that looked like a clown's outfit. "Pretty gross, huh."

"Definitely. Go with silver."

"Okay." She spun. "Unzip me, Quin. I've got to get over to makeup."

Just then, Bruce Harmon stuck his head in the door. "Okay, ladies, I'm here for close-ups." His camera, perched in its usual spot on his shoulder, swung toward Rose, who was hurrying back toward the dressing room.

"Don't you *dare* get a shot of my ass, Bruce, I'll strangle you."

Harmon laughed, twisted the gold post in his ear, and set his camera on a chair as he stepped inside. He dug into his pocket. "I just came from the Prince, Quin. You're supposed to call Marielle."

"Thanks. Who gave you the message?"

"Dina. Pissed her off, too," he chuckled. "She hates acting as a receptionist for people out on the set. Then on top of it, Gill called her and asked her to drive me out here." He crooked a finger at her, motioning her outside. They stepped out into the heat again. "Listen, can I ask you a personal question?" He spoke softly and slipped on a pair of sunglasses.

"Sure."

"What's your opinion about Detective McCleary?"

He's stubborn, Bruce. And at heart he's still a bossy cop. But other than that, he's loveable. "He seems okay. Why?"

"You think he's trustworthy?"

"I guess so, but I hardly know the man." *What're you driving at?*

Harmon looked down at the ground and kicked a pebble under the motor home. "I was just wondering what you thought."

"I don't think he's a crooked cop, if that's what you're wondering."

"Uh-huh." He looked up. "Now here's a question that

my dissertation committee's going to ask, Quin. Or one like it. Let's suppose that Marilyn Monroe's biographer back in the sixties had a video camera. He knows she's been having an affair with Bobby Kennedy. He's actually filmed them together. He hasn't told anyone about it, because he figures his role is to record facts, not judge them. And besides, you're dealing with the attorney general of the U.S., not some flunky."

He shifted his weight from one foot to the other. "Now, on the night Marilyn Monroe dies, our biographer arrives at her house while someone's visiting her. He hangs around outside, waiting for the person to split, then decides to sneak around the house to see what's going on. What he sees is a murder involving a guy he *knows* works for Bobby Kennedy. Now. His ethical dilemma is this. Does he report the murder? Does he just turn in his tape anonymously? Does he say nothing to save his own ass? What?"

"He goes to the cops."

Harmon held up a finger. "Ah, but wait, Quin. We're talking attorney general, okay? We're talking cover-up. People have been known to disappear when they mess around with government stuff like that."

"Yeah, you've got a point, but I still think he should go to the police. I mean, what the hell would've happened if Bernstein and Woodward hadn't taken a risk?"

"True, yeah, that's true." He rubbed his jaw. "I've got two bastards on my dissertation committee who can't stand me. It's the pits, I'm telling you."

Rose whisked past them, en route to makeup, and followed by the corporal. Harmon stared after them for a moment. "I should catch Rose getting made up." He stepped quickly past Quin and retrieved his camera. "Thanks for your opinion, Quin. I appreciate it." Then he dashed off through the white light. She squinted as she watched him, as his dark shaped receded against the horizon, and wondered what Harmon was keeping to himself.

"Ellie? It's Quin. I got a message that you'd called."

Quin stood outside a small roadside store, five miles from the set. It was a square concrete block building with graffiti scrawled across the sides and dirty front windows plastered with sales posters. To Quin's left, hugging the graffiti, was a rusted garbage can brimming with refuse. Flies buzzed around it. This was no-man's-land at the western end of the county: a two-lane road, a burned citrus grove across from her, a pair of buzzards circling low in the distance. It might've been Africa. Or another part of Alpha Centauri.

"I kept calling your place at the Towers, Quin, and you were never there, so I thought I'd go through the Prince. I hope it's okay."

"Sure. No problem. What'd you find out?"

"I hit pay dirt, kiddo. It really took some digging, but I've got something on Pam Spenser, that woman who was in the gossip-column picture with Gill. She was a reporter. Listen to this. It's from an article dated ten years ago." And she began to read: " 'On the morning of what would have been her twenty-sixth birthday, the body of *Herald* reporter Pam Spenser was pulled from a Davie canal. She had been raped, tortured, and shot.

" 'Spenser, who took a leave of absence from the *Herald* four months ago to investigate what she once referred to as the biggest story she'd ever tackled, was last seen at a country-western bar in Davie three days earlier. She was reported missing by reporter Pepe Moreno.

" 'Editor Howard Fast said Spenser requested a leave of absence because she was having family problems. Moreno, however, contended she was on leave so she could investigate a story. He declined to elaborate.

" 'Investigators are considering the possibility that Spenser's death is linked to several other murders. Homicide Detective Abel Laxton said this department is pursuing several leads related to serial murders.

" 'Serial killers usually kill randomly, senselessly, and

with extraordinary violence. Torture, mutilation, and sexual assaults characterize the acts. "There are," he said, "murders elsewhere in this country with a similar M.O. to the Spenser homicide, and the department is checking them all." ' "

Marielle paused. "Spenser was survived by her parents and a sister."

Quin's ears drummed, her hands slipped the length of the receiver. She fumbled in her purse for a pen and paper. "Give me the reporter's name again and the detective."

"Pepe Moreno is the reporter. Abel Laxton's the detective."

"Anything else?"

Marielle laughed. "You mean that's not enough?"

"No. It's great. It's perfect. I can't thank you enough, Ellie."

"I'll drop this stuff by your place this afternoon or tonight."

"Right. Thanks."

They rang off and Quin stood in the heat, blinking, staring at the two names on the paper. Then she called McCleary—first at home, where she got a recording of her own voice, then at the office. Ruth said he wasn't in. Quin could hear the drone of her television in the background.

"Then I'd like to leave a message, Ruth."

"Sure thing, hon. What is it?"

"Ask what he found out about a woman named Pam Spenser."

"Look, if it's real important, let me just beep him. Give me your number so he can call you back."

Quin did, then stepped under the awning to wait. The heat struck the white concrete walk, the burned fields across the road, and had bleached the color from the sky. She would roast here. They would find her charred remains out back, where the dust had blown them.

A battered van with fading red paint pulled up in front

of the store and three guys hopped out. One of them, a tall, burly fellow with a hirsute chest and a tattoo on his arm, sauntered over to the phone. He gave Quin the once-over, then picked up the receiver.

"Could you make it quick?" she asked. "I'm expecting a call."

He glanced around, his eyes sliding from her face to her feet, then fastening on her breasts as he grinned. "Quick? You want it quick? Sure, baby, I'll do it quick." His grin widened.

Great, wonderful, how could she be so lucky? She was waiting for a simple phone call and some goddamn hick comes along who now had a bulge in his pants, who was stepping toward her, leering. Quin sidestepped, closer to the door of the store. The hick loved it. He hung up the phone and jammed his fingers in the waistband of his jeans and moved toward her again.

"If you come one step closer, I'm going to scream. And I have a very loud voice." She dipped her hand into her purse.

"Now, honey, you just go right 'head and scream, 'cause that's what I'm gonna make you do, anyway. Scream. What you got in that little ole purse there, hmm?"

She drew her gun, and the hick blanched, and then he laughed nervously, as if he were trying to make up his mind whether she was serious or not. "Now, honey, why don't you jus' put that thing away 'fore you hurt someone." He patted the air with his hands, but he didn't step any closer.

Her thumb knocked the safety off. *Hey, kid, this isn't Cagney and Lacey, Miami Vice, Magnum, P.I., The Equalizer.*

"And why don't you just move your ass toward your van and get inside and close the door, friend."

He backed away. He stepped down into the road. Then he turned and hurried to the van, and a moment later his two friends came out, laughing, loaded down with beer. They got in the van and drove away, and only then did Quin begin to tremble. She returned the gun to her purse and walked over to the phone and leaned against it, so she could watch the road.

C'mon, Mac, hurry up.

Suppose the van suddenly swerved back and the three guys jumped out of the van? Suppose—

The phone rang. She grabbed it. McCleary said, "Quin?" The sound of his voice was an anodyne. "Ruth gave me your message. I never got a chance to ask Gill about that photo of him and Pam Spenser."

"Well, either you should or I will. But I think it should come from you, Mac," she said, and told him what Marielle had reported. Her eyes kept sweeping the road like radar, waiting for a sight of the van. There were only fields of quavering heat. She heard voices and noise in the background when she'd finished. "Where are you, anyway?"

"In the mall. About to check on our computers. Look, there've been some developments on this end, too. I'll stop by the Prince later to talk to Gill, then give you a call at the Towers. Maybe we can have dinner or something, okay?"

"Okay." She paused, ran the back of her hand across her forehead, wiping away perspiration. "Mac? I'm, uh, sorry I got so mad last night. When you suggested dropping the case. I'm sorry I called you a bossy cop."

He laughed, one of his low, husky laughs that brought goosebumps to her skin. "You were right."

"Friends?"

"Friends."

"I love you," she said, and hung up.

She walked quickly back to her car. Inside, she locked the doors, turned on the engine, and let the cool air blow directly into her face. Suppose she hadn't been armed? What then? Would the hick have dragged her back behind the garbage cans and raped her? Would he have called his friends? Would they have taken turns? Did she

246

emit some sort of scent that attracted incidents like this? Was it possible?

There was something intrinsically wrong when you had to resort to pulling a gun like a vigilante because some hick figured he'd get himself a piece while he stopped at the general store. Or when you had to dig ten years into the past to find a bit of information about the man who hired you that he should've told you to begin with. Or when you had to work out your differences with your husband over the phone. It meant she wasn't perceiving things clearly.

Twenty-six

MCCLEARY DISLIKED MALLS. They made him feel as if he were living in a closed environment on another planet. *On Alpha Centauri with Spin.* The air always smelled slightly stale, the plants looked etiolated, the tips of their leaves dried, bleached of color, and you could never tell from the light what time or season it was.

He hurried into the computer store, and Zack, the salesman who'd taken his order a week ago, saw him and nodded. "Mr. McCleary, I was just about to call you."

The forced smile, McCleary thought, betrayed him. It said, *Hey, buddy, I got bad news.* "We were denied the credit?"

Zack's smile flattened out like a hyphen. "They turned you down flat. Sorry."

"Who're *they?*"

Zack brought out a file, flipped it once. "The company checks people out through the credit bureau, and if they're approved, then the money comes down through Lincoln Bank in Maryland." He turned the file so McCleary could see it. "We received this on the computer this morning."

There was a brief note saying he was entitled to an explanation about the credit denial. The reasons were simple enough—a fifteen-to-thirty-day late payment on the firm mortgage within the last year and an outstanding payment on his VISA charge card.

The reasons were simple, yeah, but wrong. "I've never made a late payment on anything in my life."

Zack shrugged, as if to say there was nothing he could

do about it, that he did, in fact, hear denials from customers every day about their sins of omission. "Are your name, address, and Social Security number correct?"

"Yes, but nothing else is."

An awkward silence ensued in which McCleary stared at the credit sheet and Zack stared at him. "Look, Mr. McCleary. Sometimes there are computer foul-ups. I'll give you the number for the credit bureau we use and the name of my contact. Maybe he can help you out. Tell him you want the dates of these late payments. Then get in touch with the bank involved and take your canceled checks with you to prove their information is wrong. Make a stink."

"I intend to."

Zack, a consumer himself, smiled grandly. "Good." He handed McCleary a business card. "Here's the name of the guy I deal with. If you get the thing straightened out, give me a call."

As soon as McCleary left the store, he returned to the pay phone from which he'd called Quin. He dialed the credit bureau number. He asked for Bill Penn, was put on hold, tapped his fingers through the end of a song by Stevie Winwood, and into an instrumental by Chuck Mangione. Then a woman got on and asked who he was holding for. He told her. He was put on hold again. This time, the D.J. gave away $500 to a faithful listener. In the middle of the woman's shrieks, a voice said, "This is Bill Penn."

McCleary, praying for patience, carefully explained who he was and what he wanted, and Penn was actually cordial. "Let me call up your file, Mr. McCleary. I need your Social Security number, and spell your last name for me."

McCleary complied.

"Just a second." He wasn't put on hold. "Okay, let's see here. The firm's mortgage payment to Coast Bank was due August thirtieth and hasn't been received. The VISA payment due on September fifth hasn't yet been paid. I hope that helps."

"Where does your information come from, Mr. Penn?"

"We go through a central credit computer."

"And where does *their* information come from?"

"Ultimately, from the banks and credit card companies."

There was a finality about that word, *Ultimately*, that McCleary disliked.

"If you think the information's incorrect, then drop us a line. But I'd suggest you go directly to the agencies involved to straighten it out. Pretend they're the IRS. Go armed with proof."

Proof, evidence, lies. "Right," he muttered, and thanked Penn and hung up.

Half an hour later, McCleary was going through their bank statements while Merlin, paws curled over the edge of the desk, watched him. He found the August statement, but the checks written in the later half of the month—including the firm's mortgage payment and the VISA payment—weren't there. They would probably be with September's statement, which hadn't arrived yet.

He went into the kitchen with the bank statements, pulled the phone over to the butcher block table, and sat down. He dialed Coast Bank and gazed out the window into the yard. The blue of the pool reflected the sky, a plateau of clouds and the tips of the swaying pines. Birds fluttered around the feeder he'd filled with seed. Merlin, crouched in the windowsill now, watched the birds and opened his mouth, making odd, funny sounds, as if he were talking to them.

McCleary's gaze rose to the screen door where Kranish had stood that night. *Watching.* Kranish with his hidden video camera, *watching*.

Charlie Roberts, *watching*.

Bruce Harmon, *watching*.

And now the coincidences were stacking up, too many of them to ignore, to shuffle aside. Everett Winthrop, who'd hired Surfer Boy Roberts, was one of the vice-presidents of Coast Bank, which had fucked up his credit. Ten years ago, a female reporter named Pam Spenser had been murdered while investigating a story, and Kranish had known her, had been photographed with her, and had never mentioned her. *Night Flames* was a twenty-first-century TV movie about a money laundering scam that smacked of real-life twentieth-century Miami in which a reporter was murdered while investigating a story.

"Bookkeeping. This is Ms. Simmons."

"When will the checking account statements for September be mailed?"

"On the twenty-fifth, sir."

"I need to know if a couple of my checks have cleared yet."

"Business or personal account, sir?"

"Both."

"If you'll give me the account numbers, sir, I'll check for you."

He gave her the account numbers and floated off into the netherworld of *Hold*. When Ms. Simmons returned, she said: "Your name, sir?"

This was the *who are you?* game. "Mike McCleary. It's a joint account with my wife, Quin St. James."

"Which checks would you like to know about, sir?"

"A check written to Coast for a mortgage payment on August twenty-sixth, and a VISA card payment written on September first."

"I'm checking. . . . No, I don't see any of those payments listed here, Mr. McCleary."

"Look, they've got to be there."

"Did you mail them locally?"

No, from China. "Yes. The August payment was mailed the same day it was written—the twenty-sixth—and the VISA bill was paid in person."

"Well, sometimes they don't appear on the computer right away. Let me look for the actual checks. Just a second."

Three minutes passed. Four. Five. Merlin lifted up, arched his back, and leaped down from the desk. A full eight minutes later, Ms. Simmons returned. "I'm sorry,

Mr. McCleary. I haven't found them. Perhaps if you contacted the postal service."

"What about the September payment? There should be a copy of *that* check, since I paid it there, at the teller's window."

"I'm sorry, sir, I—"

"I'd like to speak with the supervisor."

Her sweetness soured. He could almost see her smile sucked into darkness. "I *am* the supervisor."

"Of what?"

"Bookkeeping."

"Who's above you?"

"Sir . . ."

He lost his temper then. "Look here. Today is September twentieth. The August payment was made almost a month ago. It should've appeared on the computer by now. And the other payment—"

"Just a minute and I'll connect you with Mrs. Crenshaw. She's *my* supervisor."

Mrs. Crenshaw, however, didn't want to discuss it over the phone. She suggested McCleary come in with his checkbook. "I'll be there in ten minutes," he said, and hung up.

When McCleary saw Mrs. Crenshaw's mouth, he knew he was in trouble. It was a militant mouth, all work, no play, crack the whip, we ain't got all day. That kind of mouth. He went through his explanation, including the event that had prompted his request in the first place. He could see immediately that as far as Mrs. Crenshaw was concerned, refusal of credit reduced a human being to something barely above plant life.

Her response was firm: "I'll have to look into it."

"Fine. I'll wait."

Her mouth twitched into a half smile, a smirk. "I'm afraid that's impossible, Mr. McCleary, since we're closing in"—she consulted her watch—"twenty minutes. It'll take me more than that to look into this."

"You close at two?"

"In here we do. The electronic service is open twenty-four hours, of course. You'll have to come back tomorrow."

"Tomorrow."

"Right."

"I'd like the name of your supervisor."

"Above me, Mr. McCleary, are four vice-presidents, the president, and the chairman of the board."

"Fine, I'd like to see Everett Winthrop."

Another self-satisfied smirk, then: "They've all left for the day."

"What time do you open?"

"Nine."

He stood. "Will Mr. Winthrop be here then?"

"I don't keep tabs on Mr. Winthrop, but I believe he may be out of town."

"We'll see. I'll be back at nine."

He was so thoroughly infuriated when he left the bank that he spent several moments in Lady doing nothing at all except thinking about Mrs. Crenshaw's mouth and blaspheming Miami, its banks and clerks, its supervisors. Then he drove across the street to a Rexall Drugs and from the phone booth called Benson's office.

He was out.

He called the lab to see if the results were in yet on Greg Hess' blood test. "Lab, Sergeant Benson."

"Hey, you're a chemist now?"

"Mac, Christ. I've been calling your office for the last hour. Ruth's been beeping you."

McCleary looked down at his belt. He'd turned the damn thing off. "What's wrong?"

"Greg Hess is a type O, and he's got *loooww* blood sugar, that's about what. He's our boy."

Twenty-seven

AND WHAT IS the cause of today's migraine, Gill? asked the
the physician in Kranish's head.

*The light of Alpha Centauri blinds. The glass of the
dome is actually a living substance, composed of thou-
sands of glow-worms. The glow strikes that white sand,
doctor, three times stronger and brighter than our sunlight
against snow.* Yes, the light. The light had plunged into
his eyes like hot daggers, and he'd taken another one of
his pills—his third already today—and it hadn't helped.
The agony had swept into his temple, a cathedral of pain,
and knocked him out flat. He'd fallen to his knees in the
dust, the body of Lynette the Stew rolling from one side
of his inner vision to the other, and they'd stopped shooting long enough to get him off the set and into a motor
home.

Now he lay in the cool dark, a cold cloth against his
head. Lee Ling had been here earlier because he'd refused to let anyone call a doctor, and she had done
something nice to his feet. He vaguely remembered Dina
fluttering around like a moth, fussing over him. Then
he'd told them both to go away and leave him alone.

"Gill?"

For a moment, he didn't know if the voice was in his
mind or real. He sat up and saw Quin ducking as she
stepped into the motor home.

"Can I get you anything?" she asked, looking down at
him.

Her face seemed far away, as if he were looking at her

254

from the wrong end of a telescope. "No, thanks. I took a couple of pills."

"How about a lunch tray? They're about ready to break. I can bring you one from the tent."

He swung his legs over the side of the couch. The pain followed. "Maybe later, Quin."

She sat down—not exactly beside him, but on the same couch. She was looking at the bucket of melted ice water into which he dipped the cloth for his head. "Gill, who's Pam Spenser?"

Something hot and sharp lanced through him. He wrung the cloth out. "A woman I knew a long time ago."

"A reporter?"

He nodded and pressed the cloth to his head, wishing she would go away, shut up, or touch him. Yes, that would be nice, to have Quin touch him. Quin who was McCleary's wife. One more depravity, he thought, and felt like weeping.

"Did you know she was killed?"

"No," he lied. "I didn't know her that long, Quin." He was glad the cloth covered his eyes. "I've got to lie down again."

"Oh, right, I'm sorry." She rose quickly. "You sure you don't want a lunch tray?"

"Yes, thanks. I'm sure." He stretched out again. He could smell the vestiges of her perfume. "Quin?"

"Yes?"

He removed the cloth from his eyes and stared at her, silhouetted against the door, tall and thin as a ballerina, her umber hair loose around her face. "I'm sorry." It was barely a whisper.

"For what?" Chilly words, stiff. They rubbed up against him, hurting.

"For . . . for . . . whatever. Whatever you think I've done, I'm sorry."

She came back across the room. Sat beside him. Gazed at him as if seeing him for the first time. She took the cloth off his head, dipped it in the water, wrung it out,

255

and placed it against his head again. When she spoke, her voice was softer. The chilliness was gone. "I resented you. I felt like you were trying to wedge between Mac and me, that you were . . ." She averted her gaze now and looked at her hands, which were in her lap. "That you were playing me, trying to get me to . . . to act on this attraction I had for you because you were envious of the relationship Mac and I have."

She stopped, raised her eyes.

Such weird blue eyes, Kranish mused. Like the eyes of the people on Dune who'd taken the spice. Eyes like that. He realized she was waiting for him to say something. "I guess maybe that's part of it. I guess maybe I wanted to know what you were about so I could understand how monogamy works." He laughed, but it was a sick, tired sound. "Ridiculous, huh, the games people play with themselves." He noticed they'd been talking in the past tense, almost as if they had once been lovers and were reviewing what had happened, what had gone wrong.

She touched his arm then.

For a moment, Kranish wanted to climb inside her eyes, nest there like a bird. "Why'd you ask about Pam Spenser, Quin?"

"Just looking for new angles, Gill, that's all." Her hand was still on his arm, and he wanted very much to kiss her, so he lifted up on an elbow, the pain clawing behind his eyes. Then she rose, quickly. "If you need anything, holler. I've got to get something to eat."

He watched the door open, and then she was gone. He lay back. He slept.

When he awakened, the pain was worse. It had oozed into his nose and lodged directly between his eyes. He slipped on his sunglasses, wincing as he sat up, and parted the curtains with his hand to gaze outside. He could see the huge lunch tent the caterer had set up. It rose from the white dust, dark as a bloodstain, billowing in the breeze like a sail.

He was hungry. Starved. He couldn't remember eating

breakfast this morning. He couldn't remember having eaten anything, in fact, since yesterday morning, when he and McCleary had been sitting in the dining room at the hotel.

He was hungry, but he didn't have the energy to get up and walk over to the tent. He stretched out again, the cold cloth over his eyes. He realized the television in the motor home was on, the sound droning like a giant mosquito. The midday news, yeah, that's what it was. Something about the body of Lynette Walleski, a United stewardess, being found in Biscayne Bay.

Kranish reached out, patting the table for the remote control box. He turned up the sound. The newscaster's voice was like a hot, dry wind. ". . . Ms. Walleski was last seen at the Poseidon Club Saturday night, in the company of an unidentified man and woman, who are believed to have been the last people who saw her alive. Sergeant Tim Benson of the Metro-Dade homicide division says police have identified the killer's blood type but are not releasing the information for security reasons."

Kranish groaned and struggled up. He'd forgotten about sperm checks. He'd forgotten about it because he'd been in the inky netherworld of a migraine, because Dina had been standing there saying, *You can't call the police, Gill.* He'd forgotten, and now they knew his blood type, they knew Lynette was last seen with a man and a woman. They knew. Jesus, they knew.

". . . If you have any information concerning Ms. Walleski's death, please call Anonymous Crime Tips at . . ." The number flashed on the screen, burning into Kranish's consciousness.

Type O, I'm a type O just like whoever torched Domer. He lay back, pain stabbing his head like a dozen needles. He slapped the cold cloth over his eyes, then sat up again, pressing it to his eyes, pressing until the pain seemed to ebb a little. *I killed the stew. Dina and I killed the stew. An accident. Anyone could see that. . . .* But

257

what about Domer? And Moorhouse? Had he killed them, too? Had he?

He would call McCleary, explain, and McCleary would buffer him from the cops.

Kranish stumbled out into the glaring light, into the oppressive air of the Great Hunger Desert. He put on his sunglasses again and tried to walk erectly toward the tent. A hot breeze spilled dust into his face, his eyes. The air smelled of despair; the air on Alpha Centauri had always smelled of despair. This planet needed Spin. Spin Weaver would set things right. Yeah, he, Gill Kranish, fucked things up, and Spin set them right.

Perspiration trickled into the collar of his shirt, and he paused in the shade of the honey wagons, staring at the names on the doors. Little box dressing rooms with a bunk, a sink, a shower. The stars got the motor homes, and everyone else got the honey wagons, except that his stars shared their privileges. They knew he expected it of them. The people who worked for him understood the rules. *Sure, Gill. They understand the rules so well that someone killed two of your actors. Someone with type O blood who . . .*

No, he wouldn't think about it. He would call McCleary from . . . there was no phone in the tent. He would have to use the phone in his car. He had parked it . . . *where?*

Kranish pushed against his temples with the heels of his hands, trying to remember. He stumbled away from the honey wagons, toward the limestone pit. Where was everyone? Had they left him here alone in the Great Hunger Desert to die? Had they been whisked back to Settlers' City on the shuttle and forgotten to wake him?

He paused at the lip of the limestone pit and peered into the abyss of light and dust. That dark smudge down there against the whiteness was his car, wasn't it? Funny, he didn't remember parking it there. Had the Mercedes been transported to the planet? Yes, he was sure it had. He was sure he'd watched it being driven into the belly of the cargo ship. And he recalled driving it. He slid down the scarp, the white sand burning his hands, heat rising from it in waves.

He stumbled across the desert, glancing about nervously for some sign of the crustaceans that gave the place its name. Crabs with a taste for human flesh. They were supposed to be nocturnal creatures, but already there had been four attacks in the last two months on people from Settlers' City. And he wasn't wearing boots. He wasn't armed. He walked a little faster toward the smudge. It began to assume a shape. His heart hammered wildly as his sneakers sank into the deadly sand. His skin was so moist the white dust clung to his arms and hands. The crabs would smell his fear and dig up through the sand, their pincers tapping, dancing. That awful sound would fill the light, a sound like a thousand castanets clicking, and the crabs would surround him, and then attack. Unless he reached his car.

Then he saw the smudge clearly, two bodies, side by side, blood blooming in the sand like flowers, and he broke into a run. The desert sucked at his feet, his head split open, he fell to his knees. The cop was lying on his side and might have been sleeping, except for the blood crusted at his throat like a necklace, and the blood darkening his shirt at the chest. His mouth was open in a silent scream.

A foot moved. Not the cop's foot, but a foot that belonged to the other body. He didn't want to look. He knew it was one of the crabs poking up through the sand to ravage the foot. Its pincers would tear at the shoe, digging down to the flesh. Its pincers would snap off toes like they were toothpicks. He tried to leap up, but he couldn't move. His muscles had frozen. His eyes roamed from the moving foot up the leg to the bloody torso. A piece of paper was pinned to the chest. His eyes skipped over it and fixed on the body's face. Rose's mouth was moving, her eyes were supplicating him, drawing him, blood bubbled over her lip.

259

Kranish scooted toward her on his knees, murmuring, "Rose, Jesus, Rose, oh God, Rose."

He lifted her head from the sand. Her eyes swarmed with pain. She coughed. Her lips moved, and Kranish leaned toward her, trying to hear what she was saying. "Oh Gill, poor Gill," she whispered.

He touched her face with his hand, brushing the white sand off her cheeks, afraid to pick her up, but wanting to hold her, rock her, absorb her pain. His eyes burned with tears, he couldn't breathe right, the heat filled his lungs like cotton.

"Hold on, Rose, just hold on, I'll get help, I'll—"

She shook her head, alarm flaring in her eyes. *No, don't leave me, please.*

So he sat there running his hand gently over her hair, leaning close to her as she tried to speak. The crabs had done this. Rose had ventured out here alone, out into the Great Hunger Desert, alone without boots or protective clothing, alone without a weapon, and she'd gotten disoriented. She clutched at his hand, her lips moving wordlessly.

"I can't hear you," he cried. "I can't hear you."

Then she murmured a word, a name, and her eyes rolled back in her head. He stared at her, shook her by the shoulders, shouted to her to wake up. The name she'd uttered banged against the walls of his skull, and the thin membrane in his mind between fiction and reality finally snapped altogether and he sat there, staring stupidly into the white light, rocking her, slowly. Slowly.

PART THREE

Final Cuts

"At the heart of detection is the art of listening."

—Spin Weaver

"I'd rather take a risk and fall flat on my face than play it safe and mediocre."

—Gill Kranish

Twenty-eight

1.

QUIN AND PATTY Cakes were strolling toward the limestone quarry as he explained how he wanted her to do her scene that afternoon. The heat and her full stomach made her drowsy, and it was difficult to concentrate on what Patty Cakes was saying. She kept thinking about Kranish, about their odd conversation. They reached the edge of the quarry and Patty Cakes stopped and pointed. "Hey, who the hell's down there?"

She peered through the brilliant light into the pit. She saw two . . . no, three people, and it looked like they were sunbathing in the quarry. She started to say something, but Patty Cakes made a strange, strangled sound and suddenly he was sliding down the sides of the quarry, slipping and sliding as if the hill were coated with Vaseline. Quin raced after him.

They tore across the sand. Dread balled like undigested food in her gullet as she neared, as she saw Kranish. He was sitting in the sand, rocking Rose, humming to himself, his sunglasses lopsided on his nose. Alongside him lay the body of Corporal Vic James, the cop assigned to guard Rose. The stench of blood, of feces and urine, had stalled in the hot air. Quin slapped her hands over her nose and mouth, then fell to her knees, staring in disbelief at Rose. An ache an ocean wide ripped through her. She blinked back tears. She reached out to touch Rose, to smooth the hair away from her face, but Kranish drew back and clutched Rose's head to his chest.

"No no no," he murmured.

"Jesus," Patty Cakes whispered. "Oh Christ. Gill?"

Kranish blinked and drew his eyes slowly, laconically toward Patty Cakes. His hands and arms and face were coated with white dust. Tears had left erratic trails through the dust. His eyes, once a wide, Pacific blue, were the color of faded jeans, and blank as eggs. "Crabs," he hissed. "The fucking crabs. She . . . she shouldn't have come without boots. I told her, Molly and I told her over and over again that you need to wear boots and protective clothing and have a laser. But she wouldn't listen. She would say, 'Oh, Spin, you worry an awful lot.'" He laughed, a soft, utterly mad laugh, and then his features seemed to shrink, to draw in on themselves, and he began to weep.

Patty Cakes glanced at Quin, alarm darkening his eyes, then back at Kranish. "C'mon, man. I'm going to help you up. Let's get you out of the sun." Patty Cakes spoke gently, quietly, and Kranish just continued to weep and pressed his cheek against the crown of Rose's head. "Just put her head down carefully, Spin . . . that's right."

Kranish set Rose's head in the dust, running his hand over her hair, touching her cheek, her neck where blood had dried. Quin saw a piece of paper pinned to Rose's bloody blouse. Then the light struck the head of the straight pin that held it in place. She realized it was stuck into Rose's chest. A shudder fluttered through Quin and she hugged her arms against her. She was going to be sick, she was . . .

She gently closed Rose's eyes and bit down on her lip. She started to reach for the paper, then yanked her hand back, remembering there might be prints. "Quin, give me a hand," Patty Cakes said.

He was trying to help Kranish to his feet, but Kranish was murmuring, "I've got to tell Molly. I mean, she—"

"Right, Spin. Molly's back in the city. Can you stand

okay?" Patty Cakes' voice was a murmur, a paternal coo. "Are you hurt?"

"Hurt, no, I'm not hurt. But the crabs . . ." Kranish's eyes widened in his cheeks as Patty Cakes and Quin helped him up. She averted her eyes from the dark stains in the sand around Rose, from the blood smeared from her neck to her chest, and fixed Kranish's right arm around her shoulder. Patty Cakes did the same with his left arm. "Can you make it up the hill, Spin?" Patty Cakes asked.

"The hill? Where's the hill?"

"There, see it?" Patty Cakes pointed and then adjusted Kranish's sunglasses.

"Hill, sure, I can make the hill. Molly and me, we have some things to do. We're going . . ." He frowned. "Well, I can't remember." He turned his head and looked at Quin. "Do you hate me?" His voice was a thin rasp. "Please don't hate me. I told Rose not to come here without boots, Quin, I did, that's what I told her. It's not my fault she died, it isn't, I would never do anything to Rose. Rose was my friend, my . . ."

Quin tightened her hold on Kranish's waist, and she and Patty Cakes began to move slowly toward the hill. Kranish was a dead weight, his head dropping to his chest now as he continued to weep, to beg her not to hate him.

"I don't hate you," she assured him, her voice choking. "No one hates you."

She could see people lining the edge of the pit now, figures sliding down the slope to help them, and she wanted to scream, *Where were you when Rose was being stabbed? Where the fuck was everyone?* But the heat had sucked all the moisture from her mouth, and now Kranish had passed out and his feet were dragging in the sand.

Then there were people everywhere, someone was saying, "I'll get him, Quin," and she moved out of the way. Black dots splashed across the inside of her eyes like spilled ink, and for an instant she thought she was going to pass out. But she felt a cool hand on her arm and blinked and Will Clarke's face swam into view.

"Over here, Quin, where it's cooler," he said.

Beyond him she saw police cars parked parallel to the honey wagons, and two paramedic trucks, and she didn't understand how they'd gotten here so fast. Will was saying something to her, holding tightly to her hand, and she let him lead her over toward the paramedic truck.

"He thinks he's Spin," she mumbled.

The back of the truck was open, its lid like a protruding tongue, and Will Clarke told her to sit down and then pressed a glass of something into her hands. Quin drank. Never had cold water tasted so good. She held out the glass for more, drank again. For the first time she noticed that Will now wore Centauri clothes—the silver jumpsuit that looked metallic and the thick, heavy boots.

"Are you okay, Quin?"

"Yes, sure. I'm fine. Someone's got to get Rose and—"

"There're some people down there now. Just stay put here in the shade, huh?"

Over his shoulder, she saw that the honey wagon area was swarming with people and cops. She spotted Benson, standing at one of the cruisers, talking on the radio. She saw Greg Hess in the back of the police car, his face pressed to the window. Another car arrived, and Doc Smithers and two men from the lab got out.

Now several paramedics were hurrying toward the van with a stretcher, and behind them was Dina. Quin got up, brushed off her clothes, and stepped to the side. She glimpsed Kranish's face before they slid him into the belly of the van. A face as white and thin as parchment paper, eyes closed, an oxygen mask over his nose and mouth.

An IV snaked into his arm.

Dina started to climb in after him, but the paramedic shook his head. "I'm sorry, ma'am. We have our orders. No one leaves in here but Mr. Kranish."

"Where're you taking him?" It was a demand, not a question.

He named the hospital, then closed the doors as Dina stood there, a hand balled at her mouth, nostrils flaring. The van sped away into the white dust and the light. Her arms dropped to her sides. She looked at Quin, at Will.

Before Quin could say anything, Benson had come over to them, his face damp and haggard. "We're going to be getting everyone's statements. If you'd all go over to the lunch tent to wait, please."

"Now?" Dina exclaimed. "You're going to do it now?"

"Yes, ma'am, we are."

"Why's Greg Hess in the cruiser, Tim?" Quin asked.

Benson snapped, "We just arrested him, that's why."

"*Arrested* him?"

Benson's look silenced her. She, Will, and Dina started toward the tent, none of them speaking. A numbness was spreading through her. An image of Rose insinuated itself, and she pushed it aside. Not yet. She wasn't ready to think about Rose yet.

Outside the tent, Benson pulled her aside. The harsh light slid into the deep lines that shot down from either side of his nose. "The dispatcher is getting in touch with Mac, telling him to get to Parkland Hospital. If Gill comes out of it, I want someone there to talk to him." Then, quietly, he added: "I'm sorry I snapped at you, Quin."

She nodded. She understood. "How'd you get here so fast?"

"We'd arrived to arrest Hess."

"Why Hess?"

"He's got type O blood and hypoglycemia."

"You've got actual evidence?"

"On him? No, not yet."

Quin stared at Benson.

He nodded toward one of the motor homes. "Let's go in there and I'll get your statement."

2.

McCleary spent two hours in the lobby of Parkland General, waiting for some word about Kranish's condition. He perused magazines without seeing them. He stood at the window, peering out into the long shadows, turning over his memories of Kranish like pages in a book. He slowly ate a sandwich in the coffee shop that he didn't taste, and tried not to speculate on what Kranish might've seen.

He stared out the window, into the hot streets where Miami's traffic sped, and thought about nothing at all.

He made calls.

From the West Coast offices of the Screenwriters' Guild he obtained the name of Hannah Davidson's agent. Her name was Lila Echemendia, and everything about her voice indicated that he'd better make this quick, because she was busy, busy, busy. But then he said he was calling from Gill Kranish's office and her voice zipped from an Arctic chill to Rio at noon. "Yes, Mr. McCleary, how can I help you?"

So this, he thought, was the power of Kranish. "We've run into a couple of problems with the script and Gill hasn't been able to get ahold of Ms. Davidson at her home number. Would you happen to have a forwarding number?"

"No problem. Just a second." He heard papers rustling. "Okay, here we go." He jotted it down and thanked her.

He stared at what he'd scribbled, confused that the number had a South Florida area code. He fed a quarter into the phone, dialed. There was no answer. He hung up and was about to dial the dispatcher at the station to see if there was more news from Benson, but a man behind him said, "Are you Mr. McCleary?"

He glanced around. Nodded. The man was thin, with dark, intense eyes.

"I'm Dr. Arnold. I understand you're a friend of Mr. Kranish's?"

"Yes. How is he?"

"He's in intensive care. He's suffering from acute exhaustion, and he's extremely disoriented. The paramedic said he'd sustained a severe psychological shock, is that correct?"

McCleary nodded and briefly explained. Arnold rubbed his jaw, reached into his pocket, and brought out a plastic bottle. "A nurse found these pills in his pockets. They're commonly prescribed for migraines. Does he have a history of migraines?"

"For the last year or more, yes."

"I'd like to keep him in ICU as long as he's so disoriented. I've also ordered some tests to be run on him."

"What kinds of tests?"

The PA system barked. Several nurses hurried by. The front doors opened and a rush of warm air carried in the smell of exhaust, of September.

"Blood and urine samples and a CAT scan. I realize he didn't sustain a head injury, but when he regained consciousness, he practically begged for his migraine pills. I'd like to have that checked out. Just to be sure."

"Whatever you think is best."

"Does he have any family?"

"No. His parents are dead and he's an only child. He isn't married."

"Frankly, what concerns me more than Mr. Kranish's physical condition, Mr. McCleary, is his mental state."

"The disorientation, you mean."

"Perhaps 'disorientation' is too soft a word. He's been asking for Molly, Molly Drinkwater. Now it's been a while since I've seen a Spin Weaver film, but isn't Molly—"

"Yes," McCleary said softly. "Yes. She's Spin's girlfriend."

"That's what I thought." He sighed. "The disorientation may wear off as he becomes physically stronger. We'll know more in the next couple of days."

"Suppose it doesn't wear off?"

Arnold glanced down at the floor, then up to McCleary. His expression spoke volumes about his life as a physician. "Then I would recommend a psychiatric evaluation, Mr. McCleary. Do you know who holds power of attorney for Mr. Kranish?"

"I think Patrick May, his director, does."

"Well, it's premature for that right now. Let's just see how he does. We'll keep him on intravenous feeding for the next twelve hours or so."

Arnold's beeper sounded. He smiled, shook McCleary's hand, and passed him a business card. "Please feel free to call me at any time."

"May I see him? Just for a few minutes?" Dr. Arnold was about to shake his head. "Look, I won't upset him. I just want to see him, that's all."

"All right, but it'll have to be brief, Mr. McCleary. I'm going to post a 'No Visitors' flag on his chart until he's gained some footing."

They rode the elevator to the fifth floor. The odor of disinfectant, of alcohol, depressed McCleary. Hospitals depressed him. He could hear the murmurs and beeps of the life support machines.

Kranish's room was a private one, separated from the nursing station by a wall of glass. "His vital signs are being closely monitored," Arnold explained. "I suspect we'll be able to move him out of here by tomorrow morning."

"Even if he still thinks he's Spin Weaver?"

"As long as he doesn't become violent. Go on in. But please, not for long."

He was connected to a variety of machines, and the room was a medley of sounds—beeps, drips, sighs. The television was tuned to an *All in the Family* rerun, but there was no sound. McCleary knew Kranish despised sitcoms, so he changed the channel until he found a *Star Trek* rerun. He looked down at Kranish. His eyes were open, watching McCleary.

270

"How're you feeling?"

"Like this big mother crab is sitting on my chest."

Crab? Then he remembered. The crabs were the sand critters on Alpha Centauri. "Can I get you anything?"

"Just bring Molly, okay? I asked the guy in white, I asked the woman in white, I ask and I ask and everyone says, 'Yes, we're contacting her, calm down now,' and so far I haven't seen any Molly." His eyes skipped to the phone. "Will you call her for me? Would you do that?"

McCleary suddenly remembered the day they'd had the run-in with Big Jim and his boys. When Kranish had untied him from the tree, the skin on his face had seemed white and as thin as eggshells. Like now. "Sure, I'll call her when I leave." He touched Kranish's arm. "Listen, it's very important. Did you see something?"

Kranish turned his head to the wall. "Rose was still alive," he whispered.

"Alive?" McCleary hurried around to the other side of the bed. "Did she say anything to you, Gill?"

Kranish squeezed his eyes shut.

"She did. She said something to you. What was it, Gill?"

His mouth moved. His eyes fluttered open. "The crabs got her." His blue eyes looked frosted, glazed.

McCleary patted his arm. "I'll be back tomorrow."

"You'll call Molly, right?"

"Right."

"Thanks." Then his eyes closed, and in seconds he'd tumbled back into the black oblivion of a dreamless sleep.

McCleary remained by the bed for a few minutes, watching the play of afternoon sunlight on Kranish's face. He looked, in sleep, like a kid again.

3.

Quin sighed as she slid into the hot water, the steam. It loosened the white dirt in her pores and her sorrow over

271

Rose. She could feel the ball of her emotions breaking apart like phlegm in her chest. The psychological wall she'd erected this afternoon had developed fissures. She cried a little, then got disgusted with herself because tears over a death were always for yourself, the survivor. What good did they do? So she got mad. She worked herself into a white lather of rage and then let it hiss out of her like gas.

An utter exhaustion flooded through her when the last of her anger was gone. She sat there, her toes fiddling with the knob so a steady stream of hot water ran into the tub. She must've dozed off, because her head suddenly jerked up at a noise in the hallway. She reached forward to turn off the water so she could hear better and was grabbing for her towel when the door creaked open. Her hand flew to her chest, and then she laughed nervously and sat back.

"Mac, you scared me."

He was holding a glass of wine in either hand. His smile stretched thinly, and his voice, when he spoke, seemed riddled with fatigue. "Sorry. I figured you'd heard me downstairs. Want some?"

He held up the glass of wine and she nodded.

He came into the bathroom, flipped forward the lid on the toilet seat, and sat down. He set her glass on the edge of the tub and sipped at his own. "Did you just leave the hospital?"

"Yes."

"And?"

"He thinks he's Spin Weaver, Quin."

"Yeah, I know," she said, and reiterated what had happened that afternoon, including her strange conversation with Bruce Harmon, the video historian. She did not mention what had taken place in the motor home with Kranish.

"What could Harmon possibly know?"

"Beats me. But I think it'd be worth your while to find him, Mac."

272

He told her about their credit denial and his suspicions. Her water grew tepid and she ran more. For a moment, especially when she squinted her eyes, she could see something taking shape in the shadows, something . . . Her stomach growled, distracting her, and she lost the thread.

"What I figure is this," McCleary said. "Ten years ago, a *Miami Herald* reporter, Pam Spenser, was working on a story that involved a money laundering scam. It had to be money laundering, because that's what *Night Flames* is about. And it probably involved drugs, since that's also what the movie's about. She knew Gill; we know that from the gossip column picture. She was supposedly murdered because she got too close to the story. Gill took what happened, projected it into the twenty-first century, and got a Weaver yarn out of it called *Night Flames*. Greg Hess has been arrested for the murders, and Benson swears up and down he's sure it's him, but I think he's wrong."

Quin started to say something, but McCleary asked her to let him finish. "The way I see it, there're a couple of things we've got to confirm. First, whether Pam Spenser was killed because of this story she was investigating. We can talk to the homicide detective who was on the case and also to that journalist who reported her missing and said she was working on something big. What was his name again?"

"Pepe Moreno."

"Yeah, we'll talk to him and Abel Laxton, the detective. Second, we've got to find Davidson, the scriptwriter. I want to hear what she's got to say about Gill's input into the script. In other words, does Gill know who killed Pam Spenser? Did he, like the character in *Night Flames*, split because he was afraid he'd be knocked off too? Third, I'm going to talk to Winthrop. I've got this bad feeling, Quin, that maybe, just maybe, he's tied up somehow in whatever scam Pam Spenser was investigating ten years ago."

273

Quin got out of the tub and wrapped a towel around herself. She went into the bedroom to dress, and McCleary followed. "There was a note pinned to Rose, Mac."

"I know. I called Benson when I got in." He sat at the edge of the bed, then got up, walking around the room, rubbing his neck. "It was another I Ching passage."

"From Before Completion?"

"Yes."

She opened her dresser drawers, looking for clean clothes, and felt McCleary's eyes on her. "I know what you're thinking," she said.

"Damn right I'm thinking it," he mumbled. "Christ, Quin. You and Rose both got notes, and now Rose is dead."

"Look," she said in her most reasonable voice, "I'm not staying at the Towers, okay? I don't want to stay at the Towers. There's no reason to, because we won't be shooting tomorrow anyway, and I'm not real anxious to follow Rose, McCleary."

She turned then, ready to tell him again that he was a bossy cop at heart. But his face was stretched as taut as a drum, the brows peaked, a tic beneath his eye, his mouth puckering, and the remark turned to dust on her tongue. She went over to him and slipped her arms around his neck. He buried his face in her hair, hugging her tightly.

"Are you going over to the station or anything tonight?" she asked.

"Benson wanted to bring the note over so we could see it, but I told him I'd come by tomorrow. I want to eat dinner. Watch the tube. Read. Swim. Anything but think about this."

"Oh. Well. In that case, I have some ideas on what to do," she said, and kissed him and began unbuttoning his shirt.

As if to protest this choice, her stomach growled and fussed, and McCleary laughed.

"Ignore it," she said, walking over to the bed and pulling back the covers. "Afterwards, it can have dinner, and then I'll pig out on chocolate chip cookies to placate it."

She slipped in between the cool sheets with a sigh and saw that McCleary hadn't moved. "Who's that?" he asked, pointing at the calico cat in the doorway.

Quin sat up. "Rose's cat. That's Tracy. As in Spencer Tracy. Hepburn is around here somewhere. Merlin's not very pleased with the arrangement, but what else was I going to do? Call the Humane Society?"

"Is it a permanent arrangement?" He shucked his clothes, and when he rolled in beside her, he turned on his side and propped his head up in his hand.

"Do you mind?"

His thumb stroked her jaw. "Tracy, Hepburn, and Merlin," he said, nodding slowly. "I think it's got a nice ring to it, don't you? Very mythical or something."

Then he lowered his mouth to hers.

Twenty-nine

IN THE DREAM, McCleary was in a hurry. He rushed into the house to get something, flew up the stairs to the bedroom, and when he opened the door, there were Kranish and Quin making love as a video camera whispered nearby, catching it all. He shouted something, and Quin lifted her head from Kranish's chest and smiled and said, "Please go away, Mac."

Then Kranish, without saying a word, simply raised his hand from the curve of Quin's back and waggled his fingers. McCleary ran over to the closet where he kept the .357. His fingers closed around it and he spun and then he aimed and fired, just as he had lifetimes ago when the woman had been Robin, not Quin. He kept firing, emptying the gun, but the shots hadn't killed them, hadn't killed either of them. Now they were laughing, and McCleary bolted out of the dream, blinking, the shots and the laughter echoing in the room, pursuing him.

He glanced at the clock. It was 4:38. He rolled over on his back and stared at the ceiling, remnants of the dream weaving like shadows through the quiet. He moved closer to Quin's warmth and rested his hand on her hip. Her back was to him, but in her sleep she sighed, as if something of his touch had penetrated her awareness. He closed his eyes, willing himself to sleep, but his hand slid over her hip to her thigh, loving the softness of her skin, the gentle rise and fall of muscles. His mouth brushed her spine, the sharp point of her shoulder blade, then its rounded curve, smoother than butter.

The dream image floated through his skull again, triggering something, and he suddenly knew that part of Quin's dislike of Kranish was her attraction to him. This dark revelation startled him, brought a slow burn to the hunch spot between his eyes. So obvious, he thought. All along it had been obvious, and he'd chosen to ignore it. He'd been waiting for some brilliant illumination that would explain the way she had looked for things to dislike about Kranish, and all along he should've been peering obliquely to the side, into the shadows, doing a kill flash, as Quin called it.

She turned on her back, threw an arm over her head. The covers slid to her waist. McCleary lifted up on an elbow, watching her sleep. "Quin?"

He felt rather than saw her awaken.

"How come you're up?" she asked, rolling onto her side, burrowing her face into the hollow of his neck as his arms slid around her.

"Just a dream." *About you and Gill, Quin.*

His hands stroked her back; the fabric of her nightgown felt cool against his palms. She smelled faintly of sleep, of shampoo, of desire. *Did Gill ever touch you, Quin? Did you want him to? Did you fantasize?* Was that what the conversation had been about Saturday night on the stairs in Charlie Roberts' building? About who he would sleep with if he were single? Had it been about fantasies?

His body reacted to the thoughts, and he didn't realize he'd stopped stroking her until Quin pulled back. "What's wrong?"

"Wrong? Nothing's wrong."

Her hair fell along one side of her face. McCleary ran his fingers through it. "Are you happy, Quin?" The words stuck to his tongue, and he suddenly regretted them. Suppose she said no? Suppose she laughed like she had in the dream and confessed she'd slept with Kranish? Suppose . . .

"What kind of question is that?"

"Are you?"

"I'll be a lot happier once this case is finished." She lay back, her arms folded under her head.

"But are you happy in this marriage?" McCleary rolled onto his side again, his fingers trailing across her arms, the curve of her breast, down to her ribs.

"Of course I am. Why? Aren't you?"

"I am, yeah. I was just wondering if you are, that's all."

Her laughter was warm, soft. "I'd tell you if I weren't."

"Would you also tell me if you were attracted to Gill?" He hadn't intended to say it, was astonished that he had, and now she covered his hand with her own, halting its slow journey down her arm.

"What's that supposed to mean?"

"Well, are you?"

She reached out and turned on the lamp. She was sitting up, blinking, brushing her hair away from her face, clutching the sheet against her as if his question had stirred a kind of modesty. "Are you asking me if I screwed him, Mac? Is that it?"

"No."

She rolled her lower lip against her teeth and looked like she was about to cry. "If I'm attracted to him, then."

He nodded.

It took her a moment to answer. She looked at her hands, clutching the sheet, then up at him, the blue of her eyes never failing to startle him. "Yeah, I guess I was. Before this tape business. Before . . . everything that's happened. Then today, on the set, I went into the motor home to see how he was. He'd collapsed with a migraine during shooting. And while I was in there, I asked him about Pam Spenser, if he'd known her, and he said yeah, and I asked if he knew she'd been killed and he said no, and I think he was lying. Then he apologized to me." She'd been speaking rapidly, but in bursts, as if she were gulping breaths in between. Now she paused. "I asked him why he was apologizing and he said, 'For whatever you think I've done.' So I told him."

McCleary sat cross-legged on the bed, not looking at her, trying to puzzle through how he felt about this. She rocked toward him. "I always felt excluded when Gill was around. In the beginning. He seemed to claim all your attention."

McCleary reached past her and turned off the lamp. It was easier to talk in the dark. "Excluded how?"

"Oh, like that weekend when you two went to the Everglades and you never even bothered inviting me to come along. That kind of exclusion."

"I didn't think you'd want to come."

The bed squeaked; he heard her fixing the pillows against the headboard. "Well, I probably wouldn't have, but you could've asked, Mac."

"You're right. I'm sorry. What else?"

"I don't know. Just small things that add up over a period of time. I know I haven't always been too great either, when he's been around, and I apologize. It's just that I felt so . . . so infuriated."

He reached for her hand, needing to feel connected to her. She slid down between the sheets. He began to caress her again, long, slow strokes along her arms. "And the night you asked him to stay and you stayed up talking late and all. I felt like you do when you're twelve and your best friend has defected to the enemy."

McCleary laughed, his hands moving across her back, her mouth pressed against his shoulder. "I didn't mean to make you feel that way. Really."

"I know you didn't." She whispered it, and began to cry, softly, clutching him hard against her, so hard he could feel the beat of her heart in his own. He knew the tears were in part for Rose, but the knowledge didn't make him feel any better. He shifted and kissed her eyes and mouth, tasting salt and the deep need of a hunger that seemed to have been growing in him, in them both, for days. It was a need to connect, to move beyond death and murder into the safe cocoon that was their space and theirs alone.

They didn't speak. There was only the language of bodies now, the rhythms of a different song in which muscles whispered and bones sighed, in which the blood heated up like summer. She felt different against him, her skin silkier, warmer, sweeter, as though she were a woman he did not know well, but hoped to. Even when she whispered his name, when her fingers tightened against his back and she began to moan, she was not the same woman as before her admission about her attraction to Kranish. Something in him had changed, deepened, widened—perhaps his capacity for love, perhaps his capacity for understanding, maybe both.

Afterwards, they lay side by side in the hot, tight dark, speaking in hushed tones of their pasts, both common and separate, of incidents each remembered. He told her about that winter day in Syracuse when he and Kranish had been hassled by Big Jim and his crew, and how when he'd been tied to the tree, he'd heard them raping Kranish. "And when Gill came over to me, after they'd left, I pretended like I was just coming to."

"So he doesn't know that you know?"

"No. I never said anything. It would have humiliated him terribly, Quin."

She squeezed his hand and quietly said, "I think a part of me has always envied Gill for knowing you so much longer than I have." She gave a soft, quick laugh. "Silly, huh."

"You think we got cheated out of time or something?" he joked.

"We'll make up for it. Actually, Mac, you haven't changed in fifty thousand years, not since that lifetime in Atlantis."

He chuckled, started to say something, but thought he heard a noise rippling through the quiet. "Did you hear that?" he whispered.

She sat up. "It's just one of the cats."

280

"No, it wasn't a cat."

He swung his legs over the bed, pulled on jeans, hurried over to the closet for the .357. *Like in the dream.* But this time when he turned around there was only Quin in the caliginous glow from the clock, wiggling into her robe. McCleary opened the door quietly and stepped out into the hall. He could hear the sound clearly now. Someone was in his den.

He crept through the hall, started down the back stairs, testing each step first with a tentative pressure from his foot. No squeaks. He reached the bottom step and paused, back flat against the wall. Some bastard was going through his file cabinet, a bastard who was probably named Charlie Roberts. McCleary could hear the rustle of papers, the quiet whisper of drawers opening, closing.

He stepped to the floor, sprang to the other side of the hall, and advanced, the .357 held upright but ready.

Looking for your stolen files, Surfer Boy?

The audacity; that was what really pissed him off. Good ole Surfer Boy, acting with impunity, stealing into a house in the darkest hour and then blithely going through the files. And yet, it was hardly worse than what he and Quin had done.

Maybe it's not him.

McCleary paused at the edge of the doorway, adrenaline rushing through his head. The door wasn't closed all the way, and light oozed through the crack, spilling into the hall. He looked at it obliquely, and slowly detected the movement of a shadow. Then he heard another drawer opening in his file cabinet and he kicked the door with his foot and swung into the den, the .357 aimed at Charlie Roberts' heart.

Roberts spun around so fast his foot knocked over a stack of files on the floor. Notes and invoices slid out. "Charlie, imagine meeting you here. In the middle of the night, no less. You're getting careless, Charlie. C'mon, get up. Get up nice and slow and put your hands on top of your head."

"Where the fuck are my files, McCleary?"

"C'mon, get your hands up before I lose my temper."

Roberts raised his arms. McCleary approached him cautiously and patted him down until he found his 9mm Walther. "Sit down on the couch there, Charlie. We're going to have a little talk, you and me."

"Fuck you, McCleary. I want my files."

"Move." Roberts sidled toward the couch like a crab and sat down. McCleary pulled over the chair from the desk and straddled it. He propped the barrel of the Magnum on the back of it. "So, buddy, what's going on?"

"Get off my back."

"You either tell me what's going on or I call the cops and press charges for breaking and entering."

"I could do the same, *buddy*."

McCleary grinned. "I'm afraid I don't know what you're talking about, Charlie. But maybe I can remember if you tell me about Everett Winthrop."

"Go suck an egg, man."

"Suit yourself." McCleary reached for the phone.

"Hold on. Okay. Just hold on. Everett Winthrop." A slow smile worked at Charlie's features. McCleary sensed that whatever allegiance he had to Winthrop was about to be displaced by Roberts' need to gloat. "You *are* slow, McCleary." He ran a finger alongside his nose and his smile got wider. "Had a bit of trouble with your credit lately?"

"I don't have the time or the inclination to play games with you, Charlie," he replied, and lifted the receiver on the phone and punched three numbers before Roberts came around.

"Okay, he's vice-prez of investments for Coast Bank."

"Tell me something I don't know, Charlie. Like about his interest in *Night Flames*."

"He never exactly spelled it out, McCleary, but I got the impression he was real pleased that things weren't running smoothly, if you know what I mean."

"No, I don't know what you mean. Be specific, Charlie."

"I got the impression he didn't want the movie made—not for TV, not for VCRs, not for the theaters, not for squat. When you and your wife started poking around, it pissed him off. I tried to warn you that day on the tennis court, McCleary, that you didn't want to piss the man off. But oh no, you weren't listening, were you?" Another gloating smile.

"So what was your job?"

"Like I said before, to keep tabs on things."

"On the murders, you mean."

Roberts nodded.

"You know what I think, Charlie? I think you're Winthrop's hit man, that's what I think."

"I'm disappointed in you, McCleary. I thought you knew I don't do jobs like that."

"But I bet you know plenty of guys who would."

He shrugged. "Yeah, I know a few. But if you want my honest opinion, I don't think Winthrop has anything to do with all that."

"But I bet he would've been plenty interested in meeting one of your friends if the murders had suddenly stopped, huh, Charlie."

A shrug. "He never said." He leaned forward now, a thin line of perspiration perforating his upper lip. "Look, McCleary, I'm telling you this for your own good. You do *not* want to fuck with this guy, okay?"

"Why'd he want copies of the script?"

"I don't know. Now where're my files?"

"Gee, Charlie. It slipped my mind."

Roberts leg jutted out so fast that McCleary didn't have time to react. His foot connected with the Magnum and sent it flying. McCleary leaped up, but he wasn't quick enough. Roberts was already on his feet and slammed into him, knocking him against the desk chair, which toppled as McCleary fell into the desk. Pain erupted in the small of his back; the room went fuzzy. His hands shot out behind him, and he lifted up, and then he heard

Quin's voice shouting, "Hold it right there, Mr. Roberts. Don't even breathe too hard or I'm afraid I'll have to blow your nuts off."

Roberts' head jerked toward the door. McCleary's vision began to clear. Quin held a shotgun leveled at Roberts' groin. "Okay, okay, just be real careful with that, lady," Surfer Boy murmured.

McCleary scooped up the Magnum, and aimed it at Roberts' head. "Sit down, you asshole."

Roberts sat down. Quin lowered the shotgun and dialed Benson's home number. Then she passed him the receiver and raised the shotgun again, her expression hard, almost hateful. When Benson answered, he sounded like he was underwater.

"Hey, Tim. You want to send a squad car over to the house? I've got an intruder here named Charlie Roberts. And he just sang a mighty fine tune for me, mighty fine."

"Give me ten minutes and I'll come myself."

McCleary smiled. "Thanks, Tim."

"Winthrop's not going to like this one goddamn bit, McCleary," grumbled Roberts.

"Oh, shut up," Quin snapped.

Thirty

HE AWAKENED WITH a desert in his mouth. He needed water, he needed to move, he was hungry. He knew immediately where he was, and he wanted out.

Kranish's thumb pressed against the call bell. It pressed and pressed, and almost immediately a nurse sailed into the room. She turned on a lamp and the light hurt his eyes. He turned his head to the side. "I want water."

"It's right here, Mr. Kranish." The nurse touched his chin with fingers of ice, and he glanced at the table. Now she was pouring water from a pitcher. Now she was showing him where the button was to raise his bed. Now the upper half of his bed was raised. She was treating him like an invalid.

He wanted to get out of bed, but when he tried to swing his legs over the side, he felt a sharp tug between his legs and realized they'd catheterized him. "Call the doctor. I'm leaving."

"Mr. Kranish, it's five-thirty in the morning." The nurse held the glass up to his mouth. He told her he could hold it himself, thank you, and did. He drained the glass. "Now why don't you just lie back down and go to sleep. The doctor will be in by ten this morning."

"Look, miss, I don't want to sleep. I've had too much sleep. Now get this goddamn hose out of me, because I'm leaving."

Her spine stiffened with alarm.

He looked down and saw the needle in his arm, a needle connected to a tube. And what the hell were these goddamn things taped to his chest? He yanked one off. It pulled at the hairs. The nurse backed away from the bed. He coaxed another electrode off his chest. And another. And another. And pretty soon the background whispers in the room were gone. His head hurt, but only dimly, as though the pain were the memory of pain.

An orderly marched into the room. Big man, a big, big man with shoulders that could barely squeeze through the door. "What seems to be the problem, Mr. Kranish?" Jesus, his voice was riddled with ersatz cheeriness. Kranish wanted to puke.

"No problem. I'm leaving, that's all. I'd like to speak to my physician."

Once again, he started to drop his legs over the side, but this time, the orderly whipped up the metal railing with a quick snap. "Mr. Kranish, I think you'd better just lie back down and—"

"Maybe you don't speak English, son. I said I want out of here, and I want out now. Either call my doctor or this hospital is going to have a lawsuit slapped against it. A big lawsuit. You got that?"

"I will say this just once, Mr. Kranish. The doctor will see you later this morning. His orders are that until then, you remain here, as is. The nurse can give you something to help you sleep."

"I don't want a goddamn pill."

Someone had lowered the head of his bed. Funny, he didn't remember it happening, but here he was, flat on his back again, staring up at the underside of the orderly's chin.

"Then how about a shot, Mr. Kranish? If you don't quiet down, I'm afraid the nurse is going to have to sedate you."

That term, 'sedate,' smacked of *One Flew Over the Cuckoo's Nest*. He and Rose had watched that film one night on the tube in . . . *Rose*.

He squeezed his eyes shut as it all came crashing back. He heard that soft *snap* inside him and suddenly he was on Alpha Centauri. He and Molly were strolling through the umbrageous, sweet-smelling air in a park in Settlers' City, the chalky light filtering through the thick branches.

You ready to rock and roll, Spin? Molly asked, grinning.

Here? Is it legal?

And she laughed, Molly did, and took him by the hand and led him to a small, shrouded lake with pink water. *The legend says that when a man and a woman immerse themselves together in these waters, they're linked forever, Spin. Even death can't part them.*

The nurse and the orderly were shadows at the edge of his awareness, and one of them was saying, "Mr. Kranish, I'm going to give you something to help you sleep."

Then the shadows faded away as he and Molly undressed and held hands and slipped into the warm pink waters of another world.

Thirty-one

1.

QUIN SAT ON the porch steps facing the pool, sipping a cup of coffee. Dark clouds scudded the morning horizon, and the air smelled of rain. But the weatherman, droning from the TV in the kitchen, assured everyone that nature wouldn't keep her promise, that she was tantalizing them, and meanwhile they were entering their one hundred and twenty-first day without rain. Lake Okeechobee, which supplied fresh water to most of South Florida, was eleven feet below normal for this time of year. What they needed, said the weatherman, was a hurricane.

She glanced at her watch, willing the hands to move ahead. It was 7:30 A.M. McCleary had left a while ago for the station to dig up Abel Laxton's address. The homicide detective who'd handled the Pam Spenser case had long since retired. Benson had no idea where he was and suggested they go through the Police Pension Division. So here she was, caught in limbo time. It was too early to call the *Herald* offices to talk to Pepe Moreno, and too late to go back to bed. She kept thinking about Rose, about the look on Roberts' face when she'd leveled the shotgun at him, and about the I Ching note in her pocket that Benson had brought by when he arrested Roberts. The note that had been impaled on Rose's chest.

Before Completion. She removed the note from her pocket. *The conditions are difficult. The task is great and full of responsibility. . . . If we wish to achieve an effect, we must first investigate the nature of the forces in question and ascertain their proper place. If we can bring these forces to bear in the right place, they will have the desired effect and completion will be achieved.*

There were no changing lines, only a final line that was chillingly succinct: *Success will justify the deed.* She folded the note and slipped it back in her shirt pocket. She heard scratching behind her and glanced around to see Merlin, trying to dig his way out of the kitchen. Quin opened the door wider for him and he scooted out as though he couldn't get away from the other cats fast enough. He raced over to the swimming pool, squatted at the shallow end, and drank like a cat in the wild. Quin spotted Hepburn and Tracy under the table and coaxed them out.

"C'mon, guys, you're out of Miami Beach retirement now. Go catch some mice or something."

Hepburn skulked at the door, purring, sniffing at the alien air, then stepped delicately out onto the porch steps and settled beside Quin to appraise the situation. Tracy followed, but reluctantly.

She consulted her watch again. The hands twitched to 7:36. She went inside and dialed Dina's number at the Prince. Quin didn't really expect her to be in, and was surprised when she answered. She thought momentarily of Dina with Lee Ling and Gill. Proper Dina in a video-taped orgy. "Dina. It's Quin. Is there any word on how Gill is?"

"Oh. Quin. I was just about to call you. Patty Cakes has arranged a memorial service for Rose this afternoon at the hotel chapel. At three." She paused. "About Gill, the only thing I know is that they're taking him out of ICU sometime today. He might be able to have visitors. I don't think his, uh, mental condition has improved at all, though." Quin heard the other lines ringing. "Listen, I've got to run. These phones have been pealing ever since yesterday. The news about Gill is out. See you this afternoon."

The line went dead, and Quin stood there, listening to the hollowness zipping along the line. Something about Dina bothered her, something she couldn't focus on. She tried to clarify it, examine it, but couldn't and walked back into the kitchen. The local news was now on. Quin turned up the volume as a photograph of a woman who looked like Meryl Streep filled the screen.

". . . police are asking anyone with information about the murder of Lynette Walleski to please call Anonymous Crime tips. Ms. Wallesksi was last seen leaving the Poseidon Club on Miami Beach with a man and woman . . ."

One more statistic, she thought, and switched off the television. She glanced at the kitchen clock. 7:55. Close enough. She picked up the folder of stuff Marielle had given her and flipped it open. She removed the article on Pam Spenser and walked over to the phone. It was time to track down Pepe Moreno.

2.

When McCleary arrived at the station, he found Benson standing in the hallway outside the conference room with Maia Fox and a man he'd never seen before. Maia wore one of her Molly Drinkwater outfits—a silver skirt that shimmered like aluminum foil, a black silk blouse with streaks of silver that looked damp, almost alive, and a red shawl with black lace. Her boots were also silver. He recognized them as the woman's version of the protective boots that were worn in the Great Hunger Desert to protect a person against the insidious crabs.

He wondered at the thin line between *her* perception of fiction and reality. Maybe tomorrow or the next day, Maia Fox would capitulate to the character she'd played all these years, then she and Kranish could soar into warp drive forever. Christ.

290

"Uh, this is Mike McCleary," Benson said as McCleary approached. "Gill hired him to work on the case."

The man standing rigidly next to Maia just nodded his head curtly. One good look at him next to her and McCleary knew they were brother and sister. Brother Fox had the same dark eyes and coloring as Maia, but that was where the similarity ended. His mouth was *not* infinitely intriguing; it was small, thin, and constipated.

"This is Craig Fox, Greg Hess' attorney."

"And I would like to see my client, Sergeant." Fox spoke with the hubris that seemed to characterize most attorneys, McCleary thought.

"He's being brought up, Mr. Fox. Why don't we go into the conference room." Benson gestured toward the doorway and they all went inside. "Would anyone like coffee?"

"Yes, I would," said Maia, walking over to the window.

"I'll get it, be back in a minute," Benson said to no one in particular, and left.

McCleary sat down. Brother Fox opened his briefcase and brought out some papers. No one spoke, and the protracted silence grated on him. Whoever would've thought, McCleary mused, that someday Molly Drinkwater would be standing at the windows here, in a room where McCleary had spent plenty of time during his ten years in homicide. Maia, who wasn't much like the zany, bright Molly, gazed down into the city of Miami, sunlight bringing out the auburn streaks in her hair.

"Greg had been fasting for three days, you know," she said suddenly. "That's why his blood sugar's low. It has nothing to do with hypoglycemia or whatever you people have been talking about."

Her brother shot her a look. "Keep quiet, Maia."

She whipped around. Her eyes flashed. "I will *not* keep quiet. Greg's been arrested for something he didn't do, Gill's lying in a hospital thinking he's Spin Weaver, Rose is dead, J.B.'s dead, Lenny's dead, and whoever killed them is still *out* there." She jabbed a finger accusingly toward the city. "And no one's doing a goddamn thing."

"We're doing everything we can," McCleary retorted. "But we haven't exactly gotten a lot of cooperation from you."

"I've told you everything I know. I've told Sergeant Benson everything I know. What the hell do you want?"

McCleary seized the opportunity. "For starters, why didn't you mention Gill's private collection of videotapes, Maia? You know, tapes like the one you, Domer, and Gill made not so long ago?"

Her lovely mouth dropped open. Her eyes darted to her brother, who looked startled, but only momentarily. "What's that got to do with anything?" she replied finally.

"Then you knew about the collection?"

She walked over to the table, ran her fingertips along the edge. "I'd heard rumors."

"Then didn't it occur to you that maybe whoever's trying to sabotage this film might be doing it to get back at Gill for something like a tape, Maia?"

"A woman? You think a woman committed these horrendous murders?" She laughed. "Jesus, McCleary, that's sick. That's as sick as saying Greg Hess is your killer."

"What about Irene? She's been involved with Gill, she was having an affair with Domer at the time of his death, she knows enough about cars to sabotage one. What about her, Maia? What do you know about Irene?"

"I've already told you what I know about her."

"What about Hannah Davidson?" he shot back.

She looked up, fingering the lace on her shawl, and frowned. "Hannah? What's Hannah got to do with anything?"

"You know her?"

"Of course I know her. My houseboat is parked behind her house."

Swell, that was swell. He'd been calling all over the country trying to locate the woman, and she'd been on Miami Beach. "You mean she lives on Star Island?"

292

"Sometimes. She got in last night, if you want to talk to her."

"Does Gill know that house is hers?"

She shrugged. "I doubt it. Gill doesn't pay attention to details like that. He's got too much else to think about."

"Why's she in town?"

"Because she'd heard about the murders and figured the script was going to fall apart. She's got a big stake in this movie."

"I'd like to talk to her."

"Well, you know where I live. She'll be there all day."

"I'd like to hear more about Gill's private collection of tapes," remarked Brother Fox, looking at his sister.

"It's none of your business, Craig," she snapped. Then Greg Hess was escorted into the office by Benson, who was holding cups of coffee.

Hess looked like a teddy bear that had been through the wash—black bean eyes faded, his face the color of bread. He broke into a smile when he saw Maia.

"Thanks for coming," he said.

She rolled onto the balls of her feet and kissed him hello. There was a certain dramatic flair to it, as if she were in front of the camera. Nauseating, McCleary thought.

"If you'll excuse us, please," said Brother Fox. "You too, Maia."

She went into the staff kitchen to wait, and Benson and McCleary walked down the hall to Benson's office. "Maia says Hess has been fasting, that's why he has low blood sugar. If that's true, you're going to be in deep shit trouble, Tim."

"Lawyers don't scare me, Mac. Hess' alibis are shaky. He's guilty."

"The only thing he doesn't have is a motive."

"Not one that we know about." He ran a hand over his hair. "Look, Mac, it fits. I mean, what was he doing on the set yesterday? He's supposed to be managing the production office. Okay, so he says he was delivering some supplies or messages or whatever. Well, hell, Dina Talbott could've delivered them. They arrived on the set about the same time. No, he did it, I know he did."

"You've discounted Bedford?"

"She's O, her alibis suck, but hell, she doesn't have hypoglycemia. Maia Fox I've discounted ever since I found her mysterious little pilot who confirmed that, yes indeedy, he'd taken her up in his Pitt Special when they'd broken for dinner. Besides, she's A Positive, not O. Devereaux's O, but no hypoglycemia. So there you've got it."

"According to the doc, the blood type wasn't necessarily that of the killer, Tim. Domer could've scratched someone accidentally earlier in the day."

But Benson wasn't interested in hearing about ifs, ands, buts, maybes. "Mac, I am up to my eyeballs in bullshit. There's this murder of the United stew on which we've got nothing. There are four murders connected with *this* case alone, and *one* of those murders was of a cop. You know what kinda heat that generates?"

"Of course I know."

Benson looked at him as if he'd just remembered McCleary had been in his shoes for ten years. "Yeah, right. I forgot." He paused and quietly added, "On top of everything, Vic James was one of *my* men. That makes me feel . . ." His voice trailed off, and he shook his head.

"How does Charlie Roberts fit in?"

Benson studied the floor. "I don't know yet." He looked up. "He got released an hour and a half after he was brought in."

"How?"

"Oh, he made a phone call, and twenty minutes later the D.A. was in here and bond was posted and that was that."

"Who'd he call?"

"Your friend Everett Winthrop. Or so the guard downstairs told me."

Great, just great.

"There wasn't anything I could do, Mac," Benson went on.

"I know. I'm not blaming you." He blamed the system. Its inequities seemed to be building up like a wall behind him, and sooner or later there would be one flaw too many and the whole thing would crash in on him, crush him. "Listen, I've got to see a couple of people. Could you have someone dig up Abel Laxton's address for me? Or a phone number? Didn't you say we could get his address through the Police Pension Division?"

Benson rolled his eyes. "Mac, this doesn't have anything to do with the Pam Spenser case, and besides, Laxton has been gone from the department for nine years. You don't even know for sure how well Gill knew her."

"That he knew her at all is enough. Take a look at the *Night Flames* script when you've got some time, Tim."

"Okay, so there're some similarities. But I'm sure Spenser's murder was well publicized. He might've gotten it out of the paper."

"Which is why I want to talk to Hannah Davidson, the scriptwriter," he replied, and explained what Maia had told him.

Before Benson could say anything, Craig Fox rapped on the door, and McCleary saw Hess behind him, being led away by an officer. Fox announced that his client was entitled to a second blood test. Benson told him to take a hike.

"Sergeant, my client had been fasting for seventy-five hours. As any nidget knows, fasting lowers the blood sugar. Now, either he gets another blood test today, after he's had breakfast, or I'll slap a suit against this department for false arrest so fast it'll make your ass spin."

"We have other evidence against him besides the low blood sugar," replied an undaunted Benson.

"Oh, *really*."

295

McCleary wanted to grab Benson by the arm and shove him into a closet before he incriminated himself further.

"Well, Sergeant, I will be back within two hours with an order from Judge Parker."

He walked off down the hall with his sister; Benson shot him the finger. "False arrest, my ass," he mumbled. Then he turned to McCleary. "What's a nidget?"

"An idiot, Tim."

Thirty-two

1.

THE GUARD IN the lobby of the *Miami Herald* was a young fellow with blond hair and cheeks scarred from acne. He seemed to take enormous pleasure in telling Quin she wasn't permitted beyond the desk.

"I'd like to speak with a reporter named Pepe Moreno." Her earlier call had determined that Moreno still worked for the paper and that he would be in this morning.

The guard pointed at a phone. "Call the newsroom. It's extension six-five-two."

It took three tries to get through, and then she had to be connected to another office. "This is Moreno."

He sounded like he was on his way out the door. "My name's Quin McCleary, Mr. Moreno. I'm a private detective, and I'd like to speak to you about Pam Spenser."

"I don't know a Pam Spenser," he replied, and the line went dead.

When she dialed the number again, it was busy. She hung up, drummed her fingers against the counter, tried once more. This time, a secretary answered. Mr. Moreno's calls, she said, had been switched to the front desk because he just left on an assignment.

Quin asked the guard where the employee parking was. He lifted an arm and pointed at a hallway. "If you're looking for Moreno, though, he's probably headed toward the coffee shop across the street. He always goes over there in the mornings."

"What's he look like?"

The guard picked at his cheek. "Short guy, maybe five eight or so, brown hair, skinny as a rake."

"Okay, thanks."

Quin darted back outside, into the heat, and hurried across the street to the Cuban coffee shop. The air inside the *CRISTOBAL* smelled of expresso and fresh bread. Latin music blared from a radio. On a black and white television elevated over the counter area, an Hispanic soap opera was in progress. Quin felt like a minority, the token minority, as she stood there, glancing around for Moreno. She spotted a man who fit the guard's description seated in a booth by himself, paging through the newspaper. She walked over to him. "Mr. Moreno?"

He looked a bit like Michael J. Fox in *Family Ties*, but older, perhaps in his late thirties. He was lean without thinness, handsome without arrogance. A reasonable man, surely.

"Yes?"

"I spoke to you a few minutes ago. You hung up on me."

"Look, Miss. I told you I don't know a Pam Spenser. I have never known a Pam Spenser. I. . . ."

She passed him the *Herald* clip Marielle had dropped by the house and slid into the other side of the booth. "Right there it says you were a friend of Pam's, that you were the one who reported her missing. I just need some answers, that's all."

He folded his newspaper, set it aside. His dark eyes were limpid, sharp. "And just what's your interest? You said you're a private eye. Who're you working for?"

"A man named Gill Kranish who—"

"I know who he is. The whole goddamn world knows who he is. And I hear he's flipped out and thinks he's Spin Weaver."

"Where'd you hear that?"

Moreno smiled. It softened his face a little. "Have you seen the *Herald* headlines today?" He reached for the paper, opened it. "Right there." He pointed midway down the page. PRODUCER HOSPITALIZED FOR EXHAUSTION. Above it was another article about the murder of Rose Leen and the policeman.

"Where does it say anything about him thinking he's Spin Weaver?"

"It doesn't. Sometimes it pays to have a hospital source." He sat forward. "So Kranish hired you to find out who's killing his people?"

"My husband and me, yes."

"Then what's that got to do with Pam Spenser?" Suspicion coruscated brightly in his eyes, so they looked like shiny pennies.

"Are you familiar with the story line for *Night Flames*?"

"I'm a reporter, not a TV writer, Mrs. McCleary."

She ignored his sarcasm. "I think it's based on what happened to Pam Spenser and the story she was investigating at the time, Mr. Moreno. I think it's what's behind the murders that have happened. Four murders, Mr. Moreno. You *do* know there've been four, don't you?"

He looked acutely uncomfortable, started to say something, but the waitress came over to the table and set a demitasse of Cuban coffee in front of him. She asked Quin if she wanted anything. "The same. But without sugar."

The woman left. Moreno sipped from his cup and lit a cigarette. Some of the color had returned to his face. "What do you want to know?"

"Anything that could provide some clues to this case, Mr. Moreno. Just tell me about Pam Spenser."

He lowered his eyes. When he started to talk, his voice was quiet, remote, and detached. Over his shoulder, Quin could see a blur of sunlight, cars, the *Herald* building. "Pam had the desk next to mine. Occasionally we worked on a story together, had lunch, met for drinks, whatever. She considered me a good friend." He smiled and looked up. "Something I would've liked to change, but she was involved with someone at the time. Anyway, one day we were at lunch and she told me she was thinking of taking a leave of absence so she could work on a story. A *big* story, she said. I pressed her for details, but she wouldn't budge except to say it was bigger than anything she'd ever done. She said it was going to be a book, and *her friend* was going to help her."

"Her friend?"

"That's how she referred to this man she was involved with. She'd met him at some bar in the Grove about six months before. He was from L.A., and she said he had a marvelous future in front of him. He was working on a screenplay that was going to knock the socks off the American public."

"Gill Kranish."

"Yeah, but I only found that out later, when I happened to run across a picture of the two of them in an old issue of a tabloid—not the *Enquirer,* but something with less circulation. Kranish wasn't very well known then. He had a couple of episodes of a TV show he'd directed and one movie to his credit that had bombed at the box office, but because the critics liked it, his name appeared from time to time in the gossips as a 'young director to keep your eye on.' That sort of hype."

He sipped again at his coffee, and the waitress brought over Quin's.

"Anyway," Moreno went on, "she took the leave of absence. I didn't hear from her for, oh, maybe three or four months. Then I get this call one night, real late, and she was crying. She said she had to meet with me. She was scared. *Her friend* was pulling out of the deal, and she was scared. So we agreed to meet the next night at this country-western bar in Davie. She never got there."

He looked up, his brown eyes as shiny as marbles. "That's it?" Quin asked.

"For then that was it, yeah. Her body was found three days later. Just like it said in the article. But then the homicide investigation began. Apparently there were a handful of people who knew about Pam's mysterious lover, but no one had ever met him. Interesting how Kranish managed to keep such a low profile, isn't it? Anyway, the detective who worked on the case, Abel Laxton, put me through the third degree. He thought I was protecting Pam's lover. But then he eventually realized I didn't know any more than her other friends did. I didn't know her lover was Kranish until four years ago, when I ran across that gossip column picture."

"You never went to Laxton about it?"

"He retired within a year of Pam's death. Three months or so into the case, bad things started happening to him."

"Bad things? Like what?"

Moreno sat back with a sigh. "Let's see. First it was his dog, I think. The dog disappeared, and its mutilated corpse later turned up on Laxton's doorstep. Then it was threatening phone calls, telling him to drop the case or else. Then his wife was killed in a car accident. Well, Laxton knew it wasn't an accident, but he could never prove it. Not too long after that he went to pieces. Started drinking real heavy. He took early retirement."

"Do you know where he is now?"

"No." He saw her skepticism and smiled. "Really, I don't know."

"Who took the case then?"

"For the next three or four years there were a couple of different guys assigned to it. They all started having a run of 'bad luck,' just like Laxton. I don't know what happened after that. I stopped trying to keep up."

"You never wrote about it? Never did a follow-up story?"

Moreno laughed; it was not a pleasant sound. "How old do you think I am, Mrs. McCleary?"

"Mid-thirties?"

"Thirty-nine. And I would never have *seen* thirty-nine if I'd investigated Pam Spenser's murder." He lowered his voice. "Oh, I was tempted, especially when I ran across that photograph of her and Kranish four years ago. But hell, by then Kranish was the Spin Weaver whiz kid and I was married and had a ten-month-old son. I had too much to lose. Whoever killed Pam also arranged some bad luck for the cops who took the case. And I bet you it's the same someone who's killed off his people."

"Maybe." The *something* that had bothered her before had suddenly flared up again, like fireworks at the edge of her mind.

"Where was Pam's family?"

"California. That's where she was from."

"Did you ever meet them?"

"No."

"Wasn't she survived by a sister?"

"Yeah, but I never met her, either. All I know is that she was younger. That's all I know about the whole bloody mess."

2.

Bruce Harmon leaned over the tray with developer in it, watching the picture emerge. It was one of six he'd taken from the videotapes. Enough evidence, he thought, to put a certain party right into death row. Into Sparky. Fried alive.

He would mail these and the tapes to McCleary, and then get the hell outa town. He didn't want to be around when the story hit, nor did he want to witness the demise of Kranish's kingdom.

He slid the prints into the stop bath, then into the fixer, and went into the kitchen. He retrieved the copies of the tapes from behind a ceiling panel, packed them in a box, and taped it shut. It occurred to him that he didn't have McCleary's home address. If he sent the package to the police department, there was no telling how long it might sit around the mailroom. Harmon knew about mailrooms. He'd worked in several during his long stint through graduate school. But who else was there to send them to if not McCleary?

Quin. He could send the packages to Quin care of the Atlantic Towers.

No, bad idea. The mail for the Towers came through the production office. Anyone could pick up the package. Maybe Quin's friend Marielle would accept the package and make sure it got to either her or McCleary. She said she lived in . . . where?

Then he remembered. Lazy Lake.

He dialed information for Lazy Lake and asked for a listing for Marielle Lindstrom. When he had the number, he called her. She answered on the second ring. He quickly explained who he was, and she remembered him.

"The video historian, sure, how're you, Bruce."

"Okay, thanks. Listen, Marielle. I've been called out of town. Actually, I have to go to New York for an interview with MTV and I—"

"MTV? Is that work?"

"Yeah. Well. I was wondering if you could do me a favor."

"If I can, sure."

"I'd like to mail you a package and ask you to make sure it gets to either Quin or that Detective McCleary."

"Uh, well, sure. But why don't you just send it directly to the police station, Bruce?"

"Mailrooms," he said, "are where the planet turns flat. Things tumble off the edge and are never heard from again."

She laughed. "I see your point. Look, he has an office separate from the station. Let me give you that."

He wondered why *she* would have it, but he didn't ask. When something you needed floated your way, it was safer to thank the God of Serendipity, take it, and keep your mouth shut. He jotted down the address and thanked her and was about to hang up when she said, "Is there some sort of problem, Bruce?"

Problem? Harmon almost laughed. No problem, no siree. Five deaths in two weeks, if you counted the woman rolled into the bay, but it wasn't *his* problem. He was gone from here. Gone.

"No, just that I need to take a shot at this interview."

"Well, good luck."

"Thanks again."

He labeled the package and tucked it under his arm as he rushed outside.

The sky sagged with clouds. The sun had vanished. A breeze spilled through the trees in the parking lot, a warm breeze, but it made Harmon shiver. *Someone's strolling across your grave, Brucie baby.*

He drove to the post office. Traffic blurred on either side of him as though his car were a train rushing blindly toward the future. Inside the post office he waited in a long line. Thunder cracked in the distance. He was running out. But who wouldn't? The idea of being Victim Number Six wasn't the least bit appealing. Let the cops handle it. He was turning over his evidence like any good citizen. He just wasn't sticking around for the question-and-answer period, that was all. He wasn't sticking around because if he did, Rose's killer was going to come after him. He knew it. He could feel it.

The package went overnight mail. Yes, the clerk assured him, it would arrive at the address tomorrow. But someone would have to be there to sign for it. Right, right, he said. He understood.

It had begun to rain as he left the post office, a light, warm rain that tapped the windshield of his car like a child's fingers as he drove home. He decided it was a good sign that the first rain in all these months should fall just as he'd mailed off his tapes. Relieved of his terrible burden, he started humming. He was still humming as he pulled into a parking space in front of his building a while later. Maybe he *would* go to New York and apply for a job with MTV. Why not? MTV would be a different sort of fact culling—music instead of TV movies, rock stars instead of actors. He would remain a historian.

He rushed into his apartment and continued down the

hall to his darkroom, intent on his hiatus. *Ten minutes to clean up in there, fifteen minutes max. Then it was adios Brucie baby.*

He opened the door of the darkroom, and two facts registered simultaneously—the room had been disturbed, and the hairs on his body were bristling. Then a cold liquid struck his face, the smell of the developer chemicals consumed him, his eyes caught fire, and he cried out. Stumbling back, he clawed at his face, barely hearing the door close behind him.

He groped through the room, trying to find the sink. He needed water, a cold flush of water in his eyes and then a doctor. But the pain, oh Christ, the pain was nearly unbearable and he couldn't think straight and he—

"You shouldn't have meddled, Bruce," said the voice.

He fell onto the counter, his arms swung across it, knocking aside the trays, canisters, and then his fingers closed over the edge of the sink. He grappled for the faucet. Cool water ran through his hands and he splashed it in his face, cupped it in his hands and washed out his eyes. It was too late, he could feel the chemical seeping into his eyeballs, being absorbed by the soft tissues, the nerves. But the water soothed the pain.

"I found these fascinating tapes, Bruce. It really wasn't very nice of you, always around with your camera, always *intruding.* . . . I suppose you kept copies, didn't you? I'd like them, Bruce. The copies."

Whimpering, knuckling his eyes, he squinted in the voice's direction. He could see the person now, a soft blur in the orange glow of the safe light. He blinked rapidly. The burning returned. He moved slowly along the counter. *If I can reach the door* . . . But the blur stepped toward him. Something cold and thin sliced into his stomach. The pain was like a white burning in his gut, a flare of intense indigestion, but momentary, like pain in a nightmare, and nothing compared to the agony in his eyes.

He looked down at himself, blinking, blinking hard to clear his vision. All he saw was a vague shape protruding from his belly. A knife. He drew it out, felt it leaving his gut like a knife leaving Jell-O, and the voice spumed through the fusty air. He threw the knife in the direction of the laughter, but heard it bounce off the walls. The voice scooped it up. It was ubiquitous, this voice, a god, a demon, truculent with madness.

"That wasn't nice, Bruce, not nice at all."

He pressed his hands to his stomach, his mind's eye like the lens of a camera, recording every detail, every fact. He started to laugh. The blood flowed faster from the wound and oozed through his fingers. Then the pain turned to numbness, a novocaine numbness, and he slipped to the floor, the blood still oozing. But there was no pain. That part of his brain had shut down. *McCleary will have the tapes soon. Fuck you.*

"I don't know how you figured it out, but it doesn't matter because no one else will. Because you're going to tell me where the copies of those videotapes are, Bruce." The voice lowered itself to the floor beside him, flowing over him like warm water. "I had to do it. Gill killed someone I loved very much by letting her take all the chances. So I had to ruin him, Bruce. And I'll have to kill big man Winthrop and his stupid sidekick. Them, too."

He didn't know who Winthrop was and he didn't care. The voice was cool, silken, he thought dreamily.

"But I have time. There's always time." The voice paused. Harmon sensed its gaze on him. "How're the eyes? I bet they smart, huh. But it had to be your eyes first. Because of the camera. Everyone is getting what he and she deserves. Karma, I think they call it." And the voice laughed. "You shouldn't have followed me that night to the warehouse. That was a mean and spiteful thing to do. What have I ever done to you, Bruce?"

"Too late," Harmon whispered. "You're too late," and then he laughed, coughed, and laughed again.

"Too late? No, I don't think so, Bruce. After all, I have the knife. I can either kill you quickly—or slowly, so you suffer. You choose."

But the voice had ceased to matter. In his mind, behind his now sightless eyes, he could see McCleary ripping open the package, jamming the tapes into a VCR one by one. *History, McCleary, it's history.*

"Did you hear what I said, Bruce?" The voice leaned close to him. "If you tell me where the copies of the tapes are, you won't suffer anymore. Otherwise, there're all sorts of ways to make you wish you were dead. Flaying you, for instance. Through the centuries, that's been a rather popular torture."

"I'm a historian," he whispered.

"What? What was that?"

He was floating out into the Great Beyond. He waited for the white light he'd read about, the tunnel, the faces of friends on the Other Side. It was probably all crap, he thought, but he waited anyway, and the voice pursued him.

"I want the copies of the videotapes, Bruce. I know you made copies. You're the sort of man who would. Now, why don't you just tell me where they are?" He felt the cold tip of the knife at his cheek.

"Historian," he whispered again, and then he gathered the spittle left in his mouth and let it fly. The voice grunted, he laughed, the sharp tip pressed into his cheek, and he tried to scream and couldn't.

"I have all the time in the world, Bruce," cooed the voice.

"Historian," he whispered again, and laughter bubbled from his mouth like soda water, and blackness clamped down over him and he died.

Thirty-three

THEY HAD DONE something to him.

They had wheeled him into a room, swabbed his neck with alcohol, told him not to move, and they'd plunged a needle into his carotid artery. Then they'd slid him onto another table and it had tilted like a carnival ride, and then they'd snapped pictures of his head. A nurse had stood there the whole time, holding his hand, murmuring, "Very good, Mr. Kranish, you're doing just fine," but what the hell did she know? His brain had blazed like the dome on Alpha Centauri, faces had pinwheeled through his head, his memories had been turned inside out like dirty socks.

Where was Molly? Where was McCleary? Why was there such a terrible pressure behind his eyes?

When he came to, the room was blurry, but he heard voices. *TV voices. Whose?* Yes, he would play a little game. It was called *Identify the TV voice and walk outa here alive*. The voice belonged to . . . *Spock, Mr. Spock*. No, shit, no, that wasn't right. It was Bill Cosby in *I Spy*.

His vision began to focus. He saw Cosby on the screen. "I did it, I got it right," he mumbled.

"Gill?"

He jerked his head left. He knew this woman, he did: that dark hair that rippled with light from a window, a slender, sinewy body. He had only misplaced her name. She was a friend of Molly's. She did tricks. She did . . . funny, he knew there was a special name for what she did, but he couldn't remember.

"Hi," he said.

She frowned down at him. There was something weird about her face, as if she were suffering and were afraid to let it out. "How're you feeling?"

"There's fire in my head. Is Molly coming?"

"Molly? Oh. Yes. Sure. She'll be here later." Then, more softly, her face tearing at the edges like tissue paper, she said, "Oh, Gill," and sat beside him on the bed. The tart scent of her perfume pleased him. It smelled good enough to eat. She took his hand in her own.

"They're going to take out my hose," he said, glancing at Cosby.

"Your hose. Oh. Right." She laughed, but it rang false. "I'm glad. So now you have bathroom privileges, that's good. When're you getting out?"

"Still have a hose in my arm," he said.

She touched the side of his face with the back of her hand, and for a moment there was something about the feel of her hand that was hauntingly familiar. A quick, sudden image came to mind. He saw a man who looked like him sitting in a car, and a woman, this woman, was beside him. She was holding his hand against her breast. She was saying something about a thumb trick on her nipple. She was angry. She hated him. Yeah, he could see her hate in the memory, could feel it radiating around him like heat.

He wanted to ask her about it, but now she was standing again, pouring water into a glass. He liked to watch the water falling, splashing, and imagined it in slow motion, a cascade that fractured the light, beautified it.

"Dina said she tried to get in to see you. Everyone's been trying to get in, but you're not supposed to have visitors until this evening." She glanced at him, a quick, inscrutable glance, and smiled. "So I sneaked in. Just try to keep a stunt woman out of someplace, right?"

Kranish watched as she tipped the glass to her mouth, then drank it down as though she'd been deprived of water for days, maybe weeks. Had there been a drought in Settlers' City? Was that where she lived? How come he couldn't remember?

"Someone spoke to your doctor, though," she continued when she set the empty glass down. "And he says you're suffering from a temporary amnesia. That there was something you saw which . . ."

Kranish pressed his hands to his ears and closed his eyes. If he couldn't see or hear her, then she didn't exist.

"Gill. Listen to me."

She ruined it. She touched him, and that ruined it because now his eyes were opening, now he could hear her again. "Go away," he said.

"Gill, did you see something? Was one of them still alive when you reached them? Did you see who killed them?"

Why was she leaning so close to him? Why was her hand tightening on his arm? Her nails poked into the underside of his wrist, hurting. Why was she reaching into her purse? Why—"

"Excuse me, miss, but Mr. Kranish isn't supposed to have visitors," boomed a voice from the doorway.

The woman spun. It made Kranish dizzy to look at her. "I . . . I work for him. I'm the stunt woman on—"

"I don't care if you're one of *The Golden Girls*. You're not supposed to be in here. Please leave."

Yes, leave, go away, leave me alone, you hate me because. . . A blank. There were gaping holes in his memories, black holes. Maybe he'd been lobotomized.

The woman said good-bye and left and the nurse came in and checked his IV. "I want to see my doctor."

"He'll be in at—"

"You've been telling me that since yesterday," he shouted. "Now I want to see the goddamn doctor, do you understand?"

His shouts brought two orderlies into his room at a sprint. They held him down. They were taping his hands to the bed, they were taping his legs together, and he began to scream and scream, and now the nurse was coming at him with a hypo and . . .

310

He blinked. No one was moving. The orderlies were frozen at either side of his bed, staring at the nurse, who was gazing at someone in the doorway. Kranish turned his head. A man he recognized as his doctor strolled into the room.

"What's all the noise, Mr. Kranish?" He pulled up a chair and nodded at everyone else, nodded curtly. They vanished like stick figures in a nightmare.

"They taped my hands and feet together and . . ." He stopped and stared in horror at his hands, which weren't taped. He could even move his feet. He raised his hand close to his face. Turned it over. His palm was laced with lines that he wished he could read. *Destined for wealth. Success. Sorrow in love. When you are thirty-seven, you will kill a woman, you will roll her body over the side of a houseboat and . . .*

"Oh God," he whispered, and covered his eyes with his hands.

After a while, the doctor spoke gently. "Mr. Kranish, there are some things I need to explain to you."

His hands dropped away. "My head burns. They did something to my head."

"X rays, Mr. Kranish. I'm having a specialist take a look at them. Because of your headaches." He paused. "Do you remember my name?"

Kranish thought very hard. Arnie, Dr. Arnie. No, something close to that. "Arnold. Dr. Arnold."

"Right."

"And your detective friend, do you remember his name?"

"McCleary. Sure, I remember McCleary. I've known him all my life." He sat up straighter.

"And who was the woman who just left?"

"She does tricks."

"But you don't remember her name?"

He thought about it. The only thing he could come up with was Bed. But who would have a first name like that?

"No, I don't remember."

Arnold scribbled something on his clipboard. "What about McCleary's wife? What's her name?"

"Quin."

"And your director's name?"

"Patty Cakes."

"Excuse me?"

"Patrick May. We call him Patty Cakes."

"Do you remember your assistant's name?"

"My assistant?" Kranish's eyes looked as soft as under-cooked eggs.

"Yes, the woman who manages your office."

"Something that sort of rhymes with dinner."

"And the name of the woman who plays Molly Drink-water?"

Kranish shook his head.

"And your name?"

"Gill Kranish."

Dr. Arnold smiled and wrote again on his clipboard. "Now tell me what happened yesterday, Mr. Kranish."

I had a migraine. I was in the motor home. The TV was on. News, something about the stew who . . . about the stew. I was going to call McCleary. I left the motor home. The sun disoriented me, my head hurt so much. I slid down into the quarry pit where my car was parked but it wasn't my car it was . . . "Rose," he whispered, the name lodging in his throat.

"Rose, right, tell me what happened when you found Rose."

A tightness crept into the back of his head. In his mind, he could see Rose and the corporal, the two of them lying there, bloody, the horrid sunlight streaming over them. Then Rose's foot moved and he'd thought it was a crab, he'd thought it was a crab and that he was Spin and that the crabs had killed her. But she was alive, still alive, and he'd gathered her in his arms and her mouth had moved, she had said something to him. . . .

He winced, anticipating the sudden *pop* in the tight-ness, the sudden snap that would catapult him back into the alien landscapes of light and white dust, but nothing happened. "I just can't remember what she said."

"But she said something, right?" Dr. Arnold prodded.

"Yes, I think so. I remember her mouth moving. It's like . . ." He shrugged. "I don't know, like there's a huge hole there."

Dr. Arnold jotted something else on his clipboard.

"What're you writing?"

"My observations."

"Does the Freedom of Information Act apply to your observations?"

The doctor laughed. It deepened the color of his eyes. "I'll summarize it for you." He leaned forward. "Rose told you something as she was dying. It threw you into a temporary aphasia, a memory loss. Amnesia. Whatever it was also blocked out the names of the women who are working on this film."

"How long does temporary amnesia last?"

"That depends on the event that triggered it." Dr. Arnold shrugged. "There are a great many things we still don't know about memory. Sometimes, there can be memory losses that last years, Mr. Kranish. Other times, it's only a matter of hours. Your mind threw up a barrier. What you have to figure out is the connection between what Rose said to you and why you can't remember the names of the women working on *Night Flames*."

"When can I get out of here?"

"In a couple of days. You were suffering from acute exhaustion, Mr. Kranish. Let's give your body a chance to replenish itself. You can have visitors this evening, but don't wear yourself out. I'll have your catheter removed and you'll be on a fortified diet."

"What about the IV?"

"I've got you on some vitamin supplements. We'll discontinue them tomorrow. Sound good?"

"Great."

Arnold stood, reached around the corner of the door-way, and brought back a poster, which he unrolled. It was a movie billboard for *Spin in Space*. "A friend of mine got this from a theater in the Grove a lot of years ago when the movie came out. Would you autograph it for me?"

Kranish gazed into the black field pocked with stars, into the bright orb that glowed within the field and seemed to expand, to grow. His eyes climbed and slid and soared across the letters that composed the title. He could see himself in his L.A. office, his high-tech cave, the day the billboard had been brought in for approval, eight weeks before the movie had hit the theaters. He remembered how his heart had pumped with pride, with excitement. He'd known then that Spin Weaver would one day move beyond him, his creator, and find his own place in the hearts of men. It had been that sort of feeling.

And now, as he looked at the poster, he felt the same flutter of certainty that *Night Flames* would be completed and shown on television and be nominated for a few Emmys, but that he wouldn't live long enough to see it happen. Dr. Arnold handed him a pen, and across the bottom Kranish wrote: "As Spin would say, 'If you can imagine it, then it exists, and if it exists, then you can find it.' Best, Gill Kranish."

Arnold thanked him and read it and looked up. "Just like you can find the memory."

Then he left.

Thirty-four

1.

"MR. MCCLEARY. I thought for sure you would've been here and gone by now," said Mrs. Crenshaw of Coast Bank as he was ushered into her office.

"I got held up."

"Have a seat, please. I'll be with you in a minute." She signed something with a quick flourish of her hand, dropped it in her OUT basket, then swiveled around in her chair and tapped the keyboard of her computer like a bird pecking at seed.

A bird, yes, he liked that analogy. Mrs. Crenshaw was a bird from the wrong side of the forest who'd made good because she was brighter than the other birds in her neck of the woods. She sang louder and harder than the others and pecked fiercely at those who got in her way, and by the time she'd made it, she'd forgotten what it was like on the bad side of the forest.

When she turned again, her lavender outfit rustling like plumage as she moved, her mouth went rigid. She folded her hands on top of the desk. "So, Mr. McCleary. I went through our files, and I've been unable to find those checks."

"Then I'd like to speak to Mr. Winthrop."

"I'm afraid he doesn't usually handle these—"

"He'll see me."

Oh, how that rigid mouth twitched and fussed. Through tightly pursed lips, she said, "I'll buzz his secretary."

Five minutes later, McCleary was seated in Winthrop's plush outer office, where two walls were solid glass, Miami sprawling below him. A light rain had turned her streets dark and wet, her glass buildings were slick as oil and had captured the plump pillows of clouds like mirrors. In the gray light of the rain, the sea beyond seemed imbued with a mysterious power, as if at any moment it would rear up and bring the city to her knees.

"You can go on in, Mr. McCleary," said Winthrop's minion, smiling at him, a proper but cold smile, he thought, and stepped into the sanctum.

Actually, Winthrop's office wasn't nearly as interesting as the outer area. The view was obscured by thin curtains, so he seemed to be looking into the city through a strip of gauze. The furnishings were expensive and tasteful, but businesslike, conservative. There were a number of plaques along the walls.

The surprise was Winthrop himself. McCleary didn't know what he'd expected, but it wasn't the giant of a man sitting behind the desk. He must've stood six four or five, rising against the backdrop of Miami as if he owned it. He had bear hands. A hearty laugh. A loud voice. He also had a mouth too small for the rest of him, McCleary noticed, a pinched, secretive mouth.

McCleary played it straight at the beginning, laying out his bank statements and his credit problem like a losing hand in poker. Winthrop went along with it too, oohing and aahing, rubbing his chin, consulting his computer, and making a call to bookkeeping. He finally sat back with a sigh.

"I'm afraid, Mr. McCleary, that there is simply no record of these payments having been made. I suggest you pay the bills again. It won't remedy your credit situation, but it will rectify your accounts."

McCleary gathered up his things and did his best to look defeated. "Then I guess there isn't much else I can do." He stood, and Winthrop, acting right on cue, motioned for him to sit back down.

316

"There is *one* thing you could do, Mr. McCleary."

"What's that? File a grievance?"

"No, drop the Kranish case."

So. Now it was out.

"Why?"

"For reasons too complicated to go into right now."

McCleary ran a finger alongside his nose, looked down at the floor, then up again. The giant was smiling. "I think you've been misinformed, Mr. Winthrop. My credit can take a dump for the next ten years and I still wouldn't drop this case. All you've done is whet my appetite."

He stood, and the giant did also. His smile had turned into a squiggly line like a smile in a cartoon. "I'll give you forty-eight hours to change your mind. Don't forget that Coast holds the mortgage on your firm."

You don't want to piss off my client: thank you, Surfer Boy.

"The word for that is blackmail, Mr. Winthrop."

"Call it what you like."

"Then tell it to the cops."

He laughed. It was an octave too high for a man his size. "Oh, you have proof? What proof? Your credit's bad, Mr. McCleary, and you have no proof that it should be otherwise. *But,* maybe you think that whatever evidence you have concerning the murders on the set of this little project of Mr. Kranish's will hold up in court. Don't count on it, of course. You're an ex-cop who shot his partner and left the police department under what I think most people would consider a questionable state of mind. I'm a bank vice-president. Even if your friend Benson believes you, where's your evidence? Again, in this society, everything comes back to the onus of proof, Mr. McCleary." The smile vanished. "You've got until the day after tomorrow to drop the case."

In a horse's ass, chum. He slammed the door on his way out.

Several blocks from the bank, McCleary pulled into a Texaco station and darted through the rain to a phone.

He dialed Bruce Harmon's number. As he stood there, the rain came down harder, drumming the pavement, making the air steam. There was no answer, so he called Benson to check on whether he'd found an address for Abel Laxton.

"I haven't gotten beyond the file yet, Mac. There's something weird with this thing."

"Weird how?"

"Well, first I found it in the basement in a carton marked CLOSED. Hell, that Pam Spenser case was never solved, so it couldn't be closed. I can't get the guy I need to talk to in the Police Pension office. Then Quin comes by to tell me she talked to this Pepe Moreno, the reporter who knew Spenser, and he claims the guy working with Spenser on this big story of hers was Gill Kranish, who pulled out at the eleventh hour."

Well, there you have it, Mac.

"What else?"

"The autopsy report stated that she'd been raped and tortured. The scrapings taken from under her nails pointed toward a Caucasian male with AB negative blood. Strands of blond hair were found in the car, which was abandoned several blocks from the canal on a dirt road. Protein analysis of the hair pinpointed the man's age at between twenty-five and thirty. So now the guy would be somewhere between thirty-five and forty."

McCleary knew what Benson was suggesting. Charlie Roberts worked for Winthrop, who had a definite interest in the film not being made. Roberts had blond hair. Roberts was the right age. But they had no proof he'd killed Pamela Spenser. He said as much and Benson sighed.

"But hell, Mac, a blood test would solve it damn quick. AB negative blood isn't exactly common. And if we nailed him, I bet you he'd tattle on your banker Winthrop so the judge would cut him some slack."

"*If* he's guilty," McCleary added, then told him about his meeting with Winthrop.

318

The rain came down harder, and blew in against him. He moved to the side of the phone and up against the wall. He stared out through the wall of water, inhaling the deep, clean smell. When he'd finished, Benson said, "Believe me, Surfer Boy will sing, Mac. I think you should arrange a meeting with Winthrop for the day after tomorrow, just like he wants. And in the meantime, I'll see what I can do about revitalizing this Spenser file and getting a warrant for Roberts' arrest that'll stick. Getting a warrant may be tricky, considering my screwup with Greg Hess."

"You gave up on that theory?"

"Didn't really have a choice. After he'd had breakfast, they took his blood again and sure enough, no low blood sugar." Benson's voice was pensive and rueful. "And that brother of Maia Fox's is the type to file a suit."

"Don't worry about it unless it happens."

"I'm waiting for a call. Hey, Quin wants to talk to you."

When he heard her voice, he felt suddenly warm and good inside. It was how he felt sometimes after lovemaking, when he knew he and Quin had somehow bridged their separateness. It was how he'd felt last night before that bastard Charlie Roberts screwed everything up.

They discussed their individual game plans for the rest of the day, then settled on a time to meet for dinner. She remarked how she could hear rain in the background and was he standing outside? He laughed and told her he could tell by her voice that Benson was still in the room. Uh-huh, she replied, you've got that right. It was a casual conversation, but with an undertone that told him she too had been thinking about last night. Her admission about her attraction to Kranish had somehow deepened things between them, changed their perceptions of each other and of themselves. He felt absurdly grateful. It wasn't every day you stumbled over a major revelation.

2.

The service for Rose was held in the chapel of the Prince Hotel. Patty Cakes first informed the crowd that Kranish was out of intensive care and could receive visitors. Then he gave a eulogy which was really for all those who had been killed during the course of the shooting, and ended with what Quin thought was a gallant hope at this point: that *Night Flames* would be finished and aired on NBC in the spring. There was already talk, he informed the crowd, that the network was interested in a Spin Weaver series.

As she filed out with the others half an hour later, she paused at the picture window and gazed down on Collins Avenue. Cars as shiny as bubbles splashed through the rain, most of them headed north toward the upper reaches of Miami Beach. The boats tied to docks in the canal on the other side of the street bobbed like gigantic corks. Beyond the canal lay a string of Spanish-style mansions. And reflected in the glass was the elegance of the hotel itself. It was not her world, and perhaps it had never been Kranish's either. Perhaps he'd bought into it only because he'd believed he had to if he wanted to reach the top.

"Quin?"

She turned around. Dina stood there with an Oriental woman who had a lean, lovely face and the most gorgeous hair Quin had ever seen. Enviable hair, thick and black and not a frizzy curl in sight. The woman was as slender as a blade. "Hi."

"I don't think you know Lee Ling, Gill's acupuncturist," said Dina.

"No, I don't." They went through the usual introductions, Dina seeming stiff and ill at ease, her fingers laced together in front of her.

"Mrs. McCleary, when I spoke with your husband, we discussed Gill's hobby."

She spoke quietly. People moved around them and

320

then down the stairs, and it was quiet again. It took Quin a moment to realize what she was referring to. "Right. The tapes. What about them?"

Lee Ling's expression when she glanced at Dina was both indignant and humble. "You see? I told you the truth, Dina." Her onyx eyes slid back to Quin. "Thank you, it was nice meeting you, Mrs. McCleary."

She hurried down the stairs to the lobby, and Dina started after her, but Quin caught her arm. "What was *that* about?"

Dina brushed a strand of hair from her cheek and laced her fingers in front of her again. She looked like a schoolgirl. She was wearing another shirtwaist; rarely had Quin seen her in anything different. Oh, the dresses were always colorful and beautiful and fit her perfectly, but the style remained unchanged: a tailored cut with a high collar, and buttons down the front, and prim, so goddamn prim.

"About Gill's hobby, Quin. You heard her."

"You didn't know?"

Dina laughed. "I knew about the women, yes, but about this other thing? You think I like being videotaped with . . ." She paused. Her fingers twisted at her collar. "No, I didn't know. Not until now. Excuse me, Quin."

Quin watched her body recede down the stairs, thin and slight, the sort of body a gust of wind might carry away.

As Quin headed north on the interstate toward home, she saw the El Dorado again. It had been following her since she'd left the Prince. A blue El Dorado two car lengths back. Charlie Roberts drove a Cadillac that make and color, and he'd walked out of an arrest this morning, and that bothered her. Bothered her a lot.

She switched over to the right lane. The Caddy followed smoothly, cutting through the late-afternoon heat, the rain, and the endless traffic like a scythe. She couldn't see the driver, since the car remained too far behind her and the windows were darkly tinted. She considered the possibility that she was just being paranoid. There must've been dozens of Caddys that make and color. But there was one way to find out for sure.

She waited until the Caddy was blocked in by a van, then eased into the left lane again. Her foot pressed down on the accelerator, the Toyota began to shake as the needle sprang toward seventy-five, and she sped ahead four or five car lengths. She darted in between a truck and a motor home in the center lane, so she was protected from view.

Her hands started to perspire and slipped on the wheel. She eyed the mirror anxiously. A Greyhound bus whizzed by. Then she saw the El Dorado's blue nose, edging forward. She swerved the wheel and pulled into the far right lane, keeping pace with the truck to her left, hoping Roberts hadn't seen her switch lanes.

When she looked again, the El Dorado was bearing down on her to the left, its tinted windows reflecting the Toyota. If she was going to end up as an accident statistic of twisted steel and shattered glass on I-95, it would be her own doing, not that of some shit in a Cadillac, thank you very much. She slammed her foot against the accelerator, jerked the wheel to the right, bounced onto the shoulder of the road. She sped past four cars and screeched onto an exit in North Miami.

Down the ramp she flew, the Toyota shaking like a deprived drunk, its engine straining, protesting, shattering whatever illusions she might've held about outrunning the Caddy. The light had just turned yellow. She raced through it, her left turn yawning in a half-moon. One glance in the mirror told her the El Dorado wasn't far behind.

The light at the intersection had turned red. Cars were stacking up like poker chips. The last thing she wanted was to be stalled in traffic, so she made a quick left into a shopping center. Health foods, Movie 10, Video Arcade. She zipped between two rows of cars, swung around the back of the theater, and came to a stop on the far side of a dumpster.

Quin grabbed her purse, leaped out, and ran toward the back door of an Indian restaurant. A slender, dark-skinned man was just emerging with a bag of garbage. "Excuse me," Quin murmured and brushed past him, into the odor of steamed rice, curry, and fried vegetables.

An Indian woman at a long counter was chopping veggies with a butcher knife and looked up as Quin burst into the kitchen. "Excuse me, please, you are looking for something?"

"The, uh, I'm looking for the video arcade. My son's there. I have to pick him up, see. He was going there after the movie and . . ."

She gestured with the knife. "If you please, go through there."

Quin backed toward the door, feeling as though she should bow or something. "Thank you. Thanks very much."

She emerged in the center of the mall. In front of her was a video arcade jammed with kids. To her left was the ticket counter for the ten movie theaters. A banner across the entrance said, SEPTEMBER MOVIE FESTIVAL. She dug in her purse for money and glanced at the movie choices. She almost choked. The third Spin Weaver film was showing.

She slapped down a ten. "One, please."

"Which film, ma'am?" asked the girl behind the counter, cracking her gum.

"Spin's Revenge."

"That's two-fifty for the matinee." She opened her cash drawer. "Hey, Bobby," she said to the guy taking tickets. "I need some change. Get me some, will ya?"

Quin glanced around. The mall was crawling with kids. Short kids, tall kids, fat kids with acne, all of them laughing and conspiring and smoking cigarettes and just hanging out. Rising from their midst was an adult. A man with blond hair. A man with blond hair and silver reflective sunglasses and a grin as wide as Texas.

Surfer Boy.

"Keep the change."

"It'll just be a second, ma'am. Bobby went to . . ."

He'd seen her. He was hurrying through the throngs of kids now. Quin rushed past Bobby the ticket boy. Her purse banged her hip, reminding her that the loaded .38 was inside. She opened the door of the first theater, but there were only four people inside. Not good enough. In the second theater there were maybe two dozen people. She hurried to the fourth door, where she heard cheering, and stumbled into a theater of kids. There on the screen was a life-sized Spin Weaver, running along a space station corridor with his robot cohort on one side and Maia Fox as Molly Drinkwater on the other side.

Quin flew down the aisle and into a row in the middle section. "Excuse me," she murmured as she stepped over legs, her shoes crunching against discarded boxes of popcorn and cups of Coke. "Excuse me." She found an empty seat between two different groups of kids and slid down low, so only her head showed. She hugged her purse against her and stared at the screen. Molly Drinkwater took aim with a nifty laser at the man who was wrestling with Spin, trying to flatten him. As the beam of light shot forth and struck the man, the kids let out a cheer.

A ribbon of light sliced the dark to her right as the door to the theater opened. She slid down farther in her seat. The girl next to her slapped her hands over her mouth and let out a yelp as the man on the screen burst, giving birth to tiny clones of himself that crawled out of his charred chest like baby spiders.

"*Gross*," squealed the teenage girl next to Quin. "*Gross*."

Quin turned her head carefully and saw a man moving slowly down the aisle, checking out the rows. *These people get back at you through your families:* wasn't that what Roberts had said to McCleary about his *client*? His client Everett Winthrop, vice-prez of investments for Coast Bank? *People who play for keeps, Quin. Roberts may have raped and tortured Pam Spenser.*

She nudged the girl next to her. "Listen," she whispered. "See that guy coming down the aisle?"

The girl shoved a handful of popcorn in her mouth, crunched away at it like a cow on its curd as she glanced around. "Yup."

Quin reached into her purse and unzipped the inner pocket where she kept her larger bills. "I need your help. That guy's after me."

"Yeah?" Interest seeped into the girl's voice. She looked over at Quin. "He beat you up or something?"

"Me and my kid, yeah. I've got to get outa here, and I'll give you forty bucks if you and your friends will help me."

"No shit. Forty bucks? Yeah, all right. What do you want me to do?"

Quin pressed two twenties into the girl's hand and leaned close to her, whispering her instructions. The girl whispered to the girl beside her and she to the next girl and so on down the aisle. When Quin looked back, Surfer Boy was two rows away and still advancing. She waited until he was almost even with her row, then she got up and moved quickly toward the opposite end of the row, her shoes crushing straws, spilled popcorn, ice. She dared a look over her shoulder and knew Surfer Boy had seen her. So she whistled, a long, limpid sound that cut through the soundtrack and the gloam of the theater.

The girl and her five friends heaved their boxes of popcorn and their cups of Coke toward Roberts and leaped up and started screaming. Above the ruckus, one voice shouted, *"Help, someone, help, this guy's a perv!"*

Pandemonium broke out inside the theater. Moments before Quin burst through the exit to the left of the screen, the film sputtered and died and the lights flared. She caught a glimpse of Roberts surrounded by screaming kids who were pelting him with everything from pop-corn to hot dogs. Two security guards were pushing their way through the crowd. "C'mon, break it up, c'mon, everyone back in their seats!"

Then she was outside in the hissing rain, racing toward her car.

Thirty-five

1.

THE HOUSEBOAT ROCKED gently at its moorage, protesting its restraints. The rain, which was coming down hard and fast now, had darkened the wood. McCleary saw a wet blouse and a pair of khaki shorts draped over the railing flapping in a sudden breeze like flags. Both the houseboat and the house looked deserted. There weren't any cars in the driveway, and the garage door was closed.

McCleary parked Lady in front of the garage at the end of the driveway, reached for his raincoat, and got out of the car. Seventeen weeks without rain, he thought, and then it comes down all at once, in a fury. He sprinted toward the houseboat, the ground like sponge under his feet, a wall of rain moving across the bay.

"Maia?"

A flock of gulls answered him, crying out, sweeping exuberantly through the rain and rising like kites. He peered through the door. The houseboat was longer than it was wide, with a straight view from the kitchen in front, where dirty dishes were stacked in the tiny sink, through a sitting room to the bedroom. "Maia?"

He heard a sharp peal of laughter, climbed back onto land, and crossed the yard to the screened-in pool, shoulders hunched against the rain. He was tired. He needed to sleep. He wanted to talk to Kranish. But he kept moving toward the pool.

Its sides were hidden by thick hedges with huge red hibiscus flowers that seemed to be sucking greedily at the rain. It wasn't until he reached the door that he saw them. Maia Fox, wearing nothing at all, was moving slowly around the side of the pool, under the patio roof. A video camera on her shoulder was aimed at a blond woman in the shallow end. She was floating on her back in the rain, her round pink-tipped breasts protruding from the water. Their bathing suits grew out of the terrazzo floor around the pool like colorful, oddly shaped lily pads.

"Excuse me," said McCleary, and opened the screen door.

The blonde's head whipped up so fast her hair flew around her face like wet seaweed. Her arms crossed her chest, forming a perfect X, and she backed toward the edge of the pool, sputtering, "Who the hell are *you*?"

"My favorite detective," murmured Maia, lowering her camera and setting it on the table where it was dry. She came over to the edge of the pool and sat down, dangling her feet in the water, rain splashing across her head, her breasts. "No problem, Hannah, he's cool. A little stiff, but cool. We're celebrating the rain, Detective."

McCleary moved back under the corner of the patio roof, where the rain couldn't touch him. "I'd like to ask you a few questions, Ms. Davidson."

Her arms had come away from her chest, he noticed, and only her neck was above water. She ran her fingers through her hair and quipped, "So you're a little stiff, huh?"

Maia pressed her hand to her mouth, giggled, and regarded McCleary beneath thick ginger-colored lashes. The rain beaded on her skin, her nipples hardened. "Be nice to the detective, Hannah. He wants to ask you about the script for *Night Flames*."

"I don't like cops, and I like detectives even less, so the sooner you're gone, the better," Davidson growled, and moved closer to Maia. She came to rest in the far corner of the pool, her arms stretched out on either side of her, along the edge. She kicked up her legs, flaunting her nudity, her toes pointed as if they were taped together. She was alluring, but there was a coldness about her that left a bad taste in his mouth.

McCleary walked over to the table where the camera was, plucked a towel from the chair, and tossed it to Maia. She caught it, smiling, still smiling, and draped it around her shoulders. "Where did you get the idea for *Night Flames*?"

"My muse, Detective."

"Who's your muse?"

Her cobalt blue eyes slid to Maia. "He's so boring." She said it as though McCleary weren't standing there.

Maia's India ink eyes crinkled at the corners as she laughed. "He's just doing his job, Hannah. And he doesn't fish." She and Hannah exploded with laughter at their private little joke.

"My muse, okay, Detective. My muse varies, depending on the script."

McCleary's patience frayed at the edges. "Look, I don't have time to screw around. If you don't want to talk to me, fine, then I can arrange for you to be brought down to the police station."

"My, aren't we testy." She had moved to where Maia sat and was now massaging her foot. Maia sat back on her hands so rain splashed onto her breasts, rolled down her flat tummy, and between her legs. "Okay, *Night Flames*. About three years ago, Maia and I went to one of those *boring* Hollywood parties and she introduced me to Gill. We got to talking and he mentioned he had an idea for a Spin Weaver script for TV and would I be interested? Well, naturally I was. Until then, no one but Gill's name had appeared on the scripts. But he was with his little slave, Dina, and I don't talk business with the hired help around. So I told him to give me a call the next day. He did.

"We tossed some ideas around, brainstormed for a

couple of days. He showed me some newspaper articles about a Miami woman named Pam Spenser who'd supposedly been murdered in the course of a story investigation. 'Suppose,' said Gill, 'we have two reporters, a man and a woman, who live in Settlers' City on Alpha Centauri.' "

She paused as Maia slipped into the water and watched her swim smoothly toward the other end of the pool.

"And?" McCleary prodded.

Davidson reached for the towel Maia had left at the edge of the pool, pulled it around her shoulders, and hoisted herself out of the water. She sat on the edge, fixing the towel modestly around her. "And I liked the idea. So we had them investigating a smuggling scam. Hallucinogenic plants from the Great Hunger Desert were being harvested in huge quantities and smuggled to Earth. A corrupt banker was laundering the money for the operation on Alpha Centauri. Old World money, as Gill would say. Anyway, the woman is killed during the investigation, and the other reporter, thinking he's next, flees back to Earth with his terrible secret. Spin and Molly, of course, eventually nail the banker."

And in real life, McCleary thought, Kranish was the man who fled.

"Interesting story, isn't it, Detective?" cooed Maia, stopping in front of Davidson.

"If you knew how the story evolved, why didn't you tell me a week ago?" McCleary asked, glaring at Maia.

"I'm an actress, Mr. McCleary. Not a detective. Besides, you never asked."

"Withholding information about a murder makes you an accessory to murder."

The twinkle in her eyes evanesced. "I'm not an accessory to anything. How am I supposed to know something if you don't ask? I'm not a mind reader." She ran her hands over Davidson's calves.

"Stop it," the other woman said, and drew her legs up against her.

330

"I'm sick of people poking around," Maia went on. "Benson, you, and then some blond fella shows up here a couple of days ago, asking questions. I told him to take a hike."

Surfer Type? "What'd he look like?"

"Reflective sunglasses, macho, surfer type."

"What'd he want to know?"

"About Gill, mostly." She got out of the pool and walked over to the table and sat down. McCleary tried to ignore the fact that she didn't have any clothes on. She rubbed a towel through her hair, then drew it around her shoulders. "Anyway, I didn't like his attitude and told him to leave and he said, 'Make me.' "

"You didn't tell me *this*," Davidson piped up.

"I don't tell you everything, honey." She gave her head a defiant toss. "He left when I started screaming. On top of it, I think someone was in my houseboat while I was gone last weekend. Things weren't where I'd left them." She shrugged, and now she drew a comb through her hair. "Anything else, Detective?" She stood, the towel dropped away from her shoulders, and she reached for the video camera.

"Yes. Whose camera is that?"

She hoisted it onto her shoulder and pointed it at him. "Mine. I can't say that my collection is quite the caliber of Gill's, or that I'm as obsessed by it as he is, but it does help to pass the time."

He heard the camera whirring. Shadowy reflections danced in the lens. "Smile, McCleary," she said, and something snapped loose inside him. Across the screen of his eyes, he saw a blazing Domer, the Maserati going up in flames, Rose's plump, endearing face. Then he saw Maia laughing, stroking his arm that day on the houseboat, Maia floating in some imaginary world as her goddamn camera continued to purr, the lens still aimed at him. He moved toward her, his anger blinding him to everything but a singular need to grab the camera, smash it. She giggled as if it were all a joke and told him to hold still. His hand closed over the lens and he yanked the camera away from her.

"Did your collection include a tape of J.B. Domer's last few minutes of life, Maia? Did you set his slacks on fire? His hair? Did you immolate the poor fucker and then stand there getting it all on film?"

She hugged her arms across her breasts, flattening them. The diaphanous light seemed to rob her face of beauty as she hissed, "My alibis check and just who the hell do you think you are, anyway? You barge in here, making accusations, disrupting everything. Well, this is private property, buddy, and you're trespassing. Now let me have that camera and you get the hell outa here."

"You're not listening, Maia," he said, his voice dead calm. He kept moving toward her, the camera tucked under his arm. She stopped, pressed up against the railing at the shallow end. He was so close to her he could see the flecks of amber in her irises, floating there like miniature chunks of driftwood.

"Four people are dead. Now, maybe those deaths aren't real to you. Maybe you think they happened on TV and that tomorrow Domer and Moorhouse and Rose are all going to walk in here and everything's going to be like it used to be. Well, lady, I've got news for you." He was out from under the patio roof now. Rain splashed through the screen and spilled down the back of his collar. Maia was squinting, sniffling, wiping rain from her face. "They are *dead*. Understand? That's *d-e-a-d*, and . . ."

He saw the lightning quick movement of her arm and caught her wrist midway to his cheek. Davidson was shouting something. McCleary dropped Maia's wrist, turned slowly, looked at Davidson, her perfect mouth cockling with accusations, and he dropped the camera in the pool.

It sank like a corpse.

Davidson stopped shouting. The silence filled with the sound of the rain pounding through the screen. "You fuck," Maia screamed, and then she burst into tears,

332

covering her face with her hands. "I didn't kill J.B. I didn't kill anyone," she sobbed. "There . . . there was blood in my houseboat when I got back last weekend. Spots of blood crusted on the floor. They looked like roses. It wasn't my blood." Her head jerked up. "I suppose now you'll want to go over there and take samples, won't you, McCleary. Yeah, that's all death is for you guys. A job. You take blood samples and dust for prints and you read autopsy reports and, hey, what the hell, what's one more body? You stand there telling me death isn't real for me, but you're talking about yourself."

He had stopped hearing her when she'd mentioned the blood in her houseboat. Davidson was beside her now, the two of them huddled in the rain as though they'd been placed there for punishment. "Is the blood still there?"

"Oh, sure, McCleary." She marched back over to the table and grabbed another towel. She drew it around her like a shawl, shivering. Davidson was right behind her, bundling up in the other towel. Marionettes, McCleary thought dimly. "Yeah, I found blood on my floor and just left it there. Hey, yeah, that's good. I mopped the floor, what do you think."

"I think it's time for you to leave, Detective," demanded Davidson. "We'll send you a bill for the camera."

McCleary gazed at them, standing side by side, wet and wrinkled as prunes, their faces raw with emotions he didn't understand. His anger hissed out of him and he turned, wordlessly, and stepped out into the twilit rain.

2.

Kranish barely noticed how the dozens of bouquets around his room filled the air with a scent like spring. He was oblivious to the murmur of the television behind him. He gazed out the window, where rain skittered across the glass, to the hospital grounds below. Bright yellow lamps had blinked on, vying with the gray dusk for dominion; cars pulled into and out of the lot, their headlights cutting through the gloom.

His hand rested on a letter that was addressed to the police and ready to be mailed. He felt curiously drained, emptied by the confessions he had committed to paper. *The stew's name was Lynette, and Dina and I. . . .* And to McCleary, a different letter, about a woman named Pam Spenser whom he'd met ten years ago.

But with the emptiness came an odd peace. He felt it seeping into him, straying into the dark pockets of his soul. It was the sort of peace a man felt, he thought, when he heard the cold whispers of approaching death, and was not afraid.

He still couldn't remember what name had bubbled from Rose's mouth as she had died. But the absence of the memory had sharpened his senses, connecting him in some way to the killer, as though their beings had fused at a molecular level. He knew she would come for him, just as she had for J.B., for Moorhouse, for Rose, and that she was connected to Pam Spenser. And so, unburdened of his secrets, he waited, his thoughts flinging outward like a net toward the past ten years ago.

He met Pam Spenser here in a bar in Coconut Grove, in the hallway outside the restrooms where they'd collided. Perhaps it was her ordinariness that struck him or the sharp glint of intelligence in her eyes. Maybe it was nothing more than his need to be with someone. But he offered to buy her a drink and she accepted and they sat talking until the bar had closed.

Even if she hadn't told him she was a journalist, he would've known because she made an art of listening. Her attention triggered his own need to talk, and before the end of the evening he had recounted his brief history in Hollywood: the commercial flop of his first film and his humiliation among his peers; his hiatus from Hollywood, driving aimlessly across the country, stopping, starting, stopping finally, here; his idea for a script which would wipe out his defeat when he returned. She, in turn, spoke in a low, hushed voice about the money laundering story she was investigating. They kept drinking. She asked him home.

Many of his memories of the months after that first night were as flawed as his love for her had been. But he vividly recalled how he'd become involved in the investigation and how near the end of it things began to happen that frightened him: her slaughtered cat in the driveway, the theft of her notes, the slashed tires on her car. Warnings that they were too close to the truth. His script—which later became the first Spin Weaver film—began to suffer from neglect. He suggested they drop the investigation, and she refused and accused him of being a coward. So he asked her to marry him and drop the investigation because he was returning to California. She refused, and the last time he saw her, she was sitting at the kitchen table with her head in her arms, yellow light spilling into her hair.

Five days later, her body was pulled from a canal in Davie. Kranish, afraid that whoever had killed her would come after him, packed his belongings in the car that night and fled. Again. He *had* loved her. Pam. His last stab at love. He'd blown it.

Now five more people were dead and his life had come almost full circle. He did not know who had planned his ruin, but he knew why. So he would wait and she would arrive, his nemesis, disguised as lover or friend, and they would have it out.

"Gill?"

He whirled around, then laughed. "Lee, hi."

Her dark hair glistened with raindrops. She wore slacks that molded to her hips as if they'd been painted on, a matching print blouse, and a raincoat.

"You're looking a lot better than I thought you would, Gill."

"Good doctor." Kranish walked over to the table and poured a glass of water. "We're going to resume shooting tomorrow. Patty Cakes was in earlier, and he thinks we've got enough footage on Rose to roll without re-shooting everything with a new actress."

"That's great." Her smile was thin as a dime. She shut the door. "I think we have some things to discuss, you and me, Gill."

The sight of the closed door alarmed him. But he forced himself to smile and motioned toward the chair even as his hand gripped the water glass so hard his knuckles turned white. "What's on your mind?"

3.

"Bruce?"

Quin knocked at the door again, then touched the knob. It was unlocked. She turned it and stepped into the dark apartment. "Bruce? It's Quin."

Her voice echoed in the stillness. She didn't know why she'd come here; she'd been on her way home. She patted the wall until she found a light switch, then closed the door behind her, shutting out the din of the rain. The room was the strangest Quin had ever seen. There were three pieces of lawn furniture—a table and two chairs, striped pink and white like peppermint candy cane. In the kitchen was one of everything—one glass, plate, frying pan, pot, knife, fork, spoon—and all of it was in the sink.

In the bedroom, a sleeping bag was rolled out on top of a bare mattress. Two VCRs and a TV were propped up on an old footlocker. The TV was on, but the sound wasn't. The light flickered unevenly.

"Bruce?" she called again.

Air whispered through the vents, swollen with an odd smell she couldn't identify. Unease twitched through her. She was still shaken up from her near miss with Charlie Roberts and annoyed that when she'd gotten home, McCleary wasn't there. She'd called Benson, but he wasn't in either. And meanwhile, Roberts was still out there somewhere, unless they'd issued a warrant already, which she doubted. So here she was, shivering in the chilly twilight of an empty apartment, wishing she hadn't come.

Suppose Harmon marched in while she was standing here? What the hell was she going to say to him? *Oh, hi, Bruce, listen, my friend Marielle called and said you spoke to her earlier today about a package you've sent to McCleary? And what's this stuff about you going to New York to work for MTV?*

The idea of Harmon leaving before shooting was completed just didn't figure. He was scared. He knew something, and he was scared, and whatever he'd mailed to McCleary would prove it. *So if it's gone, then what're you doing here, Quin?*

She laughed—a weak, small laugh—rubbed the back of her hand across her mouth, and walked down the hall. The door at the end was closed. She rapped on it and said, "Bruce?"

When there was no answer, she turned the knob. The muted glow of a safelight spilled into the hall, and with it, the odor, stronger now, pungent. Chemicals. It smelled like darkroom chemicals.

She nudged the door open all the way and gasped, sucking at the putrid air as she stared at Bruce Harmon.

He was flat on his back, the ghastly glow of the safelight exacerbating the raw terror in his eyes that not even death had effaced. There were overturned trays around him, canisters of film, rivers of chemicals, paper. The overwhelming odor of the chemicals had occluded the smell of feces, urine, the death smells. But it swirled toward her now, all of it, and she pressed her hand to her mouth and backed out of the room.

She turned, gulping at the air in the hall, then stepped back into the darkroom and turned on the overhead light. She saw puddles of blood, the brown stains on Harmon's shirt, the blood crusted on his cheek, the burns on his face and inside his eyes.

His eyes. Oh God, someone threw chemicals in his eyes. She squeezed her own eyes shut and pressed back against the doorjamb as her knees threatened to give out. Visions of Rose climbed through her head like braided vines. She forced her eyes open.

She moved away from the body, into the hall again. Then she turned and raced to the front room to call the station.

Thirty-six

1.

THUNDER BOOMED.

Sutures of lightning tightened the edges of the sky.

The windshield wipers sang a monotonous tune.

"You sure this is the place?" McCleary asked.

Benson consulted the slip of paper where he'd jotted Abel Laxton's address during the conversation with the director of the police pension. "Yup, this is it."

The headlights illuminated a yard that weeds had claimed. A mango tree grew at an angle to the side of the little house. The sidewalk was cluttered with damp leaves. But there was a pickup truck in the driveway, and the porch light was on. McCleary pulled up in front of the house and turned off the engine.

They got out and darted through the rain toward the house. Benson rang the bell. A man in his early sixties answered the door a moment later. He had thick gray hair, eyes older than time, and stooped shoulders. He was smoking a pipe. "Yes?"

Benson introduced himself and McCleary. "We'd like to ask you a few questions about a case you had ten years ago, Mr. Laxton," Benson said.

"And which case would that be, Sergeant?"

"The homicide of Pam Spenser."

"Read my report," he replied, and started to shut the door.

McCleary's hand shot out, holding the door open. "We need your help. Please."

For a long moment Laxton didn't say anything, didn't move. A gust of wind blew rain onto the porch. The old man sighed. It was the sound of someone who had been fleeing the past too long. "All right, come in."

They followed him into a small, tidy living room where the aroma of tobacco had permeated the air. Lights blazed from either end of the couch. A cat slumbered on top of the television, which was on, tuned to one of the early season premieres. "May I use your phone?" McCleary asked.

"Right around the corner in the hall, son." Laxton tapped his pipe against the side of the ashtray. McCleary heard him say, "So what is it you would like to know, Sergeant?" and wondered how many times in the last week he'd heard that same question.

He called the house. When there was no answer, he hung up, thought a moment, dialed again. Quin should've been there. They'd agreed to have dinner between 7:00 and 7:30, and now it was 8:00. She was never late for a meal. In fact, she had probably already eaten and had hopped in the shower. Or fallen sleep on the couch. Or . . .

He finally gave up and returned to the living room. Laxton had relit his pipe. "I was just telling your friend here that the Pam Spenser case is jinxed, Mr. McCleary. Everyone who ever worked on it had bad luck, real bad luck."

"We heard."

"You did? From who?"

"A reporter named Pepe Moreno."

"Moreno, right." His white head bobbed. "Poor bastard, I really gave him a hard time there for a while. I figured he was covering up for whoever had killed Pam." He paused and eyed McCleary, then Benson, through the smoke. "I assume you know by now that Kranish and Pam were lovers?"

340

"We've managed to patch that much together," Mc-Cleary replied, and reiterated Quin's conversation with Moreno.

"That's pretty accurate. Except that in addition to the slaughtered dog and the threatening phone calls and all the rest of it, I also got beat up bad one night by a man I never saw. He pinned a note to my shirt, telling me that if I wanted to collect my retirement, I'd best drop the case. All it did was make me more persistent. Until they killed my wife." His eyes glossed over. McCleary had the feeling the old man was peeling back years like the layers of an onion.

"When did you find out about Kranish?" McCleary asked. "I mean, that he was the man working with Pam on her story."

"Not till a long time after I'd retired. I got a call one night from a woman who said she was Pam Spenser's sister. She offered condolences about my wife. . . ." He hesitated. "What'd Moreno tell you about that?"

"That she was killed in a car accident," Benson said.

Light suffused his blue eyes. "It wasn't an accident, Sergeant. Be sure of that much." Another hesitation, then: "Anyway, this woman who said she was Pam's sister offered her condolences and then said that everyone involved with Pam's death and that of my wife would be dealt with severely. That was just how she said it, too. *Dealt with severely.* It was crazy talk; the sort of stuff you hear a lot of when you're dealing with the victims of violent crimes." He glanced at Benson. "Well, you must know how it is."

Benson nodded. "What was the woman's name, Mr. Laxton?"

"She never said. But she's the one who told me about Gill Kranish. She said she would ruin him, that it would take time, but she would ruin him for running out on Pam. Well, I didn't know who the hell Gill Kranish was. I didn't know until the first Spin Weaver film came out. And then I tried to contact him through his office in

L.A., to let him know about this call from Pam's sister. But of course he never returned my calls.

"I was drinking pretty heavy back then, and I was more interested in my next bottle than in contacting Kranish, so I finally gave up trying."

Thunder crackled in the distance, and a few moments later the living room window lit up. "Did you ever speak to Pam's parents?" McCleary asked.

"Sure. Once. The day of the memorial service. But they couldn't tell me much. They'd been living out on the West Coast and she'd been in Florida. But that's when I found out Pam had a sister, because Mr. Spenser made a remark about how Pam's sister didn't even know what had happened yet. They said she was overseas in school. On a fellowship."

McCleary asked where. Laxton rubbed a hand along the side of his face. "My memory's not what it used to be, but I think it was somewhere in the Orient. China, Japan, one of those countries."

McCleary rubbed his eyes and an image of an I Ching hexagram blazed through the darkness inside them. "So she was in school in the Orient, right?"

Laxton relit his pipe, frowned, shook his head. "No, wait, that's not right. Shit, lemme think. Pam was probably twenty-six, twenty-seven. Her sister must've been around twenty-one, yeah, that was it. She was spending her senior year abroad on a scholarship in Australia. The Orient thing was a summer trip she took. That was it."

Something clicked in the back of McCleary's mind. Something he'd seen or heard, something . . . It slipped away. "Did you ever speak to her folks again?"

"No. They went back to California, and I said I'd call them when I had any news. Well, I never had any news. But I did call them the night Pam's sister phoned me, and their number had been disconnected. I tried to track them down through information, but never got anywhere. And, like I said, I was hitting the bottle pretty bad then and finally gave up."

"Do you read the paper?" Benson asked.

Laxton looked at him askance. "Sure, I read the paper. Why?"

"Then you've been reading about the murders."

"Yeah." He puffed on the pipe, and smoke drifted up around his head. "And no, Sergeant, I didn't connect them to any of this until you gentlemen arrived at the door. And even if I had, I wouldn't have done anything about it. A man would have to be crazy to reopen that case."

"Did you have any leads?" Benson asked.

"Sure. But only one of them panned out—a connection to Coast Bank."

McCleary and Benson exchanged a look. The skin at McCleary's temples tightened. "You never checked it out?"

"Listen, son, I never had the chance because my wife was killed and my life sort of fell apart and I retired and dropped the whole thing." He leaned forward and stabbed at the air with the mouthpiece of his pipe. He squinted an eye shut against the invasion of smoke. "After all these years, I've decided I don't blame Kranish for running. If he'd stuck around town for me to question him, it would've gotten in the news, and whoever had killed Pam would've come gunning for him." He sat back, shaking his head. "Nope, I don't blame him at all. I shoulda done the same thing. Maybe then my wife would still be alive."

No one spoke. The silence inspissated the air in the room, made it seem smaller. McCleary experienced a moment of breathlessness, as though the walls were actually moving, closing in on him. He started to get up, but just then Benson's beeper sounded, breaking the mood. "May I use your phone?" Benson asked.

Laxton nodded. "Go ahead."

While Benson was out of the room, Laxton rocked in his chair and puffed on his pipe and McCleary walked over to the cat, petting it. Neither of them spoke. Air whispered through an overhead vent, and McCleary raised his face toward it gratefully.

"You an ex-cop?" the old man finally said.

"Yes."

"Homicide?"

McCleary came back across the room holding the cat. "It shows?"

Laxton regarded him with his old, old eyes, then studied the bowl of his pipe again. "It always shows, son."

Benson returned. He looked ill. "That was the station," he announced in a flat voice. "It's Harmon, that video historian. Quin just found him. In his apartment. He's dead."

McCleary rose slowly to his feet and set the cat in the chair. His muscles stiffened with tension. "Where's Quin now?"

"I guess she's still at Harmon's."

Laxton saw them to the door. The last McCleary saw of him, the moon-colored light from the living room yawned behind him. The cat was draped like a shawl around his shoulders, as if to protect him from the assault of the past.

2.

Kranish had received a handful of visitors that night, but no one except Patty Cakes and Lee Ling stayed very long. It was almost as if he had some terrible disease they were afraid of contracting. But perhaps he *was* diseased, just not in the ways that showed.

At 9:30, when the big lights in the hall winked out and the dimmers had come on, he pulled his IV pole over to the bed and slipped between the cool sheets. He felt for the letters under his pillow. Good, they were still there. He would ask a nurse to mail them in the morning. The letter about the stew would implicate . . . *her name, what's her name?* . . . well, the woman whose name rhymed sort of with dinner.

344

He was sorry about that, dreadfully sorry, but he'd lived a lie too long.

"Di-di-dinner," he said softly.

Dinner and Bed and Molly Drinkwater: three women he'd seen tonight, three women whom he had made love to, and he couldn't remember their goddamn names.

The vodka from Patty Cakes' flask had warmed his insides and made him drowsy. He dozed off. When he opened his eyes again, a hand was stroking his arm. Groggy from the vodka, he saw only a silhouette leaning over him, the white of a uniform, then hair falling alongside a face. Something was over his mouth, tape, yes, it was a strip of tape. And his wrists were tied to the railing, and his legs were bound.

He grunted.

"Oh, I'm glad you're awake," she whispered, straightening now, reaching up to the bottle connected to his IV. "I mean, I think it's only fair you should know why you're going to die, Gill."

He grunted and rattled the railing with his bound hands. She pressed her knee against the metal so it couldn't move. He tried to kick and couldn't.

"You ran out on her, Gill. On Pam. You shouldn't have done that. She loved you. She wrote me about you. She said you wanted to marry her, and it was just lies, wasn't it? It's really too easy to kill you, Gill, to let you off the hook this way. I wanted to see you after I'd ruined you. I was going to help you pick up the pieces, you know, because then we would've been even. But things got a little out of hand, and I know if I let you live you'll end up betraying me. So I can't. I'm sorry, but I can't."

And then she drew an air bubble into the IV. Kranish could actually feel it the moment it hit his veins. It raced through his blood, this harbinger of death, and he seized on his last few seconds as though the act of doing so would, in itself, be powerful enough to forestall death. His senses absorbed the potent scent of flowers, the skyless dark beyond the window, the infinite expanses of space that Spin would conquer.

Then the air bubble impacted with his heart, burning like a bee sting, and he thought: *Aw, Christ, Mac, I'm sorry.*

Thirty-seven

QUIN STOOD OUTSIDE Harmon's apartment, leaning against the railing, breathing deeply of the loamy scented air. The kitchen windows were open, and she could hear McCleary on the phone inside, talking with Marielle. He was asking her to repeat word by word what Harmon had said to her today on the phone. His voice sounded patient, but tense and brittle, as if at any moment something might break it.

She tuned his voice out. She concentrated on her hunger. On her bloating bladder. Every time an image of Harmon or Rose insinuated itself, she shoved it aside. Benson stepped outside; she knew it was Benson by the way he walked.

"Quin?"

"Hmm?" She turned, still leaning on the railing because she didn't trust herself to stand. In the exiguous hallway light, Benson looked old, but not with age. It was as if his eyes had absorbed all the horror they could and now there was simply no more room. It was burnout. It was the look McCleary had worn when she'd met him.

"If you're ready to leave, I'm going to send one of my guys home with you to stay until Mac and I are finished."

"I can wait here, Tim."

"We're going to the post office when we finish here to find that package Harmon supposedly sent McCleary and—"

"And I'd feel better if you weren't home alone," McCleary finished, walking up behind Benson. He leaned

347

against the railing to her left, his smoky eyes saying, *please cooperate*. "You were the one who pointed out, Quin, that the I Ching note you got was addressed to Quin McCleary, not St. James, so the killer knows who you are. Where you live."

"Yeah, I get the picture." She looked down at her running shoes, the tips scuffed and black, and imagined herself trying to sleep at home, alone, the house creaking and sighing around her. But worse than that would be lying in bed, telling herself it was okay to let go just because a cop was downstairs. A cop she wouldn't know who might have bad hearing or flawed reflexes. Forget it, she thought. "Maybe you should put me in jail, huh. I'd be safe in jail."

McCleary glanced at Benson. "That might not be such a bad idea."

"It's a lousy idea. I was just kidding," she grumbled. I'll go with you two to the post office."

"I don't know how long it's going to take us to find this thing," McCleary said. "I thought you had to be on the set tomorrow."

"Well, yeah, I do." She pulled him aside. "How about if I stay at Marielle's? I'd rather do that than go home."

"I guess that'd be safe." He placed a hand on either of her shoulders. She felt the heat of his fingers through her blouse. "I wish you wouldn't go back to that set. Would you at least think about it?"

She poked him in the ribs. "Hey, what happened to the bossy cop routine?"

"Don't joke. I'm serious."

"Do you want to see this case through or not?" she asked gently.

He let go of her shoulders, and she felt the loss of the connection. "I don't know."

"I mean, if we want to see it through, McCleary, then my leaving the set isn't going to accomplish anything."

I'm afraid for you, said his eyes.

I know you are, her shrug replied.

"Look, I'll go to Marielle's. Call me when you have something. Let's both think about what we want to do. If you want to pull out of the case, that's fine with me. It's up to you, okay?"

McCleary glanced at her then, and she caught the flash of his smile. "Just like that? No fight? No fuss?"

"Nope."

"Shit. A landmark."

She glued a hand to her hip. "Don't be sarcastic."

And he laughed. It was such a quick, pleasing sound that Quin smiled in spite of herself, in spite of her hunger and her fatigue and the fact that they were standing in the shadow of death, talking about death. Jesus, it made no sense at all. "Call me," she said, resting her hand against his arm, then turned to head down the stairs.

"Hey, Quin." He followed her quickly.

"What?"

"I'll walk you to your car."

"I'm not going to get mugged on the way to my car, you know."

"Indulge me," he said. So she did.

The rain had diminished some and was warm against her face. Lightning flashed in the distance, igniting a plateau of clouds, and thunder rumbled distantly. They stepped around puddles that gleamed like mirrors in the glow from the lights in the parking lot.

"I think someone should check on Gill," she said.

"Tim's going to send a guy over there to stay the night."

She nodded and started to open the door to her Toyota, but McCleary leaned her up against the car and slid his arms around her. His hands came to rest against the small of her back. "I understand about Gill, and I'm sorry I badgered you last night."

"You didn't badger me." She pressed a hand to his face, liking the feel of his beard against her hand. Rain dripped through the tree overhead, anointing her neck, her forehead, her arms. She brushed his mouth with her

349

own, and he hugged her, fiercely, and she felt a deep warmth inside. Nothing could ever rob them of that, she thought.

"Sometimes," he said, resting his chin on the top of her head, so she couldn't see his face, "I feel this totally unreasonable fear about losing you, Quin."

She squeezed her eyes shut, swallowing the lump that leaped into her throat. "I feel the same." The moment clamped down over her, heavy, weighted with truth, and she pulled back and tried to laugh as she touched her finger to his mouth. "But you're stuck with me, McCleary. Huge grocery bills, cats, and all. One more lifetime, poor you."

He kissed her then, long and hard, his hands in her hair, then he stepped back. "I'll call you," he said, and hurried back toward the building.

Quin went by the house first to feed the cats and pack some clothes. Then she drove thirty minutes north, hitting only one bad spot in traffic. She exited on Oakland Park Boulevard, and glanced anxiously in her rearview mirror. Just the usual traffic, she thought, nothing to be paranoid about.

On Andrews Avenue, part of the road was flooded. The gutters had stopped up. She detoured around a K mart, wound back, and turned onto 26th Street, and then passed through the entrance to Lazy Lake.

The world was immediately transformed. Instead of concrete, there were trees. Instead of the splash of traffic, she heard insects, water coursing through drainpipes. The streetlights were out, and the deep shadows from the banyans slewed around her. She rolled down her window because the glass had begun to fog, and a pelagic scent wafted through the car—but it was from the lake, not the ocean. She glimpsed the lake through a rent in the branches, rain caroming across its surface in the cellular darkness, the silhouettes of pines bending in the wind like plastic matchsticks.

She followed the road, now pitted with puddles, around the lake to Marielle's place. She thought, for a moment, that she saw the shimmering glimmer of headlights behind her, but then the thick trees closed in.

When Marielle shut the front door, the sound of the rain was muffled. But the wind whistled along the eaves, stalking minute cracks in the windows and doors. The house creaked, as though answering the susurrous call of the surrounding banyans and pines.

Quin, her clothes soaked from the rain, drew the tranquility around her like a shield and looked down at herself. Water puddled at her feet. Her slacks weighed twenty pounds. She glanced up at Marielle, who radiated a calm as perdurable as starlight.

"I bet you just love visits like this, huh," Quin quipped.

"If you'd waited five seconds, I would've come out with the umbrella, Quin. Here, let me take your bag. We'll go find you some dry clothes and then we eat and you tell me what's going on."

Quin followed her down the hall. "All the lights on the road are out."

"Listen, more than half an hour of rain and all of Lazy Lake short-circuits." She flung open a closet door in the bedroom and plucked out a blouse and a pair of jeans. "These should fit you, although the jeans may be a little short. If you want to take a shower, go ahead. There're towels and stuff in there."

"A shower sounds grand."

"Great. I'll make us some munchies."

Quin went into the bathroom, curling and uncurling her toes against the thick carpet, savoring her anticipation of a hot shower, food. She went into the bathroom with clean clothes draped over an arm, shucked her wet things, and turned on the shower. In moments, steam had thickened the air and the hot needles drummed against her head, her back, kneading her sore muscles like hands until she felt as limp as putty.

But nothing—not the hot water, the thought of food, or being safe—touched the tight spasm of fear that twitched in the center of her chest.

2.

McCleary and Benson stood in a room as huge as a football field, waiting for the guy in charge of the main branch of the Miami post office. He was on the phone. McCleary watched him through the glass that separated his cubicle from the room, noting two black-and-white monitors which showed mailroom workers sorting letters and packages. When Benson rapped sharply on the glass and the man glanced up, McCleary got a good look at his mouth. *Uncooperative.* Large lips, the sort that pouted when at rest, lips that said, *Don't fuck with me.*

The man nodded, but remained on the phone. "Hey, where's your beeper?" McCleary asked, pointing at Benson's empty belt.

"I left it in the car."

McCleary started to tell him that wasn't a very smart thing to do, but just then the guy in charge stepped out of his office. "Yeah?"

The guy's name was Tommy Dislitz, according to his nametag, and he wasn't impressed when Benson flashed his ID. "So, what do you need?"

Benson patiently explained what they were looking for. Dislitz grinned, his large lips rolling back as if he were snarling, exposing teeth that were as yellow as an old floor. Then he laughed and hoisted his pants over his erumpent gut.

"You gotta be kidding, Sergeant." He swept his arm out in front of him, indicating the endless macadams of runners, the jumble of mail sorters, the piles and cartons of mail. "You know how much stuff is mailed in Miami every day? And you want me to find a package mailed today? No way, pal. Sorry."

"How about if we know where it's being mailed to?" McCleary asked.

"And where would that be?"

"North Miami." He gave his address.

"Well, that helps. But it doesn't mean it's going to be easy. I gotta know roughly what time of day it was mailed, when . . ."

McCleary and Benson looked at each other. "We don't know when," McCleary replied.

Dislitz shifted his weight to his other foot and skinned the wrapping from a piece of Trident gum. "If it was mailed early morning, then it's probably been sorted and loaded onto one of our trucks. We've got eight trucks that service the zip code for the address you gave me. If it was mailed mid-morning, it's probably in a pile to be sorted and loaded onto the truck. If it was—"

Goddamned bureaucrat. "Whatever," McCleary barked. "We'll help you look."

Dislitz rolled his eyes. "Listen, guys, I'm sort of understaffed tonight. It'll arrive tomorrow. Can't this wait? I—"

"No, it can't." Benson's voice had assumed a sharp edge, but Dislitz didn't seem to notice.

"I've got four guys on vacation and nine on sick leave and— "

McCleary's patience caved in. He stepped toward Dislitz and the man backed away. It was a dance, a stupid little dance like the one he and Maia had performed. And when Dislitz was up against the wall, McCleary brushed the back of his hand across the guy's shirt and said, "Now here's the story, friend," and enlightened him about the murders.

"Yeah, okay, you made your point," Dislitz said, knocking McCleary's hand away from his shirt. He wasn't exactly obsequious, McCleary thought, but it would do. "Follow me. This is going to take a long goddamn while."

"Then let me run out to the car and get my beeper,"

Benson said, and more softly added, "If Harmon sent you a box of brownies through the mail, Mac, we're both going to be pounding sand."

3.

When Quin turned off the faucet, she could no longer hear the rain. It had stopped. A seventeen-week drought, and then the rain had come down in buckets, as if to compensate for the earlier lack in a matter of hours. The vagaries of nature were only secondary to the vagaries of marriage.

The steam wafted around her. Her pores sang, her bones sighed with contentment, she was ready to indulge herself in a giant pig-out. She stepped from the shower, wrapping one thick towel around her body and another around her head. She opened the door. The bedroom was dark. She was sure she'd left the light on, but maybe Ellie had turned it off on her way into the kitchen.

Her hand sought the switch and then froze. Blood rushed to her head, and she stepped back into the bathroom and switched on the shower again. All right, so she was being paranoid. But just in case there was someone besides herself and Ellie in the house, she felt safer letting the person think she was still in the shower.

She pulled on the clean clothes and crept into the bedroom again. Light from the hallway and living room oozed into the room. Cold air hissed through the vent, striking water beaded on her neck. She shivered. She moved toward the bed where her purse lay, where her gun was. Behind her, the shower drummed. She crept into the hall just as a flash of distant lightning illuminated the lake, snapping the outside deck and glass doors like a photograph. Then the light died and an afterimage lingered, burned into Quin's eyes: Two figures hovering in the glass—one was tied and gagged and the other held a gun to her head.

She dug her hand inside her purse, and couldn't find

the gun. A moment later a voice called, "Come out and join the party, Quin. And don't worry about your gun. I have it. Besides, you wouldn't get off more than a shot before I blew your friend's head off. And that'd be a shame. It's such a pretty head."

Quin's fingers went limp. The purse slid to the bed. She stepped out into the hallway.

Thirty-eight

1.

THEY STARTED THEIR search through the mountains of packages of different shapes and sizes that bore the same zip code as McCleary's address. As they worked, fragments of their conversation with Abel Laxton kept floating to the surface of his mind. Something about Australia. That bothered him, but he couldn't figure out why.

"Hey, I just had a thought," said Benson, looking up from his pile of packages. "Suppose Harmon sent his package overnight mail?"

Dislitz grinned. "Now you're talking. Let's check it out."

An hour later, they found their prize. McCleary tore into the thing like a kid at Christmas. Inside were two videotapes and a note to McCleary from Harmon:

> Mr. McCleary:
>   Here's my version of *Blow-up*. I was interested only in recording facts, but somehow that changed when Rose got killed. I liked her. She was a real lady. And I got scared.
>
>   Bruce Harmon

"One of you guys mind signing a release for this?" asked Dislitz, wagging a form in McCleary's face. "Just protecting myself."

Benson took it. "Here, I'll sign." He scribbled an illegible signature on the bottom of the form, handed it back. "You have a VCR in this building?"

"Yeah, right, sure." Dislitz laughed, exposing his yellow teeth. "All we do here is watch TV, and help cops."

McCleary stifled another impulse to damage the man—nothing irreparable, only something unpleasant. Like a busted jaw.

Benson's beeper, which he'd retrieved from the car, went off, and Dislitz stabbed the air with his thumb, indicating his office. "The phone's in there."

Benson and Dislitz walked off in different directions, and McCleary stood there, eyes fixed on Harmon's note. When he glanced up again, Benson was moving swiftly toward him, rolling his lips together. His face was as bloodless as a corpse's.

"What's wrong?" McCleary's voice was fissured at the edges.

"It's Gill, Mac. They've just found Gill."

The savagery of the emotion that swept through McCleary ignited the insides of his eyes and knocked the air out of him. It triggered quicksilver flashes of memories, thirty-five years of them, as though he were dying and his life were passing before him like a movie. Then a part of his mind shut down and a numbness oozed through him and his mouth moved, yes, he could feel his mouth moving, could feel impulses leaping synapses in his brain as images connected to words.

"The hospital?"

Benson nodded mutely.

They headed for the door.

The air smelled of sanitized death: that was the first clear impression McCleary had of the hospital. Then, slowly, other things registered: the number of cops on Kranish's floor seemed to outnumber the hospital personnel; the watchful patients in the doorways of their rooms looked as frail and haunted as concentration camp survivors; the murmur of voices from the room at the end of the hall; the sound of crying.

As they entered the room, McCleary recognized Dr. Arnold. He stood at the window talking to Doc Smithers. Three cops were taking statements from several of the nurses. A police photographer was snapping pictures.

McCleary approached the bed. His legs were stiff as planks. His hands felt chilled, clammy. He blinked rapidly several times, as if to dispel the sight of Kranish, the reality of death. He lay on his back, his arm still connected to an IV, but bound to his other arm with tape. Someone had thought to close his eyes, and he looked peaceful, as though he were still sleeping. McCleary sat down. He had loved this man like a brother. In spite of all that he had not known and all that he knew now, that love had not diminished. He took Kranish's hand in his own. The skin was cool, dry.

"Uh, sir," said the photographer. "I'm afraid you'll have to wait until . . ."

McCleary's head jerked up, his wood-smoke eyes black as obsidian. The photographer shut up and moved away. McCleary stared at the IV tube in Kranish's arm. He peeled back the tape that held the needle in place and removed it. Then he untied his arms. His head seemed too high on the pillow, so McCleary slid his hand gently under the back of Kranish's skull and lifted it. As he eased the pillow away, he saw two letters that had been tucked underneath it like lost teeth for the tooth fairy. They were addressed in Kranish's neat, controlled handwriting. One was to him, and the other to Abel Laxton.

McCleary slipped the letters inside his shirt pocket, and hugged Kranish to him. He seemed light and thin as a shadow. A part of his childhood broke away like a chunk of dirt from a mountain, a terrible ache spread through him, tears stung the corners of his eyes. He whispered, "Jesus, Gill, I'm sorry."

Then he got up, covered Kranish's face with the sheet, and walked over to Dr. Arnold and Doc Smithers.

"Mac, I'm sorry, I . . ." Smithers stammered, touching his arm.

"How'd he die?"

Arnold cleared his throat. "The IV had been tampered with, so I suspect it was an air embolism that killed him." He looked at Smithers as if for support.

"We found this inside his mouth, Mike," Smithers said, reaching for a baggie on the windowsill. Inside was a crumpled piece of paper, already sealed and tagged for the lab.

"What's it say?"

Smithers ran his hand over his head. "It says, 'I'm one step ahead of you.' "

The words echoed in the room, a flaunt, a challenge, a mockery. Anger surged through him, breaking the torpor grief had imposed on him. "Dr. Arnold, is there a VCR anywhere in the hospital I can use?"

"In my office. C'mon, I'll take you down there."

Several minutes later, fatigue crawling through him, McCleary popped the first tape into the machine. His insides were coalescing like milk into cheese. The hunch spot between his eyes burned bright and hard. The skin there felt as if it were sloughing off, exposing bone. A shot of the moon filled the screen, a bouncing moon like the ball on the old sing-along songs. Then the moon slid out of its black cocoon and panned a street at night. The lens zoomed in on Kranish with a young woman. A blonde. Now the moon fell toward the bay and the lights of Miami. The camera panned a houseboat. Maia's houseboat, then swept across the driveway, pausing on Kranish's red Mercedes.

The next shot was through a window. The lighting was bad, but there was sufficient illumination to see a bed and the bodies tangled there like pretzels. McCleary recognized Kranish. Dina. The third person, the blonde he'd seen earlier in the tape, lifted her head only briefly, her hair flowing behind her, a champagne river. He rewound to her face, froze it, and just then Benson came into the room.

"Mike, I've got . . ." He stopped, whispered. "It's her. Jesus, that's her. That's the stewardess, the woman who was found in the bay."

"You're sure?" McCleary didn't take his eyes from the screen. He unfroze the frame. *Dina and Gill killed the stew, Dina and Gill . . .* Australia, that was it, the thing about Pam Spenser's sister in Australia. Australia and koala bears. Oh God.

He ejected the tape, slammed the other one into the VCR. Night again. A figure dressed in black like Darth Vader moved stealthily toward a building McCleary recognized as the warehouse where the Maserati had been stored. Then the camera panned the area. Moonlight spilled over stark, concrete structures, the wire-mesh fence that surrounded the warehouse, and paused on a red Mercedes.

Kranish's car. The car Dina Talbott often drove.

I'm one step ahead of you.

McCleary swiveled around in the chair and reached for the phone to call Marielle's.

2.

Fear bloated her. Quin fought it back so it wouldn't show.

She would wait.

She would seize her opportunity.

The fear pressed hard against her bladder.

McCleary would call her, to make sure she'd made it.

McCleary would call and get a busy signal.

Her fingers twitched against the armrest of the chair. She looked at Dina.

She wore a white nurse's uniform and stood behind Marielle now, the gun pressed to the back of her head. Quin sat rigidly in a chair across from her, feet flat on the floor, hands resting on the armrests, just as Dina had

360

instructed. She had done everything Dina had told her to do. She had fetched water from the kitchen. She'd taken the phone off the hook. She'd brought in a clock from the bedroom. She had moved with the rigidity of an automaton, the stiffness of her body contrasting sharply with the luminal quickness of her mind as it seized possibilities, plans, and options and discarded them. As long as Dina held the weapon to Ellie's head, Quin was powerless.

Without power to act, without control. She clung to who she was. She waited.

". . . So you've got exactly five minutes, Quin, before I blow your friend's pretty little head off, to tell me where the copies of Bruce Harmon's tapes are."

Keep her talking. "Which tapes? The documentary footage?"

Tick tick tick, whispered the clock.

"Sure, Quin." She grabbed a handful of Marielle's hair with her free hand and yanked on it. Ellie grunted, wincing with pain. "Now don't play dumb with me, or I'll first pull her hair out by the handful."

A single lamp was on. Its light pooled in Ellie's lap and spilled over her knees to her bare feet. Quin could see the perspiration beaded across her forehead and upper lip.

"I don't know what you're talking about, Dina." Quin kept her voice quiet and steady. "I didn't know Bruce that well."

Tick tick tick. Dina glanced at the clock and smiled. "Four and a half minutes left, Quin."

"I can't tell you what I don't know."

"Then why did you go by his place tonight? What prompted you to do that, Quin?"

Make it good. "He was going to lend me an extra video camera he had so I could practice for my scene tomorrow."

A burst of wind rattled the windows. Quin curled her toes tightly against the rug. She glimpsed hesitation in Dina's face, then a strengthening of resolve. She laughed;

it sounded like a cackle. "Quin, it's a simple question, really. You tell me where the copies of the tapes are. In return, I'll kill you both quickly, without pain. Just like I did Gill."

Quin's fingers gripped the armrests of the chair. A shudder chilled her spine. The nurse's uniform, she thought dimly. "Gill?" she croaked. And then some small, final piece of the puzzle slipped into place with a neat *click*. "Pam Spenser. You're her sister, aren't you?" Quin whispered.

"Very good, Quin. And Gill was her lover." Dina's free hand brushed at something on her cheek. "He used my sister just like he used everyone. He used her to get a script, a story. And then when she got too close to the truth, she was killed by one of Everett Winthrop's men. I don't know who the man was, but I know he worked for Winthrop. And I'll get them both. But Gill had to be first because he never came forward. He used her and then he took off. A gutless wonder."

"But he didn't kill her, Dina."

Her cheeks puffed out, and something ugly tugged at the corners of her mouth. The skin on her face seemed suddenly translucent, like a paper lantern. "Don't tell *me* what he *did* or *didn't* do, Quin." The words tumbled out in a sibilant hiss, and behind them came the relentless *tick tick tick* of the clock. "He tried to mold me, control me. He tried to control everyone." She smiled. "He would've done the same to you. He wanted to, you know. Oh, he never said it, but I know how he thought. I could see how he looked at you." Her voice softened, cracked with emotion. Her shoulders stooped beneath the weight of her madness.

Beyond her, outside the glass doors, Quin thought she caught a blur of movement, a shadow. But then she knew she'd imagined it. *No one's going to get you out of this, Quin.* No dashing hero. No one.

". . . didn't find out about Pam until I . . . I got back to the States. And then I . . . I had a breakdown. Drugs, electric shock. And . . . and my parents. It killed them.

362

First my father had a stroke and then my mother died of a heart attack. So by the time I was twenty-three, Quin, I was completely alone and had lost two years of my life. It was Gill's fault. And now he's paid." Her voice turned mellifluous, sing-song. "I had to avenge Pam's death. It was only fair. It's quite an honorable thing to do in some parts of the world. Like in China."

"This isn't China."

Dina stepped out from behind the couch, leveling the gun at Quin's chest. "Don't presume to judge me." Her eyes narrowed to soft green slits; her nostrils flared. Quin could see her strapped to a table, electrodes glued to her scalp, jolts of electricity coursing through her until her body bucked in uncontrollable paroxysms.

"You sent the notes? The tapes?"

"Of course I did."

"But why the tape from Gill's collection?"

Dina made a strangled sound, as though the question were stupid and the answer obvious. "So his dear friend Mike McCleary would begin to see Gill exactly as he was."

Dina stepped away from Quin and reached into her purse. She brought out a pack of crackers. She opened them with her teeth. *Hypoglycemic. Dina's hypoglycemic, always munching on food.*

She glanced at the clock. "Two minutes, Quin."

"Harmon mailed the tapes here," Quin said quickly. "They'll arrive in the morning. And if you have any idea of signing for the package, forget it. The mailman knows Ellie."

Dina smiled widely. "Signing for it? Oh, I wouldn't think of it. We'll let Marielle do that herself. We have plenty of time to wait. I'm not in a hurry. I just want the tapes, that's all."

"Why? What's the point now? Gill's dead."

"Because I want them, that's why." She chewed delicately at the edges of her cracker, like a mouse. "And

363

since we have so much time to wait, I think it'd be a good idea if we put you somewhere safe, Quin. Stand up."

Quin stood and glanced at Marielle, who was frantically trying to tell her something with her eyes. Quin followed her gaze to the tip of a pair of scissors peeking out from under a magazine.

"I think I'll tie you to the staircase or something, Quin. That's the sort of scene Gill would've liked. I don't want you and your friend in the same room." Dina dropped the crackers on the couch. Crumbs spilled onto the cushions. It was something a child would do.

Quin glanced at Marielle, who nodded, a barely perceptible nod, and looked quickly at the scissors. Quin suddenly understood that Marielle intended to try to free herself with the scissors and that Quin should stall Dina for time.

"Okay, to the bedroom to the right, where the back stairs are."

Quin moved. *C'mon, Ellie, get loose.* She walked toward the back bedroom. "I'm quite good with this gun, Quin, especially at close range, so don't do anything."

They were in the hall now. Lightning blazed momentarily in the window, its illumination bleeding down the walls. Her legs ached from tension. Her feet were bitterly damp and clammy. But a dead calm had been growing in her, widening like the pupil of an eye, and she moved with certainty, confidence. She would stall for time.

She had reached the back stairs, and Dina told her to stop. To sit down.

Quin did. She sat down and gripped the edge of the steps with her hands, concentrating strength into her legs, readying herself.

Dina was shorter by at least half a foot.

She was thin.

Her bones were as brittle as rice paper.

She had the gun and her madness and . . . No, she wouldn't think about it. She would act. Period.

364

One blow to the solar plexus. One blow, that was all she needed.

Dina had a ball of twine in her free hand.

"Grip the railing, Quin."

"It won't work, Dina."

Her eyes deepened to a pea green. Her smile was cold, and as it widened, it became a coffin.

And then suddenly Marielle screamed, *"Quin!"* And Quin's legs flew out, connecting with Dina's chest before she'd even reacted. The gun flew out of Dina's hand and she toppled back, and Quin leaped up and ran.

She slammed open the sliding glass doors in the bedroom, stumbled when her bare feet connected with the slippery wood on the deck. She felt herself falling, grappled for the railing with her left hand, half slid down the steps to the wet grass.

Then she tore toward the lake.

Thirty-nine

1.

THE OPERATOR HAD said Marielle's phone was off the hook. McCleary told himself it didn't mean anything other than what it was. A mistake. A receiver that hadn't been returned to its cradle properly.

He continued to tell himself that while Benson dispatched cars to the Prince Hotel, while around him the world pulsed with heat, while Kranish's body was carried out. Then he called Marielle's again and the busy signal pounded like surf in his ears and he couldn't stand it anymore, he had to check, to be sure.

"If you don't hear from me in half an hour, Tim, contact the Broward P.D. Here's Ellie's address."

"How would she know where Quin is, Mac?"

"It's probably nothing. I just want to be sure."

Now he was at the Sunrise Boulevard exit, so close to Ellie's he could almost smell the sweetness of the lake, but a three-car pileup caused by the rain had stalled traffic. McCleary inched into the far right lane, thinking he could pull onto the shoulder and follow it to the exit. But three dozen other cars had the same idea and he got mired as surely as an ant in honey.

For just an instant, McCleary imagined bursting into Ellie's like a madman, only to find her and Quin sitting in the living room, sipping tea, watching the late movie, the place as quiet as a church. He wanted desperately to believe it was true. But he continued to look about anxiously, seeking a route out. The line crept forward.

2.

The dark steamed around her. The rain had stopped, but the air swelled with tropical heat. Insects buzzed. Frogs croaked. The area around the lake filled with a cacophony of sounds. Quin barely noticed. Her consciousness had shrunk to a narrow beam of light intent on only one thing. Escape.

She could hear Dina behind her, pursuing her like a nightmare as she tore toward the lake. Indefatigable Dina, her truculence a raging fire that fueled her.

A shot pierced the dark. Something hot tore through Quin's shoulder, knocking her to the ground. The pain struck more deeply than fear, and from some primitive deep center of her brain roared a fury that seized her autonomic nervous system like a giant fist, triggering the release of adrenaline, a river of adrenaline that shot her to her feet.

She clutched her shoulder, cut right, left, right again, and thrashed through a holt of bushes. Her foot caught on a root, she stumbled, fell, rolled, came to a stop only several feet from the lake, in a cluster of weeds.

Blood pumped from the wound in her arm.

Her supine body gasped for air. The agony in her shoulder lit up the inside of her head. She inched back into the bushes and peered through the dark, trying to orient herself, clutching her shoulder.

A distant bolt of lightning stripped back the horizon like old skin, and less than four hundred feet from her she saw Dina.

Quin flattened herself against the ground and slithered, colubrine, back through the weeds, down a gentle slope and into the lake. The warm water cut her off at the waist as she clung to a handful of reeds, catching her breath. Her arm screamed with pain as she moved slowly along the periphery of the lake, just her head sticking out of the water like some grotesque weed. The water's warmth soothed her shoulder. Her bare feet slid through mud every time she touched bottom.

She sensed Dina was still nearby. It was almost as if the woman's madness had sensitized her to Quin's location and tracked her like a heat sensor. Once, something slithered past Quin's hand and she nearly cried out. But whatever it was kept on going, and she continued to pull herself from one tussock of reeds to another. When there were no more reeds, she dug the fingers of her right hand into the spongy ground. Mud squished up under her nails.

Her heart pounded long and hard. Her insides steamed like the dark. Now and then she heard water dripping through the trees. Just to her right was the Randolph place. *Selling for only three hundred and fifty thousand.* Between the house and her lay a curve of land about two hundred feet long that was as bald as a desert. She was terrified of leaving the water, of being exposed. But she didn't think she had the strength to swim, and her wet jeans added too much weight to her body to attempt it with just one arm.

In front of her snaked a path to the road. From there she could circle back to the driveway, where her car was parked. No matter which direction she chose, it would mean exposure.

Where's Marielle?

Her head drummed as she hugged the edge of the shore and pressed her cheek to the ground. Her shoulder continued to bleed, weakening her, melling with her fatigue, abrading her will. Her eyelids begged to close. Drowsiness infected her. She slipped from the shore, the lake closed over her head, a huge pain screamed in her chest. She scrambled for the surface, sputtering as she broke through, gulping at the air.

When she didn't see Dina, she pulled herself onto

land, unzipped her jeans, wiggled out of them. It was like shedding the weight of an unmentionable sin, a terrible guilt. She unbuttoned her blouse and slid it off her shoulder to take a look at the wound. She nearly passed out and bent over at the waist to allow blood to rush to her head.

After a moment, she tore at her sleeve with her teeth and ripped loose a piece thick enough to bind her shoulder. She didn't know if that was what the first-aid book called for or not. But hell, she'd seen Spin do it, and didn't Kranish go by the book for his movies? Besides, she had no other ideas.

When her arm was bound, she rocked onto her knees, then sprinted at a crouch toward the Randolph place.

3.

When Lady was less than three hundred yards from the exit, McCleary pulled out of the line of cars along the shoulder. The right wheels hugged the incline, rattling over gravel as Lady eased past the line of cars. The car's grip on the gravel faltered; she slid.

He jerked the wheel in the direction of the slide, the tires found purchase, and then he gunned the accelerator and tore down the face of the scarp, the tires spuming mud and gravel. The car smacked the bottom of the incline, then raced up toward Sunrise Boulevard, having bypassed the choked exit altogether.

He tore toward Lazy Lake.

4.

As Quin reached the low iron fence that surrounded the old Randolph place, two shots rang out as clear as pain. *Ellie. Jesus, she shot Ellie.* She eased open the iron gate, her lips drawing back in a grimace as it squeaked, and then she stumbled into the yard. The canopies of banyans dripped water, and the ground was treacherous with burrs that bit at her bare feet. She made her way toward the concrete walk and leaned momentarily against the wall to catch her breath.

The bandage on her shoulder was already stained red again, but the pain had receded to a dull throb. Stiffness radiated from it, from her shoulder to her upper arm. She could barely move it. She was dizzy.

She toppled away from the wall, scurried up the walk, and reached a second gate. A padlock secured it. She had to ease her way over it, cradling her injured arm like a bird with a broken wing. When her feet sighed against the wet ground, she stumbled toward the road.

She came out below Marielle's house. Way below. The street lamps were still out, and only a dim moonlight filtered through the mountains of clouds. There were no cars. No people. She wondered if perhaps she'd died and this was the place in between life and death, the holding station.

But the dead don't bleed. She darted across the road at a crouch and moved through the brush and trees along the edge, back toward Marielle's house and her car. There was a spare key taped to the inside of the Toyota's back fender. McCleary's idea. McCleary, her orderly husband. McCleary.

Now, as she advanced, she detected a shape forming in the darkness. She blinked, moved closer, and saw it was a car, Kranish's Mercedes, growing out of the dark, plump and red as an apple, moonlight reflected in its windows. It was parked far enough off the road so it wasn't visible until you practically stumbled on it.

If Dina had left the keys in the ignition . . .

She pressed back farther into the bushes, inhaling the smell of the wet leaves and the humus scent of the earth. Her toes dug into the cool, damp ground. Had anyone called the cops when they'd heard the shots? Where was Ellie? Dina? What—

Something darted out from behind her, grazing her back, and she leaped to the side, almost screaming, and then she saw Ellie's face, damp and pale as a moon, peering at her from the loamy dark.

Quin stumbled toward her and dropped to her knees in the thick brush. Both of them tried to speak at once.

"Your arm . . ."

"I thought you were dead . . ."

Ellie pressed a finger to her mouth, listening, the tendons in her neck protruding, her copper hair exploding around her face. Then her finger dropped away. "The car, Quin. The keys are in the car, but the doors are locked. I was just about to break the glass when I heard you. I wasn't sure it was you. A car went past before, but I don't know in which direction. I think it might have been Dina, leaving in my car or yours."

Might have wasn't good enough, Quin thought. She patted the ground for something with which she could break the window. She found a large rock, and, gripping it firmly in her right hand, she slipped out of the brush toward the Mercedes.

5.

McCleary extinguished his headlights as he approached the house and stopped the car about three hundred yards from the driveway. He removed his .357 from the glove compartment, sprinted past Quin's Toyota, Marielle's VW, rang the doorbell and pounded on the door. He finally slipped around to the side of the house and got in through the utility room door, which was unlocked.

He found nothing inside.

Now he crept out into the yard, through the brush toward the lake, wanting to shout Quin's name but afraid to because Dina would hear.

The weapon was a dead weight in his hands.

He fought back a momentary image of Robin's face as she had held the knife to Quin's throat that night lifetimes ago. . . .

He heard the shattering of glass, but it was impossible to tell where it had come from. The moon had fled behind the clouds again, and the darkness melted around him like hot oil. The night pulsed with sounds. Something splashed in the lake. He moved into deeper brush, the hairs on the back of his neck bristling when he thought he heard the crack of a twig behind him. He spun, saw nothing, and moved on.

Now he heard the sputter of a car engine.

He broke into a run and headed for the road.

6.

The car leaped to life.

Quin held the steering wheel with her left hand, grimacing against the hot shoots of pain singing from her wrist to her shoulder, and slammed the Mercedes into reverse. The wheels spun impotently.

She threw the car into first, reverse, first again, rocking it out of the mud. Then suddenly it sprang forward and tore up the road. At the widest juncture, she braked, swerved the wheel so fast the Mercedes fishtailed, and the engine died.

"I'll drive. Let me drive, Quin." Marielle's voice rang out, pierced with subdued hysteria.

Quin ignored her and turned the key in the ignition again. The Mercedes shot forward, and the headlights fell on a silver Mazda RX7. *Lady*. Quin jammed her foot against the mushy brakes. They squealed like an injured beast, and the pedal went almost to the floor before the car stopped.

She threw open the door and shouted, "McCleary, Dina's still out there! We've got the car!"

Then she slid back in, popped the gear into first again, and fled down the road, knowing he would follow the sound of the engine and head for the entrance to Lazy Lake. Even he wasn't crazy enough to stalk Dina Talbott alone.

372

The tires spewed dirt and gravel and flung spicules of mud onto the windshield. She put on the wipers; mud smeared across the glass. The speedometer climbed. Blood oozed from the wound in her shoulder. Marielle was shouting, *"Slow down, slow down!"*

The Mercedes bounced over a hole in the road and came down hard, jarring Quin to the bone. The headlights sliced through the dark like knives through a melon. She thought she heard sirens as the Mercedes whipped around a sharp turn, sped beneath the canopies of trees older than she was, and she sat forward, peering through the smeared windshield. She tapped the mushy brakes, and then two things happened very quickly.

Something struck the windshield and fissures of cracks fled out from its center like threads in a spider web. "It's her!" Marielle shouted. "It's her, she's shooting at us!" Quin's foot came down hard over the brakes. It was like sinking her toes into a sponge. Nothing happened. She pressed harder. The brakes were wet. Gone.

She threw the car into third gear. It sounded like a giant grinding his teeth. Another shot ran out. A bullet struck the hood of the Mercedes and ricocheted.

Quin slammed the gear shift into second, but nothing happened, the car didn't slow. Now they were barreling toward a figure in the middle of the road, a slight, pathetic figure in a soiled nurse's uniform who was raising her gun.

"Jump, Ellie, jump!" Quin shouted.

7.

McCleary crashed toward the entrance to Lazy Lake, a few hundred yards behind Dina. He heard sirens and he heard shots and his legs pumped faster. He heard the gears of the Mercedes being ground to dust, and he burst through the trees as the doors to the Mercedes flew open. The car bore down on Dina as she fired, the headlights illuminating the ghastly horror on her face, and then it slammed into her, hurling her fifty feet outward, and careened into a concrete wall and exploded.

McCleary threw himself to the ground.

Debris rained through the air.

Greasy smoke billowed up through the underside of the banyans. Some of the dryer branches caught fire, but the flames never spread because of the wetness. But the Mercedes blazed.

McCleary leaped up and ran across the road. Marielle was staggering to her feet, dazed, her face orange in the firelight. Quin stumbled forward, Quin in a torn blouse and her underwear, Quin clutching her left shoulder. She saw the Mercedes burning, then she saw him and began to shake. She tried to walk on legs of Jell-O, and McCleary grabbed hold of her.

"What took you so long, anyway?" she asked, and then her eyes rolled back in her head and she fainted dead away.

Fade Out

Spring

THE CEMETERY WAS deserted, but everywhere Quin looked, there were sparges of color that somehow compensated for the lack of people. The acacia trees were bursting with red blooms, clusters of geraniums and zinnias grew between the graves and along the road, and the grass was so green it looked as if it had been dyed.

"Maybe we should've brought flowers or something," Quin remarked, as she and McCleary got out of the car.

He chuckled. "Flowers for Gill? No way. I brought something better."

He opened the trunk of Quin's Toyota and removed a large box from the back. "What is it?" she asked.

"You'll see."

They walked through the shaded cemetery, not speaking. A pleasant breeze stirred the branches. Dried leaves pinwheeled along the dirt road. A bluejay dipped low in front of them, chirring at their intrusion. Quin's hunger kept pressing her to reach into her purse for the apple she'd brought along, but it seemed irreverent to eat in a cemetery, so she stifled the urge and thought instead of Kranish.

In death, he'd become almost inseparable from the hero he'd created. *Night Flames* had premiered on NBC a month ago and had swept the Nielsen ratings. There was already talk about Emmy nominations. Spin Weaver would be coming to television in the fall as a series, and a biography of Kranish's life would be released around the same time, with a movie to follow a year later.

Charlie Roberts had turned state's evidence against Everett Winthrop. He received twenty years for the murder of Pamela Spenser. Winthrop got thirty-two years for charges ranging from fraud to murder. For once, Quin thought, the sentences had fit the crimes.

They stopped at Kranish's grave. There was no headstone, but out of the center of the grave grew a small marble slab with Kranish's name, date of birth, and date of death. McCleary crouched down, opened the box, and removed a spade. At the top of the grave, he dug a deep, rectangular hole about two feet long and a foot wide. Then he brought out a piece of granite roughly the same size which was covered with plastic. He set it carefully in the hole.

"A gravestone?" she asked.

"A tribute."

She helped him fill in the edges around the hole with grass and dirt. Then McCleary peeled off the plastic. Carved into the granite was:

Take it from me, a genuine genius is as rare as rain in the Great Hunger Desert.

—SPIN WEAVER

About the Author

T. J. MacGregor lives in South Florida. Her first novel in the Quin St. James/Mike McCleary series was DARK FIELDS.

The CHOICE for Bestsellers also offers a handsome and sturdy book rack for your prized novels at $9.95 each. Write to:

The CHOICE for Bestsellers
120 Brighton Road
P.O. Box 5092
Clifton, N.J. 07015-5092
ATTN: Customer Service Group